THE WHITE ANGEL

The
WHITE ANGEL

John MacLachlan Gray

❧ A Mystery ❧

Douglas & McIntyre

Douglas and McIntyre (2013) Ltd.
P.O. Box 219, Madeira Park, BC, V0N 2H0
www.douglas-mcintyre.com

Edited by Pam Robertson
Cover design by Anna Comfort O'Keeffe
Text design by Brianna Cerkiewicz
Printed and bound in Canada
Printed on paper made from 100% post-consumer fibre

Douglas and McIntyre (2013) Ltd. acknowledges the support of the Canada Council for the Arts, which last year invested $153 million to bring the arts to Canadians throughout the country. We also gratefully acknowledge financial support from the Government of Canada through the Canada Book Fund and from the Province of British Columbia through the BC Arts Council and the Book Publishing Tax Credit.

Library and Archives Canada Cataloguing in Publication

Gray, John, 1946-, author
        The white angel / John MacLachlan Gray.

Issued in print and electronic formats.
ISBN 978-1-77162-146-5 (hardcover).--ISBN 978-1-77162-147-2 (HTML)

        I. Title.

PS8563.R411W44 2017   C813'.54   C2017-902723-9
                                               C2017-902724-

AUTHOR'S NOTE

ALTHOUGH BASED ON actual events, *The White Angel* is a work of fiction, as are the characters portrayed. Any resemblance to actual persons living or dead is fragmentary and incidental. For a factual account of the Janet case and the people involved, see *Who Killed Janet Smith?* by Ed Starkins.

Although deeply offensive by today's standards, racial terms in the book are authentic to the era and should be taken as an indication that some progress has been achieved.

I

Coming events cast their shadows before them.

1924

VIEWED THROUGH THE windscreen of the Edwards Company hearse, Shaughnessy Heights is a creamy blur of laurel with garish splashes of rhododendron and azalea.

They turn onto The Crescent. On the sidewalk, backed by a cedar hedge as smooth and thick as any wall, a solitary figure hunches miserably, waiting for a sodden Airedale to relieve itself. June is a chilly rebuttal to the promise of May; and when July arrives there will be no rain at all, and the smoke and fog will bake the city like a chemical flan. From Shantytown to Shaughnessy, everyone endures the same weather. Very democratic, the weather.

Peeling an orange (he's had no lunch), McCurdy pokes his head and shoulders outside the vehicle—it lacks both doors and side windows—for a better look at Canacraig, General Hector Armstrong's thirty-room temple to himself. The colossal mansion cost more than a hundred thousand dollars to design and construct, and contains both a ballroom and a bowling alley. Rumours of concealed stairways and underground passages add a touch of mystique to the pragmatic business of transforming fish, timber and land into money.

Social functions at Canacraig are legendary—conclaves of powerful men, in which a handshake deal over brandy and champagne can change the course of a railway, and a seating arrangement can establish the price of an otter or a salmon. When someone questioned these bacchanals General Armstrong was heard to say, "If you want money to flow, you must prime the pump."

McCurdy's gaze travels upward, above the columns and portico, where a lone eagle with something furry and limp in its talons

7

undertakes a tortuous ascent, dive-bombed by shrieking crows just when it needs to concentrate. The eagle, with its escort of pests, manages to clear the Tudor Revival mansion next door; the improbably long hind legs of the dead animal sweep through a tattered rope of smoke from the stone chimney.

He tries to think up a line to anchor a poem about the aerial spectacle he just witnessed. *The eagle and the crow* comes to mind—a failed poet and a yellow journalist, a hunter of soaring imagery and a carrion-eater; all the more appropriate because he and Sparrow are on their way to pick up a corpse.

What a dreadful idea! At least he has the sense not to write it down.

He thumbs the last section of orange into his mouth and flings the peel into the gutter as the hearse turns onto Osler Street where, less than a block away from The Crescent, the architectural style shifts from an imperial chest-thump to the now-popular "ultimate bungalow": a traditional Victorian cottage swollen to twice its size, made of knot-free Sitka spruce from thousand-year-old trees and fitted with stained-glass windows. Modern, yet traditional; extravagant, but with a nod to modesty.

The hearse Sparrow is operating manifests a similar schizophrenia—it's a local copy of a Mitchell hearse but with plywood panels instead of glass. Plywood is cheap and removable, allowing the hearse to perform double-duty as an open carriage. Trimmed with carved filigree, draped with tasselled curtains, each corner fitted with at least one carriage light, the vehicle could pass, from a distance, for a private railway car.

In motion, the hearse isn't so much a conveyance for the dead as a torture chamber for the living. Its wooden chassis was mounted on the frame and suspension of a Crossley transport truck built to War Office specifications; even when functioning properly, it was never meant to carry human beings—live ones, at least. Nor is the suspension kind to the coachwork, which rattles like a load of lumber at every variation in the road's surface.

McCurdy chews up the last of his orange, licks the juice off his fingers and wipes his fingers on the white coat folded in his lap. The pain in his back has started to travel down his leg.

"Howard, has anyone bounced back to life on the way to the undertaker?"

"Not as such." Sparrow deftly shifts gears at what is, for the hearse, a hairpin turn. "But sometimes b-bodies flip over. It's unnerving, of course. In the war, corpses came to life all the time. Someone wrapped like a mummy would start kicking."

The vehicle waddles up a crushed-stone driveway, past the house and onto a patch of wet grass that already contains several other parked vehicles. Brakes screech; the suspension lets out a wheeze like a tired fat man. As is the custom, Sparrow leaves the motor running, to avoid having to crank the engine a second time.

"Here you go, Ed. Here the venal b-bastards gather to toast their fucking good fortune masked as accomplishment. Civilian b-bosses are nothing but officers in suits—they should b-be dodging Molotov cocktails."

"Molotov cocktails? Oh come on, Howard. After a rain I've seen you pick worms off the sidewalk to prevent their getting stepped on."

"Worms never oppressed anyone."

"So why *aren't* the bosses dodging Molotov cocktails?"

"B-because the workers don't want to overthrow the upper classes; they want to be upper class themselves! Besides, the Molotov cocktail was a metaphor. You're a journalist, man! Your job is to b-bring down the walls of Jericho with your trumpet, throw the upper classes into confusion and enrage the masses."

"To hell with your revolution, Howard. I've told you before, I write to pay the rent."

"Yes, yes, you're a b-bourgeois individualist. That goes without saying. But you can be useful. Revolutions aren't created by revolutionaries alone."

"That line makes no sense."

"It was Lenin's line. May he rest in peace."

"I agree. May he remain dead as long as possible."

"Shaping human history may not be your cup of tea, b-but you can still b-be of use. Scoundrels serve the cause simply by b-being scoundrels. In making your dirty little living, you expose their dirty little secrets to the masses, and the masses rise up."

"And what if they don't have dirty secrets?"

Sparrow puts one foot outside. "*Of course* they have dirty secrets. You don't live in Shaughnessy Heights without dirty secrets. And if you can't find a dirty secret, make one up!"

Stepping onto the running boards on both sides of the cab,

they take stock while Sparrow rolls a cigarette with one hand and lights up.

McCurdy tries to scratch off the orange stain on his white coat. "Obviously we're not in a hurry."

"We're not trying to *save* anyone, if that's what you mean."

McCurdy notes the police motorcycle to his right, then a recently waxed Cadillac and a battered Ford runabout. On the door of the Ford someone has stencilled the crest of the Point Grey Police, an emblem identical to every other constabulary in the Empire, with a crown, laurel, shield and local animal. Each area of the city has its own police service, whose character depends on the expectations of the surrounding community; for the Vancouver Police, the priority is to minimize thievery and violence; for the Point Grey area (primarily Shaughnessy), the constabulary exists to protect the private property of people who have a lot of it.

Like the hearse, the other engines have all been left to chug and chatter; when the two men alight on the grass, they could be next to a small textile mill.

McCurdy squints through the illuminated drizzle, beneath slate clouds so low that he feels the urge to stoop lest he bump his head.

"Why am I here, Howard? What's the story?"

"I told you on the telephone. A retrieval of a dead nanny."

"And?"

"And nothing. I had a premonition when the shout came in."

"A premonition about a dead nanny. What did she die of?"

"Exactly my thought. What *do* nannies die of?"

"Pneumonia? The flu? Croup? How the hell do I know what nannies die of?"

"Except that she wasn't sick. Sick people die in b-bed. She's lying on the b-basement floor."

"Maybe she fell down the stairs on the way to the loo."

"Then why are the police here? Do the police come when some nanny fucking tumbles downstairs?"

"Calm down, Howard, I take your point. I was playing devil's advocate."

"No you weren't. You're being deliberately obtuse. I b-bring you a story at considerable risk..."

"Impersonating an undertaker's assistant is hardly a capital offence."

"I mean professional risk. B-bringing a reporter to a scene of violent death."

"Stop whining. It's your revolution. Now help me put on my disguise."

He joins the driver at the rear of the vehicle, where Sparrow helps him squeeze into his lab coat.

"For this you b-buy the beer, Ed."

"When have you ever bought the beer?"

"From each according to his abilities, to each according to his needs."

In a single, practised motion, Sparrow opens the double doors, reaches inside, hauls out a stretcher rolled like a scroll and hands it off to McCurdy, then removes a folded white sheet, tucks it under one arm and heads for the house with a smooth, athletic stride.

"We might encounter the Faulkners, who own the place. I shall speak to the client on b-behalf of the firm. As my assistant you will obey orders, and at no time draw attention to yourself."

McCurdy swings the stretcher onto his shoulder as though it were a rifle (not that he has shouldered a rifle). "You're getting awfully rank-conscious for a communist."

"You have no rank. You're a journalist."

"And a poet."

"One chapbook. *Dozens* of copies sold."

"You want me to write tracts for the *Red Flag*. About the success of the quota system at some wheat commune in Minsk."

"The *Red Flag* has been taken over by weasels from the *Clarion*. The *Worker's Guard* is the only half-reliable voice."

"Voice of what?"

"The class struggle. Workers—as opposed to the self-indulgent children of the upper b-bourgeois."

"By which you mean me—and your fiancée, let's not forget."

"You're worse. How much is the *Star* paying you?"

"A cent a word. The next best thing to nothing."

"Newson, that fascist feck, pays you a cent for every single word you write?"

"Capped at seven dollars."

"You really have sold out, haven't you?"

"You're right, Howard. I'm on the pig's back."

2

O eggs, never fight with stones!

RELATIONS BETWEEN HUMAN beings are usually a matter of circumstance.

McCurdy first ran into Sparrow at a packed rally in the Labour Temple, with Victor Midgley of the BC Federation of Labour in full throttle over the evils of the Canadian Pacific Railway. Even his applause-grabbers were lugubrious: *Production of product will be replaced by production of use!*

Just at the moment when Midgley thrust an accusing finger at an imaginary capitalist (actually a railway clock on the back wall), in poured what would later be described as a "spontaneous mob of patriotic men"—servicemen, veterans and fascists from the Citizens League. Having convened in the Beatty Street Drill Hall (refreshments supplied by the Hotels Association), and after a stirring denunciation of communism by a frontiersman who served with Baden-Powell, the mob spontaneously left the building, proceeded to the Labour Hall and beat the living shit out of anyone they could put their hands on.

In McCurdy's experience, a major difference between the Right and the Left is that the Right *plans* better. No leader with the Western Labour Congress had paid the slightest attention to tips from sympathetic journalists about the planned attack, nor did they see any particular significance in the two machine guns recently emplaced on the roof of the Beatty Street Drill Hall.

As usual, their main problem was stupidity compounded by religion. As Scottish Baptists, the Canadian Left never lost faith that their gospel would carry the day, if only they sang it loud enough.

Accordingly, an unequal match took place between, on one side, bare knuckles, and on the other police nightsticks, horsewhips and the butts of Ross rifles—which failed to fire properly but served well as man-bashers.

To maximize public attention, organizers of these outraged, armed citizens had let it be known to the press that they planned to throw Midgley out the second-floor window as a climax to the melee—a must-see for right-of-spectrum readers, who longed for the defenestration of Saint Midgley, dogged Mr. One Big Union. Excited citizens went so far as to print advance handouts, using the language and fonts of a scheduled prize fight.

When the bloodletting began in earnest, McCurdy settled himself near an escape route and took notes on a scene in which a communist or unionist or anarchist (they draw the same adjectives) lay in the fetal position while the rugby section of the Vancouver Boating Club "gave the boots to him." Having recognized two of the brutes as off-duty policemen, the reporter was not tempted to intervene, which would result in a trip to the jail and to the hospital, in whichever order.

To bring home the patriotic lesson, two stout footballers from the Meraloma Club dragged the man to the Union Jack and held his mashed face there until he kissed it.

Then their interest seemed to dwindle, and a certain sadness came over them like a distant, troubling memory. Averting their eyes from the inert body sprawled on the floor, they drifted off in twos or threes, looking for another lefty to wallop.

McCurdy rose to his feet, put away his notebook and decided that he couldn't just let a man bleed to death. He scraped the fellow off the floor, lugged him downstairs and out the street door, and deposited him on the grassy verge, propped against a pole. Cursing the bloodstains on his coat, he'd begun to dab at them with a spit-moistened handkerchief when the victim spoke: "The patch!" he burbled through platypus lips. "You must get the p-patch!"

At first McCurdy thought the words he had heard were *musket the paths*, which made no sense. Only after several repetitions did he recognize the word *patch*—which made no sense either until he had a close look at the man's face.

The thick film of blood that enveloped his head like a condom had thinned enough that it was instantly clear what he meant by *patch,* for the eye was missing—and not only missing. It appeared as though some sort of explosion had annihilated a quarter of his face. As for the patch, McCurdy was just going to have to go back up there and fetch it.

Leaving his acquired responsibility propped up against the pole, he opened the street door, climbed the stairs, insinuated his way through the roaring melee to the site of the beating, got down on his hands and knees, and retrieved a delicate piece of moulded metal, almost invisible in a small pool of blood.

Back out on the street he hailed a taxi, bundled the man and his patch to St. Paul's Hospital, and paid the fare.

The fellow was a veteran, and McCurdy remained infinitely susceptible to guilt—of which the 1920s offered an infinite supply for the man who hasn't served.

For his part, Howard Sparrow, the beating victim, misinterpreted McCurdy's gallantry; lacking other information, he assumed McCurdy to be a fellow class-warrior, ready to give his life to social justice and a better world.

Upon Sparrow's release from hospital, the two men reconnected— and what a disappointment to discover that his saviour was nothing but an opportunist who cared only about self-expression and personal advancement.

When their differences became obvious, a confrontation occurred during which Sparrow broke McCurdy's spectacles, which meant that he had to guide him back to his hotel. It's impossible to settle a score with a blind man. With glasses like the heels of medicine bottles, McCurdy was a bullied child who kept a list of his tormentors for hypothetical revenge; since then, he has tried to style himself after James Joyce, with limited success.

McCurdy having replaced his glasses, the two men continued to meet, for no other reason than that, when it comes to drinking companions, in Vancouver a man can't afford to be too choosy.

Unless you could afford a private club, the city's drinking places were populated by veterans, thieves and muscle-bound goons, who drifted to Vancouver because they couldn't live decently someplace else. (Only to find that they couldn't live decently here, either.)

And to cement the relationship, McCurdy had seen Sparrow without the patch.

Not that such prostheses are rare. What with modern ballistics and bad luck, not to mention the human impulse to peek over the rim of a trench to see what's out there, every city in the Empire was compelled to create institutions for men who should not be seen in public lest they frighten children. Lesser mutilations were disguised with metal patches, creating Tin Nose Man, a new species named for the most prominent feature on what could be an entire tin face.

A head wound could produce other effects as well. It could literally change a person's mind, seldom for the better.

McCurdy began to wonder what had happened to Sparrow's mind when the tips started coming in. Early in their acquaintance, Sparrow left a curious message at McCurdy's hotel to the effect that he should be at the southwest corner of Hastings and Main at precisely four thirty that afternoon, and that he was to stand near the mailbox.

At 4:31 PM, McCurdy was leaning against the mailbox when he heard bells, and a pedestrian's severed head rolled past him like an uneven bowling ball. A man had slipped on wet cobbles, in front of a streetcar. McCurdy was standing six feet away, taking notes.

TERRIBLE ACCIDENT ON HASTINGS AND MAIN
Safety of Streetcars in Question
Ed McCurdy
Special to
The Evening Star

Some time after that incident, McCurdy received another cryptic call at four in the morning, and as a result was the first reporter to reach a downtown house where the deputy mayor had just died, in a bed not his own. (The house did business as a "clinic," run by three female "medical professionals" who treated gentlemen for "back pain.")

McCurdy arrived just as the covered corpse was carried out of the house and into the back of an ambulance; standing beside the open front door, he took a good enough look at the house's interior and its occupants to justify another seven dollars' worth of copy.

INSIDE A DISORDERLY HOUSE
The Shocking Scene of a Disgraceful Death
Ed McCurdy
Special to
The Evening Star

Sparrow's prescient tips were hardly a matter for the Psychical Society, however, if only because Sparrow was so often wrong. After many exhausting wild goose chases, McCurdy realized that to benefit from Sparrow's psychic hunches one would have to be psychic as well.

Journalism is a minor skill McCurdy practises in order to support the production of poetry. Unless one is embroidering a story to the point of fiction (a not unheard-of practice), reporting puts little strain on the imagination; assemble two facts, add two attributable quotes, connect them with sentences and Bob's your uncle.

To date, McCurdy hasn't produced a poem in six months.

"Howard, remind me what you know, if anything."

"The Point Grey Police called Edwards for a retrieval, a sudden death. Sudden death is unusual in Shaughnessy Heights."

"Unless it's a geezer with a heart attack."

"Not when they call the police."

Crossing the lawn, McCurdy notes a number of cigarette ends scattered about the lawn and the driveway. "Looks like the Faulkners are chain-smokers."

"We're in the m-modern age, Ed. Everyone smokes except for you."

"I'm allergic."

"That's no excuse for b-being out of style."

Across the driveway and past the garage, an empty clothesline sags between two pulleys, next to a stairwell. Four steps lead up to the kitchen, while another eight steps lead down to the basement.

McCurdy leans as far as he can over the concrete pony wall and peers down the stairwell through the door to what must be the laundry room, where he can see occupants, from the waist down—suit trousers, uniform trousers, buffed street shoes and the tail of a motorcycle jacket.

He straightens up and sits on the wall, wincing as rainwater soaks through his trousers. Beside him, Sparrow wipes a spot dry with the tail of his white coat, then sits and rolls himself another.

"So as an undertaker's assistant, what do I do?"

"Remove the deceased, obviously."

"Is that all you have to say?"

"You take one end of the stretcher and I take the other, just like in the war—b-but of course you missed out, didn't you?"

"No need to rub it in." McCurdy was refused when doctors found that he was, for all practical purposes, blind.

"Just remember that it's a b-body you're retrieving, not a sack of grain. Especially don't drop it."

"I hope it isn't obese. I have a bad back, you know."

Fanning away Sparrow's tobacco smoke, McCurdy fetches a notebook and pencil from one pocket, slips his spectacles into another, rubs his eyes with thumb and forefinger, then writes the address, date and time, together with a description of the site, holding the notebook inches from his face.

"You see b-better close up than I do. You should fix watches."

"If you want someone to thread a needle, I'm your man."

3

They are climbing a tree to catch a fish.

FROM JUST INSIDE the doorway, Constable Hook of the Point Grey Police surveys the laundry room, furnished with a tea-green Kenmore washing machine, two washtubs side by side, a table for folding and stacking laundry, and a wooden folding ironing board. On the cement floor beside the ironing board a Magnet electric iron lies on its side, unplugged, next to a Webley .455 service revolver—a man-stopper with a square grip and dull, ominous finish. Once as universal as a telephone, the weapon would fetch from two to fifty pounds on the black market, depending on the circumstances.

The room smells of fresh linen and dried blood.

On the floor lies the deceased. Someone has drawn a rough outline around her body with a piece of yellow chalk, like a child's approximation of an aura. The victim wears a denim servant's uniform and a light blue smock; her hair is a light auburn, neatly brushed, with a disorderly forelock over one open eye. The wound in the centre of her forehead could have been made by a carpenter's drill. The other side will be another matter: beneath whatever is left of the back of her skull, a sticky black pond spreads to a diameter of about two feet. Nearby, a set of women's eyeglasses lies splayed on the floor, also bloody, with a cracked star making up one lens.

Seen through a veil of smoke, with five people standing and one lying down, the room feels overcrowded. Constable Hook eases forward, his motorcycle gloves in one hand and his leather cap in the other. Constable Gorman hasn't removed his forage cap, nor has Dr. Blackwell his Panama. No need to doff one's hat when the lady is dead.

Hook's arrival goes unacknowledged by Constable Joseph

Gorman, a mound of muscle gone to fat in an ill-fitting uniform that looks as though it's been slept in. (Hook is in no position to criticize, sporting the scuffed leather vest of a dispatch rider over an abandoned tunic he found in the cloakroom; the Point Grey constabulary isn't known for its military turnout.)

Constable Gorman appears to be in the process of interviewing Mr. Faulkner and Dr. Blackwell, nodding after each response as though grateful for any answer at all. The visual image alone tells the story: Gorman in sweat-soaked serge, speaking with two civilians in three-piece made-to-measure suits, summer weight, with display handkerchiefs and knife-edge trousers. When Gorman asks a question he bows slightly, like a footman serving a round of port.

At the rear of the laundry room a stairway rises to a landing, then turns left and up to the main floor. On the landing, a woman who must surely be the lady of the house hovers over the scene. Wearing a fashionable day dress of buttercream silk crepe, she watches the room with cool, steady eyes. On a step just below, the Chinese houseboy stands at attention; a blotch of blood the colour of rust stains the front of his white shirt.

Though silent, Hook notes how the corpse manages to monopolize the room. Questions and answers are exchanged in near-whispers, as though the laundry room were a funeral parlour. Constable Gorman's pencil makes an erratic, scratching sound like a rat burrowing into a nest; he pauses to moisten the pencil between his lips in an attempt to appear thoughtful.

Constable Hook strokes the patch of hair on his upper lip, which has become a nervous habit. He originally grew the moustache for swagger, but so far it appears merely adolescent—especially when compared to Mr. Faulkner's fighter-pilot moustache, razored by a barber into a perfect chevron, an inverted set of wings.

Constable Hook clears his throat, then murmurs a greeting to Dr. Blackwell, who is the on-call physician for the constabulary. Somewhere in his forties, Blackwell has the eyes of a gambler and the burnished complexion of a man who drinks only the best; he seems to frequent the same tailor as Mr. Faulkner, and probably the same barber as well. However, unlike Mr. Faulkner, it appears he has been sleeping well.

Constable Gorman offers his colleague no acknowledgement, but continues an interview that seems to focus on the correct spelling of names, the nanny's age and length of residence—all part of the public record and a complete waste of time.

From his own experience with crime scenes (and reading Austin Freeman novels), Hook well understands that evidence, like a flower, deteriorates quickly under cover and will wither to nothing unless exposed to the open air.

"Good morning, gentlemen," he says for the second time, using his Redhat voice of authority.

Nods and acknowledgements all around, except from Gorman.

"Well, Constable Gorman. What have we so far?"

"As much as is necessary, Constable Hook. I am taking notes. There is no need for you to try and catch up."

It's now clear to Hook that Gorman thinks he has taken charge of the investigation. "Even so, Constable Gorman, I would appreciate an update. For example, have you questioned the Chinaman here?"

Gorman's eyes shift sideways. "The Chinaman is not the focus of our inquiry at present."

"Nonsense. The Chinaman was the first witness. There is blood on his shirt."

"That has been explained. He was trying to revive her."

"Who was it explained *by*?" Hook is becoming annoyed. "I didn't know you spoke Chinese."

"Explained by me." Every head in the room (except one) turns toward the sound of Mrs. Faulkner's voice.

"Wong Chi is part of the family," she says. "He came with excellent recommendations going back years, and we trust him—or have you made up your little minds that he is an Oriental and therefore guilty? Frank, be a dear and give me a cigarette, would you?" She speaks with the sort of accent Constable Hook has heard from returning Rhodes scholars, implying that nothing further needs to be said on the subject.

Mr. Faulkner produces a sterling silver case along with a matching lighter, removes a Rhodian and performs the ritual ignition of a lady's cigarette. Mrs. Faulkner inhales with a grimace; seemingly either the cigarette or her husband is not to her taste.

Gorman continues scratching his notebook. Again, Hook speaks in his Redhat voice: "Constable, do we have a statement from Mrs. Faulkner?"

"There is no need at this stage to question Mrs. Faulkner."

"And what about Mr. Faulkner?"

"He was giving evidence before you butted in."

Butted in?

"In any case, Constable Gorman, I'll take over from here. Obviously we've barely touched the surface."

"You won't do anything of the sort, Constable Hook."

"What are you talking about, Mr. Gorman? I'm the day man. It's on the order sheet. This is my investigation."

"You left your post, Mr. Hook. I took the call in your absence. I'm conducting the investigation now."

"I was just outside the door, about to eat lunch. I was ten feet away from you."

"It was an urgent situation and you appeared to be absent."

"I will have a word with the chief about this."

"Fine, constable. It's your funeral."

Hook resists the urge to seize Gorman's tunic and smash that fat face with his forehead. (As a Redhat he found it the quickest way to deal with a belligerent drunk.) The Faulkners exchange a bemused glance. Mrs. Faulkner rolls her eyes. Dr. Blackwell clears his throat. The houseboy stares at the corpse. Constable Gorman scribbles something about discourteous conduct, then turns his attention to Dr. Blackwell.

"It's cold down here, doctor. What do you make of it?"

"I believe it's because the heat hasn't been turned on." Gorman's dogged irrelevance is trying the physician's patience.

"Could it slow the process of decay?"

"Constable, the room may be chilly but it's not a meat refrigerator."

Mr. Faulkner waves his right hand with the palm down as though calming the seas, displaying a pinky ring similar to one worn by the Prince of Wales, and an air of maturity and confidence, despite the triangular pouches beneath his eyes. "I say, gentlemen, surely we should be open to all areas of inquiry. At this stage I urge you to consider any and all possibilities, to put a close to this terrible situation."

"Quite right, Frank," Dr. Blackwell says. "Quite right."

"I quite agree," Gorman echoes, glancing up with a look suggesting a careful weighing of the evidence.

Since Hook joined the force, everything he has learned about Gorman suggests a dodgy piece of work. Once a detective for the British Columbia Provincial Police Force, Gorman was "reorganized" out of the force—either for being a Liberal or for gross incompetence, depending on whom you talk to. How he was hired in the first place remains a mystery. Hook heard from someone that Gorman had been a champion bowler with the Vancouver Cricket Club; men have a tendency to mistake athletic prowess for dependability and courage.

Chief Quigley is a fan of cricket.

In any case, only a year ago Gorman was reduced to stints as a private nightguard at St. Paul's Hospital—and now here he stands, having put himself in charge of a serious investigation, tampering with evidence and contaminating witnesses.

Gorman turns to the lord of the manor, the employer of the deceased, the second witness on the scene and a potential suspect. "Do you have anything to say at this point, Mr. Faulkner, sir?"

The constable's question might as well be: *Would you please recite the speech you prepared?* Lance Corporal Hook would never have posed such an open question investigating the theft of tobacco from the stores, let alone a possible murder.

Not that Hook saw many murders in the service. With a war going on, murder seemed somehow redundant. The few he encountered involved rash action by unintelligent young men, fuelled by alcohol and with no planning whatsoever. The guilty party might as well have had it written on his forehead.

Corruption and thievery was another matter. For officers, spinning a believable lie was part of their training. To uncover criminal activity, Hook had to acquire an ability to recognize the smell of a lie, like a fart from an unidentified bottom.

Mr. Faulkner recounts his tale on cue, pausing to allow Gorman to write each sentence clearly. He might as well be dictating his memoirs.

"First, may I say that last evening was as ordinary as you can imagine. In fact, my wife and I retired early. Setting up a new office is a damned exhausting undertaking, I dare say." He turns to his wife. "Isn't that so, darling?" He fingers another Rhodian from its case and lights up, waiting for Mrs. Faulkner to play her part.

"As it turns out, though, there was nothing ordinary about it," she says, and Hook welcomes the opportunity to look at her without appearing rude.

Perhaps ten years younger than her husband, her arms are bare and her skin glows with expensive moisturizers. Hook tears his gaze upward to eye level, and realizes that she has been watching him watch her, with eyes an unusual shade of violet. He can feel his ears grow warm with embarrassment.

Mrs. Faulkner rests her hand on the houseboy's shoulder. "Wong Chi, please tell the policemen what you told me."

Constable Hook smoothes his imaginary officer's moustache and turns to Gorman. "Constable, as the officer supposedly in charge, I hope you're taking note of this."

Gorman scowls. "A waste of time. It would take a fool to believe anything a Chinaman tells you."

"It is in morning. I to peel... for dinner, batoes—no, I sorry, potatoes. I hear sound, loud sound like from car."

"Like a car back firing," prompts Mrs. Faulkner. "Wasn't that how you described it to me earlier?"

"Yes. Back fire. I look out window, see no car. Early I see Missy go down iron clothes for baby Emma. I go down to laundry, see Missy... on floor. Blood come out. I go to Missy, listen to heart. She dead. I go to telephone, telephone Mr. Faulkner at office..."

The houseboy's account peters out, either from a lack of things to say or a lack of words with which to say them. Instead, he stares at the corpse on the floor as though willing it to speak for itself.

"Not a lot of insight from our friend here, I must say," Dr. Blackwell says, studying the multiple dials of his Swiss pocket watch.

"Might as well question the family dog," replies Constable Gorman.

Hook sets his gloves and cap on the ironing table, crouches on his hands and knees and starts to crawl about. It feels infantile, especially under the gaze of Mrs. Faulkner, but someone has to do a close inspection of the floor and it isn't going to be Gorman.

Faulkner clears his throat, focusing attention back to himself where it belongs. "As you can jolly well imagine, gentlemen, it was some time before I understood what the boy was trying to tell me. Something about our nursemaid, that something terrible had happened. Of course I dropped everything and came home at once. Wong Chi was waiting for me on the lawn. He took me downstairs and I saw... what you see before you. I went to the body, felt for a pulse and found none. I listened for a heartbeat, and found none. Then I went upstairs and telephoned the constabulary, and Dr. Blackwell as well."

"In which order?" Hook asks from under the sink.

"I beg your pardon?"

"Who did you phone first?"

"I suppose I phoned the police. If she were alive, I should have called Dr. Blackwell at once."

"And why Dr. Blackwell?"

"Because he's our family physician, of course."

"Of course." *Family physician. Well that's irregular.*

Hook stands up and turns to Dr. Blackwell: "Am I to gather that you serve as physician to both the Faulkners and the constabulary?"

"That is irrelevant," Constable Gorman says. "I'll thank you to stop interrupting our line of questioning."

Our line of questioning?

"To continue, when did you last see Miss Stewart alive, Mr. Faulkner?"

"When my wife and I drove into town earlier this morning—am I right, dear? Am I correct?"

"Yes. She was standing at the back door with Emma, waving goodbye. Excuse me..." Mrs. Faulkner brushes away a tear, or possibly a stray lock of hair. Constable Hook notes that her mascara, expertly drawn, remains intact.

"It makes no difference," Constable Gorman says. "Speaking from experience, this is the most obvious case of suicide I have ever seen in my life."

"You have experience with suicides?" Hook asks.

"Forty-eight of them under my watch."

"Forty-eight suicides?"

"Correct."

"Friends of yours, were they?"

If one thing is obvious to Constable Hook, it's that the girl cannot have shot herself. Given the design and weight of a loaded Webley, he would be surprised if she had the strength to hold it up, let alone aim it backwards and pull the trigger with her thumb—and from enough distance to leave no burn marks.

Constable Gorman, who possesses little or no knowledge of handguns (neither the Provincial nor the Point Grey Police carry them), opens his notebook, writes *sarcastic and discourteous*, then squats down, knees cracking like dry sticks, picks up the revolver and holds it up to the light for examination.

"So much for fingerprints," Hook says from under the sink.

"Does anyone recognize this weapon?" Gorman asks.

"It's mine, actually," replies Faulkner. "I keep it in my desk drawer. A memento from the war."

"I thought you were a pilot."

"All pilots carried a side arm, in case our machine caught fire."

"What for?"

"So that we could shoot ourselves."

For a moment, no one can think of anything to say.

Constable Hook puts on one motorcycle glove in order to pick up the electric iron and holds the other hand close to the surface. "Which cools faster, Dr. Blackwell, a body or a clothes iron?"

Gorman slams his notebook shut. "What the devil are you on about, constable? This is an investigation, not a physics class."

"The iron is slightly warm," Hook continues. "The body is cold. Which might suggest when death occurred—assuming that she was actually ironing at the time."

"Constable, we already found out from the Chinaman that he heard a shot this morning. Is that not enough for you?"

"He said it sounded like a car backfiring. Maybe it was a car, backfiring."

Dr. Blackwell exchanges a weary glance with Mrs. Faulkner, indicating that he is being as patient as he can. "In my professional opinion, the young woman has been dead four or five hours. Which tallies with Mr. and Mrs. Faulkner's last sighting of the girl, and is more or less what the Chinaman said."

"That wasn't my question, Dr. Blackwell. Which cools faster—under normal circumstances?"

"Mr. Hook, how is that going to determine when she committed suicide?" Faulkner asks.

"Suicide, you say?" Dr. Blackwell turns to Faulkner. "Who said anything about suicide?"

"I did," Gorman says.

"Rather than start a scandalous rumour," Blackwell says, "perhaps it would be better to stick to the facts. Mr. and Mrs. Faulkner, do we know that she had a reason to commit suicide? Love affair, something like that?"

Gorman lights a Black Cat, a cheap gasper with an aroma of burning rubber. "The motive will become clear in the course of the investigation, doctor. That's what the police are here for."

"I wasn't speaking to you, I was speaking to the Faulkners."

Gorman reddens slightly, opens his notebook and writes

Blackwell—impolite and negative, with his cigarette in the corner of his mouth, head tilted back to keep the smoke out of his nose.

Faulkner strokes his chin with his left hand, providing a glimpse of his silver trench watch. "Of course I wouldn't know about her personal life. My wife here says she had callers, but none she seemed to take seriously. Isn't that so, dear?"

"Of course one can never tell," Mrs. Faulkner replies. "Most girls in this part of the world have a good many male admirers. It's not like in England."

"Did she have any trouble with your other employees?" Hook asks, indicating the houseboy. Mrs. Faulkner's knee-length skirt makes for an admirable sight, viewed from below.

"Never," replies Mrs. Faulkner, crisply. Clearly this is a woman who knows how to end a discussion. "Wong Chi is immensely loyal. As I said before, he's like part of the family."

"A Chinaman would never cause a white woman to commit suicide," Gorman says. "It's a scientific fact that we are at bottom different species. Rice-eating animals is how I see them."

As though hoping for a contribution from the deceased, Hook directs his attention there, marvelling at the girl's incandescently white skin, so white you would think it glowed in the dark; the mouth is slightly parted as though surprised or about to receive a kiss; the eyes look mistily at the ceiling, or perhaps inward, at her own thoughts—hard to tell because the irises have turned milky. The dark red spot in the middle of her forehead suggests a Hindu princess; the outline of her legs spread beneath the skirt—feet far apart, one shoe removed, defenceless—inspires unnerving sensations, even though the girl is a cadaver. Beneath an audience of men it lends a prurient quality to the situation, all the more so with Mrs. Faulkner present.

Dr. Blackwell removes a tortoiseshell case from his inside pocket, pulls out a Bond Street cigarette, snaps the lid shut, fits the cigarette into a black holder and lights up with a gold pocket lighter. Hook admires his mother-of-pearl cufflinks, not to mention his neat, pyramid-shaped moustache, and inhales the sweet smell of Virginia tobacco laced with petrol fumes—two of his favourite aromas.

"With all due respect, officer, I'm afraid you're mistaken," Dr. Blackwell says. "Look there: do you see her spectacles? One of the lenses is broken, and there is blood on the other. Obviously they fell to the floor when she was shot."

"Shot herself," Gorman corrects him.

Blackwell blows smoke toward the ceiling, sighs and shakes his head. "Officer, it's a well-known fact that people who shoot themselves always take their spectacles off first. As you can see, this did not happen here."

"That's certainly news to me," Faulkner says.

Again, Hook smells mendacity—the smell of soldiers discussing the whereabouts of a deserter or a smuggler for the benefit of an inquiring Redhat, knowing perfectly well where the fellow went. *Thought I saw him at the chapel, didn't you, Garth? Why yes, Kevin, he was on his knees in prayer...*

Blackwell nods. "It's a psychological fact."

Gorman shakes his head. "Sounds like an old wives' tale."

Hook digs a pack of Ogden's out of an inside pocket, shakes one loose, puts it in his mouth without touching it with his fingers, and strikes a kitchen match with a thumbnail.

Blackwell continues: "Had this been a suicide, one would expect her to have removed her spectacles and placed them on, say, the ironing board. And the iron might have come unplugged as she fell. Assuming that she had plugged it in as though about to start work—do you see that basket of unironed baby clothes? Why would someone who is about to commit suicide bother to plug in an iron?"

"And what is your answer, sir?" Gorman asks, poised with notebook and pencil.

"On balance I would call this a case of accidental death. The silly girl was fooling around with a loaded weapon. I can't tell you how often that happens."

"That's true," Faulkner says. "That happened to a chap in my squadron, poor fellow."

Hook tries to join the discussion. "How is it possible to shoot yourself in the head by accident?"

"By peering down the barrel, I suppose," Blackwell replies. "Or maybe she dropped it and it went off."

"And shot her in the middle of the forehead?"

"It's possible. The bullet had to go someplace."

"I've seen stranger things during the war," Faulkner adds.

While Faulkner, Blackwell and Gorman exchange cautionary

tales of loaded weapons going off by accident, Hook notices something about the dead girl's wrist. He unbuttons the girl's sleeve and pushes it up to the elbow to examine what looks like a burn mark on the skin. "Doctor, she seems to have burnt her arm."

Hook indicates the burn and receives a flicker of interest from Blackwell: "She could have burnt herself when she fell. Certainly it supports a finding of accidental death."

"But there are no marks on her shirt."

"Well, perhaps she burnt herself earlier."

"How is that possible, when there are no ironed clothes in the room?"

Gorman opens his notebook and writes: *Henpecks the witness over silly details.*

"I'll go up and see to Emma," Mrs. Faulkner says, "and leave you gentlemen to your... examination." The silk crepe of her dress rustles softly as she climbs the stairs, trailing perfume in her wake. Constable Hook tries to imagine what it would be like to smell perfume like that on a regular basis.

He turns back to contemplate the men in the room. Again he wonders about Gorman's collegial rapport with Blackwell and Faulkner. It can't be that they took a liking to him. Nobody on this earth could fail to note the man's lack of intelligence—a stupidity neither congenital nor injury-related but a case of deliberate insensibility. On the other hand, Gorman might not be as stupid as he chooses to appear; a man can be both a birdbrain and a cunning sneak, using one as cover for the other.

In Hook's opinion, the three men are too distant in profession, family background, economic circumstance, to form an alliance for any reason other than mutual gain.

When soldiers of different ranks fell into discussion as though they were equals, it inevitably revolved around a prohibited activity—gambling, extortion, theft from the stores or black marketing.

Certainly, something odd is going on. Again, his attention turns to the dead girl lying beside him on the floor. Whoever she was, she deserved better than this...

FOR THE SERVICEMAN who survived more or less intact, the Great War supplied a wealth of knowledge, training and experience. What a shock, then, to return home only to find that these hard-won skills had no peacetime value—in fact, could hobble a man for life. Automatic reactions learned in hand-to-hand combat could put a man in jail; a knack for deflection shooting, essential to a sniper, gunner or fighter pilot, served no purpose in peacetime other than bagging a duck in fall.

This was Hook's experience upon returning home to Waldo, a crossing near the American border where his father worked for the Spokane, Portland and Seattle Railway.

Waldo had no police force. Everyone knew everyone; everyone exchanged information on everyone. Everyone lived within a fence of expectations. Who needs a police force when everyone is a policeman?

Hook's father managed to swing a job for his son as an apprentice brakeman, but Hook well knew that working for the railway was the closest you can get to being indentured for life. No holidays, no days off (not even Christmas), unpredictable day and night shifts, a barely adequate salary in return for a miserable life. Two months after demobilization, he abandoned Waldo for Vancouver, a city with both policemen and motorcycles.

Today is a peculiar time for the Point Grey constabulary to be faced with a serious crime. Virtually the entire ten-man force had gone off on a picnic on Bowen Island for civic employees, leaving a skeleton staff of three, including Chief Quigley, who seldom left his office. Short-staffing was no great matter, given that the constabulary had not seen a crime of any sort in weeks; at the same time, the presence of only two active officers provided an excellent opportunity to control the precinct's response.

Wandering about the office, comatose with boredom and sickened by Gorman's acrid cigarettes, Hook ventured outside to take his mid-morning tea, leaving Gorman at the desk nibbling a dry railway sandwich.

The moment Hook stepped out the door, practically that very second, the telephone sounded and Gorman snatched up the receiver as though expecting the call.

Hook could hear only one side of the exchange:

"Here is Castle 351. Yes, operator, here is Constable Gorman. I will take the call."

"Yes, Mr. Faulkner, how can I be of assistance?"

"I see. Have you called an ambulance, sir? A doctor?"

"No need? Are you sure? Yes. Yes."

"Very good. I'll see to it. Name and address, please?"

"How do you spell that, sir?"

"Please stand by, this officer will be there shortly."

Hook returned immediately, but Gorman was already headed straight for Chief Quigley's office. He stepped inside without knocking.

At least Hook was able to write down the Faulkner address.

Moments later, Gorman barrelled out of the chief's office and outside to the police auto without a glance in Hook's direction, let alone a hint of what was going on.

At least Hook knew that *something* was going on.

He rode at speed to the address in Shaughnessy Heights, only to find Gorman contaminating the scene, coming to absurd conclusions, and chatting up Faulkner and Blackwell as though they had gone to school together.

All of this will require looking into. In the meantime, Hook knows Gorman has snookered him, and he must make the best of it.

CROUCHED NEXT TO the hot water pipe, Hook examines Miss Stewart's broken glasses and the delicate chain attached to suspend them from her neck when not needed. If she was wearing them when she was shot, why did they fly away? He directs his attention to her lovely blue, albeit frosted, eyes, staring at nothing in particular. He wants to reach out and close the lids, but can't bring himself to touch her face (how silly, to be shy with a corpse). He looks at her hand, palm up, arm splayed out as though reaching for something.

"Funny that there are no powder burns around the wound," he says.

"Nonsense," Gorman snaps. "She could have been holding the weapon well away and still have managed to pull the trigger."

"Why would she do that? Why wouldn't she just stick it in her mouth?"

"How am I to know about the mental state of a suicide?"

"On the other hand," Blackwell says, "she might have dropped the weapon with the safety switch off. A lack of powder burns is unusual with a suicide, but consistent with accidental death."

Hook takes another close look at the triangular burn on her forearm. The obvious explanation is that she burnt herself with the point of the iron; but if so, she must have buttoned the cuff afterwards—or someone else did.

"See this here, doctor? See how the sleeve covered the burn? It was buttoned, as well."

"Clearly she burnt herself when she fell to the floor. Maybe she dropped the iron and it bounced."

"Then she must have been holding the pistol and the iron at the same time. Was she a weightlifter?"

Gorman writes *more sarcasm* in his notebook.

"It seems more likely," Hook says, "that when she fell she knocked the iron *off* the ironing board."

"Could be," Blackwell shrugs.

"What difference does it make?" Gorman says. "She didn't die from an iron burn."

Hook is grinding his teeth again. "The question is, who buttoned her sleeve?"

"What do you mean?"

"After she fell and burnt herself, who buttoned her sleeve?"

"Perhaps the Chinaman did," Blackwell says. "Talk to him, why don't you?"

"This is getting us nowhere." Constable Gorman turns to Faulkner, who has been following the discussion closely. "Sir, I need to make use of your telephone on police business."

"By all means, officer. I'll show you the way." Faulkner motions for Wong Chi to step down into the laundry room to clear the way and the two men head upstairs, leaving Constable Hook crouched beside the corpse. His knees crack as he gets to his feet.

"Be careful," Blackwell says. "Some rheumatism there. You should come and see me about it."

"Do you know who the constable is calling on the telephone?"

Blackwell fishes for his cigarette case. "How would I? He's your colleague. I suppose he's reporting to his superior, as the officer in charge."

"You seem to have come to an early agreement as to the cause of death."

"Not at all. We disagree entirely."

"Yes, but you both rule out foul play. Don't you think it possible that she was shot in the head by someone else?"

"The evidence suggests something less melodramatic. Sorry to disappoint you." Blackwell adjusts his Panama hat and heads out the back door. "I'm going to have a breath of fresh air and a smoke."

Left alone with the cadaver and the Chinaman, Hook tries to think of something to say.

Dangling directly over the ironing board, the light bulb also serves as an electrical outlet; possibly she pulled the iron down with her as she fell, yanking it from the ceiling plug. Is that how she burnt her arm? Did she button her sleeve with a bullet in her head, or did she burn herself, button her sleeve, then shoot herself?

Or did someone button it for her?

The houseboy stares at the cadaver as though trying to convey a message by telepathy. Sensing that he is being watched, he turns to Constable Hook and bows slightly, palms together. Hook has no idea what the gesture means. For all he knows, the houseboy could be telling him to go to hell.

"Sir, do you speak any English? English? English speak?"

The houseboy starts to reply, but his attention turns to the doorway, at two men in silhouette. One steps inside, followed by a taller man wearing thick spectacles. Both wear white coats.

The first man looks at the dead woman as though the problem were a leaky faucet. The second is coughing and waving smoke away from his face.

"Good m-morning, gentlemen."

"Are you the undertakers?"

"Attendants on retrieval duty, sir. We pick up and deliver, like the Royal M-Mail." Sparrow nods to the houseboy: "*Ni hao.*"

Startled by the greeting, Wong Chi bows and replies in a whisper. "*Ni hao.*"

"*Dui bu qi,*" Sparrow says, and the houseboy nods.

"What did you say to him, sir?" Hook asks.

"*Hello* and *I'm sorry.*"

"What were you apologizing *for*?"

"Nothing, really. Just good manners."

"Sir, I am Constable Hook. And you are...?"

"Howard Sparrow. This is m-my assistant."

McCurdy lifts his eyeglasses and wipes the tears streaming from his eyes. The veil of smoke in the room seems almost solid.

Constable Gorman's black patrolman's boots reappear on the landing. It's another three steps to the floor, but he literally refuses to stoop to their level.

"I spoke to the chief. He agrees that we are finished here."

"Finished?" Hook fingers the small vein in his temple that turns into a wriggling worm when he gets upset. "Was that what you call an investigation?"

"Dr. Blackwell seems to have everything he needs."

"He might at least have closed her eyes."

"Blackwell is a doctor, not an undertaker."

Sparrow shakes out the white sheet and covers the body. "In any case, at this p-point it's easier said than done, sir. The eyes are frozen open."

"She is deceased after all," adds McCurdy, unfurling the stretcher.

Constable Hook can't take his eyes off her, even beneath the sheet: her white outline, the imprint of her nose, her small breasts. Already she looks like a ghost; perhaps she is one. At the base in Rugeley, men who had seen action claimed that dead comrades appeared, to find out what happened to them or to leave a message.

Certainly, the Chinaman appears to Hook as though *he* has seen a ghost.

"How long do you think she has been..." Hook finds himself unaccountably hesitant to say the word *dead* because, in truth, he doesn't *want* her to be dead.

"Rigor m-mortis starts in three or four hours, but after t-twelve hours everything starts to relax."

"Relax?"

"Unstiffen. The m-muscles unstiffen."

"Why?"

"I don't know. Ask a b-butcher. A good steak depends on it."

Dr. Blackwell blows smoke at the ceiling: "By the condition of the corpse, she has been dead four or five hours."

"So it would seem, yes," Sparrow replies, at which Blackwell gives him a look that says *who cares whether you agree or not?*

McCurdy turns to the houseboy. "Sir, you said you heard a sound that might have been a gunshot. What time was that?"

The houseboy spreads his hands and looks to Sparrow as though for a translation.

"*Dui bu qi.* Can't help you there, old chap. My Chinese boils down to *hello, goodb-bye* and *I'm sorry.*"

The exchange seems to annoy Gorman. "Sir, I'll ask you not to speak to Mr. Chi."

"Actually, it's Mr. Wong. They go last names first."

"Makes no difference to me."

"I go work now." The houseboy climbs to the landing and squeezes past the officer's bulk.

"*Zai jian,*" Sparrow says.

"*Zai jian,*" comes the reply, and Wong Chi disappears upstairs.

McCurdy turns to Constable Hook, noting the officer's uneven moustache, like a sparse caterpillar. "Did he tell you what time he heard the shot?"

"This is police business, sir," Gorman says. "I'll ask you to leave it to the police."

"Not entirely. The embalmer will need to know." Sparrow turns to face Constable Hook. "And you, officer? Any idea?"

"Ask Constable Gorman. He knows everything. Mind like a steel trap. Men like Gorman are a credit to any police force."

Constable Gorman turns to a fresh page, writes *Sarcastic!* and breaks his pencil underlining it.

For the first time, Hook is able to get a good look at the stutterer's face. It's the most impeccable job he has ever seen. The eyes match perfectly, except that one eye never blinks. To the casual observer he looks as if he can see with both eyes, but in different ways. Hook has seen many a tin nose man, but nothing on this level.

An uncomfortable pause follows, as though the attendant read the policeman's thoughts. The painted eye unnerves Hook, so that he readily answers subsequent questions, rather than invoke police business. (A veteran who escaped injury is nearly as susceptible to guilt as a civilian who spent the war at home.)

Sparrow kneels to inspect the cadaver. "Officer, according to Mr. Faulkner, the Chinaman telephoned him at his place of b-business. What time was that?"

"A few hours ago, sir," Hook replies. "Why?"

"If we can estimate when he heard the shot, when the b-body unstiffens it would simply be a matter of doing the m-math."

"Constable Gorman will do the math," Hook says. "And two and two will make two."

Having watched his inferior share sensitive information with members of the general public while slandering a fellow officer, Gorman thinks he might recommend outright dismissal. "You gentlemen from the undertaker, I advise you to be on your way, and take the victim with you. I am very close to lodging a complaint with your employer."

The vein in Hook's temple has started to throb again. "Mr. Gorman, I take it you really think the case is closed, and that it's time to clear the scene. Please make a note that I strongly disagree with your assessment."

"Mr. Hook, I'm in charge, not you. You'd be a disgrace to the uniform if you bothered to wear one." With the sharp nod of a man who has scored a winner, Gorman disappears upstairs.

Hook's right temple feels as though it is about to burst. His jaw aches from grinding his teeth.

"Here, you'd b-better take these." Sparrow hands him Miss Stewart's spectacles.

Following Sparrow's lead, McCurdy unscrolls the stretcher next to the body, stands and takes hold of her underarms while Sparrow takes her feet and they shift the body onto the army-green canvas. Hook tries not to look at the clotted mess that used to be the back of her head.

McCurdy surveys the shape lying at his feet. A white arm protrudes from the edge, as though reaching out for someone. Dropping to one knee, he carefully tucks the arm back under the sheet.

On a count of three, they pick up the stretcher. She is lighter than McCurdy expected, easier on the back.

"When they stiffen up, they get lighter for some reason," Sparrow says, as though having read his thoughts.

"Nonsense," Hook replies. "Things that are stiff are easier to lift. Have you tried to carry a mattress?"

"Some say the missing weight is the departed soul," McCurdy says.

Again, Janet Stewart's white forearm reaches out from under the sheet, palm up, as though trying to make a point: *Don't you see?*

Hook watches the white-coated attendants as they manoeuvre their seemingly weightless cargo out the door, up the steps and toward the hearse. He waits until they have cleared the steps, then climbs up after them.

Near the garage, the Chinese houseboy is collecting cigarette ends, matches, gum wrappers and other odd bits of litter into a tin pail, one by one. Very un-Shaughnessy to see such a messy yard.

For the first time in his life, Hook wishes he spoke Chinese.

He turns his attention to the line of chattering autos, like a swarm of enormous insects chewing the lawn, and... *Hello.*

Blackwell, Gorman and Faulkner have formed an intimate gathering next to the Cadillac and are so deep in discussion that they seem not to have noticed him. How convivial. In fact, Blackwell is offering Gorman a cigarette from his case, perhaps to avoid having to smell one of the officer's Black Cats.

Hook does speak English, however, and manages to catch a few sentences over the idling motors. Faulkner seems to be speaking as though chairing a debate, playing the neutral party.

"Constable Gorman seems to disagree with you, Morris. What say you?"

Dr. Blackwell shakes his head. "I tell you, Frank, the most plausible explanation is that she died by accident while fooling with a loaded weapon. Another hare-brained girl, amusing herself by tempting fate."

"Yet you still hold to your opinion, Constable Gorman?"

"I am one hundred per cent certain that it's a case of suicide. Believe me, I have seen it many times—a hysterical girl doing harm to herself. I wouldn't be surprised if it was her time of the month."

"Well maybe it's jolly good that you disagree. It will give the public something to think about. Fooling around with a loaded gun? Do you think she may have been on drugs or alcohol, Morris?"

"I have treated several girls with addictions," the doctor replies.

"People on drugs often commit suicide," adds Gorman. "Could she have gotten drugs from the Chinaman?"

"As her employer, I know that Janet was an abstainer. You can ask my wife."

Across the lawn, the houseboy has put down his pail and is now opening the garage doors, while inside an electric starter fires and a motor barks and roars. Wong Chi steps aside, revealing the chromium grill of a luxury tourer with a hood ornament like a nautical instrument.

Blackwell and Gorman turn to watch as the machine emerges like a dragon from its den.

As a motorcyclist, Hook marvels at the way a buggy with a motor can hold a man in a state of awe. It looks as though Dr. Blackwell is finally about to remove his hat.

"That would be the McLaughlin, would it not, Frank?"

"The Master Six, Morris. That is correct."

"They say the machine will do seventy miles an hour."

"Well I certainly wouldn't try it, but yes, it's true."

Mrs. Faulkner eases the McLaughlin to a stop next to her husband, allowing Blackwell and Gorman to admire the blue coachwork and three-tone livery; the two men trade a sardonic glance and a lift of the eyebrow: *What a world, that such a machine might be placed in the hands of a woman!*

Wearing a yellow silk jacket and a cloche hat, Mrs. Faulkner pulls the brake handle with one gloved hand and extends a cheek out the window so that Faulkner can step onto the running board and kiss it; he leans further inside to kiss the baby bundled in the cavernous back seat.

"Dash it all, do you really think this is the time to abandon ship?" he says to his wife.

"I need to find someone for Emma."

"You'd better fetch a replacement soon, otherwise you might actually have to take care of her yourself."

Showing no sign of having heard that remark, Mrs. Faulkner checks her makeup in the side mirror, adjusts the way her hat frames her hair, then releases the brake and abruptly guns the engine, forcing Faulkner to step back quickly lest she run over his foot.

Hook notes how capably she handles the machine, as it turns briskly from the driveway onto Osler Street. Faulkner mutters something to himself. Gorman and Blackwell tactfully turn toward the hedge and pretend to contemplate the empty badminton court next door.

The sight of Mrs. Faulkner, with her cropped hair and Cupid's-bow lipstick, puts Hook in mind of the girl on the stretcher, her white skin and long, womanly hair—at least where it was not matted in blood. Her body was as empty of life as a discarded coat, yet in his mind he sees a lovely and vivacious girl, with naturally red lips and a laugh like a dinner bell. Where does life go when it leaves the body? Does it evaporate immediately, or does it hover about like a puff of smoke, a conscious cloud?

He was taught the law of conservation of energy in school: energy cannot be created or destroyed, but only changed from one form into another. Might that also apply to *human* energy?

Having slid the stretcher into the back of the hearse, the two undertakers slam the doors shut. The man in spectacles climbs onto the running board and watches the tin nose man speak to the Chinese houseboy with his pail of cigarette butts.

He returns to the hearse and climbs into the cab. The motor's frantic valves sound like castanets as the vehicle trundles down the driveway, swaying from side to side.

4

No matter where you go, your desires go there too.

HOOK RIDES A 1920 BSA with a V-twin engine that originally came with a sidecar that he sold months ago to a pair of newlyweds from Port Moody. Freed of its poorly balanced burden, the BSA will do fifty-five miles an hour on a straight, clear road—as if such a thing existed.

As he leans into a corner he imagines himself a dispatch rider, speeding at full throttle down the pockmarked roads of Normandy, crouched over the petrol tank, spearing through a headwind, carrying orders to the front that could change the face of the campaign...

Hook joined the Corps of Royal Engineers to do precisely that. To qualify, before enlisting he purchased a 1910 Indian with a bent frame, a castoff from the Winnipeg Police Force that somehow made it to Waldo, and on the roads to and from town he taught himself various manoeuvres—swerves, high-speed wheelies, deliberate spills and recoveries—that he saw performed by so-called daredevils at the Pacific Exhibition. He incurred bruises and contusions but not broken bones; he took this to be a sign of talent.

For Hook at the time, a dispatcher on a motorcycle was the closest thing to Mercury, god of messages and motion. It never occurred to him that a man can be overqualified for action at the front.

As it turned out, following a number of interviews, someone in command determined that Hook's combination of brains and skills merited a projected lifespan of more than a week. A month later he found himself wearing the distinctive red hat of the Royal Military Police and stationed with a policing platoon at Rugeley in the Midlands, a training camp for infantry troops on their way to the Western Front.

At this point in the course of the war, Rugeley was receiving a steady influx of battalions—from Canada, Australia, New Zealand, Rhodesia and Kashmir. The heightened potential for internecine acrimony meant that a Redhat became not only a policeman but an intermediary between conflicting cultures in a global no man's land.

In the early part of the war, new recruits trained for a good two months, stabbing bayonets into potato sacks with white patches for vital organs; but with fewer live bodies in the field and a surfeit of dead ones, recruits were sent to join the fray in three weeks. Rugeley was the entry point of a conveyor belt to the meat grinder.

In the normal course of things, military police were ordinary soldiers who had been given authority to beat other soldiers to a pulp for trifling offences, whose purpose was to terrorize the men into obeying orders to the letter.

But as Hook saw it, that approach wouldn't work at Rugeley, which was not a regiment or company but a seemingly infinite procession of killers-in-training. In part, it became a matter of self-interest to adapt his behaviour to the situation. Redhats who made too many enemies often wound up in a ditch one way or the other, dead or with injuries that sent them home.

While he might use his knuckles and forehead in subduing drunks, AWOLs, deserters, thieves and bullies, Hook refrained from acts of whimsical cruelty, such as braining a man when he was down. When it came to nonviolent offenders, he taught himself methods of friendly questioning, meant to extract a confession and identify fellow travellers without having to splinter a man's teeth and ribs with his truncheon.

It began to occur to Hook that he was actually good at something other than riding a motorcycle. At the same time, the motorcycle lost none of its transcendent fascination.

On off-days he liked to race through the countryside (partridge hunters were the nearest thing to enemy fire), often in the company of some young woman he would meet in the dance halls of Stafford or Stoke-on-Trent—seated behind him, arms around his waist, her hands joined beneath his stomach, her wind-blown hair touching his face...

How he loved women, but the gap between loving women and loving a particular woman proved impossible to bridge.

Proclaiming one's undying love was an expected part of the mating dance, and most men were happy to oblige, but for Hook it resulted in little more than sadness, guilt and a used condom.

Meanwhile, his ability as a Redhat must have impressed his superiors, for late in 1917 he was transferred to the newly created Canadian Military Police Corps, the army's first legitimate police force, as a detective. Then wouldn't you know, just as he began to feel competent at his new job, Armistice was signed and the war was over.

He had had what many called a "good war" in that he returned with two legs, two arms and a face, but overall the experience was a disappointment.

Hook arrived home to a gently dying town of absent men, where one met single women at "basket socials" overseen by sharp-eyed biddies for whom all intimacies should take place with marriage in mind. A local man said to have "jilted" a girl (which might consist of failing to call a second time) gained a reputation as a cad that he and his family would carry for life. So he abandoned the Spokane, Portland and Seattle Railway and left Waldo forever, to become a policeman.

The Vancouver Police Department (VPD) rejected him because he didn't ride a horse and was therefore unable to club strikers from above. He applied to the New Westminster Police Department, but was rejected for a lack of firefighting skills—New Westminster had acquired a habit of burning down every few years.

It unnerved him how comparatively easy it was to join the Point Grey Police Force, but it made sense soon enough. The Point Grey constabulary was like the Foreign Legion, a drainage ditch for incompetents who couldn't be fired outright for various reasons.

The motorcycle allowance, though insufficient, tipped the scales. A man on a motorcycle was not watching the world go by, but flying through it on the back of a wonderful beast.

AS HE LEANS into the winding roads of Shaughnessy Heights, he mentally recites what seems to have become the official story: A Scottish nanny, the longtime servant of a prominent family, was about to iron baby clothes when she got it into her head either to shoot herself or to "play with a gun." Having made this decision, she went upstairs, fetched the weapon (somehow knowing where it was), returned to the laundry room and shot herself between the eyes, by accident or intent, without sustaining powder burns.

The fact that Gorman, to say nothing of Blackwell and Faulkner, took this absurd scenario seriously is, at minimum, a source of deep suspicion.

At Rugeley, recruits who failed to qualify for pacifist status often chose to shoot themselves rather than shoot the enemy. Hook saw enough to know what a man looked like with a self-inflicted gunshot to the face, and he never saw an instance where the shooting hand was free of powder residue.

Janet Stewart's face and hands appeared as well scrubbed as one would expect for a Scottish nanny handling clean clothes. Her face remained unmarked and lovely, even with the wound in her forehead.

As he rounds The Crescent past Canacraig, he spots a young woman in a cream dress suitable for a nanny, wheeling a pram toward the corner of Hudson Street, and on impulse he decides to interview her, thinking that nannies in the area must surely be acquainted with each other.

He leans his machine around the corner and brings it to a smart stop next to the pram, a sequence intended to indicate that this is an official matter.

She turns to him with the wide-eyed look of apprehension one might expect on a girl who is suddenly confronted by a man decked in leathers, cap, goggles and gloves, and astride a black, roaring machine.

Cutting the engine, Hook lifts the goggles to his forehead and speaks in his Redhat voice: "Good afternoon, miss. I am Constable Hook of the Point Grey Police. Be so good as to identify yourself, please?"

She has an open face, observant blue eyes and the body of a girl with a fondness for sweets. She gives him a long speculative stare, then continues to push the pram forward as though he weren't present. (In the Old Country, policemen are known to use their authority for purposes other than official business.)

He rolls the machine forward to keep up with her. "Miss, I am speaking to you as part of an investigation. An inquiry about a person by the name of Janet Stewart. Are you acquainted with anyone by that name?"

The perambulator stops. The bundle inside remains still. There is no way to know whether it's a boy, a girl or a small sack of flour.

She frowns. "Janet? Wha' of her? And wha' business is it of yours, sir?"

A spirited girl, for a nanny.

"Once again, miss, may I inquire as to your name?"

"My name is Jean Hawthorn. I work wi' the McKinley family. I am in charge of wee Billy here."

"Would you be acquainted with the young woman by the name of Janet Stewart?"

"Aye, sir. Janet is my very best friend."

She doesn't know. In his mind, Hook sees an anvil suspended above her head, about to fall.

"I'm off seeing her this afternoon," she continues. "We are to look for Dufferin."

"Who is Dufferin?"

"My family's cat. Gone since morning yesterday. He could have been snatched by a cougar or eagle is the worry, but we hope for the best."

Hope for the best. When it comes to missing persons or lost animals, Hook wishes people wouldn't do that.

A pause, while he searches for the words with which to tell her that Janet won't be available to search for Dufferin, or anyone else, ever.

"Miss Hawthorn, it's my unfortunate duty to tell you that Miss Stewart is deceased." He resists the urge to touch his attempted moustache.

He watches her face go blank and her eyes turn inward, as though trying to remember something. He can't entirely resist a feeling of power, followed by shame and self-dislike.

"Deceased?" In her Aberdeen accent it sounded like *diseased.* "D'you mean that she has...?"

"Passed away, miss, I'm afraid. That she has."

As often happens when two people are caught in a totally unfamiliar situation, there follows a moment of suspended animation; he feels a need to do something but is at a total loss as to what that might be.

In any case, he cannot offer the girl much help or comfort seated on his motorcycle. He levers the kickstand with his toe, dismounts and immediately becomes aware that she is slightly taller than him. (Hook barely made it past height restrictions in 1916. Probably he is even shorter now; English roads will do that to you.)

The young woman could be holding her breath, for her bosom remains perfectly still, but now her lower lip begins to tremble and he knows what's coming. Fortunately, he pocketed a clean handkerchief this morning.

He presents his inadequate offering. "I am truly sorry, miss."

She looks as though she might be suppressing a laugh or a sneeze. Tiny beads of perspiration glitter on her forehead, then her face collapses in tears. In one motion, she accepts the constable's handkerchief, shakes it open, wipes her cheeks and forehead and blows her nose. To steady her (the perambulator has no brake and could easily roll away), he gently takes hold of her upper arm with his ungloved hand. *A strong, well-built, straightforward girl.*

Her dress is a perfectly modest frock, well below the knee, but with elbow-length sleeves and a low neckline.

Spring is torture for a lonely man, a slow burlesque in which layers of women's clothing come off week by week, revealing patches of female flesh unseen since the previous fall. Hook feels a stirring in the trousers he would rather not experience on duty.

The pram's occupant sleeps on, undisturbed.

"Is there anything I can do to assist you, miss?"

"Janet?... Oh, dear, dear heavens..." She rests her forehead on his leather shoulder; he can smell her lavender soap.

"Miss Hawthorn, I hope you will allow me to escort you home."

She takes his arm in both hands and squeezes tight. "I would appreciate that." *A cuddlesome girl.*

They turn onto Hudson Street and walk together behind the pram, with her arm looped around his. To an observer they might be a young couple taking the baby for a stroll.

"I am sorry to question you at a time like this but, to assist the investigation, please cast your mind back: Can you think of any reason why Miss Stewart would wish to harm herself?"

"Harm herself?" Her lips form a mere trace of a smile. "Janet— *harm herself*? Not bloody likely!" She covers her mouth as though something embarrassing just slipped out.

"What do you mean, miss?"

"Janet is... was... a carefree girl wha' liked to have fun. That's all."

"Did she show any special interest in shooting guns?"

"Oh gracious, no. But she does—did—love to dance."

"Can you think of anyone who might wish to do her harm?"

"Nobody wanted to hurt Janet. Please, officer. Please may we talk about this another time?" He waits while Miss Hawthorn launches into a fresh round of tears, cursing himself for having turned into such a callous interrogator, however effective it might be to catch the witness in a moment of high emotion.

Halfway down Hudson Street, they stop at the walkway of a stucco mansion, with decorative half timbers intended to evoke Shakespearian England.

"If I may, Miss Hawthorn, I would like to speak to you again on this matter."

"When?"

Reluctantly, Hook lets go of her upper arm. "Let's wait until you are more... composed. Your observations might help to solve a crime."

"Was there a crime? Wha' has happened? How did she die?"

"At this time, I'm afraid I can't reveal that information."

"Back there you mentioned someone harming her. Was she *murdered*?"

"We have reached no conclusions as yet."

"Surely you're not after suggesting that she, that she..."

"As I say, the case is very much open. In the meantime, the police would be grateful for your assistance."

"Of course." She manages another wisp of a smile through tears, but whether inspired by the prospect of seeing him again or of assisting the police, he has no way of knowing.

"I am at your service, officer."

Constable Hook can feel his ears warming. "Well then, for the moment I shall bid you a good day, Miss Hawthorn."

"Good day to you, Constable Hook."

He backs awkwardly down the walkway to the street, pulls on his gloves and strides down the sidewalk toward his abandoned motorcycle. He forgot to ask for his handkerchief.

"Hello, operator speaking. Is this TRinity 3146?"

"Here is TRinity 3146. You have reached the Blunt residence, Cissie Braidwood speaking."

"Here is TRinity 3235. I will connect you."

SWITCH

"Cissie, can you speak on the telephone? Are you alone?"

"Alone in the house I am, Jean, and them away to the links leaving me with the brat, and him shitting himself hourly and her after me to do the linen as well."

"Did you hear about Janet?"

"Aye, they were talking about it over their coffee an hour ago. Took the heart right out of me. The poor soul."

"And a policeman telling me hardly fifteen minutes ago. I nearly fainted from the shock. He walked me home in his motorcycle uniform. Had to put his arm right around me for support."

"He didn't have his arm right around you!"

"He did. He did. Said I might help solve a crime. Imagine!"

"Well anyone could see she wasn't safe. She shouldn't a' been left alone in the house with the Chinaman. There's to be a law against it soon, I hear."

"That's as may be, Cissie, but was she really so afraid of him? She never said so to me."

"Aye, scared the life out of her he did. The way he looked at her with his big slanted brown eyes, the girl knew she was not safe. I've felt it myself in his presence, a way about him that would melt a girl's resistance if she ever let him."

"True, he is a different one. Most of them are so much shorter. From the back you'd think him a regular person."

"And him after giving her underwear and the like—disgusting!"

"She told me it was film for her camera he gave her."

"And other things too. You can trust me on that. I don't know for the life of me where he got the money."

"She was laughing when she told me about the film, Cissie. She didn't seem frightened at all."

"Oh she liked an admirer, and she weren't too particular who it was. But the Chinaman was dangerous. I saw him try to hold her hand and for a moment she let him—can you imagine? Of course the Faulkners won't hear any of it. The missus is Armstrong's daughter, don't you know, and the general running next election. They don't want a scandal over the help—especially when they left her alone with him while they were at a fancy party at Canacraig. Jessie Murray was talking about the fancy cars on The Crescent and up and down Osler. Said ye'd think the Royal Family was here."

"The general never invites my people. Puts them in conniptions, it does."

"Jean, do ye s'pose the Chinaman had his way with her while the *quality were out drinking themselves sodden? And not only drinking from what my people say. Do ye s'pose they get their dope from the Chinaman?"*

"For certain they're a unsavoury pair, the Faulkners," she continues, "he with his British manners and she with her flapper shoes and short skirts. I hear she was a sweet thing that went to London and came back with no more decency than a bootlegger's chippy."

Jean makes a mental note to contact Constable Hook. He will come over and they will sit down together, and he'll listen to every word.

5

The hardest thing is to find a black cat in a dark room—especially if there is no cat.

WHEN HE FIRST moved into his quarters on the second floor of the Colonial Hotel, McCurdy moved the desk to the window overlooking Drake Street to take advantage of the view, which seemed to approximate a microcosm of the city, minus the Chinese and the rich.

To look outside right now you could be in London, the fog is so thick—smoke, most of it. Downtown Vancouver is literally surrounded by smoke-producing entities: the railway lines north of Water Street, the honeycomb burners in the sawmills on Granville Island, Sweeney Cooperage on False Creek creating an acrid stink spiced with creosote from the manufacture of railway ties and pilings, not to mention effluent from the fish-packing plants. In June, the fumes are intensified by the low-hanging cloud that bunches up against Mount Seymour, packing and compressing the smoke until it becomes a concentrated layer of granulated charcoal. Sometimes you can't see your hand in front of your face.

Another reason to call the place *British* Columbia—and not London, but Liverpool.

A few feet below his open window a bulbous street lamp glows like a little moon, complete with halo. The headlights of passing autos drift by like the eyes of prehistoric fish. The potholes and streetcar tracks do not exist.

On the sidewalk across the street he can just make out the silhouettes of pedestrians poking their way through patches of lamp light, jostling other shadows and muttering grunts and apologies.

He reaches under the shirred paper lamp shade, switches on the electric light, and now the window becomes a black void.

He stares down at the equally blank page before him. His

inkwell is full; there are no more pencils to sharpen; he is ready, or should be. He picks up the Parker duofold he won at a high-school poetry contest the year of his graduation, an event that inspired him to change his major at university from engineering to English. Eight years later, with a single chapbook to his credit (*Ordinary Poems*, Trivinity Press, Toronto, 1920), it was a decision he has reason to regret.

He stares at the blank sheet of paper. It lies spread beneath him, begging him to give it meaning. And nothing is happening.

A few weeks ago he stowed his Underwood on the floor, on the theory that the typewriter discourages creative thinking, that longhand is the way to extract fresh ideas. Now he is forced to admit that the typewriter is not the problem and that longhand is not the solution.

There's a muscularity to the work of a young poet, being based on a single emotion, a single thought; but no matter how muscular, you can't fly for long on one wing other than to go around and around in circles.

Once upon a time, McCurdy's one wing was outrage at social injustice, of which there was ample evidence in war and peace—enough material for a lifetime, or so he thought. But there are only so many ways to express outrage, and outrage is only interesting to the extent that it comes as some sort of surprise. In the social environment of Vancouver, trumpeting the unfairness of things is like complaining that the rain is wet.

If one has nothing interesting to say about the world, the obvious alternative is to write about oneself; yet, whenever he attempts something lyrical and personal he recoils at its lack of originality. Did Tennyson not adequately deal with love, bereavement and death? Did Joyce Kilmer not adequately describe her feelings about a tree? And since the Armistice, man's inhumanity to man is a dead issue—especially coming from a poet who hasn't served.

But still he hears the rebuke implied by the blank page before him, the feeling of having let the universe down.

During an early conversation, Sparrow assessed the situation perfectly: that he was an effete individualist engaging in bourgeois introspection for want of anything better to do.

The worker is the person you rally, Sparrow said. *The bourgeois is the person you use.* Then he laughed that European laugh that says *just a joke of course*, when it really wasn't.

Their friendship sometimes strikes McCurdy as an absurd version of the Christmas truce at the Somme, when German and British soldiers gathered in fellowship, then returned to their posts and resumed ripping each other to shreds.

McCurdy cleans his spectacles with his shirt-tail and begins to write, allowing the pen to move on its own. If automatic writing was good enough for Conan Doyle, it should be good enough for him.

Outside the open window the fog becomes chilly
A whisper of drizzle
May is one's true love in a penny romance
June is a lying she-devil—a dominatrix
Sudden attacks of winter like the slash of a whip...

The pen stops on its own and refuses to continue. *Unbelievable*, it seems to say. *You can't even describe the weather without resorting to tabloid rhetoric.* McCurdy crumples the sheet into a ball, stands up and flings it sidearm out the window, into the fog.

Some time ago he began a contest with himself, the object being to land a crumpled wad of foolscap precisely halfway between the streetcar tracks. Over the months to follow, as the paper balls multiplied, the rain caused them to disintegrate into grey blobs, indistinguishable from the droppings of pigeons and gulls.

As he stares down at another white sheet, his mood darkens.

Every person has an incident in the past of such humiliation that it never fades in memory; on the contrary, it sharpens with time, and small details become needles with which to pierce one's eyeballs. To this day he can recite the *Globe* review verbatim from beginning to end. Just the opening sentence is still enough to keep him awake all night: *If there is anything to justify the general opinion that Canadians cannot and should not write poetry, it's* Ordinary Poems, *Mr. McCurdy's decidedly sub-ordinary attempt...* In a more serious vein, the critic went on to question why *Ordinary Poems* had been published in the first place, why even an upstart publisher like Trivinity Press would champion a book of poems about the lives of three garment workers at Eaton's.

The answer to that question became clear soon enough. Trivinity Press was the brainchild of a group of well-heeled seniors at Trinity

College with a connection to *The Varsity*, which had published a few of his poems under the title *And on the Left*—though at no time did McCurdy think of his writing as socialism, communism or any other *ism*, other than the egotism it takes to write poetry in the first place.

Had he not been so intoxicated by the thought of publication, he might have become suspicious. Trinity students took pride in their rapier-like, satirical wit, especially in the Literary Institute, and more especially in the Debating Society—of which his publishers served as president and vice-president.

In truth, these witty gentlemen published the book *so that it would* be panned, thereafter to become a joke, told in speeches and articles that mocked the very concept of socialist art, and Canadian art along with it.

Surely the purpose of extolling the working classes in verse, if it serves any purpose at all, is not so that they may wallow in their supposed suffering, but in order to bring home to the masses traditional British values of hard work, honesty and thrift...

Throughout that dreadful term, *Ordinary Poems* became an all-purpose straw man. In the Conservative Club and the Debating Society his poems were quoted as an extreme example of socialist absurdity, usually expressed in a scatological metaphor, the most reliable way to get a laugh:

Gentlemen, did Michelangelo work with marble, or did he work with shite? Gentlemen, why buy a book of Canadian poems when one can watch derelicts shite in an alley for free?

Meanwhile in the Department of English, professors quoted *Ordinary Poems* as a device to lighten the atmosphere, alongside McIntyre, the Cheese Poet:

We have seen thee, Queen of Cheese,
Lying quietly at your ease,
Gently fanned by evening breeze;
Thy fair form no flies dare seize.

McCurdy the poet had become McCurdy the town fool. Upon returning home at the end of term, he endured a perpetual lecture on the virtues of the insurance industry and the need for "bread and butter." (To this day, he can't face that innocuous snack without a degree of nausea.)

As much to spite his father as to exact revenge, next term he set on a different course.

Having volunteered for the position of deputy editor at *The Varsity* and gained access to library archives, McCurdy began noting similarities in phrasing, misspellings and other evidence in student essays and uncovered a case of mass cheating, including among members of the Literary Institute. It resulted in several expulsions, including the founders of Trivinity Press.

Having accomplished his goal, he finished out the term, attempted to join up for what turned out to be the last year of the war and was promptly rejected for bad eyes. Rather than endure another bread-and-butter lecture from his father, he then set out on that all-Canadian ritual for a young man at loose ends: a tour of the west by rail. Proving himself useless at farming and unwilling to turn to his family for funds with strings attached, he paid his way by contributing to the *Winnipeg Tribune*, the *Saskatoon Phoenix*, the *Edmonton Bulletin*, newspapers where the main criterion for employment was an ability to write a complete sentence in English.

Over the past half-decade he has written hundreds of poems about the vastness of the country, the inclement weather, the hardiness of farmers, the grit of railway workers and the plight of the poor, and published not a one.

Perhaps as punishment for years of bad writing, now he is a dried-up garden, a vacant lot, a burnt-out case.

MCCURDY SECURES THE temples of his spectacles around his ears, switches off the lamp, and leans forward across his desk and out the window for a look at the pedestrians and autos passing below. The fog has cleared slightly, revealing two men in dark suits scurrying along the opposite sidewalk. From around the corner a foot policeman appears with his custodian helmet and cudgel, like a life-size souvenir of England. Three men in tweed caps are smoking and conversing in a doorway—perhaps negotiating, for they grow silent as the policeman passes within earshot.

As he peers outside he can discern the outlines of ragged men in groups of three and four, loitering between buildings and in doorways, lighting dog-ends while avoiding three on a match—ex-soldiers still wary of snipers.

And of course not a woman to be seen.

Overseas, newspapers howl in outrage over the shortage of mar-riageable men and the resulting threat to the white race. When you kill off a million of your strongest and cleverest, leaving the rest physically and mentally injured, the outcome doesn't bode well for British bloodlines.

Send the women here! cries every unmarried logger, miner and fisherman in British Columbia—but no. British women, it seems, would rather die spinsters than relocate to the far edge of the earth. Except for women selling sex, women who have disgraced their families and of course Scottish nannies...

McCurdy leans further out the window to peer down at the tops of wet black umbrellas, lit from above by moon globes that resemble the entrance to a pawnshop.

He switches the desk lamp back on and begins to write—but again the pen stops on its own. *Pawnshop balls equal street lamps? A stretch to say the least!* He once heard that the three balls at a pawnshop signified two for the lender, one for the client... and now his train of thought has gone completely off the rails.

Another white paper ball sails through the night to fall between the tracks, silent as snow.

He must try something completely different.

He imagines a person arriving blindfolded from another coun-try and being led around the city; intermittently and without warning, the blindfold is whipped away and—*flash!* What does he make of what he sees? Like a blind man investigating an elephant, what does he conclude about the place as a whole?

Flash! The entrance to the Patricia Cafe on Hornby Street, whose sheet-glass windows reflect the paintwork of three gleam-ing automobiles by the curb—a Lincoln, a Packard, a REO. Sleek men and fragrant women unfold from miniature dens of leather and wood, to stroll past a red-coated doorman at stately speed, scions of the bootlegging industry, the alcohol aristocrats.

Canada's farcical experimentation with Prohibition preceded the United States by four years, which meant that Canadian boot-leggers, having already made a fortune at home, possess the infra-structure to dominate the illegal US market. Having bribed the US Coast Guard to admit whole fleets of vessels packed with booze, they play cat-and-mouse with the FBI. The resulting fortunes have created investors, philanthropists, arts patrons, developers, ne'er-do-wells, vixens, drug addicts and, of course, alcoholics...

The pen stops scratching. Goddammit, he can see where this is headed: the scions of alcohol barons as human sacrifices on the altar of excess. An old morality tale, spun from every pulpit in town.

Another white ball lands between the streetcar tracks, bounces feebly and stops dead.

With a fresh sheet he begins to take verbal photographs of the city for the benefit of his blindfolded guest, images he will later juxtapose, cunningly, to devastating effect:

Flash! All down the south side of False Creek, a clutter of tar-paper shacks float on improvised rafts, rented by ex-loggers and ex-soldiers, all injured in one way or another, who spend their time fishing for sardines, drinking whisky and washing their clothes in the salt water, or just sitting on the jetty, staring into space.

Flash! The Amputees' Lawn Bowling Club, where players stand on their stumps to make a shot.

McCurdy's pen has become motionless at the word *amputees.* Wartime Grand Guignol may have been crisp copy when there was a war to write about, but in 1924 it's the work of posers like himself...

He screws the cap over the nib, sets the pen aside and drifts another white ball into the blackness, another little round package containing yet more obvious irony, more humanitarian clucking and hand-wringing, the same material he mined to better effect in university despite the scorn it received. But more creative, certainly, than the journalese he writes today, sentences that fill the spaces between advertisements the way concrete fills a hole.

He sweeps his arm across the table, causing the remaining sheets of paper to flutter onto the floor like autumn leaves, removes his glasses and covers his eyes with the palms of his hands. *Autumn leaves? Is that the best you can do?*

AT THE END of another ghastly day, Constable Hook lies splayed like a flounder on his surplus army cot beneath the front gable of Mrs. Pinion's Gentlemen's Rooms, in a room in which much expense has been spared. A rag rug sits on the floor and a small faded picture of nothing in particular hangs on the wall. There is no space even for a proper chair.

He is smoking in his undershirt with a tea saucer ashtray

balanced on his stomach, and his head and shoulders propped against the silk pillow he pinched from the lobby of the Alcazar Hotel. He had been making inquiries about a stolen auto and the temptation was too great. Not his best moment as an officer of the law, but the pillow supplied by Mrs. Pinion might as well have been a wet cucumber sandwich for all the comfort it provided, and a complaint was answered by a dismissive clicking of her store-bought teeth.

So he stole a better pillow. One can only afford so much integrity at a salary of $32.50 per week.

With his head in a more or less upright position, he can see past the foot of his bed through the open window, past the roofs of buildings across the street, past black scrub forest, down to False Creek, which appears not as a body of water but as a wall of smoke. His mind again turns to Miss Hawthorn, with her strong arms and healthy bosom, her tears on the shoulder of his leather jacket, her aroma of lavender soap.

A bit more muscular than he might prefer—as if a man's preference makes any difference in Vancouver these days, where the population of eligible females seems almost extinct except at church. Where he might as well be in Waldo.

A few single women might be spotted at a dance hall, but that brought up the other problem: women tend to find other men more attractive than him—taller men, wittier men, men with well-groomed moustaches and skimmer hats, compared to whom he is, as his mother would put it, "dull as dishwater."

To be sure, Vancouver contains its share of ladies of the evening who are more than happy to indulge a man's taste in lips, feet or anything really. But no intelligent man can purchase an orgasm without the knowledge that for the vendor it's messy, unappetizing work, like plumbing or cleaning public facilities.

Feeling more lonely now, he forces his mind to change direction, lest he succumb to self-abuse and lose his mind or his eyesight.

He thinks back to the laundry room and the tableau he encountered there. Could the Faulkners have murdered their nanny? To avoid a scandal of some sort? Surely it would have been easier to buy her off and send her home—the usual thing in such a case. Besides, what could be more scandalous than a corpse in the laundry room with a bullet in her head?

Though Hook continues to seethe at Gorman having taken

over the investigation, it occurs to him that being treated as a
nonentity enabled him to notice a number of things that might
have escaped him otherwise, in the way that a child might observe
an "adult" conversation.

Again he thinks back to the discussion's rehearsed quality, as
though the participants were conducting not an investigation so
much as a replica of an investigation.

The fact that Dr. Blackwell serves double-duty—as chief surgeon for the Point Grey Police and as the Faulkner family physician—positioned him to arrange an agreement with a couple of
telephone calls. And without doubt, Constable Gorman has his
price; he could hardly have been booted from the Provincial Police
for an excess of zeal.

And he wonders about the Chinaman. Rather than come to
such an unlikely conclusion as suicide or accident, would it not
have gone more smoothly to blame a member of an inferior race,
someone who couldn't defend himself in English? Among the
white population the Chinese are universally viewed as a diabolical, sneaky people; the case could have been closed almost on
the basis of race alone. Yet at the merest mention of the houseboy,
Mrs. Faulkner leapt to his defence. *Wong Chi is part of the family*,
she said, in a pre-emptive tone and an acquired English accent.

With his cigarette sandwiched between his lips, he opens Miss
Stewart's spectacles, lifts them in front of his face and peers at
the ceiling. He can barely see through one bloodstained, cracked
lens. No telling whether the girl was far-sighted, near-sighted—or
nearly blind, like the attendant in a white coat too small for him.
Hook suspected the man to be a reporter but said nothing, glad to
have a witness to the exchange of horse shite in the laundry room.

Slightly unnerved, he puts aside his saucer and slides to the
edge of the cot, then sets his feet on the floor and carefully places
the spectacles in the drawer of his bedside table, the only other
piece of furniture in the room. He closes the drawer gently, as
though it contains a small animal.

As it was with the stolen pillow, he doesn't know why he took
her glasses. He just felt like it, that's all. The urge to take possession of something that had touched her, as though the spectacles
might convey something or other. Of course he will return them
to the constabulary tomorrow; if asked, he will say that he secured
them as evidence, then forgot he had them. Events at Point Grey

move at such a torpid pace that evidence tends to slip through procedural gaps and wriggle away like a minnow out of a net. This afternoon they had to delay their report to Chief Quigley because he was taking a nap, which gave Gorman—who had partaken of the brown bottle in his desk drawer—plenty of time to misplace his notebook.

For no particular reason, Hook feels drawn to the window. He crosses the room and kneels in front of the sill, which is only about a foot off the floor (his head would crack against the gable if he stood up), and flicks his cigarette end onto the street below.

Outside, wisps of grey smoke from nearby honeycomb burners drift through the air like lost souls.

6

Nothing is more visible than things hidden.

FOR SPARROW IT was an interesting morning and afternoon. After dropping McCurdy off at the Birks clock, he drove to the funeral parlour, parked the hearse in the reserved area and entered the front office without knocking.

"Hullo, Mr. Edwards. Reporting in as per instructions."

Seated behind his mahogany desk beneath a wall covered with photographs of prominent local cadavers, Nigel Edwards leaned over the desk telephone holding a burning cigarette jammed between his knuckles. With his other hand, he held the receiver to his ear. A ruddy-faced man with the spongy skin of an alcoholic, he dropped the handset back onto the cradle immediately like a boy who had been caught doing something naughty—an odd reaction for a sixty-year-old undertaker dressed for golf in plus-fours and argyle socks.

"You have the deceased?" Edwards tried to maintain frank eye contact, but his eyes kept dropping to the telephone, which looked back at him like a black, long-necked bird with a stump for a wing and a mouth like a rounded duck's bill.

"I do, sir. Miss Stewart is in the car."

"Then off with you to the mortuary. Tell Mr. Cruikshank he can proceed as usual."

"And not to the city morgue? Surely there will b-be an autopsy."

At the word *autopsy*, Mr. Edwards's pupils narrowed to pinpricks. "And why do you say that, Mr. Sparrow?"

"You mentioned the word *usual*, sir. The b-back of the girl's head, the occiput, is smashed to pieces. Most *un*usual I should say, sir."

"Don't flaunt your medical terms with me, Sparrow."

"I'm only pointing out that the condition of the deceased calls for an autopsy."

"Why do you say that?"

"Say what, sir?"

"That the condition of the body demands an autopsy."

"A violent death, Mr. Edwards. It's customary, sir."

"Sparrow, let's say a man's head has been cut off by a saw: would you call that a violent death?"

"Certainly."

"And yet surely you wouldn't call for an autopsy?"

"True, Mr. Edwards, b-because the cause in that case is known and not suspicious."

Edwards butted his smoke in a silver ashtray full of cigarette stubs, then lit up another with a silver desk lighter shaped like a bulbous gravestone. "Frankly, Mr. Sparrow, I don't think it's your decision to make, whether or not the deceased suffered a suspicious death."

"Sir, there is a b-bullet hole in her forehead."

"Neither Constable Gorman nor Chief Quigley chose to use the word *suspicious*. Nor did the coroner's office—I spoke to Mr. Brydon-Jack just now. Are you saying that a driver with a head injury knows more than two policemen, an undertaker and a coroner?"

"It was not an opinion, sir. I was speaking of precedent." *Touchy*, said a voice in Sparrow's head. *I wonder if he actually spoke to the coroner at all.* At the same time, he could sense fear emanating from his employer like waves of heat from a small furnace.

The funeral director decided to press his point further. "And what about the families? Will it do them good to proclaim their loved one a suicide? And you know how word travels—merciful heavens, if she's Catholic we'll be lucky to find a plot to bury her in!"

Sparrow had to admit that his boss had a point. True enough, the province had seen a terrific upswing in suicides since the war: vets cutting their throats while shaving, drowning on fishing trips, driving their autos off steep embankments on a clear day. Remarkable how many trained ex-infantrymen make it a practice to clean their loaded rifle with the safety off.

Undertakers are not in the business of making life difficult for bereaved families. If a grieving widow says that her husband accidentally died of carbon monoxide poisoning, so be it. Except that, in this case, the accident victim wasn't a veteran with soldier's heart but a Scottish nanny with a basket of baby clothes to iron.

Nonetheless, as per instructions, Sparrow delivered the body to Upshaw at the mortuary, who ordered it taken straight to the embalmer, as though she died of old age. When Sparrow mentioned that there had been no autopsy, Upshaw's reply sounded as though they were talking about two different corpses.

Sparrow then drove the cadaver to Cruikshank, the embalmer, to whom he mentioned the peculiar circumstances. Cruikshank (who kept a mixture of ethanol and tonic next to the formaldehyde for personal use) replied that it wasn't his problem, autopsy or no autopsy, and that in any case he wasn't about to dissect her himself. This meant that the embalmer would stuff her wounds and orifices with plaster of Paris, putting a limit to forensics.

When Sparrow called afterwards and told McCurdy the story, the reporter broke his pencil twice taking notes; it didn't require second sight to conclude that Edwards was acting under orders.

For certain, McCurdy will pay for the beer. In fact, Sparrow has invited his fiancée.

MILDRED HAS ALWAYS annoyed McCurdy, a feeling that, like the common cold, takes a different form each time they meet.

On this occasion he resents her for having come out dressed as a man—and not the girl-boy look currently in fashion (short hair, no waist, no hips, no bosom), but a transvestite getup that would put a man on a stage, in jail or in a ditch.

Had Howard forewarned him that Mildred would pull this stunt, he would never have agreed to her presence; but in all probability Howard has been kept in the dark himself.

Vancouver in 1924 is an even more miserable place to drink than it was during Prohibition. To satisfy the temperance lobby, local governments forbid the selling of drink by the glass—which means that working people who can't afford inflated government prices (half a week's wages for a bottle of whisky) are as dependent on speakeasies as ever, and the Dry Squad are far more diligent defending government revenues than public morals. Fortunately, to placate thirsty ex-soldiers, veterans' clubs were given an exemption, as were clubs for wealthy businessmen, which opened up a loophole permitting all sorts of "clubs" to materialize. Upon his arrival two years ago, McCurdy became a member of a ladies and gentlemen's club as a means of attracting young ladies, before he realized how few ladies were available to escort. And his investment continues to go to waste, even with a female present. Thanks to Miss Wickstram's taste for infiltration, they have paid a twenty-cent-per-person membership fee to the Maple, a men's-only "beer club" in the basement of an abandoned warehouse on Powell Street with unsteady furniture and soggy sawdust on the floor.

Their waiter is a red-haired ex-logger with a smashed face and without the tip of one ear, whose capacious gut acts as a shelf to support a metal tray crammed with thirty-six draught. He slams three pints on the table and holds out a palm the size of a catcher's mitt, onto which McCurdy resentfully deposits thirty cents. The waiter scoops the coins into a leather pouch and moves on without a glance at the impersonator across the table.

If he had noticed her delicate hands and the lack of a beard beneath the engineer's cap he might have discovered the ruse, but nobody can see clearly in this murky room where every occupant is puffing tobacco and half-drunk; and, in any case, he probably wouldn't care.

McCurdy is a non-smoker, not by choice. Childhood asthma prevented him from taking up that pleasant, masculine habit (though advertisements said it would be good for his lungs). As it is, he breathes enough smoke, grime and soot in the streets of Vancouver to ensure an abbreviated life.

Mildred lights another peculiar-smelling cigarette from her package of Meccas. "Who first said it was suicide?"

"One of the p-police. The stout p-purple chap."

"It was the only explanation that came out of his yap," McCurdy says. "Why would a copper do that, do you suppose? Jump to that conclusion?"

"B-because he is stupid, Ed. Or b-bought off. Or b-both."

"The doctor called it an accident. A silly girl fooling around with her boss's pistol."

"A naughty double-entendre," Mildred says, "but not to be ruled out. Did anyone suggest that someone might have shot her?"

"Nothing b-bad happens in Shaughnessy Heights, sweetheart. I thought you knew that."

"Blackwell is the Faulkners' family physician," McCurdy says. "His livelihood depends on telling his patients what they want to hear." How he envies Blackwell's Swiss watch, custom shoes and bespoke tailoring.

Mildred lights another Mecca, despite the one already smouldering in the ashtray. "I suppose everyone is eventually bought off, or frightened off—even you Eddie."

McCurdy has always hated the name Eddie. *Eddie,* as in Eddie Four-Eyes, the kid who couldn't fight until he learned to fight with words. Again, Mildred has found a sore spot and is probing it with precision.

Sparrow pokes two fingers into his shirt pocket, retrieves a cigarette paper and a pouch from the chest pocket and produces a curious, twisted cigarette. "Miss Wickstram is referring to the carrot and stick."

"Very good darling, the carrot and the stick. For example, Eddie here says he is paid to write shit for—how many cents a word was it, Eddie?"

"One cent actually, *Millie.*"

"There you are. For Eddie here, a cent a word is his price. That's the carrot. At the same time, Eddie is motivated by a fear of bad reviews—or should I say, *more* bad reviews—which is the stick."

Sparrow inhales the smoke from his roll-your-own and exhales an intoxicating puff of muggle, to be obliterated by a miasma of competing fumes. "Darling, where are you going with this? Why is it Ed's moral duty to write p-poems?"

"The poems are beside the point. The point is, to be whoring for fear of bad reviews is to be bought off and frightened off at the same time."

More smoke in McCurdy's face. First a psychological attack, now poison gas.

"You're a nasty piece of work, Millie."

"Calm down the b-both of you. The moment calls for a truce."

Mildred places her barely smoked cigarette in the ashtray beside its companion—one cigarette per nostril.

"In that case, gentlemen, I believe I shall retreat to the loo."

AS MILDRED THREADS her way between tables packed with meaty specimens of the male gender, she reflects that, for many of her classmates, this room would be seen as a veritable banquet. At graduation, they were told in no uncertain terms that there would be no marriageable suitors for them. A million dead and a million disabled in a variety of ways: head wounds, soldier's heart, not to mention injuries to the torso that precluded matrimony.

In church, at school and at home, British girls were groomed for spinsterhood as their contribution to the war effort—which for some was a not entirely unwelcome development. The curriculum at Badminton School encouraged girls to seek an independent existence. In chapel, Lenin received equal time with Jesus.

Thanks to Badminton, girls such as Mildred had assumed that upon graduation they would be pursuing aspirations of their own; once the war was won, surely the march of progress was inevitable. Unfortunately, the march of progress wandered down a dark alley, where it was set upon by thugs.

Following Armistice, job situations for women disappeared overnight. How wrong Badminton girls had been thinking that merit would rule the day, when the fact was that Britain in 1920 was in most respects the same society their mothers occupied in 1910, and their grandmothers in 1890.

What a surprise to find that in civilian society the world was still a place where girls must remain virgins (or pretend to) because they would fetch a better price on the marriage market, however bare the shelves. Mildred wonders why the pre-war practice of mail-order brides hasn't seen a revival; of course, correspondence is difficult when only one side can read and write...

Not that her education had failed to provide useful advantages. During the war, Badminton girls rose to key positions simply on the strength of being Badminton girls.

As a skill in itself, switchboard operation stood slightly above household service, requiring the ability to place a "male" jack into a "female" receptacle whose light had gone on. (Men still find the metaphor hilarious, year after year.) Any girl with ten fingers, a voice and a knowledge of English and French could become a switchboard operator with the Signal Corps.

However, this did not apply to girls who performed the service for the officer class. When it came to high-level communication, only girls of a certain breeding would do: girls with a public school education that encouraged quick thinking, physical fitness and a knowledge of world affairs, together with an ardent loyalty to her country—and above all, the proper accent.

For this rare combination of old and new values, Recruitment turned again and again to Miss Baker of Badminton School.

For their part, Badminton girls preferred to work as Hello Girls as opposed to, for example, Canary Girls, having studied enough science to know that TNT was toxic to the lungs, skin, blood and liver—and if it accidentally blew up, toxic to one's whole body at once.

As a Badminton girl, Mildred Wickstram was seconded to the War Office on Whitehall, translating and relaying hour-by-hour reports, orders, estimates and complaints, acting as a mediator between concentrations of power—a fulcrum in the tug-of-war between civilian and military command.

Mildred quickly realized that a Hello Girl in this situation possessed a degree of power herself:

SWITCH

"Yes, Central Exchange, here is 540."

SWITCH

"Colonel Havershom, sir, are you there? Hold one minute, sir, while I connect you."

SWITCH

"Sir, it's Colonel Havershom again, yes sir, from Ordinance, yes that one, shall I get rid of him or shall I make him cool his heels?"

SWITCH

"Colonel Havershom, sir, I am afraid the general's line is still busy. A call from 10 Downing Street..."

The Hello Girl knew why the general's line was busy, and why it would remain busy as far as this caller was concerned. She knew the general's likes and dislikes better than he did himself; she could intuit the severity of his anger, frustration, before he spoke a word; and though rules forbade listening in except when establishing or checking a connection, that created an enormous loophole. In reality, there was nothing to stop a Hello Girl from listening to both sides of any conversation, then piecing together the story behind it all. In that sense, the Hello Girl knew more about the internal politics of the War Office than did anyone at Whitehall. Not that she had any use for this information, but it helped to get through the day while doing a repetitive, mindless job.

Throughout the conflict, internal rumours—especially concerning the personal affairs of the higher ranks—caromed back and forth in every mess or pub, all based on something *somebody heard said*. While spying for a foreign power was a capital offence, spying *within* one's unit amounted to a national sport.

And in the middle of it sat the Hello Girl, with her headset, patches and plugs. Officers sensed her power without quite knowing why. Some fell in love with her—again without knowing why—at least for the duration of the war, as Mildred was to find out.

With the war over, officers returned to their families and resumed their proper places, manipulating the levers of business and industry. Finding themselves in an at-large position, some unseated Badminton girls chose the life of an adventuress, while a number formed close friendships with other women, exploring how a Badminton girl need not depend upon a man to fulfill her needs. Other Badminton girls chose to become nuns of a kind—dedicating their lives to securing the right to vote, to nursing, teaching and social reform. (In their off-hours these nuns could be especially wanton.)

Mildred tried all the alternatives at one time or another, until all she wanted was to put herself as far as possible from Badminton College, to go to the far edge of the earth and start over—which meant either Australia or Canada.

Immediately upon arrival, she sought employment at the Hotel Vancouver—the obvious choice.

The Hotel Vancouver was known even in London as one of the grandest hotels in the Empire, an Italianate palace covering a city block, featuring marble sinks and gold-plated faucets, where terra-cotta moose and buffalo heads lent a Canadian touch to lintels and other decorative supports.

Mildred obtained a position the way most Britons got hired: by answering questions with an accent Canadians found authoritative and "classy." In this case, she imitated Captain John Reith of the BBC, adding a touch of feminine posh for good measure.

Switchboard work at the Hotel Vancouver turned out to be the same tedium as it had been at Whitehall, relieved by listening in on other people's conversations. If caught, the worst she could expect would be a caution from the supervisor, while at best it could mean a small sum of money. (Exchange supervisors were known to relay information to newspapermen for a fee.)

The Hotel Vancouver proved a treasure trove of combustible goings-on. The fact that the Parliament buildings were situated in Victoria, sixty miles across the ocean, required cabinet ministers and high-level bureaucrats to occupy the better suites for weeks on end as an intermittent officer class, with servants to see to their most mundane needs.

Working the switchboard, Mildred takes particular interest in business and political matters. After her military experience, it makes her feel right at home.

MCCURDY STUBS OUT both her cigarettes as he watches Mildred mingling with loggers and fishermen, just one of the boys.

If this keeps up, he might have to do a bit more "due diligence" himself concerning this annoying Englishwoman. The only thing Sparrow (or anyone) knows of her background is that she has a wealthy family in Bristol. Having paid for their only daughter's posh education, for some reason they permitted her to travel alone to the edge of the world with enough money to buy stylish outfits on a switchboard operator's salary.

Was Miss Wickstram the black sheep of the family—or rather, ewe? McCurdy needs to know. He needs ammunition.

"Howard, there is no women's loo."

"Nothing to b-be done. She's a provocateur. To advance the equality of the sexes. Social justice, progress, women's suffrage, that sort of thing."

"Fine, but what happens when these women want equal pay? Housewives will unionize and go on strike. Who will change the diapers?"

"Chinese housekeepers, same as now."

"Until *they* unionize. Then it will be trained dogs, or machines."

"Evolution is in a transient stage. Women are taking on new forms, like modern art."

"Some forms are more attractive than others. What did you make of Mrs. Faulkner?"

"You mean her appearance?"

"For one thing, yes."

"Mrs. Faulkner exhibits a deliberately provocative manner."

"I agree. Did you ever see such gams?"

"Constable Hook noticed the gams as well."

"I thought his eyes might fall out of his head."

Sparrow takes a last puff, pops the tiny butt into his mouth, chews it and swallows. "A gold digger, do you think?"

"Unlikely. She's General Armstrong's daughter. What more gold is there to dig?"

"Then it must b-be about prestige. When you run out of things to b-buy, prestige is the carrot on the stick." Sparrow says this while rolling another cigarette (all tobacco this time) with his right hand, a skill common to sentries and ambulance drivers. His good eye focuses on the puddle of spilled beer in front of him, while the painted eye examines something in the distance.

"Mrs. Faulkner wants power. She wants to b-be queen of the world."

"How do you know that?"

"Why do you always ask me how I know things?"

"Sorry. Please continue."

"Mrs. Faulkner is the new kind of female. As is my fiancée, now in the men's room."

"Another bourgeois individualist?"

"More grandiose and aggressive. More species-oriented."

"What's that supposed to mean?" McCurdy signals for more beer, aware that Sparrow is well into the muggle and will be rattling on for some time. (Later at the White Lunch he will eat an entire pie.)

"That each man is a man, but also Mankind. Each woman is a woman, but also Womankind. Get the message?"

"No, I don't, but I expect it's another argument for socialism."

"Not necessarily. It's that one can b-become attached to a woman, and all of a sudden she can transform into Woman, with a capital W."

"Do you mean that she becomes a praying mantis and eats her mate after sex?"

Sparrow peers over his shoulder to be sure Mildred isn't within earshot. "In the war, remember the smart, comely, ambitious women—the nursing corps, the munitionette? Where did they go, Ed?"

"I don't know. Maybe they're in storage."

"They lost their jobs to men. So they went underground, and became dangerous."

"Tell me, how does a certain switchboard operator fit with your theory?"

Sparrow takes another look over his shoulder. "Time to change the subject. Right now."

"IS SOMEBODY TALKING about Hello Girls?" Back from the loo with a smirk on her face, Mildred turns her chair backwards and straddles it like a horse.

"Was your visit educational, darling?"

"There wasn't much to learn. Men hide from one another. Standing in front of the urinals, one might think they were counting their money."

"Your fiancé and I were discussing the Faulkners and the dead nanny."

Mildred swallows some of Sparrow's beer. "Sooner or later they'll say the butler did it. Isn't it always the butler? Especially when the butler is a Chinaman."

"Not when the b-butler works for the daughter of General Armstrong. Not with a provincial election in the fall."

"It will be a donnybrook for certain, the battle of the generals." She turns to McCurdy: "Don't you agree?"

"Excuse me, but would you mind telling me what you're talking about?"

"Just checking, Eddie, but surely you are aware who your employer will be up against? Armstrong has a formidable war chest, as you can well imagine."

"Of course." In truth, McCurdy knew nothing of the sort. During the last election he was freezing in Edmonton, and knew more about the Belgian Congo than British Columbia.

"Eddie, your boss fucking *hates* Armstrong."

"Your language, M-Mildred."

"Newson is not my fucking boss, Millie."

She lifts her eyebrows. "Really?"

"Oh all right he is, technically. But so what?"

"Armstrong was a desk general. Newson was on the front lines. Surely you've read his editorials?"

"Of course." In fact, McCurdy hasn't. Just because a man writes for a newspaper doesn't mean that he has to *read* the thing.

"Newson hates Armstrong even more than he hates the Chinese."

"I suppose you do have a point, Millie. For Newson, to accuse Armstrong's daughter's houseboy of murder would kill two birds with one stone."

"Stop it, Eddie. Your approval spoils it for me."

"B-but readers can see through the election propaganda, darling. You must learn to trust the intelligence of the common man."

She reaches out and strokes Sparrow's cheek with gentle fingers. "Dear Howard, *you* should have been a poet. You sound like Rupert Brooke."

"I resent that comparison. B-Brooke was a reservist who died of mosquito b-bite."

"In any case, darling, the mystery is why the fellow hasn't been charged already. As far as white Vancouver is concerned, the Chinese are pigtailed animals who smoke opium, eat cat meat and fuck like rabbits."

McCurdy stares blearily at his empty glass. "Opium and fucking. Sounds like a full life. Not sure about the cat meat, though."

Sparrow's painted eye investigates something over McCurdy's shoulder as he rolls himself another peculiar cigarette. "They'll get around to the Chinaman soon enough. With or without Newson."

"How do you know that?"

"A feeling. Like rheumatism before it rains..."

AS OFTEN HAPPENS in the hour before closing, the atmosphere in the beer parlour has turned. Arguments over issues such as sports and politics have accelerated into personal denunciations, angry shouts and chairs scraping across the floor, while cooler heads work to soothe the combatants as one would a frightened horse. In one corner a table has been overturned, resulting in spillage and shattered glass; its former occupants are being dealt with outside by the giant with the damaged ear.

Thanks to four pints down the neck, McCurdy has lost track of the argument they were having—something about journalistic rigour. Mildred is wearing that infuriating *I-know-something-that-you-don't* expression she reserves for such discussions: "Eddie, if you really cared about facts, you'd bother to find some—at the City Register, for example."

"Darling, stop tormenting the m-man. What does the City Register have to do with anything?"

"Take your Mrs. Faulkner, for example. When she was Miss Doreen Armstrong, the general sent her to England and enrolled her at Godolphin School. We Badminton girls called it *Godawful* School. Something had happened that nobody talks about. Something serious enough that she never came back to Canada, not even during the war.

"Not that the general abandoned his darling—on the contrary, he took her under his wing. Made frequent trips to London, made sure she became acquainted with the right people. Daddy's Little Girl she was. Even now, the two of them are as close as two coats of paint. But of course you didn't bother to look it up, did you, Eddie? Proper research being unworthy of the Rejected Poet."

McCurdy knew none of this. She has him flailing in a sea of new information.

Mildred continues. "I assume you also know that Doreen's younger sister Elizabeth is married to Jock West, MC, the war hero."

"Not to mention a DSO and DFC," Sparrow adds. "The man has more gongs than a Chinese funeral."

"Faulkner and West were with the same squadron. West shot down twenty-two; Faulkner claimed three, two doubtful. But even so, they're upper-class war heroes. So we have two heroes and a general from the same family, and an election coming up."

"You're describing a potential landslide, Millie."

"Unless the general gets on the wrong side of the Oriental question."

McCurdy rises unsteadily to his feet. His chair makes an unpleasant viscous sound as it rubs the beer-soaked sawdust floor. "Excuse me, but I have to go to the loo." *And get away from this conversation.* Some day he will win an argument with Miss Wickstram, but not tonight.

The loo stinks of beer, urine and shit. He crosses the wet porcelain floor, unbuttons his fly and leans over a ceramic facility shaped like an upended bathtub, made by a company called Adamant.

Adamant: impenetrable, unyielding.

"Mind if we have a word, sir?" asks the gentleman at the next urinal.

A familiar weariness descends on him. This is not the first time McCurdy has heard an inappropriate suggestion in a men's loo.

"Sorry, but I'm not keen on that sort of thing." He shakes dry and buttons up, averting his eyes.

"Oh, shut up," his neighbour replies. "I am Constable Hook of the Point Grey Police. And you are the fake undertaker. Just a quick word in private, sir, at the sink if you don't mind..."

NURSING HIS BEER, Sparrow watches his fiancée and his friend with his good eye, his thinking eye.

He once went to a Shakespeare play in Hanley. A man and a woman traded barbs for three hours, then married in the end. Unlikely in this case, but still...

A pity. It would make it easier for him to move on. Easier to explain.

When he first arrived, Vancouver seemed ripe for a revolution, but really the city is a hopeless case. Workers here won't get over the war for decades, let alone fight another one. Canadians are a gun-weary race.

His other reason is the painted eye. The other eye needs to understand it better, and for that he will soon head overseas once again, for an entirely different purpose.

In the meantime, if he can't beat the system, he might at least set it back a notch.

A journalist as provocateur and agitator. A telephone operator for planting and spreading information. A time bomb of explosive facts as mordant as TNT but with less physical damage.

They exit the Maple Club and head for a marginally more respectable area near Hastings and Main, for a nightcap. Their route to the Lumberman's Club takes them diagonally through Victory Square—which is not really a square, more a keystone shape—pausing near the new cenotaph, a symbolic tombstone for soldiers buried elsewhere, who left unfilled spaces in the family plot.

Carved in the stone is the legend, *Is it nothing to you,* which makes no sense until you read its partner around the corner, *All ye that pass by.*

Circle the cenotaph and the phrase repeats itself, like an insistent, ghostly chant.

Is it nothing to you
All ye that pass by
Is it nothing to you
All ye that pass by...

"Do you see," Mildred says, "how the order depends on which direction you're headed, yet it's the same question either way. Quite clever really, for a graveyard."

"A graveyard with no bodies," McCurdy says.

Sparrow lights another twisted cigarette containing a tobacco and muggle mixture. "A question with no question marks. Maybe it's by a modern poet."

Mildred accepts a light. "Gertrude Stein, maybe. *A rose is a rose is a rose...*"

71

"I'd have put in question marks," McCurdy says.

"Maybe that's why Russians had a revolution—b-because their dead are b-buried at home."

NURSEMAID'S DEATH PUZZLES
Suicide Theory Prompts Scorn
Ed McCurdy
Special to
The Evening Star

Not everyone is satisfied by the official version in the Janet Stewart case.

Authorities are privately of the opinion that the Point Grey Police and the provincial coroner, in holding that nursemaid Janet Stewart's death was due to a self-inflicted injury, are at odds with common sense and the facts.

According to an official with first-hand knowledge of the case, "There was nothing to suggest a suicide, little to suggest an accident and everything to suggest foul play." The official, who spoke on condition of anonymity, went on to list a number of circumstances that ran counter to the suicide theory, and to wonder aloud why the possibility of murder was never so much as mentioned.

"If it was suicide, we must accept that a person would be seized with the urge to kill herself, using her employer's firearm, while ironing baby clothes.

"If it was accidental, we must imagine that, in a spirit of humour or experiment, she held a heavy weapon several feet from her face, pointed it at her forehead and pulled the trigger."

Indeed, this reporter has learned that the undertaker in charge of the deceased was heard to wonder at the lack of powder burns commensurate with a self-inflicted gunshot wound to the head. "He thought it most unusual," an assistant said.

According to the Reverend Duncan McDougall of Highland Church in Point Grey, leaders of the Scottish community are extremely skeptical; some are of the opinion that, for certain prominent persons, reputation trumps justice. "It's an outrage, that a Scottish girl of blameless character should be left alone in a house with a male Oriental, at the convenience of the well-heeled residents of Shaughnessy Heights. It was a tragedy in the making and an innocent white woman paid the price."

Officials with connections in the coroner's office are likewise skeptical. "We simply cannot envisage the events as described," said one.

Said another: "It invites the suspicion that all the facts have not been brought out, that strings may have been pulled in high places for the protection of certain parties."

Chief Quigley of the Point Grey Police was strangely unavailable for comment.

7

Keep your broken arm inside your sleeve.

HAVING ONE'S NAME in print can be an honour or a curse. That is a given. The pity of it is the asymmetry: honours fade in memory whereas curses take on a life of their own.

Chief Quigley scheduled the emergency meeting for ten thirty, the usual time for his mid-morning tea. The fact that only Gorman and Hook have been called suggests that, after less than a week, the Janet Stewart investigation is going badly, in a way that additional manpower won't help. (Other members of the force are busying themselves investigating a burglary, by the usual method, which is to decide on who the perpetrator might be, then send two officers to question the suspect in a forceful manner.)

Since joining the force, this is Hook's second visit to Quigley's office. Reflexively he stands at attention, and hates himself for it. For his part, Constable Gorman exudes relaxation. To look at his smug face, he could be visiting the den of a favourite uncle.

Perfunctory nods are exchanged. Hook notices, not for the first time, how the chief's neck seems like an inadequate support for his enormous bald head.

Gorman plops into the only comfortable chair as though it were the natural order of things. Hook switches to the at-ease position, to remind the chief of his military experience.

Never has Hook seen Chief Quigley so agitated. The man literally cannot hold still—capping and uncapping pens, dusting his desk blotter with one hand while scratching the back of his head with the other. A pink and peeling rash now occupies his forehead. The chief looks like what he is: a frightened old man.

"Gentlemen, we have a crisis. And we who are most at risk must work together to bring it to a satisfactory conclusion."

Unsteadily, the chief takes a sip of tea to soothe his throat, leaving his macaroon for now. "To put it bluntly, the Janet Stewart case is in danger of causing a scandal. The public needs to be reassured that proper procedures have taken place."

The chief lights his pipe and fills his lungs. Hook stares at a picture on the wall depicting, presumably, the chief as a younger man. Gorman inspects a split thumbnail.

Quigley's empty teacup rattles as he sets it down. (Hook wouldn't be surprised if he has had a morning nip.) With a sigh, he reaches into a bottom desk drawer as though it contains a snake, and comes up with a copy of *The Evening Star*, pre-folded to exhibit a headline on page two: NURSEMAID'S DEATH PUZZLES. "Have either of you read this, this garbage?"

"Certainly not," Gorman says.

Hook demurs: "I have, sir. An abomination."

"Do you understand what he is insinuating, Mr. Hook?"

"Very well, sir. He is portraying the Point Grey constabulary as a nest of idle buffoons."

"And what do you have to say to this, Mr. Gorman?"

"The press are bloodsuckers. Surely we can find something to charge this fellow with."

"Gentlemen, the Vancouver constabulary has been waiting for something just like this to seal the case for amalgamation. They have already assimilated the Strathcona precinct and we're next in line. We must be prepared to defend ourselves."

"That's the spirit, sir," Gorman says.

"Defend ourselves with what?" Hook asks.

"We will produce overwhelming evidence of due diligence and superb dedication. We will demonstrate that the entire article is a smear, that when it comes to investigation the Point Grey constabulary is second to none."

Hook has never seen the chief expend such energy speaking aloud. It helps one to understand how the man attained his position: he *describes* police work so well.

Chief Quigley turns to Gorman. "Do you have the rest of your notes, Constable Gorman? Please tell me that there is more than what I have in my desk."

"Sir, I was subject to interference. My notes are not as complete as I would have liked." Gorman casts a venomous glance at Hook.

"No diagrams? Observations? Forensics?"

"I recorded the impediments I experienced on the ground, sir. Nobody can do a proper job under such conditions."

The chief can't hide his disappointment. "Gorman, this reads like drama criticism, not a police report. Your thoughts on the conduct of Constable Hook are clear, but what did you note, say, about the Chinaman?"

Hook was waiting for this. "The first man on the scene is the first suspect—that's a basic rule, wouldn't you say Mr. Gorman?"

"Shut up, Mr. Hook. The Chinaman has been vouched for by better people than you."

"Constable Gorman, your racial tolerance is astonishing."

"Equality is the soul of British justice, Hook."

"Amen to that, Mr. Gorman."

"The Chinks may be sub-human, but they aren't animals."

The chief absorbs this exchange thoughtfully. Sinking back into his chair, he relights his pipe, leans back and assumes the pose of a man thinking deeply.

On cue, Gorman lights up a Black Cat and stares out the window, while Hook lights an Ogden's and stares at his feet. A pleasant haze of tobacco smoke fills the room, to compete with the odour of sweat, bad teeth and old man's pajamas.

"Well? What do you have to say, gentlemen?" Quigley's eyes are watering, but not from the smoke; they glitter with the pleading intensity of a swimmer out of his depth, or a man hanging from a ledge several stories above ground. "Please gentlemen, your thoughts. We must work as a team. Otherwise..."

Gorman forcibly blows smoke at the ceiling, indicating a man of action. "I say we brass it out, sir. In my experience, these things blow over. In the meantime, we might spend an hour with the reporter. He might be persuaded to write a retraction, even an apology."

Hook leans forward to butt his cigarette in the chief's ashtray. "If I may say so, given the gaps in Constable Gorman's investigation, we don't have much to brass out."

A pause, while Constable Gorman sulks. Chief Quigley places his pipe in the ashtray; his hands flap about the desk as though feeling for an answer, then they hit the desk with a definitive slap.

"Gentlemen, here is the plan: We will return to the scene, scour the premises—and take meticulous notes."

In other words, three members of the Point Grey Police are

about to undertake a sham investigation, in which their colleagues are not to be involved.

Constable Hook isn't in the least shocked. Throughout the war, army reports made retroactive revisions on a regular basis. Without the ability to alter statistics, to transform a military fiasco into a victory, demotions would occur. Morale would suffer. The supply of new recruits would diminish.

Constable Gorman continues to toady to his superior, either because he needs his approval or because, in doing so, he serves another secretive purpose, one he shares with his well-dressed friends in the laundry room.

Or is Gorman every bit as stupid as he appears? The man was an investigator with the Provincial Police for many years, a so-called "umbrella institution" staffed by chaps who are better at keeping their jobs than doing their jobs—which seems to be Chief Quigley's forte as well.

Accordingly, the chief intends to produce "meticulous notes," the work of a hands-on officer taking charge of a sensitive, unprecedented case. In other words, they will produce a work of fiction.

As they exit the office and step into the yard, Hook wonders, is the chief stupid as well? Or are both men *pretending* to be stupid?...

Gorman inserts his stomach behind the steering wheel while the chief takes the passenger side; Hook must take the back seat as though he has been arrested. Tufts of horsehair sprout through gaps in the upholstery. A broken spring pokes his thigh. The interior houses a permanent cloud of dust, and smells of tobacco, sweat, grease and burnt rubber.

Hook would rather ride his motorcycle to the Faulkner house but feels it would be a mistake to leave Gorman and the chief alone to conduct a strategic discussion.

As in the army, a man must watch out for friendly fire.

8

In a shallow pond, bottom-feeding is key.

THE EDITORIAL ASSISTANT at *The Evening Star* has barely finished typing Nathan Shipley's latest absurdity when the telephone jangles, announcing the first of a procession of cranks and nutters eager to clog the lines and waste her time.

Shipley's prolific reporting on lurid subjects follows the same pattern, week after week. Someone always stands at a "crossroads" and something always "remains to be seen." Seemingly, writing itself played no part in his promotion to staff writer, with a cubby of his own.

Certainly the man is prolific; previous series had to do with a race of hairy men who were said to stalk the forests near Nelson, leaving footprints the size of coal shovels. To give the story the appearance of news, Shipley cited one A.L. Ostman, a prospector who claimed to have been held captive by a family of the creatures for six days. He managed to escape by intoxicating the male with snuff. Whether these hairy men are benign or malevolent, of course, "remains to be seen."

(Admittedly, Shipley's chief competition, Max Trotter of the *Sun*, is the more repetitious of the two, with his anti-communist screeds and his seeming love affair with Mr. Hitler.)

"*Here is SEymour 703. Are you there?*"

"*Hello. Am I speaking to* The Evening Star, *please?*"

"*This is the* Star. *Who are you, please?*"

"*I should like to speak to the man who wrote about the Sasquatches, please.*"

The voice on the other end, female, speaks with an unspecific European accent.

"*Your name, please.*"

"*I will not tell you.*"

"What is your business with Mr. Shipley?"

"I have information that he will be very glad to have."

"And what information might that be, miss or madam?"

"I will not tell you. I must speak to Mr. Shipley in person."

"One minute. Please hold."

Covering the speaking tube with her palm, the editorial assistant, whose name is Carla McKay, turns in the direction of Shipley's cubby, where he spends an unusual amount of time for a beat reporter. "Nathan, it's for you! Some bird with vital information!"

"Oh goddamn it, Carla, not another one."

"Watch your mouth. Men from Mars may be listening in."

"Just take down her story, would you?"

The editorial assistant buries her nose in her work, the better to avoid Shipley's terrible breath, which reminds her of a dead animal. "No I won't. I'm not a sieve for your loonies. I get the willies just typing this crap."

Shipley returns to his cubby and picks up the telephone, preparing himself for a loon on the line.

"Nathan Shipley speaking. How may I help you?"

"Am I to be speaking with the man who writes about Sasquatches and space men?"

"It's called unexplained phenomena, madam. Science doesn't explain everything, you know."

"It does not. That is why I am calling. I am in contact with Janet Stewart."

"Am I to assume you mean spiritually?"

"That is so. My name is Madame Feglerska."

"Your name is familiar. You would be the well-known psychic?"

"I am."

Ah, Shipley thinks. Madame Feglerska is indeed well known by the Vancouver Police, whom she has led on many a merry chase after corpses and buried money.

"I contact spirit guides. They relay messages from the discarnate. I have been receiving messages from Janet Stewart."

"Please continue, Miss Feglerska, you have my full attention."

"I am to conduct a spiritual gathering at the Ogilvie estate, at which she will speak."

"Have the two of you set a date?"

"Are you to be making fun of me?"

"Not for a second, Madame Feglerska."

"I would be with gratitude if you could be present to bear witness on Thursday evening at seven thirty precisely."

"I wouldn't miss it for the world."

Indeed he won't. This is how he makes his living.

As a reporter, Shipley is a writer who doesn't find news; it comes to him. He is not a hunter-gatherer but a gardener, tending his expanding acreage of unverifiable sources. The one detriment to this approach is that the reporter must befriend people he would prefer not to know.

Sometimes Shipley sees his collection of sources as a colony of misfits, witches, eccentric geeks, the brain-damaged, the fallen, the insular forlorn, who share one characteristic: they are all desperate for attention. It's enough for them that Shipley seems to take them seriously.

It frightens him that this is the congregation he has acquired.

He is working up the nerve to ask Mr. Newson for a more substantial assignment. Anything to get him away from them, at least for a while.

QUESTIONS MULTIPLY IN JANET STEWART CASE
Ed McCurdy
Special to
The Evening Star

In the absence of a proper autopsy, clear answers as to the cause of death in the Janet Stewart case have been thin on the ground.

Suspicions, on the other hand, have multiplied, having to do with unexplained skull fractures, no trace of powder burns on the skin, not to mention the complete lack of a credible motive; so that a growing proportion of Vancouver citizens are of the belief that the truth has not been told.

This undermining of public confidence hasn't been assuaged by the Point Grey Police, thanks to whom, sources reveal, there are no fingerprints to file, in fact no evidence at all to speak of, and no satisfactory report from the investigating officer, a Constable Gorman, who has refused all interview requests.

As a result, the United Council of Scottish Societies, representing fully a third of Vancouver's population, are outraged.

Reverend Duncan McDougall of Highland Church was heard to observe: "If you want to commit murder and get away with it, then Point Grey is the place to do it."

Thanks to a lack of specifics in the case, rumours have been flying back and forth like hockey pucks. Here is a partial list:

- That Miss Stewart was held captive, stripped and tortured with electric irons by devil-worshippers from the United States.
- That Miss Stewart was in the family way, and shot herself to preserve her honour.
- That Miss Stewart was blackmailing a prominent lover, who shot her to preserve his reputation.

In such an environment it's not surprising that parties have been filling the factual vacuum with their own hobby horses, and for certain political figures it has become a potential election issue.

For example, sponsors of the Women and Girls Protection Act make much of the fact that it was the Chinese houseboy who discovered the body and that he was the only other occupant of the house at the time. Is it a coincidence that members of the provincial legislature are currently debating a measure that would prohibit white women and Oriental men from working in the same household?

What really happened to Janet Stewart? Without a proper inquiry it is all but certain that the truth will never be known—which is what certain parties seem to prefer.

9

One takes the colour of one's company.

HOGAN'S ALLEY IS a cobbled lane in what is known as the "coloured part of town"—though other races live there as well—an area just around the corner from the railway station, the Pullman Porters' Club and the African Methodist Episcopal Fountain Chapel. Known as a red-light and gambling district, the street has long been a popular hobby horse for anti-vice societies.

The Elegant Parlour is one of the more popular venues, a converted stable with a carpet of sawdust on the floor and mismatched fixtures, where more than one race could be seated at the same table to drink gin and whisky, smoke muggle, eat fried chicken from Vie's next door and dance to a band consisting of comb and tissue paper, kazoo, banjo and a suitcase drummed with whisk brooms.

The venue was Mildred's idea, seconded by Sparrow. Ever the chameleon, Millie is wearing a flapper skirt and a rope of imitation pearls. McCurdy well remembers her transvestite display at the Maple Club, not to mention her getup at a labour rally, when she appeared wearing a workman's cap and a hammer and sickle pin on her lapel.

"Badminton girls dress for the occasion," she explained.

Hogan's Alley suffered a serious setback two years ago, with the shooting of a policeman by a sleeping-car porter named Fred Deal. Press accounts introduced the frightening prospect of sleeping travellers being at the mercy of "drug-addicted porters and their swinish appetites," which inspired a civic campaign to rid Vancouver of "undesirable negroes." Still, the Negro menace was a minor concern compared to the plague of Orientals about to turn British Columbia into an outpost of China.

The neighbourhood has since returned to normal. Police raids have diminished thanks to disinterest and bribery. Meanwhile, bored footless by church, tea dances and the Protestant ethic, banned from dance halls on pain of disinheritance, hordes of affluent young people have turned Hogan's Alley into an amusement park for the fast set: a centre for jazz, American food and raciness in general.

"I received a message from General Newson today."

"Did he fire you, Eddie?"

"No, Millie. Hate to disappoint you."

"But he did contact you in writing."

"Delivered by Miss Webster, his stenographer. I'll show it to you."

See me.
V.N.

"Your b-boss is a man of few words, Ed."

Mildred butts out her last Mecca. "It's management power-speak. No need to waste energy on an inferior. If she handed it to you without looking you in the eye, you're probably fired."

"How do you know that?"

"I've been fired myself."

"Fired? What for?"

"I don't wish to talk about it. You'll just have to do some research. Not your cup of tea, I know."

McCurdy lets the jab go. "Newson's secretary said I would be summoned in due course."

"The word *summoned* is a bad sign as well. You're to be called on the carpet and flayed."

"Why do you say that?"

"Because obviously he's a sadist. First he wants you to worry yourself sick, then he wants to see the look on your face when he delivers the killing blow."

Having made short work of "Big Chief Blues," members of the nameless orchestra pick up an entirely different set of instruments and ease into a curious two-step version of "What'll I Do?" As often happens in situations involving music and alcohol, it makes a suitable accompaniment to McCurdy's current dilemma.

Mildred tears open a pack of cigarettes (Helmars this time), lights up, takes a long drag and exhales the disgusting smoke across the table, leaning forward as though to improve her aim.

"By the way," she says, "I looked up Newson in the library archives. He won the DSO for, quote, 'leadership.'"

"P-posing at the edge of a trench, waving a fucking pistol in the air."

"Actually, darling, it was a bombing attack. Of course Newson was in no danger himself."

"They rarely are, darling."

"In any case, General Newson won the Vancouver City seat over General Armstrong by depicting him as a paper-shuffler. Practically accused him of war profiteering—what you would call a two-pronged attack.

"Newson won the battle but Armstrong won the war. While Newson warmed a seat in the legislature, Armstrong, thanks to his rich American wife and in-laws, invested in trees, fish, land—and now look at him: he's the king in his castle. People say he built Canacraig just to drive Newson crazy.

"Anyway, Newson serves one term, then starts playing catch-up. He partners with Colonel Grey, makes a fortune playing with other people's money and buys a newspaper. Naturally, *The Evening Star* slags Armstrong at every opportunity."

"How do you know all this, Millie?"

"I read things. Ever heard of reading?" She produces more smoke. "My point is that the game isn't over. Obviously, your boss plans to run again."

"Against Armstrong?"

"No Eddie, against the Prince of Wales. Maybe that's where you enter the picture. He wants you as... what? His verbal assassin? Attack dog? Freelancers can be useful, like mercenary troops, and when you don't need them they just go away."

A black customer in a checked suit, bowler hat and spectator shoes pulls a harmonica from his coat pocket and joins the orchestra. A gaunt chap with red hair does the same, holding a clarinet. McCurdy wonders if there is anyone in the room besides the three of them who *doesn't* play an instrument.

He turns to Mildred: "So you don't think I'm going to be fired after all."

"Frankly, I doubt you'll have the good fortune, Eddie. You'll just have to decide for yourself what you want to be when you grow up."

"I'm a poet."

"No, you're not. Poets write poems. If you're a poet, then I'm a doctor, lawyer, Indian chief—certainly not a Hello Girl."

"That was a low blow, Millie. How about an heiress with a past and a potful of money, slumming at a switchboard in a fancy hotel?"

"That was a low blow as well, Eddie."

"You two are adept at low b-blows, aren't you?"

"Blow, blow, thou winter wind, thou art not so unkind as man's ingratitude." She blows smoke for emphasis.

"Just what is that supposed to mean, Millie?"

"Just thinking about the word *blow*: to deal a blow, to blow an opportunity, to blow one's brains out, to blow over, to deal a body blow, to give a blow job..."

"Keep up the language, darling, and we will be asked to b-blow this joint."

It occurs to McCurdy that both Mildred and Howard have been smoking muggle; people mix it with Turkish tobacco to disguise the aroma. Sadly, like tobacco, muggle smoke makes him wheeze.

Sparrow holds up his glass and peers through the amber liquid with his painted eye, magnified to double its size.

"All of this reminds me of the war."

"Yes, darling. Everything reminds you of the war."

McCurdy cleans the greasy haze from his glasses with his handkerchief. He pities Sparrow, being "engaged" to a modern woman. For today's woman, engagement has acquired new flexibility. Newsreels teem with heiresses and movie stars who discard fiancés like last season's hat.

Sparrow is drunk now, and muggled as well. "Haig, Churchill, Pershing, how we cursed them whenever a Ross rifle b-blew up in someone's face, when the latest issue of b-boots were made of cardb-b-board..." He produces a battered tin of Woodbine, a packet of Vogue papers, and proceeds to roll and light a cigarette with one hand—except that his fingers lack precision and the product is damp, crooked and unsmokable. Mildred rolls him a replacement, expertly, and lights it for him.

"We thought the war was over in 1918." Sparrow removes a bit of tobacco from his tongue. "Now the b-bosses are the same b-bastards who put cavalry against m-m-m..."

"Cavalry against machine guns, yes, you've said that before, sweetheart. With enough repetition, even the war becomes boring."

"Howard is suggesting that Newson will send me over the top to face machine guns, with a defective rifle and a pair of cardboard boots."

"We'll never stop talking about the war, will we, chaps."

"B-Because the music never stopped, b-bearcat. It just changed keys."

JANET STEWART SPEAKS
Nathan Shipley
Staff Writer
The Evening Star

Anna Feglerska is a woman struggling to have her message heard and understood.

The well-known psychic, whom influential Shaughnessy matrons have taken to their bosom, experienced a dream, one that repeated itself on three consecutive nights and that might provide a solution to the Janet Stewart mystery.

Madame Feglerska has assisted the Vancouver police on numerous occasions in the past; however, in this case she was met with a summary rebuff. Nonetheless, on the evening in question, in the drawing room of a mansion on Angus Drive, the most well-bred matrons of Shaughnessy have come out in force.

Even Constable Hook of the Point Grey constabulary was seen by this reporter at the back of the room, quietly taking notes.

Having declared that she had no prior knowledge of the people involved, nor of the evidence obtained, nor of the rumours surrounding the nanny's death (indeed, she spent the past three months on Saturna Island, on a spiritual quest), Madame Feglerska seated herself in an upholstered dining-room chair and the electric lights were brought to a minimum. A sepulchral stillness fell among the spectators as the psychic closed her eyes and appeared to sink into a deep trance. When at last she spoke, her voice had a thin, spectral quality, while her accent was no longer European but quite normal.

"It is getting toward two in the morning in a magnificent home. People downstairs are drinking and dancing. The man who had met and kissed a girl upstairs has returned to the party and his social set, but he is still thinking of her as he becomes very drunk.

"Feeling an urge he cannot resist, he declares to guests that he is going to lie down, proceeds back upstairs and enters a bedroom.

"I see the bedroom. The man approaches the bed and pulls away the covers. The girl, awakened, attempts to cry out. He silences her, and there is a struggle.

"Now another man in a tuxedo enters the room and is shocked to see the first man struggling with the girl. He endeavours to pull the first man away from her, and a fight occurs. Seeing this, the girl collapses on the bed in a faint.

"The second man knocks down the first and bends over the girl to see what is the matter. He makes an effort to revive her, but as he does so the door opens and a woman enters, also the worse for liquor.

"At the sight of the man bending over the girl, the woman misunderstands the intent of his efforts and, in a fury, attacks him with a heavy object—in her hand I see a lamp from a nearby table.

"The enraged woman rains blow after blow at the man and at the girl on the bed. After that I see no more."

The gathering dispersed soon after, and Madame Feglerska retired to another room, white with fatigue. Altogether, it seemed to this reporter that the vision the psychic described to her rapt audience painted a more logical and believable picture than the theories advanced by authorities thus far.

The Janet Stewart case is at a crossroads. Which line of inquiry the police will choose to pursue remains to be seen.

IO

Only a fool argues with an idiot.

LESS THAN A week since the discovery of Janet Stewart's dead body, and already they're covering their tracks. The three officers are not here to conduct an investigation but to create the *appearance* of an investigation. The object is not to ascertain facts but, in effect, to *create* facts. That is the essence of Chief Quigley's plan, in which facts have a similar role to the one they played for Madame Feglerska the previous evening.

Seen from Hook's perspective, they are not policemen but actors *pretending* to be policemen.

Chief Quigley claims to have obtained assurances that the Faulkners will co-operate in fine style, as prominent citizens eager to assist the police in resolving this tragic event in a satisfactory manner.

Unless they are, like members of the Point Grey Police, *pretending* to be citizens. Once facts become manufactured products, anything is possible. Another legacy of the Great War. If all published air victories on both sides had taken place, there would have been no planes in the air.

In any case, their quasi-investigation has been handed a clear field. Mr. Faulkner's business responsibilities have chained him to his desk at Faulkner and Partners, while Mrs. Faulkner is busy with other, unspecified activities.

But of course, Wong Chi will be at their disposal.

The three policemen climb out of their juddering, trembling vehicle to find the houseboy standing in the doorway to the basement in an impeccable white shirt, his elbow bent in the butler pose, his hair so black it's almost blue, brilliantined and precisely parted on the right.

"Good day, gentlemen. Will gentlemen need ask more questions? Please to enter and to ask."

The laundry room looks no different than it did the last time, except for different piles of clean and dirty laundry, and the absence of blood on the floor. The chalk outline has also been partially scrubbed away—so much for the "untouched" crime scene.

Hook watches while Gorman pretends to inspect the deep double sink, the light-bulb chain and the ironing board.

Turning to the Chinaman, Chief Quigley assumes the officer's pose—feet spread, hands behind the back. "You, boy, you were the one who found the body, were you not? You. Dead. Girl. Find?"

"Find, sir?"

"Don't play dumb with us, boy. The police need answers. Now I want you to get down and show us the position of the dead woman on the floor as you found her. You. Get. Down. Floor. We measure."

"Me on floor?" The Chinaman indicates his shirt.

The chief turns to his men. "Blessed if I can talk to these people. How about you, Mr. Hook?"

"Sir, I think he understands what you said all too well." Hook unfolds a bed sheet from the folding table, lays it on the floor and turns to the houseboy. "Best I can do old chap. *Dui bu qi.*"

"Get a move on, boy. There are other ways to get your co-operation."

The houseboy arranges his body to approximate Janet Stewart's position in death. His shirt is already smeared with yellow chalk.

The chief produces a fresh notebook and a mechanical pencil, notes the date and time; then, recalling his artistic talent as a boy, begins a meticulous drawing of the body in the laundry room as portrayed by the mortified houseboy.

For lack of anything better to do, Constable Hook measures the distance between various objects, using a retracting tape measure with a photograph of Lord Kitchener, a gift sent overseas from his mother, who thought it might inspire him.

The chief pauses to inspect his drawing. "Mr. Gorman, do a close search of the floor and take extensive notes."

"First we'll need accurate measurements," Gorman replies. With a glare in Hook's direction he hunkers down on his knees, produces a retracting tape measure of his own and begins to measure and note the distances his colleague has just covered.

Hook puts Lord Kitchener back in his pocket for the time being.

The chief pauses yet again, holding his drawing admiringly at arm's length.

"You can get up now, boy. Up!" On command, the houseboy jumps to his feet, brushes off his trousers and shirt, gathers the sheet from the floor, dumps it in the laundry bin and heads for the stairs as smartly as possible.

With the chief preoccupied with his artwork and Constable Gorman crawling on his hands and knees, Hook sees an opportunity. "Wong Chi, do you think you could show me Miss Stewart's room, please?"

The houseboy stops on the landing, looks back apprehensively and nods.

"There's no suicide note, if that's what you're looking for," Gorman says from beneath the washing machine. "No need to sniff around a girl's room, unless that is to your taste."

"Actually, I was thinking of a diary. Someone told me she kept one."

Gorman turns to the chief: "He's going to read a girl's diary. Is that protocol? Seems indecent to me."

"Oh let him snoop away, constable. More material for search notes. We'll add something about finding it personally distasteful, but bold action was called for."

Hook follows the houseboy to the main floor, then up a flight of stairs to the upstairs hall. "Missy room turn right, sir."

Her bedroom is the size of an average water closet, with a cot where the toilet might be, a small chest of drawers for a basin, a narrow window beneath a low gable and, below that, a small bookcase.

Wong Chi remains just outside the door, watching uneasily. Upon entering, Hook gives the houseboy a look that as a Redhat enabled him to brass his way through many an illegal search and seizure: *Official business. Do you have any objection? No? Thought as much.*

He searches the bottom drawer, which contains neatly folded skirts and blouses, then the top drawer, which contains mysterious things made of sheer fabrics, the kind women prefer next to their skin...

And a diary. An instantly recognizable volume, with faux-leather binding and blank pages, stamped with a bookstore label

(*Springleton Stores, Diary 1924*) in embossed script. He kneels in front of the bookcase beneath the dormer window; it contains two similar diaries, embossed 1923 and 1922.

He slips 1924 into his jacket pocket, turns and speaks to Wong Chi, again in his Redhat voice: "This is important evidence. It must be secured at once."

The man's face is a mask of incomprehension, yet the hairs prickling the back of Hook's neck suggest that the houseboy understands more than he is letting on.

Hook follows Wong Chi down the hall and down the narrow back staircase to the first floor, until his escort abruptly stops and steps back, as though to allow someone to pass.

Mrs. Faulkner.

Her perfume precedes her in the way that a hiss precedes an explosion. She is wearing the same dress and, of course, the same luminous skin.

"How do you do, Constable Hook," she says with a crescent moon smile.

"I am well enough, thank you, Mrs. Faulkner, and hope you are the same." Constable Hook resists the urge to smooth his moustache.

"Is Wong Chi giving you a tour of the house?"

"He was kind enough to show me to Miss Stewart's room. She seems to have been a clean, orderly sort of girl."

"She was. You'd be surprised the way some perfectly turned-out girls can live like pigs behind closed doors." Mrs. Faulkner smiles again, showing excellent teeth. Hook smiles back, hiding his own teeth behind his lips. He glances at the houseboy, who is examining the wallpaper, a series of beige swirls like the carved ends of violins.

"Quite. Well I wouldn't know about the personal habits of... girls, being a bachelor myself..." Her perfume has already fogged his brain.

"Officer, perhaps you would care for a cup of tea? I can make tea you know, despite what my husband might have told you."

Ordinarily he would decline the offer, but his brain can't quite summon the words. "Are you sure it's not too much trouble, Mrs. Faulkner?"

"Not at all, officer. In fact it's already steeping. If you don't take tea I shall be cross with you." He follows the sway of her body into the kitchen where the breakfast nook has been set with spoons, sugar, a small pitcher of cream, a teapot in a crocheted cozy with a wool flower on top, a small plate of iced cookies, an enamel ashtray from the Langham Hotel in London, a packet of Dunhills and one of the new lighters that can be operated with one hand. Not a spontaneous occasion, but he is not prepared to object.

He waits for her to be seated—ladies first. "Mrs. Faulkner, I don't know if you are aware of this but there seem to be a number of rumours..."

"You will have to be more specific than that, officer. There are thousands to choose from."

"The rumours I'm thinking of involve a party in the house."

"There was no party in this house." Her voice takes on an edge; some things are not up for discussion. "I am ready to swear to it. Do you think I'm lying?"

"I don't doubt you for a minute, Mrs. Faulkner. It's one of those difficult questions that must be asked so that lines of inquiry can be ruled out."

"Yes, of course. It's your job to doubt people."

"And another part of my job is to chase down rumours."

"Ah, the rumours. Rumours grow like trees—haven't you noticed? The debauched party story grew out of the ground—and let me tell you, Shaughnessy Heights is fertile soil and there are seeds everywhere. Someone is always whispering something to somebody about somebody else. And like the trunk of a tree it sprouts branches: the Prince of Wales shot Janet dead while playing a form of Russian roulette; or in a fit of lechery His Majesty accidentally strangled her—except that the Prince of Wales has been in London for months. So out of one rumour grows another, and instead of the Prince of Wales we have a war hero, whom a well-meaning friend tried to stop from shooting himself. Amid the struggle the pistol fired. Our war hero may have missed his own head but he shot Janet between the eyes, with remarkable accuracy for an accident.

"Then we have tales derived from gossip, involving the sons of prominent politicians, leaders of industry. Prominent families unite to cover up an act of attempted gang-rape, during which someone pushed Janet down the cellar steps and fractured her skull: tell me, officer, when you're raping someone, do you do it upright in a cellar doorway?"

"Mrs. Faulkner, I hope that isn't a serious question."

"I meant men in general, silly. Would I invite a rapist to tea?"

"I must say I admire your keen analysis. Some of the rumours you cited were news even to myself."

"At least one of them—about the Prince of Wales, I expect—was initiated by Mrs. Harrison next door. Mabel hates the Royals. And Mrs. Cowan down the street spreads rumours almost as often as she spreads her legs."

Hook has no response other than his burning ears.

"Constable, do sit down. You look as though you've never seen a tea set before."

He slides into the breakfast nook as directed and feels his leg brush against hers; he would prefer they were at a normal dining table, preferably at opposite ends, but there's nothing to be done.

"Would you care for a cigarette?"

"I'll have one of my own, thank you." Her cigarette lighter confounds him until he sees that it works on a lever mechanism. She touches his hand to hold it steady while he lights her Dunhill, then an Ogden's for himself.

"Madam wish I pour tea?" The houseboy has been hovering nearby watching everything, as inconspicuous as the icebox by the counter.

She pours, allowing Hook a closer look at her white arm with the green and gold bracelet coiled just above the wrist. He has to physically restrain himself from leaning forward and brushing her skin with his lips.

"Cream, officer?"

"Thank you, Mrs. Faulkner, no. No sugar either."

"An abstainer, I see. A man of iron self-discipline." She clenches her jewelled fist and laughs at what might be a secret joke.

"Mrs. Faulkner, if you don't mind, a bit more about the rumours: one thing most of them have in common is a party that got out of hand."

"We residents in Shaughnessy Heights are always having wild parties—didn't you know that, officer? On Angus Drive on a given night, the air positively howls with revelry. Behind the hedges, the men are drinking whisky all night, taking illicit drugs and impregnating the nannies, while the women swill cocktails and hump the male staff."

"Mrs. Faulkner, I assure you that was not the point of my

question. It's not what happened or didn't happen, it's the rumours themselves, don't you see? Common elements that might stem from a central fact, an occurrence, however distant..."

"Officer, you talk as though rumours are things that come up now and then like weeds, when they are the very air we breathe. When you live in Shaughnessy Heights, nobody says anything to your face or gives you the slightest chance to explain yourself. The whispers happen out of hearing. You have no means of contradicting them—and after a while there is no point trying. You're not from the city, are you? Where *are* you from?"

"From a railroad town in the Interior, and I know about rumours. In Waldo, people would waste away if they had to mind their own business."

"So you know what I'm talking about—except that your Waldo can only create rumours from within. In Shaughnessy Heights we have help from all over. In Vancouver, rumours about Shaughnessy are a sort of civic sport. When they run out of rumours about the residents, they spread rumours about the dogs."

"But sooner or later the rumours peter out, don't they?"

"Nonsense, Constable Hook. You might as well try and un-ring a bell."

"Mrs. Faulkner, I will put this to you: Do you have anything to tell me that might help our investigation?"

She leans forward and puts her hand on his sleeve. Her perfume has attained a whole new level of meaning. And those violet eyes. His temple throbs. He wonders if he might have a stroke.

"Officer, I give you my word that there was no party in this house the night before Janet died."

Whether it's her eyes or her perfume, he believes her.

"Thank you, Mrs. Faulkner. You've given excellent assistance."

As he pushes away from the table he catches a shared glance between Mrs. Faulkner and the houseboy, and not for the first time experiences an uneasy sense of shared communication among people with an interest in the case—the difference being that here the rapport is between different genders, situated much further apart on the social scale even than Constable Gorman and Mr. Faulkner.

As he bids Mrs. Faulkner good day, he wonders what suspicions will come to mind when his head is clear of her perfume—other than that she is smarter than him. Descending the stairs to the laundry room, he keeps a firm grip on the handrail; her scent clings to his clothing, affecting his sense of balance. He needs fresh air to focus properly. He would never dare ride a motorcycle with a woman who smelled like that.

Standing next to the folding table, Chief Quigley has completed his drawing of the "corpse" and has begun a fresh page devoted to fictional observations about the individuals he understood to have been in the room. He has no intention of casting suspicion on the fine people who live here; at the same time, it seems safe to raise doubts about the Chinese houseboy. It's beyond him why Constable Gorman hasn't done so already.

By now Gorman has taken many measurements as well as noting the makes of the fixtures and the type of furniture, to the degree that a subsequent investigator could reproduce the laundry room in another location without a glance at the original.

"I'll do a thorough check of the grounds and take extensive notes," Hook says, to nobody in particular.

"Very good," Chief Quigley says. "We'll show that we left no stone unturned."

CONSTABLE HOOK CLIMBS the cement steps, lights up an Ogden's and perches on the low concrete wall, having dried the surface with his handkerchief. Momentarily he thinks of Miss Hawthorn, the cuddlesome nanny still in possession of his handkerchief; her image manages to break through the web Mrs. Faulkner spun around his brain.

When a man is lonely, a flirtatious married woman only makes things worse.

He turns his attention to a grey squirrel's futile attempt to raid an out-of-reach bird feeder nailed to the trunk of an English oak. For some reason it puts him in mind of his attempt to grasp the meaning of this morning's events.

To its credit, the squirrel has managed to climb onto the peaked roof of the feeder and is stretching down to reach the trough; but then it loses its balance, flips over and lands on the grass below. It then scampers about, examining things only a squirrel would think worth examining.

He pulls Janet Stewart's diary from his inside pocket, opens it at random; immediately it creates a picture of the Scottish nanny that is very different from what he imagined. Hook reads further, riveted by this young woman named Janet Stewart, whoever she was:

Arthur is good and steady, but there ought to be more than that to matrimony. Last week-end he brought me a brooch. I do not care for it and am afraid it showed. Our love affair has cooled. I'll see how long now until the end. My heart used to almost stop when he telephoned, but now I just feel bored. He is building a house in the middle of nowhere which I would rather burn down than live in.

John gave me a powder box, and a box of chocolates. In return I let him kiss me at the waterfront dance and I kissed him back with just the slightest hint of my tongue.

Hook takes out his notebook and pencil; after all, there is no more plausible suspect than a spurned lover. The absence of a surname is unfortunate, but after all this is a diary and not a statement for the police. Of course, "Arthur" and "John" would be familiar names to her best friend, Miss Hawthorn, which will call for an official visit.

My new admirer is well-off and owns a motorcar. We drove to Prospect Point in his two-seat auto and I am afraid that we parked there for quite awhile. He provided me with drinks until I feared a catastrophe.

I suppose I will always play with fire. I expect that is what the fortune teller meant when she said I have the girdle of Venus...

He makes a note of the unnamed, moneyed admirer: How many upper-class gentlemen does a nanny meet in the course of her work? With this in mind, he flips through pages of complaints—of homesickness, of the crudeness of people on the streets, of overwork and a lack of appreciation by her employers—pausing at a section devoted to the houseboy.

Wong Chi delivered presents to my room—chocolates, three blouses and a silk nightgown. At the Girls' Friendly Society, Mrs. Parker said I must beware, that the Chinaman is trying to seduce me. I am still laughing. He gave me a roll of film for my camera. He said that I was to take several photos to send home. He really cannot afford such a present...

He writes a question in his notebook: *If the houseboy can't afford film, who is behind the other gifts?*

He has smoked three cigarettes by the time Gorman comes up to fetch him.

"Constable, here is something that will interest you!" Such an invitation from Gorman can only mean an opportunity to gloat, to gain the upper hand.

Hook stubs out his cigarette on the concrete wall, returns the diary to an inside pocket and descends to the laundry room, where Chief Quigley has taken the measuring tape from Gorman and is calculating yet again the distance between the sink and the washing machine, while Gorman's enormous upturned bum occupies a corner beneath the stairs.

"You'd best look at this," Gorman calls out, creeping back from under the stairs like a toddler in reverse, then turning with a smug smile of success. "What do you make of it?" He hands a small grey object to Chief Quigley. "What does this look like, sir?"

Chief Quigley holds the object up to the light. "I'd say it looks rather like a bullet. Well done, Mr. Gorman. That's what comes of a thorough search and a professional eye."

"May I have a look, sir?"

Chief Quigley drops the small metal object into Hook's open palm, casting an amused sideways glance to Gorman. "Be my guest, Constable Hook." Hook could swear that the chief gave Gorman a wink.

"Yes, you're right, Mr. Gorman, it's a bullet. A bullet that hasn't been fired."

"What?"

"Beg your pardon?"

"Lead is a soft metal that bends on impact. A round that has hit something, anything really, becomes a slug, an irregular lump."

The chief looks at Gorman, warily: "If the bullet wasn't fired, then what was it doing on the floor?"

Gorman's face is an impenetrable mask. "A good question, sir. We will have to look into it."

Hook crouches down and rubs a forefinger into two small indentations in the cement floor. "And while we're at it, do you think we might look into these?"

To judge by the faint trace of chalk outline, one of the holes would have been situated in the middle of her head, while the other hole is just outside the chalk line.

Again Gorman gets down on his hands and knees, giving off a whiff of whisky-soaked sweat, and flicks the edge of one hole with a nicotine fingernail. "They're chips in the concrete, Mr. Hook. The cement is mixed with rock pebbles, you see, which can become dislodged, leaving a small hole."

"Concrete will also chip if it's hit by a bullet."

"But *two* holes?" Chief Quigley's eyes beg him not to produce another complication. "Mr. Hook, are you suggesting that more than one shot was fired? Surely that would imply an entirely different situation than what either you or Mr. Gorman or anyone else has suggested."

"Quite right, sir," Hook says, "but not necessarily as different as all that."

"Are you saying that she practised firing the gun before turning it on herself?"

"That is altogether possible," Gorman says. "It's something I have seen several times."

"Another possibility is that she was shot while lying down, by someone else. Someone who missed the first time."

"Missed the first time, Mr. Hook? With her just lying there?"

"Do you think it's an easy thing to shoot someone, Mr. Gorman?"

"People do it all the time, Mr. Hook."

"But not in your experience, Mr. Gorman."

"In any event," the chief says, "it seems unlikely."

Hook's headache has returned in full force. "Not if the person with the gun were extremely upset and had never fired a pistol before. Someone who had trouble lifting and aiming the weapon steadily. Someone unfamiliar with handling guns."

"For once I agree with you," Gorman says. "A woman who committed suicide. It supports my theory to a T."

Hook's head has resumed throbbing. Not for the first time, he fights off the urge to punch Gorman in the nose.

THE POLICE CAR rattles down King Edward Avenue into an area of marshy bushland popularly known as Consumption Hollow and Asthma Flats, a breeding ground for the mosquitoes that plague the residents and make the Kitsilano neighbourhood a hellhole in summer. They pass stands of alder divided into lots and displaying

FOR SALE signs, then single-storey wooden mail-order bungalows, then a series of stylishly crude cottages on the waterfront, where wealthy families spend their summers socializing at the Jericho Swimming Club and the Vancouver Yacht Club.

Jostled in all directions in the back seat of the vehicle, Hook stares with ironic malice at the patches of eczema on the chief's enormous head, then at the little roll of purple flab over Gorman's collar. How he hates them both. He is certain that the girl was murdered and, with these two on the case, the only way the murderer will be found will be if he broadcasts a confession over the radio.

Janet Stewart will rot in her grave, while speculation about what happened to her will become a parlour game. As for the murderer, it will be life as usual—thanks to the two dolts in the front seat.

Chief Quigley parks in front of the constabulary and kills the engine. "Constable Gorman? Constable Hook? I think we need a quick word in confidence." He clears his throat in a way intended to imply confidentiality. "Gentlemen, I think it best that we remain quiet about the unfired round. Someone is trying to confuse the issue, some sort of prankster, and we are not about to play their game."

Gorman blows a plume of smoke at the windshield. "In my experience, many an investigation has been ruined by a practical jokester."

"I completely agree," Hook says. "An individual, perhaps with a warped sense of humour, who has neither served nor fired a gun. Not unlike the individual who put a bullet in Miss Stewart's head."

Chief Quigley's head swivels toward the back seat. "Constable Hook, you have an unbecoming tendency to speak out of turn. Remember, despite your war experience, you are new to the force. Our priority at this time is to work as a team. Am I right, Mr. Gorman?"

"Absolutely, sir. It's a sticky wicket. I faced just such a situation with the Combined Eleven in 1912..."

KLAN RECEPTION WELL RECEIVED
Max Trotter
Staff Writer
The Vancouver Sun

On July 14th, the Vancouver branch of the Ku Klux Klan held an informal but colourful reception at their new headquarters on Matthews Avenue, a spectacle that might have been held on Hallowe'en night but which proved popular nonetheless.

According to a neighbour, "They paraded on the grounds in their white robes and hoods with black eye-holes, carrying blazing crosses, some lit by fire and others with red electric lights. It left a lasting impression."

The popularity of the American-inspired organization has soared, thanks to public concern over a possible Asian angle to the Janet Stewart case.

Among the attendees at Glen Brae were a police commissioner and a member of the legislature, who was heard to remark: "The Ku Klux Klan would be banned if it preached hatred toward Catholics and Jews but would be welcomed with open arms if it strove to free the province of Orientals."

II

No two eyes see alike.

IF HE REALLY wanted to be a journalist, his career would be on an upswing right now. McCurdy has almost single-handedly created a public outcry, a sensation that justified three pieces in *The Evening Star* in less than a week, top of the fold, all thanks to one source in the police department and another at the Hotel Vancouver who handed McCurdy his latest scoop—an inquest, on orders from the Attorney General himself, to be held within a week. More ethically ambiguous are the quotes McCurdy obtains from other "sources," all played by one Howard Sparrow—which Sparrow accomplishes with surprising ease and a keen eye for official cadence.

And in the centre of it all sits McCurdy, a spider in a web of information, waiting for a tremor.

UNLIKE A CRIMINAL trial, an inquest in this part of the world entails no opposing lawyers, no cross-examination, no rules of evidence, no mention of case law or precedents. Sworn witnesses are free to commit perjury at will without answering to anyone but, supposedly, God. Sometimes McCurdy thinks God was invented by lawyers as an all-purpose evasion tactic.

Nobody questions the joint opinion of Chief Quigley and Constable Gorman that Miss Stewart committed suicide; nor does anyone question the view of Frank Faulkner and Dr. Blackwell that Miss Stewart died while "fooling around with the gun." Nor are any of these men asked to articulate the process by which they came to different conclusions.

Nor is Edwards the undertaker subjected to cross-examination when he claims to have retrieved Miss Stewart under orders from Constable Gorman (Gorman denied this) and to have received the go-ahead from the coroner's office (also denied by the coroner). For his part, Upshaw the mortician saw no reason not to send the corpse to Cruikshank the embalmer, who performed the procedure without a second thought, despite the bullet wound between her eyes.

Nobody asks how Miss Stewart might have discovered the gun in Mr. Faulkner's desk drawer, nor why she might have chosen to "fool around" by pointing it straight at her own head. Nobody questions the likelihood that an apparently sane young woman might engage in such activity first thing in the morning, while about to iron baby clothes. The lack of powder burns, noted by Dr. Hunter, who performed an autopsy on the frozen corpse, remains a mystery requiring no explanation:

"In my examination of the body I was concerned with the lack of powder burns on the forehead. When I opened the cranium I found the bullet lodged in the brain, but no burns, as one might expect from a self-inflicted wound."

JURY MEMBER: "How did you open her skull?"

"With hammer and chisel."

ANOTHER JURY MEMBER: "You took a hammer and chisel to her forehead?"

"Yes."

CORONER: "It's the standard practice, Mr. McCrone. Please continue, Dr. Hunter."

"With the help of Dr. Mullin, I later conducted an experiment with the weapon, using the measurements of the deceased and a number of clean surfaces. We found that, given her size, if she were to shoot herself by holding the weapon at arm's length and pointing it at herself, the muzzle would have been at most ten inches from her head—in which case, the escaping gas alone would produce significant burns."

JURY MEMBER: "Which arm did you measure?"

"We measured both arms."

ANOTHER JURY MEMBER: "She aimed the thing straight at herself?"

"We believe she was shot from slightly to the right. I should mention that the body also contained a number of unexplained burns on her back and arm, and one close to her left breast."

JURY MEMBER: "Was there evidence of ravishment?"

"We could not come to a determination on ravishment. The mortician had inserted a plug, which would have obscured previous damage to the vaginal wall—"

CORONER: "I think the jury will agree that we have heard enough along these lines."

"And we examined the damage to the skull."

JURY MEMBER: "Wouldn't there have to be an exit wound?"

"As I mentioned before, the bullet was in her brain. To continue, we examined the fracture pattern and concluded that such a fracture was more likely caused by a blunt instrument to the head."

JURY MEMBER: "Could she have hit her head on the laundry tub or on the floor when she fell?"

"Unlikely. The skull was splintered to fragments. Of course there was no way to tell anything for certain once the embalmer had done his work."

CORONER: "I think it's safe to say that the fracture is of uncertain origin. Thank you, Dr. Hunter."

Spectators will not soon forget the displacement of the oath—*I solemnly swear... so help me God*—in the case of Wong Chi. Since the moral weight of a Christian oath is thought to lack the force to bind an Oriental witness, an adjustment was deemed necessary to achieve the desired effect: that the liar will hold himself answerable to the Divine.

In the case of Wong Chi it called for the Fire Oath, in which the witness's testimony is written on a piece of paper, which is then incinerated while the witness promises to tell the truth. The Fire Oath takes place in the alley behind the courthouse, to avoid fouling the courtroom. The document is in Chinese characters; it occurs to McCurdy that it could be a recipe for hot pot, though an English translation, or something like it, is provided by the interpreter, Foon Sien.

Wearing an impeccably brushed black suit and tie, Wong Sing Chi takes the stand to offer his sworn account, spoken in Mandarin. Foon Sien interprets in uncertain English, standing erect and expressionless beside the witness stand in a double-breasted suit and with a bowler hat clutched under one arm as though someone might snatch it. His muddled translations at first provide amusement, until the jury and spectators become bored and begin to chat among themselves.

Only Cissie Braidwood is able to command the undivided attention of the court. A compact girl with a small, shapely bosom, exaggerated brown curls and unfortunately rustic features (she must curse her root vegetable nose when she looks into a mirror), Miss Braidwood passionately contradicts every statement made so far, in a performance that reminds spectators of Mary Pickford challenging the king in *Rosita*.

Despite her nerves (she faints at one point, necessitating a short recess), her testimony receives a respectful silence and nods of private approval:

"Janet would ne'er take her own life, for 'tis a terrible sin, and she hated guns and wouldn't touch one for the life of her. It was the Chinaman, the one sitting over there. Him! She was petrified of him, terrified, she lived in... lived in fear of him! Engaged to be married she was, betrothed to Arthur Dawson, a decent white man. Even so, the Chinaman would whisper things to her in Chinese that she didn't understand, but ye might say she got their drift so to speak and it frightened the heart right out of her. And then didn't he start giving her nightgowns—imagine! The thing a girl wears next to her— Oh! I canna say it! Of course Janet didn't want the filthy rags but she was too afeared of him to give them back; there is no telling what a Chinaman might do once he gets a grudge in his head. She wrote diaries—look at them if you don't believe me! You'll see it was just as I say; she was a happy girl who liked white boys and they would take her to dances, and..."

CORONER: "Her diaries will not be necessary. I'm sure that the jury will agree that the poor dead girl deserves at least some privacy. Thank you, Miss Braidwood, you may step down. What is your opinion of this, Dr. Blackwell?"

"I wouldn't put much store by such stories. The young Chinaman had earned the trust of the Faulkners, was well regarded by former employers, and his local relatives are hard-working fellows employed by prominent white men. I have no doubt that Miss Stewart was fooling around with the weapon. Young people are fascinated by guns. Thanks to the war and to moving pictures from the United States, they've been hearing about guns all their lives. They want to know what it's like to shoot one. As for the lack of powder burns, from my experience in the profession I can tell you that there are many ways a person can be shot at close range without powder burns..."

While McCurdy admires Miss Braidwood's performance, none of her arguments will affect the jury's conclusion. Held against the evidence of a doctor, a prominent businessman and a chief of police, the word of a nanny carries all the weight of a feather in the wind.

After a fifteen-minute deliberation in which they mutter to one another in whispers that could easily be overheard, the jury reaches a verdict: *Death by Misadventure, Either Self-Inflicted or Accidental*—a compromise that pleases nobody and elicits a chorus of *Shame!* in a variety of Scottish brogues.

Suddenly, as though on cue, a bellowing baritone roars over these expressions of outrage, as Reverend McDougall takes the stage. Though too short to tower over the crowd, his penetrating consonants echo off the plaster ceiling like a call from the Lord: "Sodom and Judas! The blood of a Scottish girl of blameless character is at the door of every churchman who makes no protest! What is wrong with ye? Do ye not ken what is in front of yer own eyes? Are more white girls to be lost now? Will your daughters come home as fallen women—or ne'er come home at all?"

Constable Hook writes *Arthur Dawson* in his notebook as he watches the proceedings with the horrified fascination he might give to a witchcraft trial or an inquisition rite. He feels a nausea similar to what came over him at a court-martial that condemned a sixteen-year-old deserter to death by firing squad.

He needs someone with whom to share his dismay. Scanning the room, he locates the reporter writing feverishly in his notepad with a grin of appalled disbelief.

Whispering *Excuse me* and *Begging your pardon*, Hook sidles through the spectators shuffling to the exit, mostly surly Scottish women, disinclined to make way for a policeman from the Point Grey constabulary. For the moment, he's stuck behind a moving wall of sensible coats.

At last he catches up to the reporter on the first landing of the courthouse steps. Surrounded by indignant Scots women, McCurdy is diligently writing down (or seeming to) everything they say. Hook approaches, careful not to say or do anything that might suggest prior acquaintance.

"Sir, I represent the Point Grey Police. Would you be Mr. McCurdy of the *Star*, and might we have a word?"

"*Policeman* is too polite a word for you people!"

"You should be ashamed of yourselves, you policemen!"

"You have made a bollox of the entire investigation!"

"Thanks to you, a murderer walks among us!"

The constable guides the reporter by the elbow down the steps while trying to placate the tartan mob. "Thank you, ladies, for your co-operation and concern. Be assured, action will be taken..."

Having reached Granville Street, McCurdy opens his jacket and produces a half-full mickey of rye. "Would you care for a drink, officer?"

"Much appreciated. Sir."

The display window at the entrance to the Colonial Theatre has a ledge wide enough to sit on, under sufficient cover to ensure a measure of confidentiality.

"I have no glasses, unfortunately."

"I'm not particular at this point."

"How can I be of assistance?"

"I'm trying to understand the situation. I think I'm in an insane asylum."

"That's a reasonable suspicion. The question is, how big is the asylum? Vancouver, Canada or the world?"

"My colleagues fabricate evidence and ignore the obvious. The last thing on their mind is what really happened to the girl."

"A word of warning, Constable Hook: I'm a reporter. Never give me information that might identify you as my source. I would be duty bound to print it anyway."

"I suppose you mean information such as my colleague Gorman trying to plant a bullet. What gave him away was that it hadn't been fired."

"You're joking."

"Afraid not."

"Lucky for you, I can't use it. It stretches credulity beyond the limit."

They would pursue the topic if it weren't for the din emanating from a block away—the clatter of a tight snare drum, the sort you hear with pipe bands, and the clop of marching feet.

A crowd has already assembled along the sidewalk to watch. "I was wondering when they would show up," McCurdy says.

"It was inevitable," Hook replies. "The Klan are very popular in America."

"And in Saskatchewan."

"Are there Negroes in Saskatchewan?"

"In Saskatchewan they're against Ukrainians—they call them Bohunks."

"Aren't Ukrainians white?"

"White is not about skin colour, constable. Think of the Irish—the 'white niggers of America.'"

"Of course here it's the Yellow Peril, though Orientals aren't what you'd call yellow."

"In fact, the women are whiter than you and I."

"If it were about skin colour, we would be the Pink Peril."

"Please feel free to finish the bottle, officer."

Hook thinks the reporter might be an amusing chap. Unlike in a British pub, he has met few amusing chaps in Vancouver, where men prefer to talk about fish, real estate and the weather. Perhaps all the amusing Canadians were killed off at Vimy Ridge.

He tosses the empty whisky bottle into a trash bin, and by repeating the words *Police! Make way, please!* in his Redhat voice, manages to clear a path to the curb, where they watch a procession of maybe fifty men, in white gowns and conical hats, carry aloft a banner with the words KEEP CANADA BRITISH, and another urging citizens to KEEP CANADA WHITE, followed by a huge Union Jack, followed by a cross wrapped in kerosene-soaked rags. A final banner features the Klan symbol, four Ks forming a sort of X around a drop of blood—white man's blood, one assumes, though all blood is red regardless of race.

"That's quite a procession," Hook says. "When do they burn the witch?"

McCurdy watches the marchers' feet slapping up and down, never in unison—policeman's boots, brogues, two-tones. As his father (who sold insurance for Equitable Life) would say, *you can tell a lot about a man by his shoes.* "Get used to it, Constable Hook. The Klan have set up shop in Shaughnessy Heights, at Glen Brae of all places—the colossus with tits for towers. Renamed it the Imperial Palace. They hold recruitment meetings along with the Orangemen. That masked chap holding the cross is a handsome fellow from Tennessee named Wallace. They call him the King Kleagle."

"What's the fascination with the letter *K*?"

"Something to do with being the eleventh letter. Eleven disciples once they got rid of Judas."

"Really?"

"No, I made that up. But it's plausible, don't you agree?"

Some of the Klansmen wear masks with holes for eyes and what appear to be enormous earflaps on their pointed hats; most feel free to dispense with anonymity—a testament to the organization's popularity that makes one wonder about those who choose to march in disguise. By their size and gait, McCurdy identifies two aldermen and a Conservative candidate from Kerrisdale, as well as a pair of cap-toe boots he could swear he once saw on the feet of Victor Newson, owner of *The Evening Star*.

JANET STEWART TO BE BURIED DESPITE DOUBTS
Scottish Societies Up in Arms
Will the Truth Be Buried with Her?
Ed McCurdy
Special to
The Evening Star

As Vancouver prepares to bury Janet Stewart as a possible suicide, evidence has multiplied, and it has become apparent that there is much more to the case than was brought out at the coroner's inquest. Facts remain unexamined which could shine new light on the victim and the circumstances that led to her death.

The burial seems hasty, given questions that remain; indeed, one is led to wonder whether evidence is to be buried with her.

That her diary was not brought forth during the inquest may have protected the girl's privacy and reputation, but it leaves unanswered the identity of several persons in her social circle.

Who, for example, is Arthur Dawson, supposedly her fiancé, whose engagement Miss Stewart had decided to break off? Who is "John," another disappointed swain—not to mention the well-off admirer, who drives a roadster and is said to have plied Miss Stewart with liquor?

Other sources report that the Attorney General and

Inspector Forbes Caddell of the Vancouver Police Department were overheard discussing a plan to interrogate Wong Chi, the houseboy, in order to extract answers to questions that went unanswered during the inquest.

The case is of sufficient interest to have been mentioned in the British press. In an interview with the *Glasgow Sunday Mail*, Miss Stewart's father declared: "I believe my daughter was murdered to cover up the tracks of some other person. She was the victim of a carefully planned, well-carried-out plot."

The fact that such suspicions are confined to the British papers suggests a compact of silence between some members of the Vancouver press and certain prominent individuals. It is common knowledge that Scotland Yard is following the case closely. It is possible and even likely that, if and when the full story is told, it will involve a shocking number of well-known persons.

12

Life is dream-walking, death is going home.

SITUATED WELL BEYOND the city proper, Mountain View Cemetery was first established as a resting place for the dead who previously occupied Stanley Park and were exhumed when the area became a downtown recreational forest for the enjoyment of the living.

While eliminating a civic inconvenience, the reburials reflected the social organization of the city itself, locating like with like, as opposed to the ad hoc interments that had taken place downtown. Hence, at Mountain View the dead occupy separate neighbourhoods—Jews, Chinese, Freemasons, Odd Fellows, veterans, policemen and firefighters—as they decompose side by side, six feet under.

Janet Stewart's burial is to take place in one of the more recent sections made necessary by an overflow of victims—of the Great War, the Spanish Flu and the sinking of the *Princess Sophia* off the coast of Alaska.

As Miss Stewart has become a sort of saint, every effort was taken to place her in a location with some distinction. Her nearest neighbour is Joe Fortes, the beloved Old Black Joe, a locally famous Caribbean gentleman who taught children to swim for decades and whose death inspired the largest funeral procession in the city's history.

McCurdy pauses at her open grave and admires the impressive obelisk made possible by the United Council of Scottish Societies, for whom the girl has become a martyr to class and culture—the lowly servant girl sacrificed so that sons of privilege might preserve their reputations.

As minister of St. Andrew's Presbyterian, the church attended by the deceased, the Reverend James Henderson is officiating at the graveside. (The Scottish Societies would have preferred a more rousing speaker.)

Through Christ our Lord, Janet Stewart lives on—not only in the memory of all who knew her, not only in the hearts of her employers whom she served with diligence and honour, but in the mansions of our Father in Heaven, there to gaze at the light we have yet to see...

McCurdy writes a subhead—*Scottish Martyr*—then turns his attention to the Edwards Company hearse as it backs gingerly toward the grave, its rear doors open and Sparrow on the running board, facing back, steering with one hand. As soon as the hearse creaks to a stop, six men of the Scottish Societies, in kilts and sporrans, step up to do their duty as pallbearers, lifting Miss Stewart's coffin by its handles onto a platform with thick ropes attached. Grasping the ropes, they raise the coffin, transfer it to the open grave and carefully lower it, guided by two Chinese gravediggers in wide-brimmed straw hats.

With the decisive thump of wood hitting solid earth, one of the pallbearers is moved to intone a short, heartfelt denunciation: "The blood of a Scottish girl, of blameless character, is at the door of every churchman who makes no protest!"

Unsurprisingly, the outspoken pallbearer turns out to be the Reverend McDougall, who has decided to reprise his success at the inquest. Unfortunately, he is almost immediately drowned out by the wail of a piper squeezing out "Braigh Loch Iall."

McCurdy shoulders his way past a group of young men who have come to chat up Scottish nannies who need comforting; he wonders if her fiancé and the mysterious John are among them, not to mention a swell with a roadster.

He reaches Constable Hook, who is scanning the crowd, no doubt with the same purpose.

"Recognize anyone, constable?" he mutters out of the side of his mouth, like a spy in the cinema.

"Miss Hawthorn and her friend—blast, I forget the name..."

"Cissie Braidwood, the belle of the inquest."

"I see the Faulkners have left the houseboy at home."

"Very wise. Some might find his presence in bad taste."

"Instead they brought Jock West, the war hero." Hook notes the airman's moustache, which must have been trimmed by Faulkner's barber. It suits West better, though, with his long, straight nose and high forehead; except for the tailoring, Faulkner is a coarser animal altogether.

"The woman next to him would be his wife." McCurdy notes her resemblance to Mrs. Faulkner, though she appears more haggard. It's not difficult to tell when a couple isn't getting along.

"What do you make of those chappies over here?"

"Too young for the war, more Miss Stewart's age. Some of them could be admirers, I guess. From her diary she seemed to have a platoon of them. Along that line, it turns out that Arthur Dawson is a logger from Gibsons. I plan to conduct an official interrogation, if and when we manage to track him down."

"Do you suppose she was 'engaged' to Arthur and John at the same time?"

Until the diaries, it hadn't occurred to Hook that Miss Stewart might be less than pure. It was the same with the young women of Waldo, such was their aura of virginity. Is it possible that Canadian girls are no more virtuous than their English counterparts? If so, the ladies of Waldo must be laughing at him to this day.

This view of her character, true or not, in no way alters the constable's need to expose her murderer. He still wishes she were not dead, and can feel her presence from time to time.

Among the semicircular crowd, Hook locates Miss Hawthorn, in a dark dress that slims her waist while complementing her bosom. The dead being out of reach, better focus on the living.

He slowly but systematically makes his way in her direction, squeezing between a delegation from the Rebekah Lodge and a group of city councillors.

Moving to within a few feet of Miss Hawthorn, far enough to convincingly express surprise upon seeing her, Constable Hook removes his cap and joins the congregation in reciting the Lord's Prayer.

For his part, McCurdy has situated himself among the group of young men, who don't show the least interest in saying the Lord's Prayer. "Pardon me, gentlemen, but would one of you happen to be Arthur Dawson?"

Receiving a chorus of shrugged shoulders in reply, he asks, "Is anyone named John? Does one of you own a roadster?"

Another empty pause, as though he is speaking in Swahili. "I don't suppose any of you gentlemen happen to be engaged to Miss Stewart?"

They turn and face him as a group, with the vacant, indifferent stares of cows peering over a fence.

13

Now is all there ever is.

MILDRED LIKES TO watch him sleep, until he starts screaming. Right now he's sleeping like a baby. A baby with one eye open.

If it weren't for its solid walls, Sparrow's room could be a field officer's tent: comfortable but minimal, ready to be packed up and transported at a moment's notice. Except for the bed—which is larger than a field cot, Mildred is glad to say, for he sometimes thrashes in his sleep and she needs room to dodge the blows. (At present he has fallen into a gentle, post-coital slumber that will last at least a half-hour.) The room is notable more for what isn't there than for what is—no personal mementos, no medals, no pictures on the wall, other than a framed poster advertising a cruise ship, supplied by the landlord.

Earlier in their engagement, when she summoned the nerve to ask what had happened to him, it took him some time to find the words to begin; soldiers don't talk about their wounds, mostly because turning it all into a story diminishes the experience, makes it seem like fiction.

The ambulance he had been driving was a Rover Sunbeam, a name that implied wandering and light, which seemed odd in an environment of smoke and mud. Unlike at Vimy, the triage station was supposed to be five hundred yards from the trench but this was not possible, thanks to a disagreement between field commanders, who wished their men to be treated as speedily as possible, and medical staff, who would rather work outside the trajectory of battle—not only for their own sake but also their patients, who preferred not to be blown up a second time.

Thanks to their commander's zeal to treat the wounded speedily (he would later receive a commendation for this), the triage station sat practically on the field of battle, forcing medical staff to examine wounded men while rounds whistled overhead, and a continuous caravan of stretcher-bearers delivered their ragged shipments of flesh.

When the 105mm howitzer hit, Sparrow had been shouting words of encouragement to a patient with a small mark in the abdomen but hopeless disaster around the exit wound—*a bee sting in front, pot roast behind*—when he heard a sharp sound as though someone had dropped a glass bottle into a porcelain bathtub. Overhead, a barrel of whitewash tipped over and it seemed that everything in the world turned white.

He emerged from a coma in the City of London Military Hospital, on a ward where mirrors were banned, where men who somehow managed an illicit peek at themselves were known to collapse in shock. Large-calibre guns could reduce parts of human bodies into pink fragments, and even the smaller rounds made for truly startling shrapnel wounds, every one an open canyon with shattered bone at the bottom. Thanks to modern weaponry, handsome young men became monsters in a fraction of a second.

Like anyone who was not there, Mildred cannot truly envisage any of this; certainly she has no desire to see what is under Sparrow's patch.

The facial prosthesis was to be fashioned of galvanized copper one-thirty-second of an inch thick, "the thinness of a visiting card" according to the gentleman who measured him, who added that compared to others he had seen, this was a pimple.

Then the Tin Noses Shop went to work. Located in the 3rd London General Hospital, its proper name was Masks for Facial Disfigurement Department—another desperate improvisation in dealing with unforeseen trauma to body, mind and soul. Weeks later, Sparrow and his fellows walked out of London General wearing precisely formed grey metal masks and patches that made them appear like partially completed metal sculptures of themselves. From London they travelled by omnibus and ferry to the Lauren Studio for Portrait Masks in the Latin Quarter of Paris, where artists from L'École des Beaux-Arts endeavoured to match dead metal and living human skin.

Here Sparrow's journey took another turn, whose meaning Mildred feels she has yet to fully comprehend.

He was assigned to a Mademoiselle Petard, a young woman with precise features, opalescent skin and intense, dark, hooded eyes that seemed to appraise everything they saw. For two weeks she worked on his patch and its representation of an eye, a canvas the size of a railway watch. They never spoke beyond *hello* because he had no French, and in any case she seemed to have no particular interest in who he was, only in the nine square inches she covered in layers of paint, using a fine brush that couldn't have contained more than a half-dozen bristles. Never once did she look into his good eye; yet something convinced him that she knew him better than anyone had ever known him before.

Apparently, this was never discussed. Nothing was. Each morning Mademoiselle Petard would arrive, greet Sparrow, lay out her colours and begin work with the focus of a watchmaker. In the process, he examined her as well; his good eye watched her face and nothing else all morning and afternoon, as she made and evaluated one stroke, then another, then blended the two with a cotton-covered finger, her face so close to his that he could smell her skin and hair, could have kissed her if it were another situation and his face wasn't a crater on the surface of the moon.

She never pronounced her work finished, nor did she say *adieu*. Late one morning her superior dropped by to say that she had left Paris and that she wished him good luck.

It seems obvious that there was unfinished business between them.

It would be wrong to say that Mademoiselle Petard gave him his face back; rather, it was a new face, and more. The patch somehow altered everything.

Back in London, he watched carefully the reactions of strangers and acquaintances who no longer looked at him as though he were a pitiable monster but with a curious sense of wonder.

Sparrow told Mildred that he still faces a long journey before he will understand who or what he has become. He made it clear to her early on that he would not complicate the situation by taking on a lifetime companion, which would mean having to read another face. She is fine with this, or at least that's what she tells herself. When his search takes him to another country or continent, they will remain a mystery to each other (Sparrow doesn't delve into her past, having enough of his own), which is infinitely preferable to knowing a person all too well, knowing things one wishes one didn't know.

She is never sure what aspect of Sparrow's personality is a

result of his injury and what is innate. Sometimes it seems as though a kind of indiscriminate pruning took place; Sparrow can cut through a complicated argument, yet have problems putting a simple sentence together. And he seems prescient at times, the way dogs sense a coming earthquake and sharks head for deeper water before a hurricane.

One thing is certain: Mildred can't for the life of her imagine what Sparrow was like without the patch.

Certainly, the injury did not diminish his sexual drive. On the contrary, he seems to have acquired special skills, thanks to intuition and a long association with nurses. He can maintain an erection seemingly at will, though she's never quite sure what or whom he's thinking of at the time. After sex he falls asleep like a cat in the sun—until the dreams arrive. Then Mildred will watch helplessly while he flails about and cries out, or rather, screams.

At the moment he has begun to mutter some sort of poem, composed of diverse wartime imagery: trench foot, jungle rot, dressing stations, triage, rats, shrapnel, grey-back lice, saltwater lice. Soon he will confer with the ghosts of men with monstrous wounds, men reduced to shell-shocked paralysis, men who could not force their bodies to climb up the ladder but stood there frozen and were shot on the spot for cowardice. From Sparrow's sleep-talking, Mildred has acquired a dreamlike understanding of the war, a war that must itself have been like a dream.

Driving a hearse is the perfect occupation for a man like Sparrow—good clean work, the damage over and done with, nobody wounded or screaming in pain, nothing to do but tidy up.

The first time they made love, they lay on his white duster coat between two enormous trees on English Bay. He looked up at a patch of clear sky and asked, "Why is the moon such a shade of white, and why is its mouth open? Is it in shock?" She sat up and looked him in the face and wondered which eye had seen the moon.

14

The fish sees the bait but not the hook.

MCCURDY IS ABOUT to upchuck everything he has eaten today, either on the floor of the tram or on the head and shoulders of a seated passenger. It's a mystery to him how people spend a half-hour jammed upright in a crowded trolley on a hot day without vomiting all over each other.

The Main Street tram, like an elongated garden bug, judders erratically toward the city, down a ribbon of graded dirt called Main Street, which causes the pain in his back to flare up again.

After twenty minutes wedged between two damp gentlemen in kilts exuding a miasma of tobacco smoke, shaving lotion and stale body odour, desperate for fresh air, he leans toward the open window until his chin practically rests on the cloche hat of a seated female mourner, whose perfume is not helpful. Peering outside, he avoids the blur of trees that would turn his stomach and rain disaster on the unfortunate lady beneath him.

Outside the window, an Alvis open two-seater honks its Lucas horn unnecessarily, its driver and passenger grinning with smug satisfaction as it spits up a swirl of exhaust and dust, forcing tram passengers to cover their noses with their handkerchiefs, and passes the tram as though it was being towed. Then a black Wolseley passes with the crest of the Vancouver Police on its door; then two expensive autos from Shaughnessy Heights, an Aster and a blue McLaughlin Master Six—the latter driven by one Frank Faulkner, in a funereal black suit and tie, with his wife in the passenger seat and someone male in the back seat, his head obscured by the landau roof.

Further north, the tram ride becomes more bearable as Main Street enters the city proper and the dirt surface turns to asphalt, and second-growth firs give way to utilitarian buildings the colour of dust. From here Main Street becomes more and more self-consciously impressive, until they reach Broadway and Main, where the Lee Building and the Bank of Montreal stand together like an architectural Mutt and Jeff—the brick-and-stone Lee towering overhead and dripping with finials, and the squat Bank of Montreal, the two separated by a tangle of criss-crossed tram cables, telephone lines and electric wires.

Mountains in the near distance have taken on a pink-orange hue in the late afternoon light—a scene that, rendered in a painting, would be in extremely poor taste.

McCurdy hops off the tram at Hastings Street in front of the Carnegie Library (Rome and Paris, interpreted by an Englishman). He welcomes the steadiness of solid ground, and is grateful for the outdoor atmosphere—a blend of industrial smoke and rubbish, as opposed to the tram smell of sweat, perfume and incontinent farts.

Before undertaking the twenty-minute walk to his digs, he decides to step into the Lumberman's Club, where he remains an honorary member, thanks to a piece in *The Evening Star* about the exploitation of loggers for which he interviewed former members of their union, now extinct. What gave the piece its zip was his subjects' fascination with the Grand Guignol of logging injuries—a parade of split torsos and multiple amputations that would cause a seasoned medic in the trenches to wince.

Honorary membership in the Lumberman's Club is likely the closest McCurdy will ever get to a private club.

Seated at square tables in a room the size of a small diner, members play cards, drink rye whisky and smoke; on the tables are columns of betting chips at various heights, each chip stamped with the club label. The members wear sweaty lounge suits that have withstood physical labour, worn with a pair of logger's boots laced partway up. (Unlike in the Cariboo, in Vancouver a man can expose his ankles without masses of suppurating bug bites.)

A pong of ingrained smoke and sweat seeps from the plaster walls and the spruce floor, an odour that, as with boxers' gyms and army barracks, will remain as long as the building stands.

Leaning over the bar, McCurdy orders a double rye from Truman MacBeth, an ex-miner with a face like a boiled soup bone, in ragged tweeds and a brown Derby with shiny patches on the crown. Like his customers, the bartender wears his hat at all times; should the Dry Squad undertake a raid (there is always a technicality) necessitating a fast exit, it would be a shame to lose one's hat.

McCurdy arranges his face into a working-class expression; in the Lumberman's Club, a whiff of condescension can get you a punch in the mouth.

The bartender has a cigarette tightly wedged in so that it waggles up and down when he speaks. "G'day Ed, what'll it be?"

"Walker's if you don't mind, Truman. Fine weather today."

"She is that. More rain this weekend, though."

"So I understand. Make it a double."

"The Chinaman had to have something to do with it, wouldn't you say?"

To a recent visitor, the bartender's question might seem out of the blue, but the fact is that in recent weeks the Janet Stewart case has become a conversational topic requiring neither introduction nor explanation—like today's weather, an upcoming election or the Asahi Tigers, a winning baseball team comprised entirely of Japanese. (In Oppenheimer Park, fans cheer for players they would never allow in the house.)

"Could be the Chinaman did it, Truman, but he'd have to be awful stupid. Can you imagine murdering someone when you're the only two people in the house?"

"Some fella was on about that last night. Something about a party."

"That's one of the rumours. That a wild party was going on upstairs."

"No, this fella says the party was at Canacraig."

"Are you sure, Truman?"

"Sure about what?"

"That it was Canacraig? When the general throws a party it's posh but hardly wild."

"That's what struck me too. All I heard tell was there was a wild party. This guy James says he heard it from some fellow worked in the general's kitchen."

Everyone's a reporter. McCurdy refrains from rolling his eyes. "So it's possible there were *two* parties going on—one at Canacraig and the other in the house where she was murdered?"

"That's what it sounded like—a party *and* a drug orgy, but in different houses." The bartender shrugs. It's not up to him to decide what the truth is.

McCurdy wonders: if there was a party at Canacraig, would the general not have invited his daughter and son-in-law? And how does any of this square with the Faulkners' testimony at the inquest—that they retired early?

Like a primitive deep-sea creature, the story is expanding and splitting into other stories, independent organisms that swim off by themselves. McCurdy realizes it might be worthwhile to submit a think piece on the evils of rumour. He reaches for his notebook— and finds a piece of paper in his pocket that wasn't there before.

"Anyway Ed, that's just something I heard," the bartender continues. "James says his friend seen it with his own eyes, and he's a good egg."

McCurdy tips the bartender a quarter, then unfolds and reads the note. "Thank you, Truman. Your help is always much appreciated..."

MCCURDY MEET AT CORNER BY PEKIN CHOP SUEY
EIGHT O'CLOCK NO FRIEND WITH YOU
BIG STORY FOR YOU

The paper appears torn out of a notebook not unlike McCurdy's, and although the sentence reads like pidgin English, it's possible that the writer deliberately phrased it that way.

Obviously someone slipped the note into his pocket while he stood in the tram. Only, there were no Orientals on the tram; in the current social climate, any tram occupied by a white woman would be cleared of Asians, if one dared to board at all. On the other hand, although the message may have been slipped into his pocket by anyone really—male, female, white, coloured—it doesn't follow that the writer *isn't* Chinese. Nothing is too obvious to be true. The request that he come alone has an ominous ring, but the source might be camera-shy, or witness-shy, or any of the other reasons to be shy about speaking to a reporter.

Though feeling no more courageous than usual, curiosity gets the upper hand.

McCurdy glances at his pocket watch, downs the rest of his whisky and heads for the door.

EASILY THE BIGGEST restaurant in Chinatown, the Pekin Chop Suey House occupies the busiest corner on Pender Street, one floor above the Chinese Freemasons Society, also known as the Chee Kung Tong, the most powerful tong in the province, with huge interests in silk, porcelain, spices, teak, tiger's testicles and other medicinal products. By day, heard through the open balcony doors, negotiating businessmen lift their voices and goblets over lunch; by night, the restaurant caters to smart sets of all races, headed to or from Shanghai Alley.

Situated at the western edge of Chinatown, Shanghai Alley was once Chinatown's social centre for theatre, music, opera and acrobatics. Having gone considerably downmarket, the street is now a popular destination for the louche set, an Oriental version of Hogan's Alley, where the arts exist side by side with the vices of the day: gambling, prostitution and opium. From the second-floor windows on Shanghai Alley, one might hear someone practising on an erhu or doing exercise dances from the Han Dynasty, along with the sounds of serious, intense gambling—the rattle, clack and snap-snap of tiles, dice, buttons and beans, the steady mutter of prayers, the cries of triumph or despair.

Protecting this gambling Mecca, a sophisticated human relay network has been established from the intersection of Pender and Main, through a series of glassed-in second-floor balconies, to the gambling halls of Shanghai Alley—efficiently enough that, should the VPD arrive, they will find not a trace of a bet.

McCurdy winces at the odour of spinach and bok choi. The Chinese have a taste for many unpleasant things, but for someone of Scottish descent, the most difficult to accept is the eating of near-raw, insufficiently boiled green vegetables, like goats nibbling from a bush. To any white Canadian of Scottish descent, it's self-evident that cooked food should be brown.

He leans against a lamp-post, takes out his notebook and pencil, and surveys the sidewalk traffic, made up mostly of men in fashionable double-breasted suits, smoking pipes and fat cigars, men who have put China well behind them. Since the Chinese Immigration Act, one no longer sees pigtailed coolies straight off the boat; at most, one encounters a mixture of East and West—silk shirts with frog closures accompanied by fedora hats, Oxford trousers and traditional black fabric slippers.

Nearby, a less integrated member of the community, perched on the sill of a ground-floor window in a baggy collarless shirt and a hat too small for him, watches his dapper countrymen come and go with despair on his face, wondering how he will ever make the grade and, if he doesn't, how he will ever get home.

A procession of electric trams clatters by, clanging as though marking the rounds of a boxing match.

As the sun dips behind the curved rooflines, McCurdy glances at his pocket watch: eight o'clock. As the moon globes overhead fade up, gutter grime and garbage are lost in shadow while imparting a deluxe quality to building decorations that would otherwise seem cheap and garish. Red paint becomes blood red, gold leaf seems to glow on its own, and the buildings themselves seem to breathe like mythic beasts.

A man with dark, southern Chinese skin saunters past, dressed in a tailored cream suit with a gold chain between the chest pockets of his vest and an impeccable Panama hat, trailing an aroma of brilliantine and swinging an ebony English walking stick. Behind him walks a man in a broad-brimmed hat like a sombrero and with a cigar permanently fixed in his mouth.

Across the street, past the tram tracks and the steady stream of bicycles, mounds of Chinese vegetables are displayed on three-wheeled carts and in the heavy baskets suspended from yokes across men's shoulders.

A Yellow Cab pulls up in front of McCurdy to within three feet of the lamp-post, and the rear passenger door swings open, seemingly on its own. McCurdy steps onto the running board and slides onto the velour seat, shiny in patches from the friction of multiple arses. He pulls the door shut and turns to view his seat-mate, a middle-aged Oriental in a black silk shirt with mandarin collar, a homburg hat and a steel-grey boxcar moustache. Instead of black slippers he wears two-tone spectator shoes.

"Would you care for cigarette, Mr. McCurdy?"

Chung Young Lee extends an open case made of green enamel. "Dunhill, very good English brand."

"Thank you, but I don't smoke." McCurdy regards his companion with a certain dread. As a "community leader," Chung Young Lee is not to be taken lightly, a man about whom much is rumoured but little is known. To the white community his business might be only vaguely understood, but it is general knowledge that bribery and intimidation are tools of his trade, and that half the Vancouver Police Department owes him favours.

Up to now, members of the press have remained beneath his

notice. Whatever McCurdy has done to merit his attention, it can't mean anything good.

"Ah. Too bad, Mr. McCurdy. Tobacco very good for lungs and heart." Chung Young Lee removes a Dunhill, taps one end and lights up with a silver petrol lighter.

"It's been a long day, Mr. Chung, so if you don't mind let's make this brief. Do we have something to discuss? Otherwise, I'll get out here if it's all the same to you."

"Ah, but I have something good for you, Mr. McCurdy. Excellent quality. Something very special."

The taxi accelerates down Abbott Street, then turns onto Hastings, passing Cunningham Drugs and Leonard's Cafe. Chung Young Lee leans forward to speak to the driver in Mandarin, then turns to McCurdy, tossing his half-smoked cigarette out the open window onto the streetcar tracks.

"I love summer. Is it not so with you? The flowers—lilies very lucky. I think the Asahi team will win this year. Fishing very good for sockeye and chinook..."

"I've heard enough," McCurdy says, and turns to the driver. "Stop here, please."

Unnervingly, the taxi doesn't even slow down. In fact, it accelerates sharply, to prevent McCurdy from opening the door and jumping out.

East of Main Street, Hastings Street is a series of tiny vegetable and grocery stores, then a line of low-roofed frame bungalows, more like barracks than houses. From here the car turns abruptly left, down a narrow road toward the railway tracks. McCurdy can see the sawtooth outline of the mountains, and the occasional flash in Burrard Inlet indicating a buoy, or perhaps a small vessel...

He suspects that the meeting might not go well.

"It is always good to make new friends," Chung Young Lee says, but in place of a handshake, he holds McCurdy's arm with both hands in a surprisingly strong grip. "Allow me please to introduce you to Mr. Chow."

As the taxi slows to walking speed, out of nowhere appears a man the shape of an upended boxcar, a mound of muscle and bone with a face as expressive as a death mask, who steps onto the running board and extends two crane-like arms through the passenger window. Long, narrow fingers imprison McCurdy like a set of handcuffs.

"Do you mean to murder me?" McCurdy feigns indignation, resisting the unbecoming urge to beg for mercy.

"It's never wise for Chinese to murder a white man, Mr. McCurdy. Better to show him the light. Relax, please."

McCurdy's spectacles are taken away and something is inserted into his mouth, a soft, wet cloth that gives him no choice but to inhale the pungent vapour like sweet, hot tar—and suddenly all concern over the situation disappears while his entire body melts into the seat cushions.

He feels no pain, in fact pain and distress have become unimaginable. Gradually, his two companions loosen their hold, for there is no longer any question of a struggle. A rush of pleasure rolls over him in a wave.

To call it dreaming would be an understatement.

Seated in the back seat of the taxi, McCurdy topples forward—but he doesn't hit the seat in front of him; he continues to fall into a black void while his body softens into ectoplasm, so that he can now twist himself sideways and literally float over the lap of the man seated beside him (he doesn't seem to even notice), then through the open car window. In his present state, intention turns into reality with only a slight delay, so that now he is floating forward, at speed or in slow motion, in control, experiencing sights and sounds he has never seen or heard before, yet which present themselves as real life on a new level, in shimmering colour, searing reds and tropical greens. Neon railway tracks streak past Powell Street to Main Street, past a crowd mingling near a spaghetti tangle of trolley tracks—*Can't you see me, just a few feet over your heads? I am not invisible, I can see my own hand in front of me—in fact I can see without glasses!* After a lifetime wearing spectacles, for the first time he can see peripherally; the world is not something to be viewed through twin windows, it's a continuous, three-dimensional dome!

Hovering above Pender Street, he watches the Yellow Cab taxi containing Chung Young Lee head west; he glides just behind the rear window as the machine turns left onto Shanghai Alley and they both disappear through the wall of a building...

Oh, Jesus! What a burst of happiness comes over him, floating in mid-air while joy pours from the depths of his spirit in waves of revelation. Here is the secret of happiness—happiness that can be bought for a shilling and kept in one's vest pocket, ready to be enjoyed; peace of mind, delivered by courier to your door. McCurdy soars higher with each wave of pleasure, then descends into a cottony warm cloud, or shroud, protected from fear, worry or regret, truly happy for maybe the first time in his life...

15

A man can dig his own grave with his teeth.

TRUMAN THE BARTENDER points to the muscular fellow seated at a corner table. "That would be Dawson over there. Said he caught a ride from Gibsons Landing—on a fishboat by the smell of him."

"Thank you, Mr. MacBeth, for your assistance."

"Always a good citizen, Constable Gorman, and expect to be treated as such."

"What do you mean by that, sir? Are you being sarcastic?"

"Just an expression, officer. No sarcasm intended."

Hook watches the exchange, noting how effortlessly Gorman has managed to make an enemy of the bartender. He moves quickly before his fellow officer can do likewise with Dawson.

The man in question does in fact reek of fish oil, but his hands aren't those of a fisherman; instead, he is missing the tip of his left forefinger, a carpenter's injury if there ever was one, and the knuckles are swollen and scabbed—the knuckles of a street-fighter.

"Sir, would your name be Arthur Dawson?"

"It is."

"I am Constable Hook, and that is Constable Gorman over there at the bar."

Hook notes the man's prominent ears (emphasized by the white skin of a five-cent short-back-and-sides haircut), and his sun- and wind-damaged face. With his broad shoulders straining the seams of a shiny serge jacket he could pass for an athlete, except that he is working his way through a triple serving of rye.

"Is there a problem, officer?"

Hook imagines what is to come. As when breaking the news to Miss Hawthorn, he envisages an anvil suspended by a thread, a shattering weight of dreadful information about to crash onto Dawson's head.

In a matter of moments he will be a changed man. And Hook detests himself for the faint pleasure he takes in breaking bad news, like a sadistic fortune teller. He would rather the job went to someone else, but the last thing he wants is for Gorman to take the lead; it would be like performing surgery with a hacksaw.

As a Redhat, Hook learned how surprise can prove useful in questioning a suspect: establish a rapport with the fellow, chat him up, lead him on—then, at just the right moment, throw him off balance with a fact he didn't know. This takes time and patience, but it produces results.

"Would you be engaged to a Miss Janet Stewart, sir?"

"I am. How'd you know that?"

"We are with the Point Grey Police. Could you give us some idea of your whereabouts over the past few weeks?"

"I sure can. I have been in Roberts Creek for the past two months. Harry Roberts himself will tell you. I seen him over at the mill every other day."

"What do you do over there, Mr. Dawson?"

Dawson's expression brightens, though a slight wariness remains. "I'm building a house. My fiancée and I plan to live there when we're married. She thinks it a bit out of the way, but Vancouver prices have gone through the roof. And besides, these days there's a steamer every few hours for the price of a ticket."

"Oh, she'll get used to it, I'm sure. Women are adaptable creatures."

"Well let's hope you're right."

"And when did you arrive in Vancouver?"

"Took a ride on Willy Parken's gillnetter two days ago. Willy put me up in his shack in Strathcona."

"And I take it you haven't called on your fiancée yet?"

"I was attendin' to other business. Why are you askin' me these questions?"

Dawson signals Truman for another whisky. Behind Dawson's back, Hook signals *make it a double*.

Unfortunately, in facing the bartender Hook momentarily turns his back on Gorman, who leans down to within a foot of Dawson's ear with his lipless smile: "I'd suspend work on that house if I was you, sir."

"Shut up, Mr. Gorman. Shut up at once." Hook wishes to heaven he could vault the table and clamp his two hands around that fat neck.

"Why do you say that?" Dawson's eyes remind Hook of a dog about to be shot. "Officer, what are you saying?"

"Constable Hook, I see no reason why you choose to beat around the bush with this man. Mr. Dawson, I say that you won't be needing the house because you're not engaged to Miss Stewart anymore. Why? Because she is dead."

He is enjoying this, Hook thinks. He read somewhere about medieval villages bidding on condemned criminals for the pleasure of torturing them to death. Such entertainments were depicted as evidence of a brutal past, now overcome thanks to Progress.

Not so, if Gorman is any indication.

"*Dead?* Officer, what do you mean, dead?"

"Sir, I mean dead. There's no other meaning. Your Miss Stewart is dead. Don't you get newspapers in Roberts Creek?"

"No."

"Well there you are, then. Damned nasty for you to find out this way. We'll leave out the dreadful gory details 'til later..."

With no other way to stop this torture, Hook grips Gorman by the arm, drags him aside and hisses, "Thank you very much, Constable Gorman. Thank you for making this entire interview irrelevant."

"There was no point to your questioning. It was nothing but conversation."

"That *was* the entire point, you idiot. I was establishing a relationship of trust."

"Let go my arm, sir, or I will report you for assault of a fellow officer. Constable Hook, I don't hold with this psychological claptrap. In my experience, a good shock will do the trick. Put a nightstick up a man's arse and we'll know what the truth is."

Dawson appears as if someone whacked him in the forehead with a ball hammer.

"A fool, fool, such a fool..." He looks into the distance and repeats these words to himself at five-second intervals, with slight variations, making no move toward the whisky Truman set before him. His eyes are sucked backwards into two tunnels converging somewhere deep in his head—the eyes of a man who dozed off on sentry duty or mislaid his weapon and would be executed in an hour.

THE WRITING ON THE WALL
Ed McCurdy
Special to
The Evening Star

Janet Stewart was a naive young Scottish woman, cast upon distant shores, separated from her loving parents far across the sea.

Now she lies in a faraway grave. As the recent inquest demonstrated, Miss Stewart would be alive today were it not for the willful blindness of everyone connected with the case.

Despite the protests of her closest friends that she lived in terror of her employer's other servant, Wong Sing Chi, no attention has been paid to the Oriental's possible involvement. A factor in this omission, scandalous if true, may be that her wealthy employers, Mr. and Mrs. Frank Faulkner, favoured the houseboy and ignored her pleas for protection.

We hope it is a coincidence that Mrs. Faulkner is a daughter of General Hector Armstrong, who is expected to run in the upcoming election. Such a scandal might cast doubt on his avowed support of the Women and Girls Protection Act—otherwise now known, fittingly, as the Janet Stewart Bill.

Surely it's apparent that, for the sake of decency and safety, no young white girl should be left alone and unprotected in a house with a Chinaman. As a result of the Chinese Immigration Act (a prudent precaution against rampant breeding), almost the entire Chinese population consists of single men—human tinderboxes, cauldrons of lust.

According to one highly placed official, Mrs. Faulkner was heard to describe her houseboy as "like one of the family." Mrs. Faulkner expressed no such sentiments toward the Scottish nanny lying dead at her feet.

It seems that British standards have become entirely foreign to the profiteers of Shaughnessy Heights, who behave as traitors to their race, exploiting loopholes to avoid the head tax and the quota, thereby avoiding having to employ white men who require a living wage and cannot subsist solely on rice.

As an example, we might cite the prominent fish-canner

who pays the head tax for his Chinese coolies, then collects it from them in cheap labour and at high interest, or the white merchants who profit from businesses they would scarcely put their names to.

It is well known that a prosperous individual on Hudson Avenue made his first fortune by inventing a quick way to get rid of weevils in cast-off hams that had gone bad. He travelled from town to town, collecting hams crawling with vermin, cured them of their weevils, smoked them—and sold them to Chinese restaurants. Think of this when next you tuck into a bowl of Jinhua Ham.

And of course we must not forget the thriving drug trade, West to East and East to West, which would scarcely exist were it not for an unsavoury alliance between Chinese business and white investment.

It is a fact of history that, in situations of rampant abuse and injustice, a single event can galvanize working people to action and bring a ruling class to its knees. The suspicious death of Janet Stewart, together with the farcical inquest that followed, may add up to just such an event. It is no wonder that the good people of Shaughnessy Heights, through their apologists in the press and their lickspittles in government, are urging the public to remain calm.

At this crisis point in the life of the city, plaudits are due for the Scots, for their public spirit in prosecuting the case of their ill-fated countrywoman. Whether the wealthy employers of Shaughnessy see fit to do likewise.

16

There are always ears on the other side of the wall.

"Hello, operator speaking. Is this TRinity 32-33-55?"

"Here is 32-33-55. Mrs. Frank Faulkner speaking."

"Mrs. Harlen West is calling. I will connect you now."

SWITCH

"Doreen, I do hope I haven't caught you at an inconvenient time."

Mrs. Faulkner knows this trick, how "I hope" works as a coded threat, a form of blackmail, a way of holding one's potential disappointment over someone else's head. One of the many reasons why she detests Shaughnessy women.

"Actually, I was just going out the door."

"No. You must listen. Jock is upstairs. He's been drinking heavily."

"Hardly a rare occasion I should think, Lillian." She slides a Dunhill from a silver cigarette box on the coffee table and lights up, bracing for a tiresome conversation.

"Pardon me for saying so, Doreen, but you're hardly in a position to judge. In any case, Frank must come and speak to Jock immediately. He's in a bad way, and I'm afraid he will do harm to himself."

"But why bother Frank about it? Where is Elizabeth while Jock is flailing about?"

"Elizabeth is out of her mind with worry. The doctors have put her on sedatives."

"I see."

"No, my dear, you do not see. My son is saying dreadful, awful things about people dear to us both. Things he has never said before, not even the burning pilot compares to this."

Jock has a number of war stories he tells at various stages of impairment, the most maudlin of which concerns a dogfight in which he made a firing pass against an Albatross and, when he came out of the dive, saw the enemy plane in flames. Immediately the enemy pilot stood up in the cockpit of his burning plane, saluted and shot himself in the head. It's a tiresome story and Doreen doesn't believe it.

"*What sort of nonsense is he raving about this time, Lillian?*"

"*He has been attacking Elizabeth, his own wife, accusing her of dreadful things—obviously, he is experiencing hallucinations from the war. We have had to have* him *sedated as well, and kept away from the servants. Savage rumours seem to spread on their own in this dirty city. Do people really hate us that much, Doreen?*"

"*No, it's the press. They thrive on negativity. But you can be sure they receive plenty of material from our neighbours.*"

"*Everyone keeps harping on and on about your nanny. I tell you, Doreen, they're making her out to be Saint Felicity herself.*"

"*Janet was a Baptist, actually.*"

"*That is hardly the point. They're blowing it up out of all proportion, turning her into a martyr. One piece in the* Star *suggested that the entire Armstrong family is tainted by this—that your houseboy is a suspect and you are protecting him!*"

Doreen read the *Star* article, which was purportedly written by a freelancer but had Newson's fingerprints all over it, top to bottom. It was surely due to the coming election. *The dirty tricks have begun early this time around.*

"*Doreen, are you there?*"

"*Yes Lillian, I'm here.*"

"*Will you* please *tell your husband to speak to Jock? I'm afraid he will do harm to himself. Frank is the only one left who can talk sense to him.*"

"*I will, Lillian, certainly. At once.*" Then *I'm going to have to speak to Daddy.*

"*Hello, operator speaking, TRinity exchange. Is this FAirmont 3519?*"

"*Here is FAirmont 3519. Frank Faulkner speaking.*"

"*I will connect you now.*"

SWITCH

"*Frank, are you there?*"

"*Doreen, didn't I ask you not to call except in an emergency? I'm in the middle of an important—*"

"*This is an emergency, darling, I assure you. Jock is at his parents' home and he's gone off his nut again. Lillian is absolutely hysterical. Elizabeth has taken to her bed. But what's more worrying, much more worrying, is that Jock's raving has taken a new tack, and it sounds like a dangerous one. You'd better take him in hand before he says or does something really stupid."*

"Damn it. Poor Jock. Let's not discuss this on the telephone. Leave it to me and I'll be there in an hour."

At her station at the Bayview exchange on Seymour Street, operator Helen Digby takes meticulous notes, which she will deliver to her supervisor Olga Minn, who will deliver them to Carla at *The Evening Star*. For this she will receive a bonus. Of late, calls to and from Shaughnessy Heights are of particular interest to the press.

Faulkner replaces the receiver on his desk. "I apologize for the interruption. It's a family matter."

"Family always more important than business." Chung Young Lee produces a green enamel cigarette case. "Care for cigarette, Mr. Faulkner? Dunhill, very good English brand."

"Thank you, I believe I will," Faulkner replies, and lights both cigarettes with his own lighter.

"Family come first. Friendship second. Everything else very far below. I see that you are upset by worrying news—worry is very bad for health. Better to continue discussion tomorrow maybe—yes?"

17

A leader is only as good as his advice.

"Hello, operator speaking. Is this TRinity 320?"
  "Here is TRinity 320, operator Colin Hanson speaking."
  "Here is TRinity 3235. I will connect you."
  SWITCH
  "Colin, here is Mrs. Faulkner. I need to speak to my father at once."
  "I will connect you to his office, Mrs. Faulkner. Please hold the line."
  SWITCH
  "Dermot Scarfe here. May I ask who is calling?"
  "Doreen Faulkner here. I need to speak to my father at once, please."
  "I'm afraid he's in conference, Mrs. Faulkner. For what time would you wish to arrange a meeting?"
  "Now, please. I want to speak to him now."
  "The general gave specific instructions—"
  "Are you looking for excitement, Dermot? I need to speak to my father at once."
  "He is with paid consultants, Mrs. Faulkner."
  "Yes, yes, time is money, do you think I haven't heard that a thousand times? We have a serious problem, and please do not take this personally, Mr. Scarfe, but I am very close to becoming annoyed with you."
  "I apologize, Mrs. Faulkner. I shall look in on the general at once. Please remain on the line..."

With a familiar feeling of dread, Scarfe opens the office door with a discreet murmur of a cough.

General Armstrong casts him the withering look that sent many a good officer fleeing to the mess for a stiff one—feral eyes, a nose like the prow of an icebreaker, a forehead like a polished knob atop a battle-axe.

"God fucking damn it to hell, Dermot, who gave you leave to

barge into this meeting?" The general doesn't raise his voice; his tone is more like the sadness of a hanging judge.

· "I am dreadfully sorry, general, but it is your daughter Mrs. Faulkner on the line. She insists on speaking to you as an immediate priority and won't take no for an answer. She says it's about *another project*, and I was given to believe you would understand. If I am wrong..." Scarfe thinks, *I might as well go to the garden and hang myself.*

"Blast. Very well, in a moment. Carry on, Dermot."

Scarfe exits, closing the door softly as though afraid to wake a sleeping infant.

The general faces the two gentlemen across his desk, paid experts in lumber mills and meat-packing. Already they have abandoned their chairs and are easing their way to the door like two house cats in the presence of a Doberman.

"That will be all for the moment, gentlemen. What do you say we reconvene in a half-hour? Wait outside, or feel free to use the lounge downstairs if you so wish." This is spoken in a tone suggesting that only a fool would take him up on the latter offer. Nothing irks General Armstrong more than to pay an extortionate hourly rate for professional councillors to lounge in his easy chairs, drink his whisky and frig themselves.

BORN ON AN Ontario farm, General Hector Armstrong became convinced at an early age that he carried greatness within him—so utterly convinced that he began constructing his autobiography even while a schoolboy, part of a lifelong saga of accomplishment that would live in the public mind forever as a sort of immortality.

Built of concrete—not of wood like its neighbours—Canacraig is General Armstrong's triumphant edifice, his Taj Mahal. Future generations will regard the estate as proof that here lived a great man, a leader, a man who stood above other men. The building needs only to be sealed in to serve as a mausoleum, with Armstrong's office serving as a tomb for the great man. Replace the desk with a coffin and the room could be left as is, forever.

The office decorations form a narrative of splendid achievement. On the west wall, surrounding a stained mullioned window that would not be out of place in a chapel, letters from eminent persons speak of his spectacular career as a self-made businessman, buying government-owned prairie grassland, then selling tracts to prospective settlers at a spectacular profit, funded by wealthy American investors who paid for his army of land agents. In this way, the general managed to create an entire industry top to bottom, dedicated to the buying and selling of land, at a time when the population in the territories was about to triple.

He bought the land for next to nothing because the Government of Canada was concerned about incursions by the Americans, and because many of its members, including Sir Robert Borden, the prime minister, were allies of General Armstrong—part of a network of friends who supported one another in war, business, politics and law.

(The office contains no reference to his marriage into the wealthy family in Philadelphia that produced a flow of capital when business faltered; it would be inconsistent with the overall theme.)

On the east wall, the windowless wall, pride of place goes to the framed medals grouped around his Companion of the Order of the Bath, accompanied by photographs of Armstrong in uniform, posing with General Haig and Major-General Trenchard in front of the War Office. Nearby, framed headlines announce press cuttings of victories: inspiring tales of valour, many of which were ordered up by Armstrong himself in his role as Information Officer, to buck up national morale.

And of course the legions of horses, together with accounts of how Lieutenant-Colonel Armstrong re-engineered the remount commission as a private sector business, enabling the acquisition of some eight thousand of the animals in a variety of transactions. The campaign was a splendid success; the Royal Commission later cleared him of any wrongdoing whatsoever.

Amid this tale of accomplishment and triumph, one failure stands out in Armstrong's mind like a festering boil—not in war nor in business, but in politics. It was his first and only serious loss, unassuaged by subsequent success. He remains determined to erase this blot in his *curriculum vitae*, if it means becoming Prime Minister of Canada—not an unachievable goal.

"Doreen, are you there?"

"Daddy, is there an operator on the line?"

"It's a private line, lassie."

"There is no such thing as a private line, Daddy. Colin? Dermot? *If either of you are on the line, disconnect at once or there will be consequences."*

She waits in silence until she hears an almost inaudible click. *"Daddy, we must do something about the* Star. *They are getting out of hand."*

"Yes. I expected an attack, but not this early in the game. What is Victor firing at us this time?"

"He is framing Wong Chi as an election issue."

"Framing in what sense?"

"They're using him to instill an impression in the public mind that you are soft on Oriental exclusion."

"What do they want me to do, go over there and hang him myself?"

"Nothing that specific, unfortunately. Vague impressions are impossible to refute. But if he is able to define you at this stage, your image might never recover."

"My image, Doreen?"

"Your face as the electorate imagines it when they read about you in the newspaper. The mental image they conjure up. Public relations, Daddy—don't pretend you don't know what I'm talking about, you and Lord Beaverbrook were pioneers in the field."

"That was war, darling. We called it propaganda."

Armstrong chooses a cigar from the humidor on his desk, chews off the end and spits into a crystal ashtray.

"Remind me, Doreen, why we are protecting your houseboy—if that is indeed what we are doing?"

"Don't ask, Daddy. So that you can truthfully say that you know nothing about it."

"Could you give your old man a hint?"

"It's about controlling the flow of rumour. There is a crucial differ-ence between spreading a rumour and feeding a rumour."

"And what rumours are we talking about, lassie?"

"Frank is in pharmaceuticals, as you know. And I try to help him in my small way. There have been changes in the laws governing the industry, and poor Frank is at his wit's end trying to keep up."

"We had the same situation in Supplies and Services. One was always having to bend the rules this way and that."

"Whatever we say about them in public, Daddy, for the present it's imperative that we maintain good relations with our Oriental friends. Negotiations are at a delicate stage. It would be suicidal for Frank to abandon Wong Chi at this time."

"Strike a balance, I can see that."

"Trotter at the Sun *is ready with a piece on Newson's war record— evidence of bad judgment, willingness to sacrifice men to make a name for himself and all the rest."*

"That will be helpful. Setting the record straight, sort of thing."

"That sort of thing, yes, Daddy. With certain embellishments, of course."

General Armstrong opens a drawer, withdraws a crystal glass and a bottle and pours himself two fingers of Scotch. There is something about modern politics that makes him feel tired and old. Is that what public life amounts to—a public exchange of nasty tricks? Is a political career nothing but a shell game, a version of three-card monte?

"Daddy? Are you there?"

"Still here, lassie."

"We need to talk about Jock. Things have become more serious. I'm afraid he's lost his mind."

"What does Elizabeth have to say?"

"Nothing. She has taken to her bed because of his ravings. We might have to cut our losses and tell Lillian to commit him."

"Out of the question. Jock is not sick. The man is a drunk and a malingerer. How he managed to rack up a score like that is beyond me."

"Daddy, it's vital that we present him as a war hero. As is Frank, if you push it a bit. A photograph could win the election by itself—three heroes, standing side by side to save the province from culpable mismanagement. Framed that way, the fact that Jock suffers from soldier's heart is a badge of honour."

"Soldier's heart is a civilian fabrication to justify cowardice."

"Daddy, I beg you, please don't say anything like that to the press."

"OH, FRANK. THANK God you're here." Standing in the front hall with one hand on the door handle, Elizabeth smiles vaguely and presents her cheek for a kiss. When Faulkner last saw her at the burial she was like an overwound clock about to seize; now she has the languid, medicated look of a person who is no longer entirely present, who has retired to a private room inside her head. She peers behind him at the front door, bewildered and slightly annoyed. "Is Doreen not with you?"

"I'm afraid my wife is busy—shopping or some such."

She frowns. Faulkner has always found Elizabeth to be petulant and peevish when things don't go her way. Like spoiled children, the both of them. "Frank, where's Doreen? I need my sister. Jock isn't the only one who's in difficulty, you know."

"Where is Jock, by the way?"

"Oh, I don't know. Lillian has gone out for medicine. I suppose he's upstairs."

"No I'm not," says Jock, standing unsteadily on the landing of a winding staircase. Next to the landing is a set of double doors made of glass panels leading to an elevated sun porch; the lighting from behind displays his handsome profile to good advantage, although when he turns to look down at their visitor his face is noticeably puffy and florid, and there are stains on the front of his blue smoking jacket. He makes no attempt to disguise his slurred speech. However, Faulkner is pleased to see that he has kept his airman's moustache in good order; at least he has retained some semblance of turnout.

"Hullo, Frank. Have they brought you down for a spot of babysitting?"

"Good to see you, old chap. How have you been keeping?"

"Keeping secrets, do you mean? The place is crawling with them, don't you know."

"Not as such, but perhaps we might have a word or two in private—if you would excuse us, Elizabeth..."

"Of course, Frank," she says with another unconcerned smile, then turns and begins to drift toward the back of the house. "I'll tell Dotty to make tea."

"Don't bother on my account, darling."

"Yes, it's quite all right, Elizabeth. We'll just have a private chat in the library." She continues on her way without indicating whether she has heard them or not.

"Do you think she can manage? Is Lillian here?"

"I think she went out. Or perhaps not. It makes no difference either way."

Situated to the right of the front hall, the library is a corner room with windows on two walls, covered by sheer curtains and velvet drapes; another wall contains a fireplace that has been screened in for the summer, while the fourth wall is occupied with bookshelves displaying the spines of impressive leather volumes, including the complete works of Scott, Tennyson, Dickens and Kipling. Faulkner takes a winged chair next to the fireplace; at a recessed nook in one corner, Jock West retrieves two glasses and pours three fingers each from a cut-glass decanter. He manages to set glasses and decanter on the walnut coffee table without spilling, then flings himself into an overstuffed sofa and lifts his Scotch in Faulkner's general direction. "Cheers, old trout. To absent friends."

"Yes. To the empty chairs at mess: Knowles. Williams. Steadman..."

"Shot down the day he joined the squadron. Chapman. Hall... *Age shall not wither them—*"

"*Nor the years condemn...*" West can't continue. He leans back and looks at the ceiling, tears streaming down both cheeks.

"Now now, old chap, buck up. Time to keep a stiff upper lip. All that is in the past."

West drinks half his whisky in one go. "No, it's not! Not one bit of it, do you understand me? Not one bit of it is in the past. The war continues. In the mind—don't you see?"

"No, Jock. It's not the war I'm talking about."

18

To make income out of phrases is politicians' work.

"Hello, operator speaking, TRinity exchange. Is this SEymour 330?"
  "Here is SEymour 330. The Hotel Vancouver, operator speaking."
  "Here is TRinity 320. I will connect you now."
  SWITCH
"SEymour 330, Hotel Vancouver, are you there?"
"Here is General Newson. I wish to speak to Attorney General Cunning, please."
  "I will connect you, general."
  SWITCH
"Hello, are you there?"
"Here is the operator speaking. Is this Suite 1420?"
"Suite 1420. Gordon Cunning speaking."
"Hotel Vancouver, here is General Newson."
"Do you accept a call from General Newson?"
"I accept the call."
"I will connect you now."
  SWITCH
To prepare for this call, Gordon Cunning, Attorney General for the Province of British Columbia (his third cabinet post) and a rising star in the Liberal Party, has chosen a chair next to the north-facing window with a view of the mountains. Nothing like mountains to buck up one's nerve—always a prerequisite for a meeting with the general.

Meetings have provided the secret of Cunning's success thus far. In cabinet, many ministers come better prepared for the topic, but none comes better prepared for his audience. Public opinion is divided on whether Cunning is good-looking, but no one disagrees that he is a fine speaker and possesses a resonant singing voice, a rich baritone that can bring tears to grown men with his rendition of "Danny Boy." As well, his legs are shown to advantage beneath a kilt, which serves him well at Scottish events. (*He ha' a brawny set of legs on 'im.*) In fact, by this point in his career, Cunning has so impressed his riding and his peers that it would be the height of churlishness to mention that he was born and brought up in the southern United States.

Nor does it hurt that he serves as Grand Master of the Grand Masonic Lodge for British Columbia and the Yukon.

But as a politician in the modern age, Cunning's greatest strength, the one that will surely put him in the Premier's Office, is his way with the new machinery of political power: the radio, the newspaper, the telephone. On radio, Cunning's voice reaches a wide audience of voters far beyond his own riding of Omineca, and he knows how to write speeches with this in mind. As for print, his succinct statements to the Vancouver press are often sufficiently broad-based and well crafted to be quoted above the current premier.

Another advantage is his understanding of the telephone. With practice, Cunning has learned not only how to sound convincing on the telephone, but how to steer a conversation, to establish intimacy, to learn much while revealing little.

As an only child, the Attorney General developed a keen awareness of how he appeared to others. He knows, for example, that in one-to-one personal encounters men tend not to "take to him." They don't like his style, regarding him as icy and condescending; even his good looks become a detriment, the face of a smooth operator, made worse by his unfortunate surname. He often felt tempted to have it changed legally, especially when he first entered politics; but who is going to vote for a man running from his own name?

Instead he chose to tackle the name issue head on. Throughout the election and his first term of office, every speech included at least one self-deprecatory remark, joking that it made him appear smarter than he really was. (His stump-speech phrase *Cunning I am not!* would elicit a laugh from the stupidest dullard in the province.)

For the upcoming meeting, Cunning thanks God for the telephone.

The caller on this occasion is General Victor Newson—war hero, long-serving Liberal and owner-publisher of *The Evening Star*. The general is dangerous on many levels, the greatest being his ability to guide a man, knowingly or not, into serving his purpose. Like a forest fire, his abundance of contagious energy (not to mention money, advice and means of subtle blackmail) can eddy a man into acceding to an agreement he doesn't know he made until it's too late to turn back.

The Attorney General lights a cigarette and plans the conversation.

Like its owner, *The Evening Star* is the most Liberal-friendly newspaper imaginable, one that reports Liberal failures with sadness and Conservative failures with glee. Amid the dirt, blood and bodices, the newspaper follows a solid Liberal line day after day, serving the public as a propaganda pamphlet, spiced with sex, death and advertising.

This morning, the Attorney General requested a "conversation" with Newson over the Janet Stewart case, to address the possibility that two Liberal institutions, *The Evening Star* and the Attorney General's Office, were working at cross-purposes; the point being that it would be terrible for the party to face the coming election wounded by friendly fire in the form of opinion pieces that undermined voter confidence in the government.

General Victor Newson, DSO, Order of St. Michael and St. George, Companion of the Order of the Bath, holds a number of firm opinions; the reason he bought *The Evening Star* (other than to make a profit) was to give voice to all of them. Few post–Boer War developments in the colonies have sat well with Newson, especially Bolshevism, unionism and Asian immigration, not to mention Irish Catholics, who genuflect to the Pope before they will swear allegiance to their King. The repeal of Prohibition especially outraged this deep-pocketed teetotaller. *The Evening Star* badgered the Attorney General until he was forced to sign off on Newson's temperance resolution, with a pen in one hand and a glass of whisky in the other.

This time the shoe is on the other foot: Cunning wants something from Newson. He wants *The Evening Star* to turn down the volume on the Janet Stewart case until he can establish in the public mind that the Attorney General of British Columbia is firmly in the saddle. His public image depends on it.

"Here is the Hotel Vancouver operator calling, Mr. Cunning. Are you there?"

"Yes, here is Gordon Cunning."

"I will connect you now."

SWITCH

"General Newson, are you there?"

"I have been here waiting for some time, Mr. Attorney General. Yes, I bloody well have."

"We're being run off our feet, sir, managing the affairs of the province."

"Bullshit."

"I can tell you're in fighting form, sir. Excellent. And I must admit, your take on Asian immigration is spot on. It's a resonant issue, a Liberal issue, and the voters will pay attention."

"Fuck your resonant issue, Gordon, we have bigger fish to fry. Do you have a frigging clue what is happening in this city? An Oriental has committed murder and he is being protected by the family of that son-of-a-bitch Armstrong."

"Good grief. Does your newspaper have proof of this?"

"Not as such, but we are gathering evidence and it all points in that direction."

"What evidence do you mean, general? I don't doubt you for one second, but a lack of evidence turned the last inquest into a fiasco."

"That's immaterial at this point. The Evening Star is responding to a public concern that threatens the election outcome—because the situation is not being kept under control by your office, Mr. Attorney General, sir."

"That's as may be, general, but—"

"The Star's mission is to flush out the facts. Your mission is take control of the agenda. And you, may I say, have failed in this regard. For guidance, people are turning to the Asiatic Exclusion League, clairvoyants and the Ku Klux Klan. What they are not turning to is the Liberal Party of British Columbia!"

Cunning has no immediate answer to this so he switches tactics, leveraging his rank as a Mason—the one arena in which he outranks the general.

"Missed you at the Lodge last week, general."

"What? What did you say?"

"I said we missed you at the Lodge. The Worshipful Master from Olympia spoke about company spirit and teamwork, hands across the border sort of thing. Such an inspiring man. I was hoping you might introduce him."

"*Did he serve?*"

"*I don't imagine so, the man is at least seventy.*"

"*If he didn't serve, why should we listen to him?*"

"*Quite right, general. We must never forget the men who gave up their lives so that we can serve in office.*"

The pause that follows suggests that his last phrase didn't come out well. Cunning wonders if Newson has cut the connection.

"*General, are you still there? I wonder if we might turn to another matter; in fact it's the reason I scheduled this call. It's about the Janet Stewart affair.*"

"*Affair? Mr. Attorney General, I should say that it's a bit more bloody serious than an affair!*"

"*Indeed, general. The Scottish Societies don't like what they see and have called for an official inquiry. To calm them down, I undertook an investigation and found the results of the inquest highly dubious. In my view, neither accident nor suicide is supported by the evidence. Nor, needless to say, did an inconclusive verdict satisfy the public. Court proceedings are expensive—and as you know, general, our first duty is to the taxpayer, who expects value for money...*"

"*Who the hell is the taxpayer? Who the hell is not a taxpayer? Why do you insist on spouting such twaddle?*"

"*Let's call him the voter, then.*"

"*The voter expects what we tell him to expect.*"

"*Indeed, sir. Which brings us to the prospect of a second inquest. This office is in favour, provided that it settles things in the public mind for good. Which brings me to the Star's repetitive focus on the Oriental question.*"

"*Mr. Attorney General, there is no question that the Chinaman murdered her.*"

"*That may well be, sir, but as far as the Liberal Party is concerned, the issue is not whether the Chinaman murdered the nanny. What matters is the public suspicion that a highly placed individual is protecting an Oriental—a suspicion, I might add, that your newspaper has done nothing but encourage.*"

"*And let me tell you, Cunning, that influential person is none other than General Hector Armstrong. This will be revealed in the fullness of time.*"

"*And I wish you Godspeed, sir. In the meantime, the last thing my ministry needs is to appear soft on the immigration issue. As I say, already the Scottish Societies are muttering in their porridge and spreading rumours—and they are my constituency, sir. They are my base, to be protected at all costs..."*

CALL FOR SECOND INQUEST IN JANET STEWART CASE
Attorney General Must Respond to Public Outcry
Ed McCurdy
Staff Writer
The Evening Star

The Attorney General of the province stands at a crossroads: one road leads to re-election, the other road leads to ignominy and disgrace.

A decision by Mr. Cunning to call a second inquest into the death of Janet Stewart would come as a godsend to all concerned, and Vancouver citizens would commend him for it with one voice.

At the same time, in ordering a re-examination of the case, Mr. Cunning would be taking a considerable gamble. If the second inquest proves as fruitless as the first, public respect for the police, for the Attorney General's Office and support for the party he represents will plummet.

Everything depends on his response to the Oriental question. Should he continue to treat the Chinese houseboy with kid gloves, the mysterious Oriental who supposedly "discovered" the dead girl, Mr. Cunning will show himself not only as an irresolute defender of law and order, but also as an uncertain ally in the effort to keep British Columbia white and British.

A firm verdict must be reached. An inconclusive outcome would be fatal. The Scottish Societies will no longer stand for vague assurances that there is an ongoing investigation. These good citizens want answers—now.

As a prominent official speaking on condition of anonymity was heard to say: "If nothing comes of it, you can be sure that heads will be on the chopping block."

On the other hand, if a second inquest were to succeed in unmasking the villain, the Attorney General will have cornered the Scottish vote and, by extension, won the next election.

A long-time member of the Scottish Societies himself,

Mr. Cunning has tried to leave no doubt as to where he stands. "The Janet Stewart case is more than a criminal investigation. It points to the urgent need to protect the white race from intermingling with Oriental blood. We have every reason to combat a trend that will inevitably result in race deterioration. If the Janet Stewart tragedy awakens white British Columbians to the danger of mongrelism, we will have reason to be thankful."

Fine words—if the Attorney General speaks as though he truly means what he says. But Cunning also faces huge political risks in calling a second inquest. Whether the Attorney General is as canny as his name suggests remains to be seen.

19

Like throwing stones at a man in a well.

AT THE POINT Grey constabulary, the two officers escort Dawson to his cell, relieve him of any means of suicide (including his trousers) and lock the barred door, then beetle straight for the chief's office to lodge separate complaints, leaving the prisoner sobbing into his shirt front.

Quigley sits behind his desk smoking a pipeful of what smells like horse manure, while scratching an eczema spot on his forehead. "Gentlemen, I believe it's customary to knock before entering the office of a superior."

Hook tells himself that he must hold his temper at all costs. "I beg your pardon, sir, but we have an urgent problem."

"I disagree that it's a problem at all," Gorman counters. "Constable Hook here is making a mountain out of a molehill."

"Perhaps so, gentlemen, but whether we do or don't have a problem, I see no reason not to follow protocol."

"Sir, on the Janet Stewart case we have a person of interest in the cell, but Constable Gorman has made a mess of him."

"A mess, Constable Hook?"

"A psychological mess, sir."

"And what sort of a mess is that?"

Gorman lights one of his disgusting Black Cat cigarettes, striking the match with a yellow horn of a thumbnail. "It's the sort of thing universities dream up, sir. Constable Hook was about to serve the suspect afternoon tea."

"Ha! Good crack, Mr. Gorman!"

Hook doesn't find it the least bit funny. "Sir, I was securing his confidence in order to extract information he might not otherwise reveal. It was part of our training in the army—but of course Mr. Gorman wouldn't know about military interrogation techniques, having never served."

"I take offence to that," Gorman says. "Back home, many civilians served with valour and distinction."

"But not you, Constable Gorman."

"Gentlemen, gentlemen, let's not sink to petty bickering. Continue, Constable Hook."

"Sir, my colleague here informed the suspect that his fiancée is dead without giving him any preparation whatsoever. In the service I interrogated looters, smugglers, rapists, thugs, embezzlers and attempted suicides..."

"Good heavens! Among our own troops?"

"Put bluntly, yes. And from experience I tell you that you can't shock a man like that and expect a single word that comes out of him to be of any use at all."

"You are saying Constable Gorman could have been more tactful."

"To put it mildly, sir."

The chief scratches another spot on his head, whose bulbous shape makes his ears look as if they have slipped down. "And what do you have to say, Constable Gorman?"

"Sir, I protest Mr. Hook's characterization of events. In my long experience with the Provincial Police I have snagged many a miscreant with a good shock, a good sharp jab to the kidneys just to see what he has to say. A piece of terrible news is no less effective than a nightstick."

"Like a fast leg bowl, you mean."

"Correct sir, well put."

"This is not entirely cricket, though. Constable Hook, in your experience with military methods, where do we go from here?"

"I should like to speak with Mr. Dawson alone, sir. We were making headway before Gorman opened his beak."

"Then carry on with the suspect. I can't tell you what a feather in our caps it will be if we actually nab the culprit."

Having won the point, Hook heads back downstairs to the cells. Poor Arthur Dawson is about to receive another shock, every bit as nasty as the one administered by Gorman.

20

Fetch the moon from the bottom of the sea.

AS HE FLOATS to the surface, first he notices a smell: rather pleasant, slightly sweet, with a waxy overlay and a slightly acidic edge,
infused with the spicy aroma of green tea steeping on a stove. He
tries to identify the smell while staring at his closed eyelids—until
he notices that the bed he occupies is not the least bit comfortable,
certainly not a bed you would want to sleep in. The stabbing lower
back pain that travels down his left leg sends a signal that he has
been lying in the same position for some time.

Would it be worthwhile to open his eyes now?

With both hands he feels about for his glasses. His fingers grope
with accelerating urgency. His glasses are missing!

With the panic of a man who loses his pocketbook in a foreign
land, he rifles through the pockets of his jacket and trousers—and
comes up with his pocketbook. Somebody has taken his glasses
but not his money, a signal that, whatever has been done to him,
it was not from thievery but malice.

Having no alternative, he opens his eyes, but to no effect. With
or without glasses, there is nothing to see but coal black air. Fear
resurfaces like a dark crawly thing from under the earth. Better
had they taken his pocketbook, his clothes, his left arm—anything
but his glasses.

The bed seems unusually low. When he levers his right foot
(nearly numb) over the edge onto the floor, his legs give him no
leverage with which to hoist the rest of his body. With great
effort, as though it were a sack of potatoes, he heaves his torso
to a seated position, then waits for the lightheadedness to pass.

Now crouched on hands and knees (the floor seems to be made
of hardened earth), he leans forward, and despite the pain in his
joints manages to attain an upright position—and cracks his head

on the ceiling, hard. It's now clear to him that this place is either a root cellar or a room meant for very short people, or both. As his eyes adjust to the dark, he squints into the watery blur that passes for his field of vision, in the negligible flicker from what appear to be kerosene lamps hanging from the ceiling, then takes a tentative step forward—and promptly cracks his shin on what is either a sill or a low table. As he blunders ahead, he reaches out with one hand to steady himself and clutches what can only be a human knee, small and bony like a skeleton with skin, beneath a pair of loose cotton pants. The owner of the knee mutters an expression of annoyance in a language other than English.

Murmuring an apology, McCurdy shuffles forward, waving his arms from side to side ahead of him to avoid a collision. By now his pupils have dilated sufficiently that he can discern the unmistakable shapes of a series of low beds, with people lying on them in what could be a primitive hospital ward. He stumbles again and his left hand hits a wall, dank and slimy as though slugs have crawled all over it; he feels his way along the wall until he runs into a line of coats hanging from hooks, beneath a number of hats which tumble to the floor as he pushes past.

Now he can feel heat coming from a stove, lower and wider than the usual potbelly stove, from which emanates an aroma of green tea and burning coal. For fear of touching the stove, he splays both arms again and takes the blind man's position, steps forward, cracks the same shin on another bed, stumbles and feels his way along what seems to be a row of legs belonging to another row of inert bodies, lying side by side on a long mattress like chickens at market. Beyond the mattress he hears the soft wet sound of air being sucked through a tube, and smells the odour he noticed upon first awakening—not unlike the handkerchief or whatever it was that either Chung Young Lee or his enormous friend put over McCurdy's nose and mouth before he fell into that deep void of blackness and light.

Groping further along, he feels his way past another coat on a wooden pillar, then another wet wall, continuing along the wall until he reaches a corner. He pauses, then turns a corner and catches a glimpse (sensed more than seen) of a tiny, fuzzy patch of light—his first glimpse of daylight. Sidling along the wall, he moves toward the light, which appears to come from a tiny window, or at least a hole of some sort.

Now it occurs to him that throughout his journey through this cellar (or whatever it is), a venue seemingly populated by prostrate men, nobody has spoken to him, much less tried to stop him. He is not a prisoner, unless whoever put him here assumed that, without his glasses, he might as well be chained to a wall.

The light is indeed coming from a tiny window, set in a door with a rough iron handle. He pulls the handle with both hands but the door holds fast. He runs the tips of his fingers around the edge of the doorframe (acquiring a splinter in the process) until he reaches a rusted deadbolt. By peering at the mechanism from a distance of about an inch he can make out the catch, which clacks open after a few short, painful jerks.

He pulls the door open to face a blinding mist punctuated by objects moving back and forth, and a burst of human and mechanical sound...

He steps outside, takes two steps forward and slams into a wall, face first. He turns left, takes a few more tentative steps and blunders into a lamp-post. He turns toward the sound of traffic and stumbles forward, then reels back, buffeted by a chorus of warning honks. He turns toward what he thinks is the building he just left, but having lost whatever sense of direction he had, trips over the curb and falls into the gutter.

Over his head, a trolley clangs repeatedly, like the bell at a boxing match.

Splattered with mud and weaving like a sot, McCurdy receives no sympathy or help from other pedestrians as he tries to make his way through the foggy haze, knowing only by the audible transition of annoyed voices from Chinese to English that he is headed out of Chinatown. At last he makes out the domed silhouette of the Sun Tower, which provides a point of navigation with which to gauge the location of his hotel.

Once inside, of course he can go by the familiar sequence of odours as he passes through the lobby (if there is someone behind the wicket, they choose not to offer assistance), up the stairs and down the hall, where he fumbles for his keys without success, until he discovers that his door is already unlocked.

He gropes his way past the bed to the window, leans on the desk—and is momentarily gobsmacked when he feels the unmistakable shape of a pair of glasses, his own glasses, waiting for him.

He wraps the temples around his ears and his heart swells with gratitude at the familiar sight of hard-edged reality. He looks down at the familiar desktop, at his pen, ink bottle and sheaf of foolscap writing paper—and at the small box that has been placed there along with his glasses. It is wrapped in brown paper and tied with twine, like a present.

21

Never give a sword to a man who can't dance.

CONSTABLE HOOK PEERS through the bars at Arthur Dawson, seated on the iron cot with his arms covering his head. Naturally, the man is in a downcast state of mind thanks to Constable Gorman's shocking news—or perhaps due to a bad conscience as well.

Hook pauses to accustom himself to the universal jail smell, a combination of sweat, tobacco, urine and despair; he then unlocks the cell door and enters, leaving it ajar. If Dawson makes a run for it, he won't get far.

Few prisoners are so depressed that they will refuse the offer of a cigarette and a match. As a friendly gesture, Hook offers him two Ogden's; without looking up, Dawson puts one in his mouth and the other in his shirt pocket. Hook strikes a match on the cot's iron frame, lights the prisoner's cigarette and shakes the match out. He is a powerfully built man; his eyebrows join over the bridge of his nose and are sufficiently thick as to form a continuous fringe. Still, it is not an unhandsome face, and there is nothing sinister about it—although of course one can never tell.

"Mr. Dawson, how did you and your fiancée meet?"

His eyes grow soft, even poetic; the man is not as crude as he appears. "We was at the zoo, some mates and I, by the bear cage. She walks by with a stroller, and we all bow like gentlemen as a joke because she was so pretty, we was just chaffin' you know. And it made her laugh. So she went with us for tea."

"She went for tea with a group of strange men?"

"Bold for certain, but in a sweet way, innocent like, know what I'm saying?"

"I think I do."

"By the time I went back to Roberts Creek I was fair smitten. She were such a pert little thing, pretty even with the spectacles."

"Remind me, what do you do in Roberts Creek, Mr. Dawson?"

"Logging mostly. And building a house for us..." Arthur Dawson's cigarette trembles. His eyes grow watery.

"Buck up now, Arthur. You're not the first man to fall in love, and not the first to suffer a loss. Remember the war."

"Indeed, sir, you're right. Anyways, from that moment on, not an hour went by of day or night when I didn't think of her."

"As you put it, you were smitten."

"Yes I was, and am now. Vancouver is a whole day's travel, but I were back the next week, and I took her to the Orpheum, and to Love's Cafe, and I asked her to marry me. She said she would—but later I seen she was only playing a part, like in a photo-play. Down deep I knew Janet would no more marry me than join the slime line in a cannery. She were so easily bored, don't you see."

"And yet, despite that, you started building a house?"

"There is no explaining acts of the heart, sir."

"Very true. All the same, I'm sure she must have held you in great affection."

"Oh she did that, all right. Janet had affection to spare. Two months later I come into town on a Saturday, unexpected like, and I do the dance halls looking for her—the Viking, the Prom— and I seen her at the Waterfront dancing with John Lake, close, cheek-to-cheek like, and touching in other places too..."

"Who was that, did you say?"

"John Lake's his name. From back east. Deals in automobile parts—some say stolen. Fancies himself a ladies' man."

"Was John Lake a friend of yours? An acquaintance? If I was you, I'd be as mad as the deuce."

Dawson's hands become fists. "Oh, I were mad all right. But it was not as bad as the other thing."

"What other thing, sir? Take your time, I can see that this is hard for you."

"She had a toff on the side. I learned it from one of her friends, name of Cissie. I knew she was dancing with other men, but this..."

"How did Cissie know this? Did she see them together?"

"Janet told her. Told her she was doing things with him she wouldn't do with me..."

"Who was this rich man? Are you shaking your head because you don't know, or because you won't say?"

"I don't know. But if I find out, he will be in no condition to chat up anyone."

"She pushed you too far, I can see that, Arthur. Nobody can blame you if you went into a blind rage—"

"But I blame myself, sir. I blame myself for being such a fool as to go on with the house. Thinking she would someday want a home of her own—even in Roberts Creek. Janet didn't want to go to Roberts Creek, don't you see. She wanted to go to Paris."

CHIEF QUIGLEY'S HEAD threatens to topple forward, as though it's too heavy for his neck. His eyes glitter behind swollen pouches like a small hunted animal that has not had a good night's sleep in days. As he looks up at Constable Hook, the eyes take on the pleading quality of a man desperate for good news.

"Sir, you're not going to want to hear this," Hook says, "but after six hours of interrogation I can reach no other conclusion than that Mr. Dawson was not the murderer."

Chief Quigley strokes his forehead as though feeling for a hole. "Oh dear Lord Jesus Christ. Are you absolutely certain, Constable Hook?"

"There is no other possible conclusion, sir. He hasn't accounted for the past few days, but he has proof that he was in Roberts Creek on the night she died."

"Roberts Creek? Could he have made a quick trip overnight?"

"Roberts Creek is on the other side of Howe Sound, sir. A day's travel. We need to send someone to corroborate his timeline, but I believe him. One of the witnesses is Harry Roberts himself."

"The Roberts of Roberts Creek, presumably."

"Correct."

"The deuce, constable. This is such discouraging news. I had hoped to hear that we were about to lay charges. Wouldn't that have been a feather in our cap?"

"It would indeed, sir. At the same time, one would hate to hang an innocent man."

"Of course, of course, that goes without saying." The chief's tone is by no means definitive on that point.

"And of course we have yet to locate John Lake, supposedly another of her swains—the landlady at his rooming house hasn't seen him in days. As well, I should warn you that the interview opened another line of inquiry. One that could get rather messy, I'm afraid."

"To be frank, Constable Hook, I'm too tired for another line of inquiry, especially a messy one."

"I have located one of Miss Stewart's diaries."

The chief winces. "Diaries? She kept diaries?"

"I have one in my pocket right now."

"Who knew of these diaries?"

"It's public knowledge. You'll remember that it was mentioned at the inquest."

"For God's sake, why isn't it front-page news? Not enough dirt for them?"

"On the contrary, sir. Having read parts of the document, I believe Miss Stewart's life may have been more, shall we say, *racy* than readers have been led to presume. As for the inquest, the diaries weren't judged relevant—the victim isn't accused of anything, she isn't under investigation. Which is worse, to fail to solve a murder or to ruin a young woman's reputation?"

"Heaven help us. Are you saying that she had been engaging in..."

"So it would seem, sir. On that score, the embalmer wasn't helpful, not by reaming her out and stuffing her like your Christmas turkey."

"Surely John Cruikshank wouldn't do that on purpose—destroy evidence? I've known the man for years."

"There would have to have been a compelling reason for him to lower his standards. The same is true of Mr. Edwards, his employer. Not to mention the Faulkners. Mrs. Faulkner is a daughter of General Armstrong as you know..."

At this point the chief seems to have reached some sort of limit. "Constable Hook, I see that you have your suspicions, but I hope you're not about to kick a wasp's nest just to see what flies out and who gets stung, because if that turns out to be the case, I want to be standing well clear..." The chief pauses for breath. "Do you understand my meaning, Mr. Hook? You are on your own."

"I do understand, sir. In the army we called it *command deniability*. It was an accepted part of the chain of command then, and it will be the case here. It's my duty to ensure that you may deny all knowledge, in complete honesty."

"Did they really do that sort of thing in the army? Shielding officers from their mistakes?"

"Worse than that, sir. Some would say that it's how we fought the war."

22

If you see in your wine the reflection of someone else,
don't drink it.

THE CORPSE SPARROW retrieved this afternoon was an elderly recluse whose relatives seldom came to call. The body turned out to be a bit ripe, not to say liquefied.

As a result, he received permission from his superior to take the hearse for an outing and air it out. Of course, given that the vehicle has no windows or passenger doors, the odour clears in seconds, so that by the time he reaches the Hotel Vancouver nothing remains but the usual aroma of rotting carnations and dusty velvet.

The unwieldy vehicle pulls up in front of the staff exit on Howe Street just as Mildred opens an unmarked door and steps onto the sidewalk. She stops a moment to breathe the downtown air and analyze its contents (wood smoke, auto exhaust, horse shit, rotten fish, creosote) the way a sommelier would parse the nose of a glass of claret; at this moment, the worn brake shoes screech and the woodwork rattles unmistakably as the hearse lurches to a stop—and here he is.

This sort of coincidence happens frequently enough that she has begun to see it as normal.

Sometimes to Mildred it seems as though, in Sparrow's brain, the course of a life takes place not as a sequence but as co-existing bubbles of individual events, wafting about in the air: past, present and future, bumping and conjoining into clusters. Sparrow's left eye provides a convenient explanation for such occurrences, except that to attribute such events to a paper-thin piece of painted tin is less than satisfactory.

Stepping past a line of taxi drivers leaning against the fenders of their vehicles, Mildred reaches up and takes hold of the overhead strap, pulls her skirt tight with her other hand to avoid giving the boys a show and vaults into the passenger seat. (Here in the centre of town the sidewalks teem with men; if their thoughts could manifest themselves, every girl who walked down Granville Street would be stripped naked by the time she reached the Birks clock.)

"Howard, how do you do that?"

"Do what?"

"You know what I'm talking about. It is eerie, the way you time your appearances."

"Maybe it's you who's doing the timing. How am I supposed to know any m-more than you?"

Sparrow steers the hearse down Georgia Street to Stanley Park, then down a narrow dirt road to Coal Harbour; he turns down a track that was once a logging road, and before that an Indian path, and before that nothing. He parks the vehicle in an open space littered with the remains of cedar posts in the shape of what must have been the big house (a communal building the size of a skating rink), and the caved-in remains of tiny shanties whose inhabitants were chased away when their property became Stanley Park. Nearby, Indian totem poles from up north have been installed, sculpted from monumental first-growth, rot-resistant red cedars, one of them at least fifty feet high, displaying an eerie hierarchy of sea monsters, demons, sea birds with improbable beaks supported by toothy animals, crouched, mouths agape, wide-eyed faces staring out from between their fangs, and with an eagle on top, about to ride a thermal current to heaven.

They have visited the site together many times. Sparrow says that totems, rooted and unearthly at the same time, retain prehistoric, magical powers. It's as though their presence satisfies a compartment of his damaged brain, an eye for things that are worldly and otherworldly at the same time.

For certain, their occult presence awakens another aspect of his anatomy—and hers as well.

With the side panels closed, in an atmosphere of cedar bark, pine needles and dead flowers, the hearse becomes a mobile cabin, an ornate bunkhouse with a soft, velvet floor. He hasn't yet so much as kissed her, yet she is more than ready for him; he is on fire, and she wants to be burnt. (Sometimes she feels as though she could never be happy without running a slight fever.) Neither gives a thought to the simultaneous presence of sex and death, only to the urgency of the moment. She hurriedly unbuttons her shirt, slips out of her skirt, removes her bandeau (doctors claim the fashion will cause the end of breast milk and the enfeeblement of a generation), then reaches for her garter and stockings—he has ruined more than one pair of knickers when she failed to get ahead of him. Now that her breasts are freed and her knickers are off, the garters can stay where they are because he has begun to work on her the way he likes; when she closes her eyes she feels as though he has several hands that touch her everywhere at once, and more than one mouth, gliding swiftly, sucking gently, so that getting his fly undone becomes the most important thing in her life. Now she kneels before him, unbuttons his trousers and underpants, and takes his penis in her hands and lips. Now he is lying full-length on top of her; she loves his weight, loves to be crushed beneath him...

A REDDISH SUN angled high and from the west transforms the inside of the hearse into a plant conservatory; in the damp warmth the smell of old flowers becomes overpowering, decadently erotic, in bad taste somehow.

There comes a point where body heat becomes oppressive. A girl from the northern hemisphere can only stand so much eroticism, floating in a heated bubble, naked and slick with sweat, welded to a man like two layers of wet parchment.

That and his left eye, staring at her. If only there was some way to make it blink.

Mildred gathers her scattered underthings and puts them on, an awkward procedure like dressing in a tent; when she thinks about it, life with Sparrow is exactly like living in a tent—contained, temporary, providing some shelter but mostly the illusion of shelter, something not meant for heavy weather.

Except that she doesn't want shelter. She wants its opposite: exposure to the elements. She wants to be in the open. She wants knowledge of what had been denied her since she entered Badminton School—to understand life in the real world, outside the protective circle, beyond the family name.

Isn't that what running away is for?

She climbs out of the hearse and makes her way to the salt

water, where moss gently smothers the rocks and tree trunks so that they never see the sun. Now she turns back to the forest and notices what must have been an Indian hunting path long ago.

Following the path, it comes as a surprise to find how quickly the atmosphere shifts. As she steps gingerly forward, the surrounding trees darken, and what was a clear sky becomes a grey canopy high overhead. Vines obscure the surrounding trunks and coil about gnarled roots; the ground is thick with ferns and toadstools and lumps of decaying plants and sloughed-off tree bark; menacing branches await, twisted and dry, often cleverly hidden, flexed and ready to snap at her face as she passes by. The same primal greenery is repeated over and over again, the forest getting deeper and deeper with each step down what may never have been an Indian path but just a deer trail leading nowhere. She feels no wind, hears no sound beyond the intermittent chatter of an insect or bird. When she steps on a branch, the crack reverberates like a gunshot in the hollow air.

She stops to look back—and there is no path to be seen.

When you climb a mountain, going down is always more difficult; in war, a retreat can be more devastating than an advance. For a moment, here in the woods, she feels that age-old wilderness panic—*I'm lost!*

And they call this a park? In England, parks have wide paths and swards of grass and beds of flowers. Parks are not places where one can die of exposure or starvation or be mauled by a bear.

She doesn't think she is afraid, at least not yet, but she gasps aloud when she hears his voice.

"Jesus sweetheart, I'll b-bet you don't even have a compass."

"I have no sense of direction, darling, compass or no compass. It's the story of my life. How did you know I was here, in this spot?"

"You know there's no point in asking. I just knew."

He takes her hand and together they walk through the ferns. She can make out the path now. She feels safe but resents him slightly for what could pass for a rescue.

"It's funny how we're afraid of b-bears and cougars, when we're the most dangerous animals around."

"Maybe that's why everyone is so nervous. We're scared of our own shadow."

Now in the real world, standing by the moss-covered rocks,

she looks up at the patch of real sky as he gently takes her arm and shows her the way to the hearse.

ONCE INSIDE, AND sufficiently calm, she holds up a copy of *The Evening Star*. "I see that our friend has either sold out or gone insane."

"Yes, something must have happened. I'll speak to him."

"When?"

"When he agrees to open his door. I don't know how he files this shit he writes. The telephone is in the hall, so that the neighbours would hear, but they say he never leaves his room."

"Even if they missed him, I'd have heard something from the Bayview exchange."

"Jesus. Does a m-man have no privacy anymore?"

"Did you have privacy in the army?"

"Of course not."

"Well, then."

"What you want me to do, Mildred—break down the man's door with my fucking foot?"

"*Staff writer* he's called now. Did you see that? I think it gives us a clue as to what's up."

"You think he's become Victor Newson's b-bum-boy?"

"I doubt *he* would put it that way."

"Darling, I can't believe Ed would turn into a toady. He saved my life."

"Maybe his reason was less than noble. Perhaps he just saw you as a useful source. An informational pawn."

"He's my friend. I know him."

Mildred rolls her eyes. Scrape the surface of any Englishman and there's a Boy Scout underneath. These chaps weren't created by God but by Lord Baden-Powell.

"Well darling, shall we go speak to McCurdy?"

"I'd rather not. If what you say about him is true, he deserves to be shot."

"Do you have a firearm?"

"Not as such. B-But I could throw him out the window like they did to Victor Midgley."

"Well then, perhaps it would be better if I spoke to him myself."

"No, that's not what's going to happen."

"What makes you say that?"

"Because the idea is ridiculous. March into a man's hotel room alone? Out of the question."

"You think it would be indecent? Sometimes you can be so sweet."

"Darling, please."

"Are you afraid Ed McCurdy will rape me?"

"No, but someone might. The b-building is packed full of licentious men."

"That's ridiculous, Howard. You talk as though men are walking erections, searching for a cunt the way elephants root for peanuts."

"An absolutely disgusting image, darling."

"Actually, I find it rather touching—the single-mindedness of it, the lack of insight, the bewilderment. Face it, Mr. Sparrow, there is nothing more earnest than an erection."

"Especially if the owner is holding a knife to your throat."

"Don't be dramatic. The reason Ed doesn't open the door is because he doesn't want you to punch him in the face and break his glasses again."

Howard thinks about this. Given McCurdy's radical shift of editorial viewpoint, together with his promotion to staff writer, it should come as no surprise that the bugger has gone to ground. Any discussion between them now seems certain to come to blows and, yes, his glasses would be broken again.

Sparrow decides to give McCurdy the benefit of the doubt for the moment. Maybe he has gone funny, acquired some rats in the attic—and if so, Mildred might be of use. Usually, a man will straighten out somewhat in the presence of a woman, though Mildred might not necessarily have that effect.

THE HEARSE CLATTERS its way over the Granville Bridge, turns onto Drake Street and stops directly in front of the entrance to the Colonial Hotel.

"What do we do, Howard?" Like Sparrow, Mildred is wearing a dowdy white duster coat several sizes too big.

"The manager will come out before long. No hotel wants a hearse parked in front of the main entrance. A lot of men check into hotels to b-blow their b-brains out. Your military man likes to keep things orderly. Nobody wants to leave a b-bloody mess for the family. Hell for the cleaning staff, of course..."

"Please darling, I think you've made your point."

"Excuse me, sor!"

The gentleman at the curb to her left glares at Sparrow as though she were invisible. Mildred notes a pair of worried eyes, a receding hairline and a strawberry birthmark shaped like England, or maybe Japan. He speaks in a North Country accent.

"Sor! Sor! You can't stop here, this is a passenger pick-up area—do you not see the signs, sor?"

Mildred speaks up in her BBC accent, catching the manager off guard. "My driver sees the signs perfectly, sir. This is Mr. Sparrow." She gives the manager her most patronizing smile; he would tug his forelock if he had one.

"I am Miss Wickstram, Mr. Sparrow's superior, and we are here to fetch one of your guests."

The manager looks at her with increased alarm: first the hearse, now a woman with a posh accent.

"One of our guests, madam?"

"Yes indeed. A dead one. My colleague and I are from Edwards Funeral Services, and I believe the body is in Room 214."

"Mr. McCurdy? Surely you're not telling me that Mr. McCurdy is, is..."

"Dead? We think so, sir. A call came an hour ago. We believe the voice was that of Mr. McCurdy himself—that is, before we were cut off, so to speak."

The manager steps back, shaking his head as though from a blow. "Not Mr. McCurdy! Shorely there is some mistake, madam."

"You do have an Edward McCurdy as one of your guests, do you not?"

"He has been with us for months. You might consider he's a long-term resident."

"Yes, well our information is that, metaphorically speaking, he has checked out for good. Is that not so, Mr. Sparrow?"

"Yes, Miss Wickstram. And b-by his own hand I fear. Of course you would prefer it kept quiet, and I don't b-blame you. Unfortunately, the room will b-be a mess. I trust your cleaning staff are used to the sight and smell of b-blood and b-brains."

"No! He can't be dead, sor! Mr. McCurdy was on credit and he did not settle his bill! Oh dear God, I s'pose you better come in have a look."

The manager leads them into a small lobby consisting of a carpet of indecipherable colour and pattern, a patched horsehair chesterfield, two club chairs of scuffed leather, a check-in wicket, and the pungent, medicinal odour of disinfectant. A wide wooden shelf next to the wicket supports a guest book and a superannuated plant. Above the wicket is a portrait of King George.

"Take over would you, Cora?" The manager barks at a woman with a mop and an empty pail, who drops her implements with sarcastic finality and disappears through a narrow door next to the staircase; a moment later she reappears, framed by the wicket, looking sullen and overworked.

"Sir," Sparrow continues, "has Mr. McCurdy b-been entertaining visitors of late?"

"Only the delivery boy from Chang's Market."

"And he hasn't come out of his quarters?"

"Said he wasn't to be disturbed. Didn't let on like he were going to kill himself, though. Seemed happy and content."

"Many of them do," Mildred says. "Once you make the big decision, it's a load off your mind."

Past a racked fire hose and a sand bucket filled with cigarette and cigar stubs, a wide, curved staircase leads to a mezzanine floor containing tables and chairs, presumably where a spartan breakfast is served during strictly limited hours. Now it is deserted and bare, with the lingering smell of burnt toast, stale coffee and rancid butter. A much narrower staircase, redolent with disinfectant (evidence not of sanitation but of vomit and urine) leads to a second floor that smells of dirty carpet, stale smoke and old man's dentures.

Knock, knock, knock.

Getting no answer after the first knock, the manager becomes sufficiently unnerved to produce his master key and unlock the door—but having done so, he can't seem to bring himself to look inside. The extra work entailed by a messy suicide is too much to contemplate right now. So when the door swings open, he leans against the opposite wall and examines the carpet. "I'll allow you professionals to take a first look, if it's all the same to you. I once walked in on a chap who hanged himself in the wardrobe. The thought of it gives me nightmares still."

"Not a pretty sight sometimes."

"I tell ye his face was as black as your hat."

Stepping into McCurdy's room, Mildred notices the smell—not like a cigarette or a pipe; nor hashish, nor muggle.

Mildred looks back at Sparrow, sniffing the air. "What is that, darling?"

"That, Miss Wickstram, is opium. Do you see the pipe over there on the desk?" Sparrow indicates McCurdy's desk, on which sits a long-stemmed pipe, next to a spirit lamp and a bowl of some sort of paste. Also on the desk are a fountain pen, a bottle of ink and a stack of typewriter paper topped by a pair of glasses. The typewriter sits on the floor beside the desk like an abandoned dog (the battered Underwood looks as though it had been thrown against a wall). McCurdy has, for some reason, given up the typewriter in favour of longhand.

Beyond the desk and on the windowsill sits a near-empty box of Cadbury's chocolates; on the floor beneath the window is a pile of empty candy boxes, which directs Mildred's attention back to the sweetish smell in the air.

"Curious. I thought Mr. McCurdy's lungs were too delicate to take smoke."

"Opium isn't smoke, darling, it's vapour. Some say it's good for the lungs. B-but not necessarily for the b-brain."

As evidence, Sparrow indicates the man presently lying on the bed, legs and arms akimbo, asleep or possibly comatose, atop a cotton bedspread the colour of a washrag.

To look at McCurdy it's clear that over the past several days he hasn't kept himself in the best of shape. He has visibly lost weight and his skin has taken on a yellow cast. In fact he could pass for an Oriental, were he wearing a union suit and not a tank top and a pair of striped cotton boxer shorts, frayed but fashionable, with three mother-of-pearl button closures at the fly to ensure modesty.

Lying on his bed like a beetle on its back, he appears vulnerable, almost childlike. It has never occurred to Mildred to attach such words to McCurdy—*pretentious* certainly, *defensive* more often than not, but hardly sensitive, and certainly not childlike. Or perhaps all men appear like children when asleep; certainly that is true of Sparrow, when he isn't screaming.

"Let me talk to him," she says. Sparrow nods briskly and backs out of the room, to reassure the manager and to stand by, for it remains possible that our man has well and truly flipped.

Nursing is, after all, women's work, though he would never say this out loud.

Mildred perches on the edge of the bed and reaches over to take hold of McCurdy's wrist. He has a slow but normal pulse and his chest is moving up and down, so it's simply a matter of patience. To pass the time she surveys the room, starting with the faded linoleum floor—maroon and bilious green, littered with sheets of writing paper scattered willy-nilly about.

She leans over, picks up a sheet of paper and reads. It's a poem, handwritten in ink, and she can't help but admit that it's... not all that bad. Like T.S. Eliot, he writes about *bereft loneliness*, not as articulated emotion, but as a feeling that can only be approximated as a series of remarkably sharp images that both stand alone and interrelate, creating a composite picture that encapsulates the everyday isolation and loneliness of life in the modern world.

At the same time, Eddie is no Eliot, nor is he a Yeats nor a Pound nor a Siegfried Sassoon. These days, the competition is stiff when it comes to verse; you can be very good and second-rate at the same time.

She hopes she never has to tell him this.

She gets up and walks about the room, collecting sheets of paper and snooping about. Despite a washrag of a rug and the baked-on patina of nicotine coating the wallpaper, McCurdy has attempted to create something of a homey atmosphere. On one wall hangs a photograph of Dickens and another of Sassoon, while another wall contains a framed illustration in which a priest balances a cross on his nose. She wanders over to the wardrobe, which contains an array of suits, shirts and ties, all more or less equally bedraggled (frayed shirt collars, worn trouser seats), yet clean, well-brushed and with professionally repaired elbows. She has already identified McCurdy as a vain man for whom appearance is integral to personal dignity—*clothes make the man.* (When she once asked about his attention to haberdashery, he replied that his father had dressed well, making it sound as though it was the only good thing to be said about him.)

She returns to her place at the edge of the bed, and this time the slight motion of the mattress has an effect on the sleeper. His eyelids open slightly, revealing the pupils—bright pinpoints even in this light, like a snake peering out of a crack in the wall. When he mobilizes his lips to form words, the groan that emerges is deeper than normal; when he finally manages to articulate a sentence he seems unnaturally calm, unruffled, as though her presence comes as no surprise at all.

"Pardon me, Miss Wickstram, I believe I must have drifted off. What was it we were discussing?"

"We were talking about why you insist on lying around in your underwear."

"Do I?"

"So it seems, Eddie."

Noting that this is indeed the case, McCurdy eases himself off the bed, staggers to the wardrobe and produces a lounge robe made of threadbare jacquard. He crosses to his desk, puts on his glasses and turns to face her, keeping his distance.

"That's better," she says. "I hardly recognized you without your glasses."

"My glasses. Yes. Thought I lost them, until the delivery boy... ah. It's all coming back to me now. We weren't talking about anything at all. In fact, you weren't here. Mildred, what are you doing in my room?"

"Sparrow was worried about you. He thinks you've gone berserk. He thinks it calls for an intervention."

"And he sent *you*?"

"With their own sex, men tend to express emotions with their fists."

"I don't understand. What is there to discuss?"

"Your work, Eddie. And the fact that nobody has laid eyes on you for days."

"I've been working."

"Indeed, and you've been prolific, yet you've made yourself scarce. Are you trying to avoid us?"

"I'm writing day and night, Miss Wickstram. I can't be disturbed."

"Except by the Chinaman."

"What Chinaman?"

"The delivery boy who brings you opium."

"Oh. Yes. I use the medicine as a stimulant for the imagination."

"For when you write your dreadful articles?"

"I'm writing poetry, Millie. I'm a poet again. I'm through with hack reporting."

"Did you write them in between propaganda assignments?"

"What?"

"I said, did you write them in between vile pieces for *The Evening Star*?"

"Not vile enough, Mildred. When I last checked, I was at the point of being fired."

"So I've heard you say. But it hasn't stopped you from being promoted. You're on staff now."

"I'm *what*?"

"It says so under your byline: *Staff Writer*, it says."

"You're talking about articles written by *me*?"

"Under your name, yes. Did you intend to use a pseudonym?"

"Damn. I wondered where the money was coming from. Somebody kept slipping envelopes under the door."

"To pay the delivery boy?"

McCurdy's eyes have closed, exhausted by the effort of thinking, as opposed to dreaming. "I wondered where the money came from. I used it to make certain... purchases."

"Eddie, as poetic as it may seem, it's not healthy to remain stoned continuously."

"I beg to differ. I've never felt better in my life."

Mildred stands up and steps into the hall. "Howard, you'd better come in. I think we have a problem."

23

Women and cats listen while asleep.

STEWART GIRL MAY HAVE BEEN MURDERED
Confidential Report Contradicts Inquest Verdict
Ed McCurdy
Staff Writer
The Evening Star

The Janet Stewart case is at a crossroads.

A government official has confirmed that the case remains very much open and no theory has been discounted, least of all the possible guilt of Wong Chi, the houseboy who was the first on the scene and therefore a "person of interest"—avoiding the word *suspect,* in order to spare the Chinaman's feelings.

According to an official close to the Attorney General: "Many voters are under the impression that the first inquest reached a pre-determined conclusion. If the same thing were to happen a second time, in an election year, it would be a disaster."

Continued the official: "I should say that a second inquest is almost a certainty—but only if authorities are satisfied that the Chinaman is to blame."

Whether or not that turns out to be the case remains to be seen.

"Here is SEymour 703. Who are you, please?"
"Here is the operator. Am I speaking to The Evening Star?"
"Here is Miss Carla Hunt, receptionist at The Evening Star."
"I have a Mildred Wickstram from the Carnegie Library."
"I will speak to her."
SWITCH
"Here is Mildred Wickstram."

"And here is The Evening Star."

"May I please speak with Mr. Ed McCurdy?"

"I am afraid he is not at his desk. Would you care to leave a message for him?"

"It's about his overdue books. There comes a point at which it verges on theft. We are on the verge of calling the police."

"I must tell you that he hasn't entered the building in weeks. It is a mystery how he files his reports."

"In order to dictate them over the telephone, would he not have to go through you?"

"Of course."

"Well then how do you *think he files his reports?"*

"Maybe he drops them onto the editor's desk after hours. Maybe he dictates them to Nathan Shipley by mental telepathy. Sweetie, it's not my job to track down freelancers who borrow books."

"Except that he's not a freelancer, he's a staff writer. Staff writers are, as a general rule, seen around the building, no?"

"Staff writer? McCurdy is a staff writer?"

"It says so in The Evening Star. *Have you not read it?"*

"It must be a misprint. Thank you for bringing it to our attention."

Carla rings off and immediately calls for Shipley. "Nathan, someone other than McCurdy has been writing under his byline. Do you know anything about this?"

Not writing, taking dictation. Shipley breathes a miserable sigh and reaches for the bottle in his drawer. If rivals find out what he has been doing for the sake of a promotion, he will never live it down.

CONSTABLE HOOK TERMED his interview with Jean Hawthorn "a mere formality" when in truth it is even less than that, since Miss Hawthorn's information amounts to hearsay from beginning to end—the horse's mouth (as it were) being Cissie Braidwood, who virtually convicted Wong Chi of murder while giving evidence at the inquest.

But Miss Hawthorn is both comely and reasonable, and seemed open to further contact. At the same time, since the connection between them was established as part of an official inquiry, he feels it wise to continue on that basis—correctly, as it turned out; her employers are sufficiently impressed (or intimidated) to free her for the afternoon.

As Miss Hawthorn shows him into the sitting room, Hook stops himself from complimenting her on her dress (half-sleeved, tea length, showing generous sections of arm and calf), as it would seem over-familiar. He can feel his face redden at the images in his mind, which he conceals by pretending to admire the room: the floral carpet, the arched fireplace, the sooty portrait of a whiskered ancestor, the mantle displaying small photographs of young men in uniform. Bookcases on either side of the fireplace contain photograph albums covered in quilted velvet; he opens one, to find that it contains tintypes of cadavers in their coffins. Returning the ornate volume gently to its place, he notes the complete works of Tennyson, Scott and Kipling, unopened, their bindings stiff as saddle leather.

"Your employers must be avid readers, Miss Hawthorn."

"'Tis not something I noticed, Officer Hook. But true for you they have excellent taste in books. Is that the same thing?"

The unexpected question catches him off guard. Was she smiling when she said it? Is this some sort of test?

"I suppose it depends on the books," Hook replies, without the slightest idea what he means.

"Certainly, 'tis better not to read at all than to read trash, wouldn't you agree?"

"Well, I suppose one person's trash is another person's..." Lacking a clue how to complete the thought, he produces his notebook and pencil and clears his throat. "I suppose we should get to business."

"Of course, sir." She settles into a wingback chair, crosses her legs and indicates a nearby couch. "Please sit down, officer. Ask me what you wish."

"Miss Hawthorn, in your opinion did Miss Stewart have any enemies? A spurned lover, perhaps?"

"She carried on with more than one man at a time, 'tis true, but none 'a them seemed to object—not even poor Arthur Dawson. Janet was always very clear to him where she stood."

"I'm surprised Mr. Dawson took it so well."

"That's Vancouver for you, Mr. Hook. For every girl in the city there are a hundred desperate young men. A girl can have a dozen admirers if she wants."

"Have *you* had a dozen admirers, miss?" Hook can feel his ears redden.

"Certainly. But I've had them one at a time."

Hook wonders what he would make of that remark, were he a bit more... *suave*. "As to Miss Stewart, were there any potential enemies?"

"Cissie Braidwood says that Janet was petrified of the Chinaman, that he touched her and made improper suggestions in his own language."

"Did Miss Stewart speak Chinese?"

"Nae, and neither does Cissie. In any case, I seen him take her hand once, and was she ever mad!"

The interview is going as well as could possibly be expected, though it only adds to his confusion. Is it possible that murders occur in which the butler actually did it? Is it possible that the houseboy shot Miss Stewart with his employer's weapon at a time when they were the only two people in the house? Could a Chinaman be that impulsive, or stupid?

Hook once arrested a corporal covered with insect bites from head to toe; he had hidden a huge sack of stolen sugar under his cot and a hole had opened in the sack, whose contents attracted every insect in the barracks, including bed bugs and gnats...

So far, so good: however official its stated purpose, their interview has taken on an amiable quality, the only problem being that Constable Hook is at a loss as to how to move forward. While the war was on, young men and women mingled with objectives in mind that had nothing to do with marriage and children and a home on a tree-lined street. There was a frankness in such affairs, a sense of urgency that is absent in peacetime, now that people have all the time in the world.

"Is there anything else you have to tell me, Miss Hawthorn? About the case, I mean."

"Well there was one other thing, officer. It may be of nae significance at all."

"Please speak freely. One never knows what might prove useful later on."

"Well as it happens, Mrs. Faulkner has asked if I might work for them part time, as a nanny for the wee one, until they find a replacement."

Constable Hook tries to remain calm. "And is that agreeable to your employers?"

"Seemingly it is. The McKinleys are not overfond of the Faulkners, but they like to economize."

"Miss Hawthorn, we must make every possible effort to keep in contact. You could be our eyes and ears at the scene of the crime."

Scene of the crime. For Miss Hawthorn, the phrase produces a little shiver inside. "Of course I am eager to assist the police in any way I can."

They stand up in unison and exit the room side by side; then she stops him at the door with an unexpected question.

"D'you like riding a motorcycle, officer?"

"Pardon me?"

"Your motorcycle. Is it... fun?"

Again, he can't interpret her half-smile other than as a ball thrown to him, to be caught and thrown back.

"Would you like to ride on a motorcycle, Miss Hawthorn?"

The moment the sentence escapes his mouth, Hook wants to grab it back and eat it before it reaches her ears. His own ears are burning, utterly certain that he will receive a curt demur. What an outrageous suggestion from an officer on official duty!

"Wait until I fetch my hat."

FOR THE OUTING, Miss Hawthorn wisely has chosen a cloche hat with a narrow brim that fits snugly and will not fly off. As well, it focuses attention on her eyes, and goes well with her tea dress.

He is about to suggest that she might find it chilly in the wind even in summer, but refrains from doing so, thinking that she might find it necessary to nestle against his back as a shield. And her summer dress will require her to ride sidesaddle, a more precarious position that will require her to wrap her arms around him and hold on tightly for dear life.

As they speed past the shops on Broadway, pedestrians turn to watch, mildly curious at the sight of a man and woman together on a motorcycle. Though Miss Hawthorn clenches her skirt modestly between her legs, the fabric of her dress flutters in a way that reminds one of flight—an escape or elopement.

Steering clear of the Point Grey constabulary, Hook follows Fourth Avenue as far as the turnoff to Spanish Banks, a stretch of beach from which one can contemplate the city. Seen from across the inlet, Vancouver appears as an enormous greyish-brown smudge, an amorphous, squirming organism emitting a dull, monotonous moan accompanied by irregular whistles, honks and shrieks. Behind the city, a line of mountains jag upward like a set of fangs.

As they park the motorcycle, Miss Hawthorn remarks that the sight reminds her of Liverpool.

Though Hook cannot think of any good reason why it would remind anyone of northern England, he is not of a mind to doubt Miss Hawthorn's word. He nods as though he understands exactly what she means, and is rewarded for it when she takes his arm. They stroll down the path beside the beach, past the nets of Italian sardine fishermen to the point near where Captain Vancouver is supposed to have first landed and declared the province to be part of England. The natives did not object to this because it made no sense. To the Squamish and the Salish, Vancouver and his crew were alien life forms that might as well have arrived from another planet.

Away from Shaughnessy Heights and with nothing but seagulls to eavesdrop, Miss Hawthorn abruptly changes the subject. "I'm afraid I couldn'a be too frank with you at the house there."

Her tone causes him to wonder if they might be still on official business. Did she agree to come with him only because it would take her away from listening ears?

"Why is that, Miss Hawthorn? Do you feel you are under some sort of surveillance?"

"It is not like it's upfront. But word gets around something fierce, don't you know. The trees pass it on, seems like; make one enemy and you've made a hundred."

"With rumours flying as they are, it sounds like you have taken a sensible precaution."

"It was not as if I wanted to withhold something from the police, don't you see."

"Of course not. In any case, you can speak freely, and I shall forward the information to Constable Hook, anonymously."

This makes her laugh—not a titter or a giggle but a rich sound with a trace of wickedness in it.

"Cissie Braidwood said she heard from Jessie Murray about a party the night before—fancy cars driving by at midnight. And Jane McClellan said she was awakened by the baby in the wee hours and hearing traffic. Looking down from the nursery window, she could see no more than they were big and shiny. Their house is on Angus Drive, so she couldn'a see Canacraig itsel'."

Hook begins to stroke his moustache, then thinks better of it and retrieves his notebook and pencil. "So was there really a party at the Faulkner house after all?"

"Not likely, I wouldn'a think—not with a do at Canacraig. Mrs. Faulkner would be nae competing wi' her own da. Cissie Braidwood says it all proves that the Chinaman did for her while their people was out living the high life."

Hook thinks about this. If it is wrong to blame a man because of his race, it would be just as wrong to think him innocent for the same reason. And just because something is stupidly obvious doesn't mean it's not true. Chinamen can be murderers, just like everybody else. On the other hand, unless the Faulkners are the heaviest smokers in Canada, *someone* left those cigarette butts in the backgarden. Or were there *two* functions going on that evening, a party and... something else?

His interview with Miss Hawthorn must continue. Such a stimulating young woman.

WITH ITS NEON coffee cup over the door, the White Lunch is a popular venue for casual dining, featuring a white semicircular buffet, faux-marble tabletops and the assurance (as the name suggests) that food will be prepared and served by and for members of the white race.

Hook and Miss Hawthorn are having coffee and cake following their motorcycle ride, and the subject turns to cinema, as it inevitably does in modern conversation, especially when the photo-play features a modern theme. The moving picture on this occasion is *Zaza*, in which a woman unwittingly falls in love with a married man. Miss Hawthorn remarks how extramarital affairs have become commonplace in England since the war—except that, more times than not, the wife finds out and says nothing while the husband carries on doing what he likes.

"I hope you're not speaking from experience," Hook replies. "I would hate to think..."

"Mr. Hook, what are you implying?"

"Nothing. Absolutely nothing. Miss Hawthorn, I am a yokel from Waldo. You are from Liverpool, a sophisticated city woman..." He knows he is laying it on thick, but feels a need to change the subject at once.

She rolls her eyes; he can't tell if this is a good sign or not. "Nonsense. I grew up in Nantwich, a dusty old museum of a town.

During the war my sisters and I worked in Liverpool, in the ship-yards, and I would never go back to Nantwich again."

"I feel exactly the same about Waldo."

"There, ye see, we have something in common. Now let's look for something else. We were talking about the cinema. Do you go?"

In fact, Hook seldom attends the cinema because it means going by himself. However thrilling the entertainment, eventually the projector beam goes dark, the curtain falls and he leaves the theatre to face another wet night, feeling more desolate than when he entered.

"Actually, I am very fond of the cinema."

"Who is your favourite star?"

"I would have to say Buster Keaton." Keaton is the first male star who comes to mind; to cite a female would be impolitic in the extreme. "And you?"

"Gloria Swanson is, in my opinion, the most beautiful actress in the history of the world."

"I have no doubt that she may well be."

"And fearless. It's a miracle the censors haven't stepped in. Do you know that *A Society Scandal* is playing at the Pantages? It's supposed to be every bit as good as *Zaza*."

"I didn't know that, no."

"Miss Swanson plays a woman who plots revenge on her husband's divorce lawyer, who blackened her name in order to win the case."

"Lawyers are cynics. No doubt he richly deserved it."

"Well we won't know, will we, 'less we go to the photo-play."

"Would you like to go?"

"I think we hae plenty of time to see the 4:30 matinee, though we will miss the acts beforehand. Not a great loss, I wouldn'a think. The photo-play is the main thing, don't you agree?"

"I do indeed, Miss Hawthorn. One hundred per cent."

THE PANTAGES THEATRE is a turn-of-the-century landmark on what was once called the Hastings Great White Way, now making the transition from vaudeville to moving pictures—an uneasy adjustment from three-dimensional to two-dimensional enter-tainment. For this reason, Hook wonders why Miss Hawthorn has chosen the mezzanine, with sight lines that have lowered its status, resulting in its informal designation as Chinese Heaven.

For this showing the mezzanine is almost completely empty, as Orientals tend to take little interest in the emotional problems of white people, on screen or off; for that reason it seems obvious that the tiny clump of Chinese men in the centre section have come for a private meeting over something other than Gloria Swanson.

Miss Hawthorn has chosen the loges section to the left, with its private seating. Maybe she likes the feeling of sitting in a private opera box, Hook thinks, like an upper-class aesthete. In any case, the four-seat compartment provides privacy, despite its inferior, lateral view of the picture onscreen.

As they settle into their seats, the last live act of the evening is about to complete his performance: an Al Jolson imitator in blackface who performs a creditable medley of "Swanee," "My Mammy" and "California, Here I Come," accompanied by a young, intense pianist, working alone in the orchestra pit.

Miss Hawthorn pats the seat beside her as though to make sure he doesn't wander off, and they sit together in silence while the set changes occur and the screen drops from the fly gallery.

Below them, spectators in the orchestra section converse in a skittish semi-whisper, anticipating the spectacle to come.

Not long ago, loge seats in legitimate theatres were viciously expensive lounges in which rich men and women drank champagne while watching the show, but the movies changed that, especially when Chinese Heaven meant a racially segregated audience. Now the loges have become distinctly déclassé, with a slightly unsavoury reputation as a place for louche assignations.

Being from Waldo and coming from wartime England, Hook knows nothing of this. In peacetime, the veteran is not only out of place but out of date as well.

In this atmosphere of silence and dark, the most incidental physical contact—in this case, arm against arm—becomes more intense and meaningful.

He will always remain uncertain as to who initiated the first kiss, which lasts an extraordinarily long time, pausing only so that they might catch their breath; in fact it's possible that the entire episode to follow takes place in the span of a single kiss.

The projector whirls forward and a long cone of intense, dust-stained light illuminates the screen, while the seemingly indefatigable pianist pounds out a solo from the Russian repertoire.

When they pause in this, their first kiss, they glance down at what is happening inside the proscenium arch; the screen descends and the newsreels begin, and the spectacle of photography in motion temporarily hypnotizes them, as they stare goggle-eyed at images of world events so distant they might have occurred on Mars:

Someplace in Europe, a man with slicked down hair and a Chaplin moustache enters prison for some reason, wearing a trench coat and waving a stiff-arm salute to a seemingly friendly crowd, behind a police barricade.

To go by the onion-topped buildings, an event takes place in Moscow in which a bald man with a Van Dyke beard lies on a white lace pillow, his childlike hands poised side by side on his stomach as though he is about to play the piano.

A man with the jaw of a bulldog and a helmet-like forehead, with the thumbs of his tight black gloves thrust under his Sam Browne belt, stands in a circle with a group of other men wearing uniforms and white gloves, listening to a man in a turban who is backed by a group of men wearing cylindrical hats with tassels...

Still feeling the warmth of that first kiss, Hook eases his left arm behind Jean's shoulder. She responds by placing her right hand on the nape of his neck. Like early winnings in a betting game, he fears that it might be false encouragement, but he must play on.

With his left hand he first touches, then holds the swollen softness of her right breast beneath her tea dress; she does not object or push his hand away, and surely she noticed. Then, as though to counter his momentary doubts, she changes position in her seat so that now her left breast is pressed against his chest, as though waiting its turn...

They are both flushed and breathing heavily, yet he isn't certain how to proceed from here—they are after all in a theatre, with seats and not a bed—until in one abrupt, unforgettable motion, Jean pushes her right hand straight down the front of his trousers, seizes his erection (bolt upright in her honour), squeezes gently and pulls. Already excited beyond endurance, he ejaculates immediately. As soon as it is finished, she retrieves her hand from his trousers with a normal, matter-of-fact half-smile on her face.

"Now we can watch the photo-play," she says.

One might think she had just milked a cow.

24

First cross the river, before you tell the crocodile he has bad breath.

MCCURDY DOESN'T FEEL at all well this morning. At first he thought he might be coming down with the flu, what with the nose-blowing and nausea, symptoms that might have been held at bay with infusions of opium. A week ago he could order it to his room as though he were in a swank hotel calling the concierge. He would be feeling fine right now, were it not for certain people sticking their noses into a man's personal business, viewing him in his underwear and revealing a deplorable fraud being carried out in his name.

Nausea.

"Are you all right, Mr. McCurdy? Can I help you?"

Every joint is a little factory of pain. For the love of God, why did he accede to Miss Wickstram's demands? There he was, resting in his bed in a luxurious slumber, pain-free, entertained by the most pleasurable photo-plays the mind can project. Why did he let her convince him that remaining in Paradise would be a cowardly capitulation to Victor Newson, enabling the general to use his byline as a megaphone?

And what does it matter whether Victor Newson wins or loses? Either way, his bones will be in the ground in a quarter-century, along with just about anyone else in this filthy rathole of a city at the end of the earth, where dogs eat dogs and grizzlies eat everything...

On the positive side, Miss Wickstram seems to have put aside their personal animosities—temporarily, at least. She brought soup, sandwiches and muggle tea, and sat up with him through sleepless nights and raving nightmares.

While he lay in a cold sweat, teeth rattling like castanets, she would read his poetry aloud, pronounce it *not bad*, then suggest revisions. Together they edited the lines and line-breaks for voice, and she typed them on his Underwood, packaged and mailed them off to Macmillan in Toronto. (He has only a hazy memory of this...)

"MR. MCCURDY? CAN I fetch you a glass of water, Mr. McCurdy?"

"I beg your pardon, madam?" The waiting room features two prominent portraits: one of Newson in full uniform, and one of King George IV. The woman at the desk has a forthright, seen-it-all face he associates with rural schoolteachers and triage nurses at the Somme.

"I said, can I help you, sir? You seem unwell."

He endeavours to appear confident and relaxed while his mind quivers at the other end of the scale. "Ah, Miss Webster. Good to see you again. You might remember having given me this note some time ago." He fumbles in his pocket and produces a small paper ball, which he flattens and smoothes out as best he can.

See me.
V.N.

As though suspecting a forgery, Miss Webster examines the note far longer than it can have taken her to read it.

"Ah, yes, Mr. McCurdy, but that was weeks ago."

"I've had the flu."

"Ah. Good. Fine. Excellent. Please excuse me, and I'll alert the general. Would you care to sit down?" She motions to a rather comfortable-looking chesterfield. In an instant he finds himself seated on its cushions, as though her gesture alone propelled him across the room.

But oh, there is so much to be anxious about! Life offers an unlimited supply, right to the end. Of course it would be bearable if one knew when and how it would end, but nobody ever does, does one? The war taught us that anxiety is a condition of normal life; we know it on the cellular level, that anxiety is life itself...

He deepens his breathing to hold down the panic. When you withdraw from an opium habit, anxiety is your constant companion.

The other problem with a drug habit is that drugs are not given free of charge. Well perhaps at first, but soon they begin to cost money, and the rate increases along with one's required dosage, so that the inevitable day arrives when one wakes up one morning with neither drugs nor money—and the symptoms begin.

His present situation was inevitable, with or without Miss Wickstram.

While waiting for Miss Webster to return, he notes the decorations on the wall—Companion of the Order of the Bath, Commander of the Order of St. Michael and St. George, Distinguished Service Order. Surrounding the medals and citations like a chorus of well-wishers, framed photographs from Newson's military career give evidence to the depth and greatness of the man: as a nineteen-year-old, in the cork helmet and khaki uniform of the Boer War; with his battalion at Ypres; walking with General Currie during an inspection of some sort; with the King on a Bren Gun carrier; on parade during President Harding's Vancouver visit. A studio photograph of the great man looks down at him from an adjacent wall, as though assessing McCurdy's value as a human being; the lighting emphasizes the long nose, the clipped moustache and the enormous cleft chin, jutting into the future.

McCurdy takes a deep breath and steps forward.

Newson's inner office could be mistaken for a command centre in Flanders—a stark space dominated by an enormous map of British Columbia, except that the province is divided into ridings and not battle zones. (No doubt, in Newson's view, they amount to the same thing.)

The general sits behind a field table (not a desk), unnaturally erect, in a three-piece suit with a regimental striped tie, taking notes with a fountain pen—a favourite pose employers adopt to establish hierarchy, forcing the employee to stand and wait while more important business receives attention. (McCurdy wouldn't be surprised if Newson were writing *The quick brown fox...*)

"Be seated, Mr. McCurdy," mutters the general without looking up—a welcome order, even if the only chair available is a plain oak straight-back item that would give a man hemorrhoids in a half-hour.

Anxiety gives way to a confusion of emotions. Despite his instinctive dislike and distrust of the man, he retains the writer's hunger for praise and wants General Newson to think well of him, to tell him he is a fine journalist doing capital work.

A long pause follows while McCurdy sweats and stews. *Dear God, this would be so much more bearable with at least some muggle tea to steady the mind!*

The general screws on the cap of his fountain pen with care, sets it aside and swivels his icebreaker jaw in McCurdy's direction. "Good to meet you at last, Mr. McCurdy. I have read your work with interest." In a gesture that is meant to be playful, he points toward the writer with his forefinger, hand in the shape of a pistol. "You, my lad, are a writer."

"Thank you, general," McCurdy replies, unclear why he should regard this as a compliment.

"From the way you handle quotes, I gather you have written plays."

"I have, sir. Several." This is a lie, but something about the general's manner discourages correction.

"The way you make people speak, it sounds like something they might actually say."

"That's because they said it, sir." Another lie, but let them prove it.

"But surely a journalist doesn't simply take dictation."

"No, general, one has to make sense of it. People try to say what they mean, but they don't always succeed."

"Exactly. You have a journalist's ear." The general points at his own ear, using mime to ensure understanding.

McCurdy is not above a bit of toadying. "That's the trick of it, sir. The way people speak is part of what they are saying. The style is the content, you might say."

The general's forefinger again snaps into action like the barrel of a pistol pointing at McCurdy's nose. "You have a calling, Mr. McCurdy. To inform, warn, inspire. To awaken readers to current conditions that benefit nobody but communists, Chinamen, criminals and red Indians. Do you not agree?"

McCurdy doesn't quite follow. A painful throbbing has taken over where the spinal cord meets the brain. "You make a valid point," he says.

Now the throbbing gives way to another overwhelming wave of anxiety, a deluge of dread. He would rather throw himself out the window than endure an argument with General Victor Newson. He focuses on the military imagery on the wall, for inspiration, and finds none. The palms of his hands are so wet as to soak through the knees of his trousers.

"Your pieces on the Chinese question," Newson continues, "go straight to the crux of the issue. They echo the stand this newspaper has taken."

"Stand on what, sir?"

"On the Asian question. The Chinese question. The Women and Girls Protection Act."

All this rings a bell; suddenly he remembers why he came. "Perhaps we might discuss that, sir. As a question of... journalistic approach."

"Exactly. Well put. Surely if the experience of the Great War teaches us anything, it's that a controlled hostility, applied by disciplined men under good leadership, is what will save the British race from extinction.

"Since the end of the war, all discipline has been thrown aside. We are left with nothing but civilians, with their blithe assumptions of a 'right to life.' Our men are being feminized, emasculated, reduced to breadwinners while the female feathers her nest." McCurdy feels his eyes tearing up. In withdrawing from opium, the body sheds water like an overloaded sponge.

The general leans forward. "I see it's an issue about which you feel deeply, son."

"What?"

"It has brought tears to your eyes, lad. I'm impressed and moved."

"I beg your pardon?"

"Of course I realize and accept that you will not always agree with our official position. That sort of give and take is what gives a newspaper its pep. Keeping that in mind, Mr. McCurdy, I'm offering you a position as staff writer. Do you accept?"

"That is extremely flattering, General Newson, and I thank you. There is only one problem that I can see."

Newson's eyes seem to coat themselves with a film of some sort. "And what might that be?"

"It has to do with the recent articles you mentioned, on the Chinese question."

"Yes, each one a fine piece of writing, I've said that. What's your point?" His tone suggests that the general is mentally glancing at his watch.

"Well you see, sir, the problem is that I didn't write a single one of them."

"What's that you said?" The film over his eyes has turned to transparent steel.

"I didn't write them. They were written by somebody else."

"Under your name?"

"Under my byline, yes. I have a suspicion as to who it is, and that he was working under guidance."

"It would be extraordinarily unprofessional of you to direct someone else to do such a thing."

"It would, if in fact that was the case. When the forged pieces began to appear I was drugged and detained in Chinatown. I assume they've been running ever since."

"The devil! Obviously you managed to escape."

"I did." In fact, *escape* is hardly the right word, but McCurdy lets it pass.

"Well McCurdy, that is extraordinary. You're telling me that someone submitted reports under your name and without your knowledge."

"That seems to be the case, sir, yes." McCurdy uses his handkerchief to wipe the sweat from his forehead and the back of his neck, and to blow his nose. "And it's no small thing. You see, general, the words written under a writer's name are all that will be left when he dies. To have someone else take his name is like demonic possession."

The general leans so far over the table that he might as well be lying on it. "Mr. McCurdy, it's clear, to me at least, that you were abducted by Chinamen working for someone who felt threatened by something you wrote. If you feel you have been misrepresented, that is all the more reason for you to continue. Otherwise, words not your own will have carried the day."

"I don't understand, sir. Please go over that again."

"Not necessary, Mr. McCurdy. Just consider whether you wish to join us as staff writer. If not, so be it. If you do decide to remain with us, the only condition has to do with Armstrong. *General* Armstrong if you prefer—a desk general who never heard a shot fired unless it was at a ceremony. A man who married into American wealth and uses it in such a way that he will one day own British Columbia. By incremental contributions of money he will one day own the Conservative Party of BC and then run for premier!

"Armstrong is a conniver, a swindler, and he must be stopped.

This is the editorial position of *The Evening Star*, and if that is unacceptable to you, I advise you to resign at once and apply for a position with the *Vancouver Sun*. They love him there.

"In any case, a substantial fee is waiting for you at the reception desk—whether as incentive or as severance is entirely up to you. And now I have other work to attend to."

Newson stands and extends his hand. McCurdy dries his palm and shakes it. Newson's grip is firm and forthright, and he maintains eye contact without blinking, exuding leadership from every pore. At the door McCurdy glances back at the general, fountain pen in hand, his face a mask of concentration, hard at work for the betterment of mankind: *The quick brown fox...*

A DISTURBING SPECTACLE
The Second Inquest into the Death of Janet Stewart
Ed McCurdy
Staff Writer
The Evening Star

Monday, September 1, 1924

DAY ONE

9:00 AM. A shocking scene greets this reporter upon arriving at the Law Courts, as a monstrous throng stampedes across the lawn to the marble steps, a solid mass of frenzied humanity crammed against the low granite walls, while the stone lions above them avert their eyes—British symbols of fortitude and courage, overlooking a scene more appropriate to a stoning in Arabia than to a centre of English Common Law; a scene made all the more astonishing by the race and gender of the participants themselves: female members of the Scottish race, in summer hats and gloves, well-scrubbed and covered to the ankles, wrists and neck as though dressed for Kirk on a Sunday morning, their full-throated voices speaking to heaven in favour of an unspecified justice.

9:30 AM. Two bailiffs push open the doors and the stairway becomes a sluice up which, like a school of salmon thrusting instinctively, the throng surges, then splits among three pillars and unites again to shoot like water from a fire hose through the open front door. Once inside, they contribute to a scene of utter chaos as citizens unfamiliar with the building search desperately for the Coroner's Court, where the mystery of Janet Stewart will be unveiled; it is almost as though Miss Stewart herself might come back to life. Their cries back and forth for direction are magnified by the marble surfaces into a cacophony of predatory screeches, hisses and quacks.

Again, this reporter confronts the shocking fact that this confused, enraged mob consists almost entirely of women— as though the gentler sex, having broken free of womanly restraint, has now broken free of civilization itself.

Down the central hall, a wedge-shaped cordon of uniformed policemen escorts a procession of officials to the courtroom. The uniformed presence temporarily cows the ladies into something like normal human behaviour, but just as they cross the rotunda, a well-dressed woman throws her arms into the air, shrieks: *The girl was murdered! The girl was murdered!* and falls into a delirium, inspiring hundreds of voices to respond with unison moaning, a kind of chant, like a congregation of witches.

For the unfortunate male caught in this crush of enraged womanhood, it is a frightening experience.

A half-dozen bailiffs are needed to escort the witnesses, jurors and attorneys to the Coroner's Court, buffeted by a whirlwind of abuse from hostile matrons who see no reason why the coroner should receive preferential treatment over concerned citizens such as themselves.

What have you to hide in there?

Communists!

By this time the bailiffs have filled every spectator chair in the courtroom and have managed to clear the last of the holdouts into the corridor and shoulder the door shut. The proceedings are far behind schedule, late enough for a court adjournment so that the jury may reconvene at the morgue to view the cadaver, which has been exhumed and laid out for that purpose. Then they will reconvene at Leonard's Cafe for luncheon. The extended recess infuriates spectators to such a degree that officials of the court are effectively held hostage until a clerk of the court promises to locate subsequent sittings in a larger courtroom.

11:30 AM. This reporter will spare the reader most of what we witnessed in the morgue—the remains of a once lovely girl lying on a bare table, her face like a cracked eggshell. One of the doctors exhibits the location of the burns on her arms and torso, though they are no longer recognizable as such, and of course we are treated to what is left of the fracture at the back of the skull. Another helpful physician illustrates the path of the bullet by passing a piece of wire through her skull. The bottom half of her body has, to use the argot of the profession, liquefied.

After leaving the morgue, court officials repair to Leonard's Cafe, where lunch is served to those jurors who still have an appetite.

Without reproducing the circuitous route by which the various lawyers extracted information and admissions from various witnesses, this reporter will summarize the outcome—not in order to spare the reader's stomach but to spare himself the tedium of going over the testimony twice, since most of it is a word-for-word encore of what was said during Inquest Number One.

2:00 PM. Coroner Brydon-Jack seats himself and declares the session in order.

In front of the rostrum, a long evidence table contains an array of bloodstained clothing, a pair of shattered spectacles, a .455 revolver, an iron, a matched set of diaries and other items pertaining to the case. To the side is a special section for officers of the court; opposite the rostrum a full barrister's bench accommodating Crown counsel, as well as lawyers for the Faulkners, the Scottish Societies, Wong Sing Chi and the Chinese Benevolent Society.

Seemingly, everyone with an interest in the case felt it wise to retain legal representation.

The only group unequipped with legal armour are members of the Point Grey constabulary (Constable Gorman and Chief Quigley), and they will surely end up the worse for it.

Constable Gorman in particular suffers a grilling, having

changed an essential detail of his story by denying having instructed the undertaker to embalm the body. As well, he continues to believe it more likely that the wound was self-inflicted, though he concedes that it could have happened by accident.

In response, audible hisses echo among the spectators, who readily see his purpose in softening his previous testimony and allow for later wriggling:

"Constable Gorman, is it true that you made the statement: 'This is the most obvious case of suicide I have seen in my life?'"

"No. I never said that."

"So you didn't believe this was a case of suicide?"

"I continued to maintain an open mind."

"But you did and do believe it was suicide."

"I do. And Chief Quigley entirely agrees. But I am willing to be proved wrong."

"When did you telephone the constabulary after viewing the situation in the laundry room?"

"About ten minutes after I got there."

"Why did you telephone so soon?"

"My place was in the office. I telephoned the chief and he sent Constable Hook over. When Constable Hook arrived, I dropped the matter and left him to it."

"All the same, before leaving the scene for the office, you did an investigation and made notes. Dr. Blackwell says you made a search."

"I have no control over what he says."

"What notes did you make, then?"

"I commenced to make notes for my own benefit."

"What became of them?"

"I suppose I threw them in the wastebasket. These were personal notes. It was not my place to take notes officially."

"Are you saying they were grocery lists, that sort of thing?"

"That sort of thing, yes sir."

Dr. Blackwell takes the witness stand after Constable Gorman and reiterates his previous opinion word-for-word: that, to judge by the body temperature, Miss Stewart died approximately an hour and a half before his arrival.

Following Dr. Blackwell, Mr. Frank Faulkner delivers a smooth, confident performance, restating his agreement with Dr. Blackwell that Miss Stewart died while "fooling with the gun."

At this point a notable departure occurs. Mr. Abbott, acting for the Faulkners, requests to enter as evidence a telegram from Mr. Faulkner's sister in London, informing him that she had seen Miss Stewart target-shooting with a pistol. The coroner refuses to table an unsigned piece of evidence, but as far as the jury is concerned the point has been scored.

4:15 PM. The last witness of the day, Mrs. Doreen Faulkner, takes the stand in a modest but elegant late summer dress and hat, appearing unaccountably fragile, as though the entire proceedings are too much for her. She speaks in a timorous whisper. On several occasions the coroner urges her to speak up so that the jury can hear her testimony.

No need for concern, however. When audible, Mrs. Faulkner's story is a verbatim repeat of her testimony at the first inquest—that Miss Stewart was a "cheerful girl," that she was "of good moral character" and that she expressed no fear whatsoever of the Chinese houseboy, Wong Sing Chi.

Before adjournment, however, Crown counsel manages to extract from Mrs. Faulkner an acknowledgement that she is the daughter of General Hector Armstrong, a possible candidate in the upcoming election.

CROWN COUNSEL: "And is it true that you frequently advise your father on political matters—tactics and the like? Some wags have suggested that you are, in effect, the general's brain."

CORONER: "Stop the laughter please."

MRS. FAULKNER: "No sir, that is ridiculous. My father and I do not speak about anything of that sort."

DAY TWO

Perhaps out of disappointment that the previous day's session contained so little new information, a much-diminished crowd has gathered on the steps of the Law Courts on Friday morning. Therefore, most are able to gain entrance to the inquest, which has been moved to an assize court that boasts not only more seats but room at the rear for a standing audience.

Unfortunately, the assize court is visible from outside through cellar windows, so that a second audience now presses against the panes, making it necessary to keep the windows closed and curtained. Consequently, the courtroom becomes an airless oven within the first hour, while people outside pound the safety glass and shout insults. Tempers grow short all around, and witnesses will suffer periodic bombardments of catcalls, whistles and hisses all morning.

9:30 AM. The first witness of the day, Mr. Edwards the undertaker, directly refutes Constable Gorman's testimony of the day before. According to Mr. Edwards, he received clear instructions from the officer to embalm the body. The undertaker takes it even further, adding that he telephoned the coroner (the official at the head of these proceedings), who told him to go ahead.

This testimony places a new burden on Coroner Brydon-Jack, who was in fact the coroner on the telephone. This initiates a curious exchange between Mr. Brydon-Jack and Mr. Edwards, over what had in fact passed between them.

"Mr. Edwards, didn't I say to wait a little while?"

"Not that I remember, sir."

"I'm sure I did."

"I assure you, sir, that's not what I heard."

"I think the witness's memory is incorrect."

"Not in my opinion, sir..."

The foregoing exchange seems to have set the theme of the session as a whole—that no two witnesses entirely agree on anything. Nor is it clear whether the testimony of any particular witness derives from what was observed at the time, what the witness prefers in retrospect, or from one or another of the hundreds of rumours circulating through the city ever since.

As an example one must consider Chief Quigley, who seems to have changed his mind about whether he agrees with Constable Gorman, appearing to distance himself from the testimony of his underling, whose reputation, if he ever had one, lies in ruins.

"Chief Quigley, did Constable Gorman tell you that of the forty-eight cases of suicide he had known, this was the clearest case he had seen?"

"Yes, he did."

"Yesterday he denied having said this."

"I can't help what he said yesterday. Several times he told me it was suicide."

"He mentioned the number forty-eight, you say. Did he cite any of these cases?"

"No."

"Given the facts, or lack of facts, would you have permitted any embalming before the body was viewed by the coroner?"

"Most decidedly not."

"So as far as you are concerned, Constable Gorman did this on his own?"

"It appears so, though someone might have put him up to it."

Following Chief Quigley, Dr. Archibald Hunter, who led the autopsy after Miss Stewart's disinterment, helpfully produces a human skull on which to illustrate the cranial fractures. He has no firm opinion as to what caused them, whether it was a bullet or a blow to the head. Nor does he make anything of the lack of powder burns.

However, he has determined that, if she shot herself, Miss Stewart must have either held the gun backwards at a distance of at least ten and a half inches from her head, or turned it upside down with the hilt upward from a similar distance; he describes the latter as "the most comfortable position," to a chorus of rueful laughter.

Nor can he explain how she had managed to tuck the hot iron under her arm when she fell.

Dr. Hunter steps down without having expressed a firm opinion on much of anything, and any opinions he did elucidate are promptly contradicted by subsequent medical witnesses, Dr. Baird and Dr. Curtis, who have been summoned to provide commentary from an impartial viewpoint.

Dr. Curtis finds it strange that Miss Stewart would fall on her back with her arms arranged neatly beside her body.

"You don't think she would be lying there in such a composed state unless she was put there by someone else?"

"I do not."

And whereas Dr. Hunter took the view that with severe burns one would expect to find the clothing burnt as well, Dr. Curtis thinks it perfectly possible that her skin could be burnt without singeing the dress. Neither doctor, however, was able to replicate his interpretation in an experiment.

Dr. Curtis steps down, leaving behind a consensus on one thing only: that Constable Gorman is guilty of something, whether incompetence, corruption, stupidity or laziness—faults of equal seriousness in the Scottish mind.

Thanks to this procession of conflicting experts and authorities, facts have lost all value. From now on, giving testimony will be a matter of convincing the jury that one version is true—not with evidence but by the force of one's performance on the stand. In other words, the courtroom has become an audition and witnesses are would-be actors in a photo-play.

In that respect, Dr. Curtis is handily upstaged by a series of nannies, whose mutual agreement re-aims the beam of suspicion from Constable Gorman to Wong Sing Chi.

Misses Baron, Field, Parker, Kendall, Hawthorn and Harper agree on everything, as though a meeting had taken place beforehand. Miss Stewart is described as a "light-hearted," "cheerful," "witty" girl (these adjectives are used more than once) who, on more than one occasion, expressed misgivings about living under the same roof with the Chinaman. According to Miss Field, the victim once said, "He hates me and I hate him." Miss Parker agrees that there was no love lost between the two, while Miss Baron takes the theme a step further—that Miss Stewart was "deathly scared" of the houseboy, an observation echoed by Miss Kendall, who recalls how Miss Stewart "lived in fear" of Wong Chi and on several occasions complained that the Chinaman "touched her hand" and made "improper suggestions that left her speechless."

Miss Hawthorn recalls having seen a similar incident in which Miss Stewart picked up a pile of wet laundry and threw it at him. The spectators laugh heartily at the story, but then grow sombre, remembering the murdered corpse in the laundry room. Thus, in a classic case of guilt by association,

Wong Chi's presence in one laundry room scene increases the likelihood of his involvement in the other.

Rehearsed or not, the nannies give a fine and consistent performance. Yet it is Cissie Braidwood who, as in the first inquest, steals the show. Indeed, one might say that her performance starts with a bang—the sound of her head hitting the floor of the witness box as she falls in a swoon before uttering a word.

While the court clerk revives Miss Braidwood with a glass of ice water, Coroner Brydon-Jack deems it an excellent time to adjourn for the day.

DAY THREE

9:30 AM. We are pleased to report that the crowd of three hundred has recovered its sense of decorum, perhaps thanks to an editorial in the *Vancouver Sun* expressing concern over the threat of mass unrest (though the possibility of a Bolshevik uprising led by Scottish women seems remote).

Miss Cissie Braidwood has fully recovered from the previous session. Ushered to the stand by none other than Reverend McDougall (who for once refrains from one of his hellish jeremiads), she is ready and even eager to point her finger at Wong Chi: "One of the last things she said to me was that for three days she was afraid to enter a room where he was, and I don't blame her, I was afraid of him myself. Looking at him yesterday was what put me in a faint."

Mr. Stickler, acting for the Chinese Benevolent Society, steps up to the witness box with an item from the exhibit table, one of Miss Stewart's diaries, and demands to know, if Miss Stewart was as petrified of Wong Chi as all that, why her diary makes no mention of it.

Mr. Stickler then reads a list of admirers' names. It is longer than anyone expected.

"Miss Braidwood, didn't it seem strange that she spent so much time writing about her admirers?"

"She had to do something while she was in fear for her life."

This reply receives applause from the spectators, not because it makes sense but because it returns to the subject they wish to hear about: the sinister behaviour of the Chinaman.

"And what about the unnamed wealthy gentleman who, and I quote, 'provided me with drinks and hugged and kissed me so I got mushy and feared a catastrophe'?"

"Ginger beer and like that, but the only catastrophe she feared was from the Chinaman."

Again, mutters of approval from the spectators, and by their expressions it appears unlikely that Miss Stewart's array of lovers made an impression one way or the other.

Mr. Stickler turns to another section of the diary, in which Miss Stewart records how Wong Chi helped her wash and bottle fifty pounds of strawberries and how, later on, he gave her a silk nightie and two camisoles.

"Does this suggest she was afraid of the Chinaman?"

"I know what she told me. I don't have to read it in a diary."

Miss Braidwood's firm response draws a chorus of whistles, cheers and hand-clapping, until Mr. Brydon-Jack threatens to clear the courtroom. (Later reports in the *Vancouver Province* will portray Miss Braidwood as "full of spunk, with the courage of a modern-day Joan of Arc.")

Sensing the futility in this line of questioning, Mr. Stickler makes one last attempt to establish his original point:

"Miss Braidwood, you are not answering the question: If she was so terribly afraid of the Chinaman, would she not have put it in her diary?"

"If she knew she was going to be murdered, she would have written more. As it was, I suppose she didn't have time."

"No further questions," Mr. Stickler says, appearing annoyed and bewildered.

When the inquest adjourns for the noon recess, only one witness remains to testify: Wong Sing Chi, whom the spectators, and indeed all of Vancouver, have already found guilty thanks to the performance of a "spunky" girl.

1:00 PM. Whereas at the first inquest Wong Sing Chi swore under the Fire Oath, on this occasion, apparently to ensure a stronger commitment to the truth, the Chicken Oath is to be administered. Though some spectators express shock that such a ritual would occur in a part of the British Empire, they are swayed by the coroner's argument that a Chinaman's oath is worthless unless administered in his own terms.

This reporter remains skeptical as to whether the Chicken Oath is genuine. It seems more likely that, in private, Orientals are laughing at us behind their sleeves.

The oath is administered as follows: After the noon recess, bailiffs usher Wong Chi to an exterior passage where they have arranged several incense burners around a chopping block. He is given a sheet of parchment identical to the one issued for the Fire Oath, which he reads and then signs. Two bailiffs then light matches and set afire the incense and the parchment, while a third fetches a live chicken, whose head is placed on the block. Then, before the coroner, the jury and the press, Wong Chi is given a cleaver, with which he cuts off the chicken's head.

Looking fit and surprisingly calm, Wong Chi's only concern seems to be not to soil his impeccable black suit, white shirt and tie.

Witnesses are no clearer about the significance of the gesture than is the unfortunate chicken.

Back in the overcrowded, stifling assize court, Wong Chi takes the stand. His demeanour remains serene, considering the malice emanating from the spectators, who have convicted him of murder and are impatient to get to the hanging.

A translator stands by—Foon Sien, who acted in the same capacity during the first inquest, wearing the same double-breasted lounge suit and bowler hat, and speaking in the same opaque English.

For his part, Wong Chi seems perfectly capable of speaking for himself, in sentences that do not necessarily connect. At other times he lapses into Chinese, so that Foon Sien must step in with a translation so puzzling that it might as well be in a third language.

"It is in morning I peel earth vegetables no, sorry, batoes, hear loud burp spending from auto..."

In essence, the jury and spectators are receiving a literal repetition of the story he gave the first inquest and to the Point Grey Police, as well as to every newspaper in the city:

He was peeling potatoes. He heard a loud noise and ran down to the laundry room, where he found the body of Janet Stewart.

We will spare the reader the rest of the tale, which has been repeated so often that, to whites and Orientals alike, it is as familiar as the route to one's workplace. However, some exchanges between the witness and counsel deserve quotation, if only because this reporter found them puzzling:

"You do not remember her going downstairs anytime that morning?"

"Come down or not, I don't know, didn't see."

"Until the shot, you never knew of her being downstairs?"

"She took some clothes down to the basement."

"I asked you if you knew she was downstairs earlier that morning, and you said that you did not."

"Ten o'clock is not early. Five o'clock early."

"Why did you say a moment ago that you didn't know whether she was downstairs or not?"

"Sometimes I don't see, then I don't know."

"But as far as you do know, she was in the basement from ten until you heard the shot."

"I was peeling potatoes."

"We understand that, yes. And you heard a shot?"

"Shot, yes."

"What did you do?"

"I stand at sink, peeling potatoes."

"I mean after you heard the shot."

"Go downstairs. Missy on floor..."

Later in the afternoon, the questioning turns to the house-boy's relations with the nanny:

"Did you and Miss Stewart ever quarrel?"

"I bake her a cake."

"Did you ever touch her?"

"I give her film for her camera."

"Were you and Miss Stewart fooling with the gun?"

"I do not understand."

"You and Missy fool with gun, gun go off, Missy hurt?"

"I do not understand *fool*."

"Playing with the gun, like a toy?"

"Toy? No toy. Real gun, go off."

And on that note, the coroner calls an adjournment until tomorrow morning, when the jury is to arrive at its verdict.

DAY FOUR

9:30 AM. Day Four begins with a replay of Day One. Already over five hundred souls have crammed themselves between the two stone lions and up the steps with such force that one can envision the collapse of a pillar that brings down the entire edifice.

With the opening of the doors, the onrush of humanity puts one in mind of cattle clamouring down the chute to the abattoir. For these spectators, the worst that can happen will be an inconclusive verdict.

As it turns out, they are not disappointed:

"We find that Janet K. Stewart was on June 26, 1924, willfully murdered in the course of her employment by being shot through the head with a revolver in the basement at 3381 Osler Street. By whom it was fired we have insufficient evidence to determine..."

There is no question whether spectators are saddened or elated—from the roar of approval and applause one would think the Asahi Tigers had won the pennant.

EPILOGUE

The euphoria expressed by the Scottish Societies and their sympathizers following the verdict of Inquest Number Two lasted for approximately two days, by which time one glaring fact appeared on the mental horizon like a harvest moon: that the murderer had not been publicly identified, even if there remained no doubt who he was. It is one thing to cry murder and quite another to name, convict and hang the murderer. No politician or administrator will sleep soundly until that happy event comes to pass.

25

A man who makes a mistake and doesn't correct it makes another mistake.

HE SAID HE would pay for the room, and that he would provide her with spending money.

He'd better.

Florence looks over her room, and it is acceptable—clean, with a double bed and not a cot. A girl will come in once a week to change the sheets. It's a nice enough room, but no nicer than her room at Canacraig, just a bit bigger. She would prefer something more posh, in a hotel with a proper reception room and uniformed staff. The clerk downstairs is a one-armed veteran with whisky on his breath. When she told him her name, he looked at her as though she were a certain kind of woman.

Which she most certainly is not.

She would like a room with a carpet and its own bathroom, not just a sink and a commode. She would like a telephone with which to call Front Desk and order food, and someone to bring it up to her on a tray, with a thick white napkin and heavy silverware.

Someone to wait on her, for a change.

He said he would come at seven and it's now seven thirty. She is wearing her new dress, just to show him. She imagines what would have been said or done to her at work if *she* was this late for anything. At the least, she would lose her day off; at the worst, she could be fired. Now she can't be fired, because she has quit. She wishes she had a picture of the head Chinaman's face when she told him.

Five quiet knocks on the door, as agreed.

"Who is it?"

"Florence, it is I. Who did you expect?"

She knows who it is, but doesn't like to be taken for granted. She opens the door. "I was expecting you earlier, that's all."

"I do apologize. My auto was caught behind a streetcar, and I stopped to buy some things. I thought we might have an indoor picnic." He produces a paper carrying bag from Spencer's department store, places it on the dresser by the door, reaches inside and extracts a bottle of gin, a bottle of French vermouth, a jar of olives, bread, pâté—and, to her astonishment and delight, a small cut-glass bottle of Chanel No. 5 eau de parfum.

Resisting the impulse to cry out, she calmly accepts the jewel-like container and reads the label. Never in her life has she been given anything so posh, nor expected to be, but she does not make grateful noises, nor does she throw her arms about his neck. If she is to be a lady, she must act like one.

"Thank you. Very nice, I must say."

She runs a forefinger over the bevelled cut-glass, then unscrews the square crystal cap and applies the tiniest drop on the inside of one wrist, then rubs her wrists together, the way she has seen it done by her employer at her dressing table. She inhales the perfume; her wrist smells like a mysterious, intoxicating flower—what man wouldn't fall in love with a woman who smelled like that?

"What do you think?" she asks, extending her wrist for him to smell. "Do you like it?"

He inhales the scent and kisses the spot on her wrist. "It's you," he says. "And so is the new dress."

He reaches into the bag and produces two martini glasses. He pours gin and just a few drops of vermouth into each one. "I thought we should drink a toast," he says. "Pity there's no ice."

Then why didn't you bring some? "Maybe next time," she replies, sips her drink, smiles and wonders if he has noticed her lipstick— the Max Factor lady showed her how to apply a perfect Cupid's bow, using the stencil provided.

"It's a bit stuffy. Do you mind if I open the window?" Without waiting for an answer, he crosses to the window and lifts the sash as wide as it will go. "There. That's better."

Yes, she thinks to herself as she sips her drink, crosses to the window and contemplates the fire escape opposite. *And it would be much better with a view of the water and not the alleyway...*

The near-full gin bottle slams into the back of her head just above the neck, so that she crumples to the floor like a cut puppet without time even to wonder what happened.

He uses the gin bottle as a hammer—two more strokes to the same spot. He chose Gordon's Gin not for its quality but because it comes in a thick, square bottle—much sturdier than the vermouth bottle on the dresser, which would have smashed to smithereens.

26

Complication is rarely welcome.

"Hello, operator speaking, SEymour exchange. Is this SEymour 330?"
    "Here is SEymour 330. The Hotel Vancouver, operator speaking."
    "Here is SEymour 120. I will connect you now."
    SWITCH
    "SEymour 120, are you there?"
    "Yes."
    "Hotel operator speaking."
    "Here is Inspector Forbes Caddell of the Vancouver Police Department. He wishes to speak to Attorney General Cunning, please."
    "I will connect you now."
    SWITCH
    "Attorney General Cunning speaking. Who are you, please?"
    "Here is the hotel operator. I have Inspector Caddell on the line. Do you wish to make the connection, sir?"
    "One moment please..."
    Attorney General Cunning lights a cigarette, his thirty-fifth that day. He wonders how much longer he can endure this feeling that he is no longer leading events, that events are leading him. And now he must deal with Caddell—an undeniably stupid man, but a skilled bully with an animal cunning that must be negotiated carefully lest he sink his teeth into the back of one's neck. He pours himself three fingers of Scotch and repeats to himself three times the phrase recommended in *As A Man Thinketh*, his current guide to leadership: *Man is the master power that moulds and makes, shaping what he wills...*
    "Operator, I will take the call."
    "I will connect you now."
    SWITCH
    "Gordon Cunning here. Are you there?"

"Here is Inspector Forbes Caddell of the VPD. We have a situation I believe you will want to know about, sir. It concerns the Janet Stewart case."

"Oh dear God, doesn't everything?"

"A maid at the Balmoral Hotel was disposing of a load of kitchen rubbish and she found a corpse."

"A dead body?"

"A corpse would be a dead body, sir, yes that's right."

"Don't be sarcastic with me, Mr. Caddell. The maid found a dead body in a garbage can?"

"No, technically the dead woman was behind *a garbage can. The maid smelled something other than garbage, if you get my meaning, and followed her nose."*

Cunning wonders whether Caddell has the wit to execute a pun; either such word play is coincidental, or—perish the thought—the man is not as stupid as he makes himself out to be.

"Why are you telling me this, inspector?"

"Directly above, about four floors up, a window was open wide."

"So in other words the individual jumped. It sounds simple enough."

"Not quite as simple as we both might wish, sir. The door to the room was open—just a crack, but you would say it was ajar. Either she left her door open or someone else did. In any case, the room had been ransacked and there was no sign of a purse. Sir, I'll be blessed if I'll risk another version of the Janet Stewart affair."

"I couldn't agree with you more. But I think there is room to explain the situation, given the gap between her death and the discovery of the body. It seems obvious that someone else took advantage of the open door to pilfer her effects. Frankly Inspector Caddell, I fail to understand why you bring up this item of routine police business."

"Well sir, there's another thing."

"Damn it, I might have known." The Attorney General is beginning to wonder whether Caddell is enjoying the twisted sense of power that comes with delivering bad news.

"Well sir, we checked with the front desk. It seems the deceased's name was Florence McNeil, and the address she gave when she checked in was 1449 Armstrong Avenue. As you know sir, there is only one residence on that street."

"Do you mean she worked for General Armstrong?"

"Correct."

"What do they have to say about it at Canacraig?"

"According to the staff, those few who spoke English, a Florence McNeil did work there for several months but quit suddenly, less than a week ago."

"At the hotel, did you learn anything else from Front Desk?"

"Only that a gentleman came to call on two occasions."

"Was it a Chinaman? That would certainly be helpful."

"He was white, sir. Well groomed, I was led to understand."

Cunning takes time to recite in his mind: *Man is the master power that moulds and makes, shaping what he wills...* There comes a time when bold action is called for, and this is one of those times.

"Now inspector, I want you to listen carefully."

"Yes, sir."

"Are your men reliable?"

"What do you mean, sir?"

"Can I count on their discretion? This is of crucial importance."

"Sir, my men are the finest policemen in Canada."

"That's not what I asked, inspector."

"They are trustworthy men, sir."

"I'll take that as a yes. Now listen, Mr. Caddell. We have a situation where the public is in a state of panic over the murder of one Scottish girl. If it comes out that another Scottish girl has died under suspicious circumstances, there will be chaos. A Bolshevik could do no more damage to the province, do you understand me?"

"I believe I do, sir. But surely we can't ignore it entirely. If the press were to get hold of it..."

The mere idea of the press causes Cunning to touch wood, and to pour himself a dram.

The inspector continues: *"At present, our preliminary report suggests that she died either by suicide or in the course of a robbery."*

"Not good enough, inspector. It's still too much like the Stewart case. Given that she wasn't found until she started to smell, the room could have been robbed by anyone."

"Sir, no matter who robbed the room, still our options are suicide or murder. There's nothing else available. Which do you prefer, sir?"

"What about accidental death?"

"You mean she leaned too far over the sill? That sort of thing?"

"Something like that, yes. Could we suggest evidence that she'd been drinking?"

"Do you mean a bottle in the room?"

"Or by the garbage can."

"Well I suppose there were bottles by the garbage can. There usually are... Yes, I see that the report mentions a broken gin bottle on the ground not far from the victim."

"A servant girl with a known nervous disorder quit her position suddenly, left her employer without leaving a forwarding address and fell out the window of a downtown hotel in a state of extreme inebriation. Perhaps there was a romance gone sour as well—I refer to her well-groomed gentleman caller. Of course, no names are to be reported until the family has been located and consulted, which could take weeks."

"Very good, sir. That will be the story."

"I'll leave this up to you. I have complete confidence in your judgment."

"I appreciate that, sir."

"Inspector, amid the uncertainty, confusion and incompetence, I have come to believe two things."

"And what would those be, sir?"

"One, that the Chinaman is our key to the entire Janet Stewart case. Two, that he knows far more than he pretends to. What is more, he is being either paid or blackmailed into lying, either on his own behalf or that of someone else. It's imperative that he be persuaded to tell the whole truth."

"That might not be easy, sir. They are natural liars. It takes a good deal of persuasion to get the truth out of them. It's a scientific fact that Chinamen are tougher than any white man—they work harder, can do with less food and are insensible to pain."

"That is true, inspector. But there are times when a threat is so dire one must push the boundaries."

"Believe me sir, the men at VPD push the boundaries on a regular basis."

"Within the rules of conduct, of course."

"Sir, we are here to enforce the law, not break it."

"Well put, Mr. Caddell. By the way, as you know, an amalgamation of the constabularies into a single force is a priority with my department. A united force will need a leader with your courage and discretion."

"Always willing to serve, sir."

Not on my watch, thinks the Attorney General. "In the meantime, inspector, we must be careful that we are not seen together, and speak only in general terms on the telephone. The city is buzzing with

rumours. Rumours are a serious threat to public order, don't you see.
They change the way the voters interpret things, the way they view
those in charge. Believe me, inspector, we must not underestimate
the danger here. Many fine careers are at risk."

ANOTHER DEAD SCOTTISH GIRL
Ed McCurdy
Staff Writer
The Evening Star

As though the city were not sufficiently alarmed by the lack
of a resolution to the Janet Stewart murder after two inquests,
a second death has occurred with suspicious similarities to
the first, both in the death itself and in the police response.

This reporter has learned that Florence McNeil, a Scottish
girl formerly employed by members of the Armstrong family,
was discovered behind the Balmoral Hotel, having fallen out
the window of her room. According to the staff at Canacraig,
Miss McNeil left her position without notice, shortly after
the Janet Stewart murder came to light.

A hotel employee confirmed that Miss McNeil had
received at least one male caller at the hotel, but gave no
description other than that he was white.

The Vancouver Police have determined the matter to be a
case of accidental death brought on by inebriation. The fact
that the room she occupied had been stripped of valuables is
taken to be the work of an opportunistic, unrelated intruder.

The public has become accustomed to such willful blindness within the Point Grey constabulary, but expect more
from the Vancouver officers who have spearheaded the drive
to municipal amalgamation.

As with the Janet Stewart murder, the Attorney General
has taken no meaningful action. Instead, sensing an election
issue in the making and in order to appease the Scottish
Societies, Mr. Cunning has chosen to throw taxpayer dollars
at the problem in the form of an additional $3,000, to sup-
plement the $2,000 reward already put in place by the Scots.

If $2,000 was not sufficient persuasion to whomever might
possess knowledge pointing to the identity of the murderer
or murderers, it is difficult to imagine that an increased

payoff will induce some hitherto undiscovered witness to come forward.

Surely two questions cry out to be asked and answered: Are similarities between these two deaths coincidental, or is something more sinister at work? And more urgently, are young Scottish women at the mercy of an unknown predator still at large?

"Hello, operator speaking, TRinity exchange. Is this SEymour 330?"
"Here is SEymour 330. The Hotel Vancouver, operator speaking."
"Here is TRinity 320. I will connect you now."
SWITCH
"SEymour 330, Hotel Vancouver, who are you please?"
"Here is General Armstrong. I wish to speak to Attorney General Cunning, please."
"I will connect you, general."
SWITCH
"Hello, who are you please?"
"Here is the operator speaking. Is this Suite 1420?"
"Suite 1420. Gordon Cunning speaking."
"Hotel Vancouver, here is General Armstrong."
"I will speak to him."
"I will connect you now."
SWITCH
"Here is Attorney General Cunning. General Armstrong, are you there?"
"It has taken an unbecoming amount of time for you to close the file on Janet Stewart, laddie. I am beginning to wonder if I placed my bet on the wrong horse."
"Good to hear your perspective, general. I completely agree that the case has become an enormous headache, made worse by the leaking of sensitive information..."

27

A den hides the criminal, not the crime.

AT MILDRED'S INSISTENCE, they take the tram all the way to English Bay, where they find an empty log near the bathhouse to sit on. On the beach, women and men lounge about in a variety of costumes reflecting their views about exposing one's skin to the sun and to public view. (Not to mention a desire in this climate not to let sunlight go to waste.) Many of the men wear business suits with the trousers rolled to the knee as though attempting to tan their shins; other men and women have opted for wool jersey tank suits that bare the arms, shoulders and legs.

"I love the beach in summer, don't you Eddie?"

"Not really. Too much sand." McCurdy dislikes the sun as well; lacking prescription sunglasses, the glare does nothing for his frayed nerves.

"This one reminds me of Brighton," she says. "The sea breeze— and it even has a pier."

Shading his eyes with one hand, he turns to look past the bathhouse at the industrial-looking pier pointing its finger at Kitsilano on the opposite side, with its dowdy excuse for a dance hall at the far end. As for sea breeze, Mildred's cigarette smoke is winding straight up as though they were in a closed room. He loosens his tie and wipes the sweat from his face: "I hope this isn't one of your little performances, another spy act. Your costumes are bad enough."

"I'm at a stage where it isn't wise to be seen with reporters." She retrieves another cigarette from her purse and lights it while grinding the first one underfoot. "We in the information business must remember that there are persons who don't like to be informed upon."

"Dear God, you're not a Hello Girl anymore, you've become a professional eavesdropper. A mercenary spy."

"It's impossible to dress properly on a Hello Girl's salary."

"Ah. Might this have to do with the family money? For some reason has the tap become a trickle?"

"Your instinct is commendable." She examines her cigarette as though it contains reading material. "The general strike at home, you know, martial law and all that. Another kind of war. Sparrow would love it, but unless you're a communist, London has become a poor city in which to go about your business."

He watches a group of swimmers emerging from the water. Soaking wet, their wool bathing suits sag and droop in ways that are boldly revealing and unattractively odd at the same time, with udder-shaped protuberances full of seawater under the arms and between the legs.

"Well, what have you found, Millie? I don't have to mention that it had better be good."

"Good enough that it will cost you ten dollars."

"Surely you're not serious."

"Otherwise I shall have to offer it to somebody else. Max Trotter would give me more."

"Your price is obscene."

"You may be right. We'll see what the market can bear."

"Oh for God's sake, at least give me the gist of it!" McCurdy fears he is sounding desperate—not only does he continue to suffer withdrawal-induced jitters, but the entire Janet Stewart inquiry has reached a dead end, a tangle of conflicting theories and thorny questions.

"I'm hurt by your lack of trust, but very well: It seems that, before enlistment, Frank Faulkner was the co-owner of an import-export business, Faulkner & Humphrey. They bought and sold narcotics as freely as you would any other commodity. Unfortunately for Faulkner & Humphrey, during the war, controls were placed on morphine, cocaine and heroin. In order to exist as a legal enterprise, Faulkner & Humphrey were obliged to follow an entire new regime of restrictions and regulations, which they did—or appeared to...

"Now that will be five dollars please, and five upon publication, remember. I hope you realize I'm giving you a deal."

Muttering under his breath, he retrieves his notebook and his pocketbook from the side pockets of his coat and counts out five bills, which she folds into a neat wad and stows in her purse. A nearby couple, lounging beneath a parasol, notices the transaction and the man whispers something that causes the young woman to giggle.

"Very well, shall I continue?"

"I hope so, Millie."

Along with her cigarette package she takes a small notebook from her purse containing scribbled names and numbers. "Here's where it becomes rather juicy, I think. A little over a year ago, British revenue agents boarded the *Orthrys* in Hong Kong Harbour, searched the effects of a passenger named Tiew Yui Kim and seized over a hundred and fifty pounds of uncut, high-grade cocaine, and the same amount of morphine, in bags sewn into the framework and springs of Tiew's antique furniture.

"Among Tiew's effects was a letter from H.M.F. Humphrey, Mr. Faulkner's partner, offering to sell the Tong Say brothers forty-six hundred pounds' worth of cocaine."

She produces a fresh cigarette and lights up, taking her time at it; McCurdy has no doubt she is tormenting him on purpose.

"Six months later, His Majesty's Customs intercepted a letter from Humphrey & Faulkner offering a Chinese entity, the same Tong Say brothers, eighty-seven million doses of a coded drug. The letter imprudently mentioned having—and I have the quote—'complete control of the supply chain.' According to ship's records, Frank Faulkner chose that moment to return home to British Columbia, in sufficient haste that he would surely have had no time to establish business connections here in the city of his birth."

A pause, while McCurdy takes notes, which he has been doing feverishly since she opened her beak on the subject.

"Miss Wickstram, may I ask how you gathered this valuable information?"

"It's called *research*, Eddie—an alien concept to self-styled poets. Badminton girls are trained in it. And I have classmates overseas—there is such a thing as the telegraph. We in the colonies are not as isolated as some might wish."

Mildred rises to her feet. "Now shall we return downtown?"

"Actually, I need to make it to an appointment that will take us in opposite directions. After all, we must be discreet."

Hearing that last sentence, the couple beneath the parasol giggles once more.

THE YELLOW CAB turns onto The Crescent, passes Canacraig, heads down Osler and deposits McCurdy at the curb. The house could pass for a cottage in the Cotswolds, were it made of brick and stone and not spruce and cedar and located near cultivated hills and not jag-toothed mountains and primordial forest.

Thanks to Miss Wickstram, he now sees that the owners of the house have ample reason to seek inconspicuousness.

When McCurdy lifts and drops the absurdly heavy brass knocker, the sound nearly damages his eardrums. He really shouldn't be doing this—at least not yet. He should have waited until his senses returned to normal.

His return to so-called reality has been an agony of paranoia and angst. Moment by moment, he has faced two choices: tough it out or return to heaven; and the second, preferable, choice is moot—partly because of Miss Wickstram's persistence and partly because he could no longer afford the habit.

Again, the deafening clang of the knocker echoes off a hardwood floor, followed by the soft swish of Oriental feet.

The door latch clicks. The door swings open.

"Yes, please?"

McCurdy noticed earlier that the houseboy stands tall for a member of his race, but the figure in the doorway towers over him like a Greek statue—well muscled, with the sort of wide, strong jaw that can take a punch.

"Is Mr. Frank Faulkner at home? Your employer? At home? Employer home?"

The houseboy does a shallow bow. "Very sorry, sir. Mr. Faulkner not at home."

"You are Wong Chi? Wong Sing Chi?"

"I am Wong Sing Chi." The houseboy seems puzzled. *Why would a white man care what my name is?*

"I am Ed McCurdy of the Vancouver *Evening Star*. I write. *Evening Star*."

"Evening star?"

"Newspaper. Called *Evening Star*. I write." Absurdly, he mimes the act of writing longhand.

"I ask Mrs. Faulkner. Wait. Please. Sorry." The houseboy softly shuts the door. The soft swish of feet recedes down the front hall.

Seconds later McCurdy hears the advancing clack of a woman's high heels; it hurts his ears the way the knocker did.

Wong Chi, I am familiar with Mr. McCurdy and will speak to him, says the voice within.

Yes of course, Missus. I am nearby.

The door opens, and now it's Mrs. Faulkner who is standing majestically above him, wearing a pale green lace dress not at all like your mother's lace; it clings to her body and displays small, arbitrary patches of perfect skin, not to mention her bare arms, inviting kisses from wrist to shoulder.

And her perfume. McCurdy has nothing but respect for its power. If mustard gas smelled like this, soldiers would not have been breathing through piss-soaked handkerchiefs.

A good thing he prepared a speech, otherwise he would just stand there, taking her in.

"Forgive me for disturbing you, Mrs. Faulkner. My name is Ed McCurdy and I work for *The Evening Star*. I would like to ask you, if I may, a few questions about Janet Stewart. So that the public will look at it from your point of view, don't you see. As a journalist, I deplore the one-sided nature of our reporting on the case so far. Your side—and Mr. Faulkner's too, of course—has received scant attention, and I'm here to restore a sense of balance."

Her expression suggests that she doesn't believe a word of this. "You wrote that rot beforehand, didn't you? And revised it as well."

"I don't know what you mean."

"You're McCurdy, the poet, aren't you? You wrote *Ordinary Poems*."

McCurdy is at a loss to reply.

"How on earth would you know that, Mrs. Faulkner?"

"*Ordinary Poems*. Such a modest title for such an interesting collection. It received some favourable reviews, you know."

"I make it a point not to read the reviews," McCurdy lies.

"And then you seemed to disappear."

"I had to find a job."

"Could you not find something more... more worthy of your talent than *The Evening Star*?"

"To be honest, no."

"A pity. Would you like to come in?"

McCurdy has been gobsmacked. When an attractive woman mentions to a writer that she has read his work, he is hers. In this case, the effect is not lessened by her perfume, nor her lace dress, sweeping against her backside with each step. For McCurdy, time and motion have taken on a gelatinous, muffled quality, like the inside of an aquarium.

A vaporous light trickles in through mullioned windows, echoing off the varnished wood and the crystal chandelier, as they sweep into a living room furnished with faux-Tudor beams, faux-Constable landscapes and faux-Stickley furniture.

McCurdy surreptitiously takes out his notebook and pencil. He has become adept at taking notes without looking, beneath a table or even behind his back.

"Please sit down, Mr. McCurdy. I'm sure you wish to speak to Wong Chi, but his English is not good. And besides, I won't let you."

McCurdy takes the chair opposite, brown wood and pink velvet and very hard on the back.

"Madam like drink, please?"

McCurdy turns, startled. The houseboy has been standing there for some time.

"Yes please, Wong Chi. What would you like, Mr. McCurdy? Wong Chi knows how to make every cocktail known to man."

"I'd like a planter's punch, please."

"Ah, a test. Such a skeptic. Wong Chi, a planter's punch for Mr. McCurdy, and I will have a gin rickey."

"I will make. Excuse, please."

"Your houseboy has learned a valuable skill, Mrs. Faulkner. Your guests must love him."

"You talk about him as though he were a trained monkey."

"You'd be surprised how many people like their servants to perform party tricks."

"They must be your readers. The way your paper views Orientals—as an inferior species, swarming the province like ants or rats."

"I say let the ants have it. At least they co-operate with one another."

Mrs. Faulkner cocks her head sideways with a half-smile. "You're here to chase down some more rumours, aren't you?"

"Just trying to establish some facts, actually. For example, if I may ask, what is your husband's business these days?"

"Frank exports and imports antiques for the Asian market. That's as much as I know. I'm his wife, Mr. McCurdy, I take care of his household and social obligations—and little Emma, of course. We keep a traditional home."

"So he has nothing to do with pharmaceuticals?"

"Not anymore I shouldn't think—too complicated, he says, there's entirely too much bureaucracy nowadays. But then again, as I said, I'm his wife, not his business partner."

"That would be Mr. Humphrey—who has got himself in a spot of trouble, back in England."

"You've been doing your research, I see. Or *snooping* might be another way of putting it. Mr. McCurdy, why don't you ask me questions I can actually answer; like whether or not there was a party the night poor Janet died—which I can tell you, with absolute certainty, there was not."

"I wasn't about to suggest there was."

"But you *think* there was." Her smile hardens slightly: "And by the way, I know you're taking notes under the coffee table. Such a sneaky profession you've taken up."

"People have drinks, please?"

The houseboy materializes with a tray and two glasses: one contains a pale green liquid that matches (coincidence, surely) Mrs. Faulkner's lace dress and silk headband; the other is a brownish-orange. She leans forward to pick up her drink; he follows the trail of her perfume down to her wrist, with its delicate green and gold bracelet.

His hand trembles slightly, and he spills some of his drink on the houseboy's immaculate sleeve. "Oh blast! How clumsy of me! I am very sorry, Wong Chi. *Dui bu qi.*"

"It is no matter. Easy to clean."

As the houseboy heads for the door, McCurdy's attention returns to his companion, now semi-reclining on the chesterfield.

"Would you care for a cigarette, Mr. McCurdy? They are very good for calming one's nerves."

"I'm afraid I don't smoke."

"Why ever not?"

"Asthma. Doctor's orders."

"Silly doctors," she says, retrieving a cigarette from a silver box. "Would it kill you to give me a light?"

He picks up a silver table lighter. Unused to the one-handed type, he makes a hash of lighting up, so that she is obliged to steady his hand with hers.

She takes a deep drag, blows a thin stream of smoke between

Cupid's-bow lips, tilts her head and smiles, as though about to express something kittenish and whimsical.

"I have a confession to make, Mr. McCurdy. I detest this city. Everything smells of burnt sawdust and rotten fish—and always the fucking mountains and the fucking bloody sea to remind you that you can't escape, you've a moat on one side and a fence on the other. The men stink of sweat and bad teeth, and women over thirty look like mailboxes. The place is a filthy hole, Mr. McCurdy—and so far you seem to fit right in. But I like you anyway. Any Canadian who at least tries to be a poet can't be all bad. Would you like another drink?"

"Thank you but I should be going. Unless you'll reconsider and let me interview your employee."

Again, Mrs. Faulkner executes her lovely smile. Someone peering at them through the window would think they are having a delightful conversation. "Mr. McCurdy, I watched you newspapermen grind Janet Stewart's reputation into the dirt. Let's spare Wong Chi for now, shall we?"

She puts a hand on his arm. Again, that perfume.

"Frankly, I wonder why you came."

MCCURDY CROSSES THE lawn onto Osler Street and strides purposefully toward The Crescent and Canacraig. The back of his neck can feel her watching him through the front window, just inside the chintz curtains, casting beams in his direction until he passes the neighbour's cedar hedge, thick as a wall, and is out of sight.

He has a plan, or thought he did a moment ago. Gradually his brain unscrambles sufficiently to remember.

Stopping next to the sculpted hedge, he listens to the ratchety sound of lawnmowers rolling over surrounding lawns, counts to a hundred, then retraces his steps as far as the Faulkners' driveway.

He made no mention to Mrs. Faulkner of his previous incarnation as an assistant undertaker, or the fact that he knew the way to the laundry room.

He crosses the lawn and makes his way down the cement steps to the basement, where Wong Chi will surely be dealing with the stain on his white shirt. Sure enough, there is the houseboy in an undershirt, bent over the laundry sink, scrubbing away.

"*Ni hao,*" McCurdy says, hoping to put Wong Chi at ease, except that the man nearly jumps out of his skin. (He should have at least cleared his throat.)

"*Dui bu qi.*" His second Chinese apology of the day.

While the startled houseboy grips the edge of the sink for support and catches his breath, the reporter opens a packet of Ogden's he brought for such a purpose, a tactic recommended by Constable Hook.

"Would you care for a cigarette, Mr. Wong? Cigarette? You like? Good for nerves." (Again, he wonders what it is about the houseboy that causes him to talk like a Chinese immigrant.)

"Yes, please." Wong Chi accepts a smoke and a light.

"Please tell me where you're from."

"I come from China."

"I know that. But where in China? Where family?"

The houseboy submerges his shirt in the soapy water, sits on the stairs to the first floor and draws the smoke deep into his lungs, where it seems to do him good.

"Why you interested, Mr. McCurdy?" he asks.

WHO IS WONG SING CHI?
Ed McCurdy
Staff Writer
The Evening Star

Amid the torrent of facts, rumours and outright lies concerning the Janet Stewart case (it has become nearly impossible to tell the difference), surprisingly little is known about the Chinaman said to occupy a central position in the mystery— Wong Sing Chi, the houseboy at the Faulkner residence.

It was Wong Sing Chi who heard a shot fired, discovered the body and informed his employer. He was the Chinaman Miss Stewart is said to have feared, who gave her presents and referred to her as *Missy*. And yet, other than as a sworn witness, no reporter has taken the trouble to speak to the man himself.

Not that it was an easy task. Like most members of his race, Mr. Wong speaks a pidgin English lacking both connectors and modifiers, a patois consisting solely of nouns and verbs, not necessarily in the correct order.

Still, we persisted. It being a proven fact that the recognition of a language outstrips one's ability to speak it (even for native speakers of the King's English), it seemed reasonable to assume the same discrepancy among our foreign friends.

It became clear early in our interview that this is no pig-tailed coolie but an athletic, vigorous, educated man with a sense of propriety and style, who understands far more than he chooses to reveal. Always polite, he seemed to answer questions readily and without guile.

In a long and confusing interview, this reporter was able to glean the following facts:

Born in Kiangsu Province, somewhere between Nanking and Shanghai, Mr. Wong attended school in Suchow before emigrating to join relatives in British Columbia—cousin Wong Gow, a servant at the the Canacraig estate, and Wong Ling Sai Ken, another relative who has been in the employ of the lawyer Harry Stickler for nearly twenty years.

Four and a half years ago, Mr. Wong returned to China for an extended stay, and within a year married his fiancée and fathered a child.

At that time, his province suffered crop failures and political turbulence. After a year, like many Orientals, he realized that to support his family he must return to British Columbia. Having landed, he found a position as houseboy for the Faulkner family, and has been sending money to his wife ever since.

Seemingly, these facts should suggest it unlikely that, as a loyal family man, he would behave in a predatory way toward the nanny with whom he worked on a daily basis. It seems equally unlikely that, on a houseboy's salary, he could have afforded the expensive gifts he is said to have given Janet Stewart, while sending money home to China. (A Chinese houseboy earns as little as a third of what would be paid to a white servant.)

Of course, nothing will allay the suspicions of many that the houseboy is a murderer and that Chinamen are, in the words of the Attorney General, "a great influence for evil on white girls." Mr. Cunning can always be depended upon to lend substance to the public mood of the moment; in the current environment, facts, like servants' wages, are a devalued commodity.

28

The spectator sees more of the game than the player.

See me.
  V.N.

"This is complete and utter rubbish! It should never have made it to print! Explain yourself, boy! Explain to me why I shouldn't fire you at once, and why you're not writing for the *Chinese Times!*" General Newson's voice seems to rattle the windowpanes, and his jaw juts out even further than it did before; McCurdy wonders how he manages to chew.

"Sir, I realize that the piece is at variance with the paper's official position on Asian immigration, but I remember you saying that intellectual give and take is what gives a newspaper its pep."

"I'm not pleased at having my own words thrown back at me, lad."

"I apologize, sir, but there are other developments looming, developments suggesting that an over-reliance on the Chinaman-as-rapist theme might leave the *Star* out on a limb."

"Whatever do you mean by that? What sort of a limb?" Newson's eyes narrow at the prospect.

"Two things. One: that far less respectable papers have taken up the same theme. *The People*, which I don't have to tell you is the lowest sort of tabloid, has printed a story by a Dora Bates, an obvious pseudonym, who claims to be a close friend of Miss Stewart. According to Miss Bates, Wong Chi is a member of a secret society of Chinese villains who seduce girls by putting them in a trance, then addicting them to opium, then selling them as white slaves to traders from Hong Kong."

"I take it you mean that the sex-fiend angle is becoming shopworn."

"To put it mildly, sir. It could devalue *The Evening Star* by association with an inferior marque—a pity, when another bomb-shell is about to fall on Shaughnessy Heights that will blow the Armstrong campaign to kingdom come."

As expected, this is music to the general's ears. His smile has all the warmth of a wolf eel. "Another bombshell, you say? Rocket attack sort of thing? What sort of thing are we talking about?"

"It has to do with Armstrong's son-in-law."

"The so-called air ace? I've always viewed his record with suspicion."

"No, the other one. The so-called businessman."

"A slithery sort of chap, I should say. Please go on."

"I believe Frank Faulkner has been smuggling dope in partner-ship with a Chinese tong, and that Wong Sing Chi has been acting as an intermediary. This explains why the Faulkners protect him at every opportunity."

"Have you found *evidence* for this?" Newson's emphasis suggests a broad definition of the term.

"In my interview, Wong Chi mentioned two relatives who have resided in Vancouver for a long time. According to one of my police sources, the two Wongs mentioned are part of the Chee Kong Tong, the Chinese Freemasons, led by a man named Chung Young Lee. There is a photograph in the police files. I believe Mr. Chung and I once met. In fact, he gave me a lift in his car."

"The *Star* will want to take a balanced approach. In backing away from the Chinese angle, we don't want to appear pro-Oriental."

"Then tell Nathan Shipley to write another evil Chinaman piece—under his own byline this time. To produce balanced coverage and add pep."

"Shipley is a hack. If articles were written under your name—and I'm not saying there were—why would you think it was him?"

"Shipley is nothing if not consistent. Everything is at a cross-roads, and the future remains to be seen. At the same time, I agree that the argument itself would not have issued from Shipley's brain. It had to come from someone far more intelligent."

Flattery, followed by a veiled threat—establishing McCurdy as a man after Newson's own heart.

"I like the angle of attack you suggest, son. But I still don't see how it answers the main question: Who killed Janet Stewart?"

"With all the commotion over side issues, general, does anyone really *care* anymore?"

A VANCOUVER TRAGEDY
Nathan Shipley
Staff Writer
The Evening Star

Vancouver stands at a crossroads between action and inaction, and the consequences of inaction are already plain to see.

In a home in Vancouver, a man and his wife (for the sake of privacy we will call them the McKinleys) sit at either side of the kitchen table in a state of hopeless despair. The man stares with unseeing eyes at the floor, while the wife openly sobs into her handkerchief.

Only a week ago did they hear the news that their daughter has made a runaway marriage. For parents an elopement is always a shocking event, but there was something unusually sad about this instance. Their daughter, the apple of her father's eye and only eighteen, ran away and married a Chinaman. The horror of it turned them sick. Their girl, with her beauty, her daintiness, her gumption, has become Mrs. Wong Fu.

The wife went off in a dead faint when the letter came from Seattle, where their girl had gone to stay with a friend. Wong Fu was an old schoolmate, who helped their girl with her sums and won her gratitude.

For another week, nothing could lighten the misery and shame of her parents. They waited wretchedly for the next letter. But when a letter did come, in a dirty, unstamped envelope, it was more of a shock than the first:

Daddy, you must help me. Wong has four other wives and they are beastly to me. They watch me every minute. I can't go out alone. I think I am in Victoria but am not sure, there is something wrong with my thinking. Please come as quick as you can, Daddy, or I shall die.

What are they to do, when the official position is one of laissez-faire? Thanks to a do-nothing government, these good, hard-working people may never see their daughter again.

The government has begun to consider a piece of landmark legislation to establish and affirm that British Columbia is, at its heart, white and British.

Such legislation will come too late for the McKinleys.

It remains to be seen whether other white families can be spared the same fate.

AS MCCURDY CLIMBS the stairs to Chinese Heaven, he hears a newsreel concerning the opening of an Egyptian tomb. It sounds interesting, but by the time he reaches the mezzanine Egypt has been abandoned in favour of two young Americans who murdered their rich cousin in order to commit the perfect crime, "in the interests of science."

He pauses to listen to details of the case (he can never resist a true crime story), but just as he feels tempted to bring out his notebook, the program abruptly switches to a proposed solution to the Sasquatch mystery, in which the so-called monsters are revealed as an Indian band called Seeahtiks, a race of hairy aboriginals never under seven feet tall, some fully eight feet in height. Unnamed scientists in white lab coats attest to certain "facts": that the Seeahtiks hunt and kill their game entirely by hypnotism and that they deceive pursuers by ventriloquism, throwing their voices this way and that.

McCurdy listens as he hurries up the stairs to behold the goliaths onscreen; what he sees are the blurred shadows of huge two-legged creatures, or possibly men on stilts, striding clumsily between two trees. Suddenly it occurs to him that, if the printed word could be a pack of lies, and if photographs could be doctored, then the same could be done with newsreels—reporting nonexistent discoveries, threats and crimes, placing the viewer in a nonexistent universe...

Above his head, a horizontal cone of light shaped by a cloud of dust casts its beam on a new kind of window—a square, two-dimensional opening onto the wide world, real or created. In the end it doesn't matter which.

Turning to face the horizontal arc of the mezzanine, he can make out the round heads of a scattering of Chinese men; they aren't looking at the screen but seem to be conducting some sort of business.

Scanning the seats, he sees nobody resembling Constable Hook. He leans against a velvet seat back and waits for his eyes and his mind to adjust—a difficult task with the constant flickering glare on the other side of the balcony railing.

As the theatre becomes somewhat visible in the alternating

gloom and glare, he considers the loges just beyond the balcony, once the most expensive seats in the theatre, now dark and forlorn.

At last he can make out Hook's shadow, seated in the second loge to the left. *A cunning choice for a private meeting—how did he think of it?* Feeling his way along the fabric wallpaper, three wide steps take him down to the box, once a luxurious womb of velvet and gold-painted wood, now more like a tiny, musty, rotten boat.

"McCurdy. Good of you to see me on such short notice."

He takes the seat next to the constable and takes a closer look at his face. "By God, Hook, you shaved your moustache."

Constable Hook puts a forefinger to his upper lip as though checking it himself. "I did, yes. Most observant of you."

"A wise decision, I think. Facial hair isn't for everyone."

"If you don't mind, could we change the subject?" It's true that the moustache was a failure. The final blow occurred when Miss Hawthorn termed it *scratchy.* "Mr. McCurdy, we need to speak about your article. It was called 'Who Is Wong Sing Chi?' I only just took a look at it. Things have been hectic at the station."

"It was not a success with my employer, I'm afraid. Barely made it into print. For balance, Shipley wrote one under his byline, dictated by the general himself."

"You people do that sort of thing?"

"Journalists occupy a broad ethical spectrum."

"Seemingly."

"I must admit, using the name *Wong* for the villain was a nice touch on Shipley's part. The houseboy's family name becomes synonymous with Oriental lust."

"It's a very common name."

"All the better."

"In any case, your article about the houseboy proved to be of use."

"To whom?"

"To the case."

"You don't say."

"You quoted the houseboy saying that upon his arrival he was taken in by relatives. As it turns out, the relatives really do exist— in the Criminal Records sense. In fact, the VPD know them well."

"You're with the VPD now?"

"The Point Grey constabulary has no criminal records to speak of. For that we would have had to arrest criminals."

On the screen below and to the right, an item appears about

recent modern inventions: a wristwatch that unscrolls tiny maps; an automated erotic peep show; a gadget for massaging the eyeballs.

"Seemingly, a Chinaman can be a member of more than one tong at the same time. Wong Chi's uncles are Freemasons, but also members of the Hop Sing Tong, located in San Francisco, Seattle and, it seems, here. It's associated with a thug named Salt Water Goon."

"Wherever do they get these names?"

"Apparently Goon is a pillar of the drug trade. Such a lucrative business, now that there are more illegal drugs than ever before."

"Do you know, constable, I said something along those lines to General Newson. At the time I was making it up as I went along. But of course, just because somebody makes something up doesn't mean that it's untrue."

"It sounds as though the police should have a chat with the houseboy. McCurdy, you think he has enough English for an interrogation?"

"More than you might think, Constable Hook. In fact, I think he's been making fools of us all along."

29

He who rides a tiger is unwilling to dismount.

WONG CHI HAS been looking forward to a quiet night on his own.
The part-time nanny, Miss Hawthorn, is in charge of baby Emma.
Mr. and Mrs. Faulkner thought it best not to leave him alone with
the child—the devil knows what rumours might spread. And
the Faulkners can later point out that it does not frighten Miss
Hawthorn to be under the same roof as their houseboy, thereby
casting doubt on Cissie Braidwood's accusations.

Mr. and Mrs. Faulkner have gone to a political gathering at
Canacraig and will not return until late; he has locked the doors
and secured the downstairs windows, so there is nothing for him
to do until tomorrow morning, when he will assemble breakfast
and light the furnace. (Despite the summer weather, the house
can be chilly in the early morning.)

Nothing remains to bother or worry him other than the sick
feeling in the pit of his stomach that has been plaguing him since
the *xnoigsi* of Missy. He has no other explanation for the hollow
churn beneath his rib cage, the clenched fist in the belly, the
persistent image of red blood on the cement floor, other than the
memory of total helplessness. What could he do? What could a
Chinese contribute to the situation that would be acceptable to
the *gweilo*?

He finds no remedy for his feelings but sleep, the hours when
he is set free of the earth, when his soul leaves his body and
passes through a curtain of air, soaring into the dream universe.
In dreams he might encounter horrifying symbols (a black rain-
bow, a bear, a biting dog), but these seem preferable to the fears
of waking life in a land that is becoming more foreign the longer
he remains.

Situated just off the landing between the laundry room and

the main floor, his room consists of an army bed, a small dresser with a kerosene lamp, a wooden crate for laundry and that is all. The walls and bed frame have been painted war-surplus green and his bed smells like laundry soap. The floor is covered with worn linoleum whose pattern no longer makes sense, if it ever did.

An unlovely room. Still, the moment he closes the door this ceases to matter because, having no window, the room affords the most complete darkness outside the grave; it becomes no place in particular, an area of pure space, in which all outcomes are known...

He has nothing to distract him, yet he is unable to fall asleep. (Something tells him that if he slept, his dream would be an inauspicious dream.) Instead, he puts his mind in the realm of memory, the realm of lived events. He makes this excursion regularly, not just to preserve the past in his mind (who his people were, where he came from, what he did there), but to give his mind a rest from negotiating the peculiar perils of the New World.

The will to win, the desire to succeed, the urge to unlock one's potential: Confucius saw these as noble qualities, but Wong Chi does not think they hold the same significance here. Few *gweilos* came here because they wanted to unlock their potential—soldiers least of all. They had seen their potential. Most whites come because they want to escape—someplace else, somebody else, an unendurable condition.

He thinks of Suchow and his town, Chin, where it was normal to be Chinese, and where the rare sight of a *gweilo* (other than his tutor Sai Zhenzhu, some called her Miss Buck) would at first be taken for a ghost, until they drew close enough for a person to smell their *gweilo* scent.

A few things in Vancouver remind him of home. When he looks at a mountain sometimes he thinks of Dragon-In-The-Clouds, though without the stone Buddhas; the war memorials remind him that Suchow was a battlefield; the unusable stretches of sand at low tide remind him of the land surrounding his village, now that the Yellow River has chosen another route...

He closes his eyes and tries to doze off. He mocks himself for his monkey brain, his worrying.

What the universe delivers must be accepted. One works with what one has.

For Wong Chi, the inquest was a revelation. These *gweilos*

with their pronouncements of "good" and "bad," "right" and "wrong"—what did that explain? To go by what he saw and heard—nothing. Do the *gweilos* wish to live a harmonious life together? Seemingly not.

A place for everyone and everyone in their place. That was another thing Kong Fuzi would not have said had he lived in Vancouver. Or maybe he would instead have written, *No place for everyone, and nobody in their place.*

Wong Chi knows he is not the only out-of-place human being in Vancouver. In his years in the New World, he has not met a single person who felt they really belonged here, that they were *in* place. For the most part, they wander about alone and unconnected, like spiders without a web.

He reflects on home and on what he has left behind—how the story he told the newspaperman was almost true, with only some things missing. He reflects on what he might look forward to, should both his waking actions and his sleeping dreams be auspicious.

He falls into a light sleep. For a moment he flies to China, the Celestial Empire, his home...

HIS EYES OPEN wide when he hears the crash and sees the darkness shattered by a rifle butt, which literally splinters his door in half, and suddenly he is no longer in China but in his army cot in the New World, staring up at three men in white robes who wear what look to be pillowcases over their heads, with holes for eyes.

The leader continues to heave his axe at the splinters as though chopping firewood. More visitors in sheets appear but only one more can fit into the room; he too has hidden his face with a pillowcase. The second man squeezes past the man with the axe and pulls Wong Chi roughly to a seated position, tearing his undershirt, then twists him sideways and pushes him off the bed onto the linoleum floor, on his knees.

The leader holds the axe above his head, ready to chop. "Do you want it, Chink?" he whispers in Wong Chi's ear. "Do you want it right now?"

Go ahead, Wong Chi thinks. *Dying is not important. To die would be like turning off an electric switch...*

The hooded man with the axe swings the implement, narrowly missing his head and hitting the floor so hard that the handle breaks. Now the man steps outside to make room for a third pillowcase man who enters with ropes. The man who threw him off the bed reaches down and twists his arms behind his back, while the new visitor ties them at the wrist and above the elbow, almost pulling his shoulders out of their sockets and making his elbows stick out like the wings of a trussed chicken. The two men lift him to his feet and push him out the door; a third man ties a blindfold over his eyes and they march him downstairs, through the laundry room and out the back door.

30

Confusion is the planning of desperate men.

"Hello, operator speaking, SEymour exchange. Is this SEymour 335?"

"Here is SEymour 330. The Hotel Vancouver, operator speaking."

"Here is SEymour 120. I will connect you now."

SWITCH

"SEymour 330, are you there?"

"Yes. Hotel operator speaking."

"Here is Inspector Forbes Caddell of the Vancouver Police Department. He wishes to speak to the Attorney General, please."

"I will connect you now."

SWITCH

"Attorney General Cunning speaking."

"Hello, this is the hotel operator speaking. I have Inspector Caddell on the line. Do you wish to make this connection, sir?"

"I will take the call."

"I will connect you now."

SWITCH

"Here is Gordon Cunning speaking. Are you there?"

"Hello, Mr. Attorney General. Caddell here. I wish to bring you up to date on the Wong Chi disappearance."

"We will have to speak carefully."

"What do you mean, sir?"

"Let us say that I'm not confident the telephone is secure. Certain confidential matters have found their way into the press."

"Do you think it's the operator?"

"Very possibly, but there are so many operators, there is no telling which one—if indeed it's only one. For all we know, maybe they're all listening in at once."

"Would you prefer us to meet in person, sir?"

"Absolutely out of the question. We could be at the top of Mount

Seymour and we would be seen and probably heard. Speaking in very general terms, tell me how things stand at present."

"Well enough so far, sir. The Chinese Benevolent Association is convinced that the, the... What term should I use?"

"'The package' will do."

"They think the package has been... stolen. They are about to call an Indignation Meeting, whatever that is. I assured them the VPD is doing everything possible to find the package. Then Trotter of the Sun came to call and we advanced the theory that the package has run for it and tried to make it look like theft—the point being to steer public speculation in several directions at once."

"Excellent, Forbes. I look forward to these rumours. Max Trotter is not the sort of journalist to be hobbled by facts."

"And the other papers are pitching in as well. Already I have heard say that the, er, package, is dead. Some say bone fragments were found in a furnace—a detail from another case maybe four years ago, but it needs to be investigated. Another theory has it that the package is on its way to China on the Empress of Australia. So we contacted Customs. They wired the captain, who has ordered a search. As rumours multiply, to learn the truth will require a, a more thorough questioning in certain quarters."

"I will leave it to your discretion, inspector. But please remember, the last thing we want is a martyr."

31

Ghosts fear men more than men fear ghosts.

THE CAR LURCHES its way up and down a series of roads, either to a distant place or on a circuitous route to confuse the blindfolded man. Wong Chi is lying face down on the floor in front of the back seat, with a shoe pressed down on the small of his back. The foot trembles; the man who owns it is nervous.

Wong Chi does not feel nervous because he is certain they are going to kill him. The only question is when and how. Death is not the problem; it's the unfortunate preliminaries.

But the man with the foot on his back is not a killer. In addition to the tremor he exudes the odour of fear, on top of the usual rancid *gweilo* smell.

Wong Chi's shoulders ache from the ropes that hold his elbows behind his back; he cannot relax, and the trembling foot on his back will not allow him to move. To distract his mind from the present discomfort, he views the darkness before his eyes as infinite space through which to travel home, to the Celestial Empire...

Reality returns all too soon. The auto comes to a stop, the door opens and someone hauls him outside and onto his feet—too abruptly, for his legs collapse and he falls on his face in the dirt. Above him someone curses, then follows a bruising kick—hard enough, he suspects, to have cracked one of his ribs. As he gasps from another blow, he feels a sharp pain there.

Two men pull him to his feet, then lift him by the elbows up a set of steps and across what is probably a verandah, then through what sounds like a screen door into a room with a slippery linoleum floor. The room has the vinegar smell of a kitchen that has been recently cleaned.

In what could be the middle of the room, he is pushed onto a wooden chair and his arms are retied behind it. His ankles are lashed to the legs of the chair, so that now he is completely immobile. Someone behind him tears the blindfold off his face.

He finds himself in a room that was once a kitchen but is now completely empty, whose windows have been covered with black paper. By the light of a single kerosene lamp hooked to the ceiling, he sees he is surrounded by a tight circle of men in white robes and pillowcases. He can discern eyes through holes in the fabric. The eyes are moist like the eyes of fish. The only man without a mask is Foon Sien, the *egun* who served as interpreter at both inquests. He wears the same suit and vest, and his bowler hat. Wong Chi throws him a sharp, inquiring look. Foon Sien replies with a shrug: *What do you expect? This is my job. It's what I do to make a living.*

A pillowcase head leans close to his face and the man inside shouts: "Now listen, boy, we want to know one thing and you can go free: Who killed Miss Janet Stewart?"

"I am sorry. I do not know. It was morning, I was... b-batoes—"

"Bastard!" The man strikes the side of his head so hard that he topples onto the floor, chair and all. Luckily, he lands on the side where the ribs are not broken, but now he can hear nothing from his left ear other than a metallic hissing sound. The man bends down and yells accusations into his face in a voice that reminds him of one of the lawyers at the inquest: "You killed her, didn't you? You tried to roger her and when she wouldn't have you, you shot her with your boss's gun!"

"I to peel... for dinner, batatoes. I hear sound, loud sound like from car."

Another voice joins in. "You dirty Chink! You animal!"

More kicking. Because he is still tied to the chair his kidneys are protected, but his chest and face take a beating.

"Give me a gun and I'll put an end to the bastard!"

"I look out window but see no car. Early on I see Missy go down to laundry room..." The voice repeating the explanation is no longer his voice; Wong Chi has withdrawn far back in his mind where he crouches, observing everything.

The three men continue to kick him wherever they can find a place to kick.

"Missy iron clothes for baby Emma!..." His distant voice sounds like a child, crying.

More ribs broken. His attempts to explain only serve to

infuriate them more. His eyes will not open now. He thinks of his destination, his ancestors waiting for him...

Either the *gweilos* have become bored kicking the same man in the same places, or maybe they are just tired, or maybe he is asleep and can feel nothing. Or maybe he's dead.

HE IS NOT dead; he knows this because the voices are not from the celestial kingdom.

This isn't getting us anywhere.

I'm not game for this.

It's been two days. If we keep it up, we'll kill him.

Chinks can take pain way better than a white man. Ever heard of the death of a thousand cuts?

So what do you want, red-hot irons? Are we supposed to stick pins in his eyes?

We've been told we're not to make a mess of him. I don't know how many times I've said that.

Already he looks pretty bad.

So what do we do?

Take him upstairs and keep him awake. We take turns on guard. Sooner or later he'll talk.

Wong Chi takes stock of their conversation and is not encouraged. An incompetent torturer will only succeed in making a mess. The Five Punishments are specific and well known in China, but these punishments are for obtaining confessions to crimes, not for obtaining information. The *gweilos* do not understand the unreliability of information gathered by that means. Nor do they know just how hurtful it is to the soul to intentionally inflict pain on a helpless person. A certain kind of man can do this, but such men are born that way. It is not a job for a normal man.

After more discussion, two *gweilos* untie him and frog-march him upstairs to what looks to be an attic, whose window, like the kitchen windows, has been covered with black paper. Two *gweilos* put him in another chair while a third shackles him to a chain bolted to the floor. In the dim light he can make out a rocking chair in one corner containing another *gweilo* in a white sheet, cradling what looks like a cricket bat.

"If he goes to sleep, give him a good one," says one of his captors as they head downstairs, leaving him at the mercy of his solitary guard, in policeman's boots and swinging the cricket bat for practice.

WONG CHI POSSIBLY IN USA
Max Trotter
Staff Writer
The Vancouver Sun

The disappearance of Wong Sing Chi has the Vancouver Police Department on the horns of a dilemma: Did the murder suspect in the Janet Stewart case flee? Or has he been kidnapped?

Sources close to this reporter suggest the latter.

Notwithstanding, if the Chinaman has been kidnapped, who are his captors? Are they men who believe him to have murdered Janet Stewart? Do they intend to kill the Oriental as a form of frontier justice? Or do they wish to interrogate him until he reveals what he knows about the crime? Or was the axe handle found in his bedroom, together with the shattered door, intended to make it *seem* that the Chinaman had been abducted—a scenario consistent with the suspicious circumstances surrounding the death of Janet Stewart?

The answer may lie in a report by a sharp-eyed motorist who spotted the Chinaman, wearing a cap and a dark chinchilla overcoat, in the back seat of a large touring car, speeding to New Westminster.

From New Westminster, the auto was seen to cross the Fraser River Bridge to a point near the American border. Having been spirited across the line, the Oriental was met by a Seattle taxicab, waiting to pick him up and carry him south. The driver of that taxicab was a member of the biggest gun-running gang in the Northwest—notorious extortionists who plan to extract information from Wong Chi with which to blackmail the murderer.

Whether the Chinaman was abducted by gangsters, or whether he participated willingly, is up to the VPD to decide.

WONG CHI IS lying on the floor, on his side, still tied to the chair. After hitting him in the head and face with his cricket bat as if it were a practice ball, the *gweilo* returned to the rocking chair and sank into a torpid alcoholic slumber. Wong Chi also dozed off. He dreamt of monsters in pursuit, indicating an overheated system...

He opens his eyes. The man with the cricket bat has left the room. *How much time has passed?* He counts four teeth scattered in front of his face like tiny pebbles. He closes his eyes and goes back to sleep.

He is awakened by the cold, hard kiss of a gun pressed against his forehead. "You want the same treatment you gave Miss Stewart? Do you, boy?"

"It's in morning," he replies. "I to peel... for dinner, batoes... no..."

The finger pulls the trigger. *Click.*

"Lucky one, boy, try better next time."

"Like a car backfire. I go down to laundry, see Missy... Blood coming out of head, I go to Missy and listen to heart. She dead. I go to telephone..."

Click.

Wong Chi flinches, but not so much. He has begun to wonder if these are empty threats, if there are any rounds in the gun at all. As inexperienced as his abductors are, it seems more plausible that the *gweilo* with the pistol is not a heartless man, that he is only imitating one.

"Kill me, sir. Kill me and I will be dead and nothing will matter."

Again the man pulls the trigger, but this time he hesitates first. *Click.*

CAR CHASE LEADS TO STARTLING REVELATIONS
Max Trotter
Staff Writer
The Vancouver Sun

New information has surfaced concerning the mysterious disappearance of Wong Sing Chi, thanks to an alert private detective who claims to have witnessed the Chinaman bundled into the trunk of a car near Pender and Main Streets.

The agent, who must remain anonymous for fear of reprisals from both criminals and government officials, followed the speeding vehicle for several hours, to a site in the interior of the province not far from Ainsworth known as the Cody Caves.

At this point, the Chinaman was forced out of the trunk

and frog-marched into the woods toward the caves. Here the witness lost sight of the group. However it seems certain that he was taken to one of the many limestone caves in the area.

Further investigation by this reporter suggests that one of the Cody Caves may have been the hiding place where machine guns and German arms were later found by agents after the war, relics from the early days of the conflict when the Kaiser, hungry for British Columbia's natural resources, planned his great coup, and his chosen lieutenants stood in readiness for *Der Tag.*

Wartime officials chose not to disclose this shocking episode, so as not to frighten the general public and slow the recruitment drive. The episode remains a military secret.

The Janet Stewart case, and the abduction of Wong Sing Chi, may lead to a hitherto unsuspected threat from within— then and now.

"Hello, operator speaking, SEymour exchange. Is this SEymour 330?"
"Here is SEymour 330. The Hotel Vancouver, operator speaking."
"Here is SEymour 120. I will connect you now."
SWITCH
"SEymour 330, are you there?"
"Yes. Hotel operator speaking."
"Here is Inspector Forbes Caddell of the Vancouver Police Department. He wishes to speak to the Attorney General."
"I will connect you now."
SWITCH
"Attorney General Cunning speaking."
"Hello. Here is the hotel operator. I have Inspector Caddell on the line. Do you wish to make the connection, sir?"
"I will take the call."
"I will connect you now."
SWITCH
"Attorney General Cunning speaking. Are you there?"
"Here is Inspector Caddell. Just keeping you informed about the current situation."

Something in the inspector's voice tells the Attorney General that he won't like what's coming.
"I assume this is about the package."
"What package do you mean, sir?"

"*The package. For delivery. There is a need for privacy. We spoke of that earlier.*"

"*Yes, of course, the package. I am sorry sir, there have been new developments and I am run off my feet.*"

"*What new developments?*"

"*To put it straight to you, the, er, package has been released.*"

"*The package has been what?*"

"*Released, sir. Just an hour ago.*"

"*So I take it we must have what we need.*"

"*No sir, actually we don't. In fact, my colleagues were able to obtain no new information from the package.*"

Cunning's head begins to feel constricted, as though he is wearing a hat a few sizes too small. "*Then why in sweet Jesus—*"

"*No need for swearing, sir. It was a medical issue. The package incurred a severe injury. The team was required to call for medical assistance.*"

"*So what did your goons do to the package?*"

"*My colleagues—and I would ask you, sir, not to call them goons—they exercised their best judgment. If I remember, sir, you made some mention of the danger of martyrdom...*"

"*Inspector, don't shove my words in my face. What the hell happened?*"

"*Well sir, as I said, the subject incurred a number of injuries. The individual was unruly and abusive. Brought it on himself is the truth of it.*"

"*Inspector, don't take me for an idiot. Please hold the line while I attend to something.*"

The pressure in the Attorney General's head has moved to his chest, along with a general feeling of nausea. He pours himself three fingers of Scotch and drinks it down. It provides little relief.

"*Inspector, when your colleagues released the package, in whatever condition, where did it go?*"

"*Our determination is that a policeman found the package sitting in the middle of Point Grey Road.*"

"*A policeman. Thank God we have police.*"

"*Except that it wasn't a member of the VPD. It was a member of the Point Grey constabulary. Another case for amalgamation if you were to ask me, sir.*"

"*Damn your amalgamation, inspector, if you don't sort this out.*"

"*We are doing our best, sir. In any case, it seems that a Constable*

*Gorman ferried the package to the Point Grey constabulary and
called a Dr. Blackwell."*

*"Ah, Blackwell. A solid man, Blackwell, and a friend of the Liberal
Party. First good news I've heard so far."*

*"In the meantime, we have detained the package on charges. As
a lawyer, what do you suggest we charge him with, sir? Given his
condition, we'll want to keep him under wraps for awhile."*

*"Oh for God's sake, inspector, you created this situation. Do what
you think best."*

MILDRED TAKES A special delight in their primitive attempts at
coded discussion. During the war, she listened to exchanges that
could be mistaken for gibberish, but when translated and unpacked
would reveal casualty estimates far beyond what was reported
to the press, or unacknowledged risks presented by defective
equipment, or the fact that a suicidal charge, later described as
"unsurpassed in valour," had served no military purpose at all.

How she longs to broadcast what she heard over the wireless,
to be Howard's metaphorical bomb. Her fiancé was right about
that. And she has to admit that perhaps McCurdy deserves a
modicum of respect. With bodies buried in the mud, muckraking
can be good honest work.

And easy work, too. Compared to what she overheard at
Whitehall, these are schoolboys playing mumbly cat in the garden.

"Hello, operator speaking, SEymour exchange. Is this SEymour 152?"

*"You let the telephone ring fourteen times, operator. I counted
every one of them."*

*"I am told this is an urgent call, sir. With whom am I speaking,
please? Are you Mr. McCurdy?"*

*"Here is Logan Price, and I'm tired. My door is next to the hall
telephone. I'm not McCurdy and I'm not his receptionist either."*

"The call is urgent, sir. We thank you for your co-operation."

"I hope you go to hell."

"Thank you, sir. I will hold..."

Left to dangle by its wire, the telephone bangs against the wall
several times.

"Here is Ed McCurdy. Are you there?"

"Here is SEymour exchange, I have a Miss Wickstram on the line."

SWITCH

"Eddie? Are you there? Because I have something to sell."

32

A man's enemies are not demons, but human beings like himself.

THIS HAD BETTER be good. More important, it had better be worth five dollars.

McCurdy climbs out of the taxi in front of the Point Grey constabulary (half-timbered in the British style, to fit into the neighbourhood), pays the driver through the window and recognizes the two-tone Cadillac Opera Coupe parked outside as belonging to Dr. Blackwell, who never seems to be far away when there's a situation involving the Faulkners. Next to the battered Ford police car he is pleased to see Hook's motorcycle, knowing that the constable will be available for later reference.

Inside, it seems that the houseboy's appearance has roused even Chief Quigley, who has climbed out of his bed and into his dress uniform, for photographic purposes. At present he is standing outside the open door of his office, in close conference with Dr. Blackwell, Constable Gorman and Constable Hook; hearing McCurdy close the door, all four gentlemen turn simultaneously and conversation stops as though turned off by a tap. "I'll see you down to the cells, doctor," Gorman says, casting a baleful look at McCurdy, and the two disappear down a set of stairs at the far end of the outer office.

He greets the remaining two policemen, careful not to give the slightest hint of a prior acquaintance with Hook. "Good evening, officers. McCurdy of *The Evening Star.*"

Chief Quigley grimaces, as though a foul smell has wafted into the room. "This is police business. What in hell are you doing here?"

"I have received a report that the Chinaman has been found. In journalism, the early bird gets the worm."

"Very clever of you, I'm sure. Give me a moment, would you?"

The chief disappears into his office and almost immediately returns with a handwritten sheet of paper, which he hands to Constable Hook.

"Mr. Hook, we have a prepared statement. Be so good as to read this to Mr. McCurdy. And there will be no questioning. Do not elaborate, and that is an order." Quigley's face has become blotched as though allergic to the possibility of questions. He turns on his heel and returns to his office, leaving the door open so that he will not miss a word.

Hook clears his throat, feeling like an idiot: "At approximately twelve midnight, the officer on telephone duty received a call from a citizen to the effect that a man was staggering about at the lower end of Point Grey Road near Marine Drive. By coincidence, Constable Gorman, who was off-duty at the time, happened to be parked nearby. The person wandering down the road turned out to be Wong Sing Chi. The man was injured and in a confused state. Constable Gorman then drove the Chinaman to the constabulary, locked him in a cell and notified Dr. Blackwell, who came at once."

Constable Gorman, having surfaced from the cells and seeming to take issue with this version of events, takes over the briefing. "That is incorrect, Mr. Hook," Constable Gorman says. "It was not coincidence in the least, nor was I off-duty. While on patrol I was stopped by a motorist who reported a man who was either drunk or insane, and possibly dangerous. I acted in the interests of public safety."

Hook massages one temple, as though he has a headache. "Mr. Gorman, I am reading the official statement from Chief Quigley. If you wish to dispute his account..."

"You are reading it in a sarcastic tone, Mr. Hook. It creates an entirely wrong impression..."

Chief Quigley has re-emerged from his office, sensing that the briefing has gone awry. "Suffice it to say that the arrest was made in an exemplary manner by one of our best men."

"Does that suit you, Gorman?" Hook says.

Gorman is about to retort when Dr. Blackwell emerges from the cells below. He is about to accompany the chief into his office when the main doors open and another officer appears, whom McCurdy recognizes as Inspector Forbes Caddell of the Vancouver Police Department, along with a rotund man with a wary squint and the ears of a small Indian elephant. Like the chief, Caddell is in full uniform as though prepared to pose for photographs. "Good evening, gentlemen. Chief Quigley, I am informed of a break in the Janet Stewart case. Please bring us up to date at once."

The blotches on Quigley's face merge into one deep red stain. "Inspector, I'm afraid you are out of your jurisdiction—and out of order as well. Please be so good as to—"

"Chief Quigley, you are quite mistaken. At this time I am not acting in my capacity with the VPD, but as official consultant to Judge Condon here—who has been assigned to the case by the Attorney General. Show us into your office, would you, so that we can speak privately." Caddell casts a withering look in McCurdy's general direction.

Judge Condon leads the three policemen and the doctor into Chief Quigley's office and sits behind the desk as though it were his own. The door shuts, but almost immediately Constable Gorman emerges and heads back downstairs to the cells.

Moments later, Gorman reappears, escorting, or rather assisting, Wong Chi up the stairs, across the floor and into the chief's office. McCurdy is shocked by his appearance. His face is swollen almost beyond recognition and has a sickly green pallor. His clothing has stiffened with dried blood.

The door to the office closes again. Momentarily, McCurdy wonders whether the interrogation is to continue, followed by a charge of "attempted escape."

A pause, then Constable Hook reappears wearing an exaggeratedly official expression. "Sir, this is a delicate police matter and I'll have to ask you to leave the premises."

McCurdy speaks in a voice loud enough to be heard throughout the building: "Certainly, officer. Glad to co-operate, and thank you for your assistance."

As they reach the door, Hook whispers: "The silly buggers have charged the Chinaman with murder."

PROTESTS RING HOLLOW AFTER WONG CHI ARREST
Interrogation Produces Valuable Clues
Max Trotter
Staff Writer
The Vancouver Sun

Chinatown is in a ferment of propaganda concerning the

Wong Chi arrest for murder, whipping up sentiment against white authorities supposedly responsible for this "miscarriage of justice."

The Chinaman's lawyer, Mr. Harry Stickler, is likewise crying outrage at the fact that the suspect has been held incommunicado at Oakalla Prison. For their part, officials at the prison assure the public that he is physically fit but mentally confused and unable to give a clear account of himself, despite the presence of a capable interpreter, Mr. Foon Sien.

To these complaints, Attorney General Cunning has answered thus: "He is to be held incommunicado only until we have time to catch our breath. The investigation continues, quietly and persistently, led by Inspector Caddell of the Vancouver Police. It is a difficult process because of the many rumours that have caused embarrassment and delay. We do not wish to compound the confusion by opening the gates to further speculation."

To this, Inspector Caddell added the following: "I assure you that the arrest was no accident. It was undertaken by the Vancouver constabulary, as a result of efforts by myself and the Attorney General's department."

According to unofficial sources, a private detective agency carried out the initial abduction, paid for by a concerned citizen who wishes to remain anonymous. It is safe to say that the Chinaman had a lively time of it, so that justice might be served.

In the process, constant questioning and the application of the third degree produced invaluable information. From a reliable authority, this reporter has learned that officials expect to be able to show a jury that Wong Chi fired the bullet that killed Janet Stewart, thereby clearing the case once and for all.

33

When legs fail you, fight on your knees.

OF ALL HIS humiliations as a poet, McCurdy's worst was the note from Macmillan.

He hoped that the lateness of the publisher's response indicated interest, or at least indecision; on the contrary, their response was as clear and cold as ice:

Thank you for your submission. Unfortunately, it is not for us. Cordially, A. Miller, Assistant Ed.

Condescension wafted from the typesheet like dime-store perfume. How he would have liked to throttle A. Miller and pluck out his eyes! But no. Writers are expected to deal with rejection the way a seal shrugs off sea water. Did Melville, Proust, Joyce and Poe grind their teeth to powder over letters such as this?

Yes. They probably did.

But there comes a point when a writer grows bored with the injustice theme—an unfair advantage, a prejudicial elite, the conviction that his rejection is someone else's fault; a sense of injury that develops into a form of masochism in which the stooge serves up both his back and the knife with which to stab it.

And for what reward? An obscure literary prize, a sale of a hundred copies, a royalty cheque for five dollars? Sour grapes, possibly, but true nonetheless.

In a sense, this perfunctory rejection of his latest, much improved verse has done McCurdy good, in that the question "Why write poetry?" has become "Why *publish* poetry?"—especially when opportunities present themselves for an adept writer, publications in which it is the writer who cracks the whip.

Poetry is an antique medium; the future, for good or ill, is in newspapers.

As he explains this to Miss Wickstram, he finds it unnerving that she offers no counter-argument, no stiff-upper-lip anecdote, no reference to yellow streaks and white feathers, no shirker accusation, no authenticity lecture.

She watches her cigarette as though it held the answer: "Which is better, do you think, in the scheme of things—a muckraker or a poet?"

"Well, to begin with, a lot of poetry is muck."

FOR SOLDIER AND working man alike, change is never gradual. You sneak a glance over the parapet and suddenly you're a monster that frightens the children. The soldier lights a cigarette and suddenly he has no head, or steps on a land mine and suddenly he could be spread on a sandwich. He comes home a hero and suddenly he's just another bum.

As a civilian, McCurdy's version of change was gentle by comparison. A week after receiving his rejection letter, still seething with resentment, he began to reread the manuscript—objectively, analytically, as though it had been written by someone else; and suddenly he found himself in complete agreement with A. Miller, Assistant Ed., Macmillan & Co. Were he an English teacher he might have given the work a B, neither spectacularly good nor spectacularly bad, a notch or two above average; worth pursuing, but useful only to oneself and perhaps a few indulgent friends.

Seated at the table across from him in the Ladies & Escorts Club at the Alhambra Hotel, Miss Wickstram wears a non-smile of mixed emotion, and a terrible thought occurs to him: When she championed his submission, did she know he would be rejected? Is Miss Wickstram a sadist? Or did she want to set him free?

He contemplates this curious woman as she drags on a cigarette, blows a smoke-circle with Cupid's-bow lips, then looks downward as though worried about her gin fizz. Meanwhile to McCurdy's right, well into the muggle, Sparrow stares into his half-full beer glass with his good eye.

Change is in the air.

In Sparrow's mind the bubbles in his glass become steam and a train is shuddering away from the station with one passenger car containing a lone passenger: him.

Decisions were easy during the war, if only because you made so few of them. Mostly someone ordered you to do something and you did it. You might be killed, but at least you didn't have to decide whether going out and getting killed was worth doing.

Civilians will never understand how life in war makes for a stable, uncomplicated existence, however short. To the men in service, the war *was* life, the world, the only place to be. Each day Sparrow put on the same uniform, took orders from the same ranks, drove to the same battlefront and separated the same dead from the same wounded. (The dead all looked the same if they looked like anything at all; the wounded required the same sequence of procedures.)

Then the war ended, and suddenly a man is required to make decisions with insufficient information—or worse, suddenly discovers that he has already made a decision without knowing it, has taken orders from some inaccessible part of the brain.

The train, with Sparrow in it, disappears.

McCurdy sips his planter's punch, which is inferior to the houseboy's concoction: "I hope the both of you realize we're infecting the entire room with melancholy. Even the bartender is down in the dumps."

No response from Sparrow. Miss Wickstram lights a cigarette and closes a curtain of smoke. Another long silence engulfs the table, broken by the creak of wicker, the click of lighters firing up and the liquid murmur of cocktails consumed.

Finally Sparrow speaks, *sotto voce*, as though confiding a secret: "I need to take a p-piss." Without looking at either of them, he sidles past the two salesmen at the next table in striped suits and two-tone shoes, conferring with two young women wearing cloche hats and denture-like smiles.

McCurdy returns his gaze to Miss Wickstram, whose neglected cigarette languishes in the ashtray, sending aloft the acrid fragrance of burning rubber. Interpreting her expression, McCurdy faces three possibilities: that she is suffering from an allergy, that she has caught a cold or that she is crying. But not sobbing: her face remains perfectly composed despite intermittent teardrops, like a miracle Madonna in a Spanish cathedral.

Aware of his gaze, she picks up her cigarette and puffs heartily, with the defiant yet resigned look of someone who saw something coming, and here it is.

McCurdy fans away the wall of smoke. Now she is watching

him: *Do you have anything to say? I thought not.* He averts his gaze to the wall decorations in the Ladies & Escorts Club: antlered heads of deer, bears, moose, big-horned sheep, bison and mountain goats, as though a local hunter has taken it upon himself to kill every large animal in British Columbia. These trophies hang among murals depicting canals, stone bridges and open, pastoral valleys, suggesting an idealized European countryside—a land with no mosquitoes.

Miss Wickstram dabs at one eye with a handkerchief. "You're being patronizing, looking away like you're embarrassed or something."

"No, I'm being polite. Try to see the difference."

"Whichever one it is, stop it."

"I will if you'll put out your cigarette."

"Didn't you know? Girls are permitted to smoke in public these days."

"Yes, and you're allowed to fart in public as well."

After a moment's thought, she drops her cigarette into her cocktail glass. "There. Is that better?"

"Actually, it smells worse than when it was lit."

He faces her across the table in a spirit of negotiation, of give and take. The first item is to verify the facts: "Howard told me he was thinking of relocating—he seeks other opportunities, that sort of thing. I get the impression that you'll not be going with him."

"I'm not invited. I'm not relevant."

"So it's back to the revolution?"

"I don't think so. He'd like to be there, but mostly it's about the eye. It's seeing someone else."

"That is a witty remark."

"No, it's a literal observation. He mentions her more often now, as though preparing me for something. Plus-wise, well, if you've been there before, you know when you're there again."

"Yes. There's a sameness to rejection. The feeling that you don't exist. *Sorry, you're not for us.*"

"In this case, *Sorry, you're not for me.*"

"Yes. But it's the same thing, somehow."

They both stare into their drinks as though they contained some sort of message. "Do you mind if we change the subject, Eddie?"

"Gladly. You first, Millie."

"How is the Chinese houseboy doing?"

"According to the medical report he has broken ribs, a fractured skull, a punctured eardrum, several missing teeth and a dislocated shoulder, as well as various bruises and contusions. In yesterday's *Sun*, Trotter described him as 'confused but in good physical condition'—which is true, for a man who's been tortured for nearly a week and then charged with murder."

"You realize that there is not the slightest chance that the houseboy will be convicted—at least, if evidence means anything anymore."

"So it would seem, unless the VPD has an ace up its sleeve."

"More likely a case of command dementia. I witnessed it myself in the upper ranks during the Somme offensive, the 1918 version. They're run out of ideas. They're down to their brain stems. Frankly, it's a pleasure listening to them."

"You're saying that the houseboy's trial is like flipping over a flat rock, just to see what crawls out from underneath?"

"Quite. Very good, Eddie. Not that there is a plan per se; just another mind-bubble from overpaid, stupid men, flailing about..." She trails off as though detecting something in the air: "He's coming back. I'm afraid I have to leave."

McCurdy wonders, *does everyone but me have a sixth sense*?

She rises. "It's the eye. It's starting to give me the creeps."

McCurdy tries to imagine life without Sparrow: "Could we stand it, just the two of us, in Vancouver, staring across a table, you blowing smoke in my face—with no stutterer to intervene?"

The edges of her mouth (impeccably drawn) turn somewhat upward. "Relations between people are mostly about circumstance, don't you think, Eddie?"

"Yes. I remember someone saying something of the sort. In fact, I think it was me."

SPARROW RESUMES HIS seat, just as Miss Wickstram hits the street. "Where is she off to?"

"Away from you, apparently."

"Change seldom happens smoothly, Ed."

"So I've noticed."

"She assumed I would b-be here forever. Always a mistake in these unsettled times."

"Especially when the gentleman is after a phantom artist somewhere in France."

"It's not Mademoiselle Petard I'm chasing. It's something else."

"What?"

"I don't know. Do you?"

"Do I what?"

"Do you know why you do things?"

"Other than out of pure self-interest, every once in a while a sort of common decency comes over me. And you?"

"I like a good fight. The coal miners—two million strikers from John O'Groats to Land's End. Government goons and armed b-blacklegs on the docks. There's another war on, matey, might as well join up."

"A strike on that scale will require many ambulances. It's a wonder you haven't gone already."

"I don't like to leave things hanging. A dead girl is counting on us to... do something."

"I quite agree. Annoying, isn't it? So what are we to do?"

Sparrow rolls a cigarette with one hand and lights it with the other; the smell is of cheap tobacco and not muggle. "I didn't go to the bog. I was on the pay phone, doing you a favour. I called a few people about a story going around the limo and taxi drivers. B-By the way you owe me eight nickels."

"This had better be good. Rumours go two for a cent in this town."

"Except that this one is true. I know it."

"How? How do you know?"

"Why do you always ask that?"

"Of course. You've had another mind-bubble. Case closed."

"Remember, just b-because it's a rumour doesn't mean it's a lie."

"You're trying my patience, Howard. Please go on."

Sparrow leans forward and exhales, giving his asthmatic friend the full benefit. "The word is out among the drivers—ambulance drivers, even the truck drivers eating lunch at Atkinson's Diner— that Jock West is in the b-bug house. He was raving like a lunatic. My chap says they had to p-put a straitjacket on him."

"They took him by ambulance?"

"Hired a Cadillac limousine. The driver worked at Canacraig."

"We must go to Essondale at once. I'll get a taxi."

"No p-point. Only family members allowed. No reporters admitted—especially not you. Is it true you were macking on Mrs. Faulkner and she slapped your face and threw you out?"

"Another rumour, Howard. What a surprise."

34

When you know there are tigers, don't go there.

IT BEGAN AS soon as they sat on the Faulkners' capacious chesterfield, the kissing, and now they are horizontal and it's barely mid-morning. Hook had planned only for a pleasant conversation and can scarcely believe his good luck.

He has managed to slip his hand beneath her blouse, where he discovers neither a corset nor even a liberty bodice, as was always the case with English girls; instead she is wearing what feels like a knotted kerchief covering her two breasts separately and lifting them by means of straps, which explains their prominent shape despite their exquisite softness. It excites him almost beyond endurance. He slides his hand beneath the fabric and touches her nipple with trembling fingers; her breathing becomes a soft purr as he kisses her neck just below the earlobe.

Sick with desire, his rigid penis pressed against her thigh, his temples throbbing with blood, he feels beneath her skirt with his free hand, up her thighs to her knickers (shorter than the English kind), which elicits a soft groan, then he feels underneath...

As though he just pricked her with a sharp object, Miss Hawthorn sits bolt upright, pushes him away with both hands and deals him a stinging slap across the face.

Clearly he has gone too far. He knows this now.

"I don't know what kind of a girl 'tis you think I am, but unless you watch your manners you'll find out pretty quick! I am a decent girl who intends to marry a gentleman and I will have no truck with anything less—and you a policeman, for mercy's sake!"

Suddenly she grows icily distant, arms folded over her bosom. She could be looking at him from a lifeboat while his ship goes down.

"I sincerely apologize, Miss Hawthorn. I became carried away by the moment and took liberties I had no business taking. If you'll please forgive me, I promise you it will never happen again."

She performs an almost imperceptible shrug, as though to say, *Well, what do you expect? He is, after all, male.* "I accept your apology Mr. Hook, but I will hold you to your word. And if it happens again—"

"Believe me, Miss Hawthorn, I would rather shoot myself."

"Fine."

He catches himself marvelling at her pride in herself, her sense of personal destiny as a human being who could bear children and could love a man until they both died.

"In any case, Mr. Hook, we should put ourselves in order. Mrs. Faulkner is shopping and could return at any moment."

"And is Mr. Faulkner at his office? It is, after all, Saturday."

"He is overseeing a shipment of furniture for his export business. It's to be delivered to a warehouse on East Hastings Street."

"A warehouse, did you say?" Hook can barely refrain from reaching for his notebook, which would be poor form under present circumstances.

"Heard him myself, I did, giving directions on the telephone. He said something about a gorilla, which made nae sense at all. I wasn't eavesdropping, mind, the baby and I were in the same room, couldn't help meself hearing."

"God bless you, Miss Hawthorn."

He holds her close. With one strong hand she grips the front of his trousers. Her blouse smells like rain.

AS HOOK'S MOTORCYCLE crosses Granville Bridge toward Hastings Street, the rain feels needle-fine and soft as cotton as it drifts through a watery sun. The breeze feels summer warm and smells like damp newspapers. Heading north, he speeds past unemployed men loitering on the sidewalk like figures made of damp papier mâché, useless for work that requires a sound mind or body and called "loafers" by Mayor Owen, an ex-blacksmith who likes to muse about creating a "civic rock-pile."

Avoiding the slippery streetcar tracks, he turns up Hastings Street, passes the Amputees Association, then Mrs. Olsen's Rooming House and Leonard's Cafe. East of Main Street, blocks of Chinese vegetable and grocery stores, then a series of storage sheds, then a factory—home of Gorilla, a company that manufactures logging equipment. Next door to the factory sits an inconspicuous wooden building with a false front, with no sign in front or over the entrance, more like a pioneer post office than something you find in the warehouse district near the water.

He pulls up, switches off his engine and plants the kickstand in the hard dirt beside a set of wide wooden steps. The narrow front door is unlocked and, like the entire facade, windowless.

The interior turns out to be much larger than it appeared from outside, an enormous rectangular space with walls painted white, like a huge icebox containing stacks of antique furniture along one wall. Across the room on the other side of the loading bay, four Chinese men are in the process of stripping chairs and chesterfields down to their frames; along another wall, hardwood skeletons have been neatly piled opposite the finished antiques. Nearer the loading bay is a huge bin containing mouldy horsehair and stained fabric awaiting disposal. In the far back corner, crates have been stacked with *Faulkner and Partners* stencilled on one side.

Hook notices the absence of replacement stuffing and fabric; perhaps that part of the work remains to be done elsewhere, or maybe the material is to be delivered later. He imagines a team of Chinese women arriving at sundown and working throughout the night sewing soft packages into the upholstery.

Whatever is going on, there is not much he can do about it. The VPD is unlikely to devote man-hours on a stakeout, based solely on the opinion of Constable Hook of the Point Grey constabulary.

One of the Chinese workers sees him standing by the door and quickly withdraws into what looks to be a back office. Being unarmed, out of uniform and out of bounds, Hook deems it prudent not to initiate a meeting, especially when a man emerges from the office who is the tallest Oriental he has ever seen and whose muscular arms remind him of gantry cranes.

Hook turns smartly, hurries outside, kickstarts his machine and heads toward Main Street.

He is halfway past a block of greengrocers when a roadster just behind him honks a repeated *ayooga*, telling him to speed up despite the fact that he is already doing thirty miles per hour. He does a shoulder check: as though prodding him forward, the Studebaker's front bumper and swan ornament are perhaps two feet behind his fender. He accelerates to full throttle, weaving around traffic at Main and Hastings—and his front tyre blows.

On a straight path, the machine could be safely brought to a halt, albeit with difficulty, but in mid-turn it immediately begins to fishtail so that steering becomes impossible. Having no other option at this speed, he dumps the machine on its side, lifting his lower leg while grasping the seat and handlebars, while the machine spins beneath him like a top, until a rough patch in the cobbled road surface causes him to lose his grip, fly off his machine and skip along the street like a stone on a pond (thankfully away from oncoming traffic), coming to rest on his back beneath a parked taxi in front of Cunningham Drugs.

For what seems like a long time he lies on the cobbles, waiting for the world to stop spinning, staring at the taxi's undergear inches above his face and mentally checking for injuries; turning his head carefully he sees his goggles, which, miraculously, remain unbroken.

To his left, the wheels of the Studebaker pull up beside him and come to a stop. The door opens and a pair of slippered feet appear, the footwear favoured by Chinese workers. Hook twists his head sideways at an odd angle and stares into space with half-closed eyes—imitating, as best he can, a man with a broken neck. He envisages Janet Stewart, on the laundry floor, eyes staring into the distance. He holds still... A pause. Someone kneels on the road, bends over and peers beneath the taxi, then stands, apparently satisfied that Hook is either dead or satisfactorily injured. A moment later the door slams shut, the Studebaker continues on its way and Hook is left to assess the damage.

IT TAKES HIM the rest of the day to sort things out. He feels lucky that there is anything left to sort.

After a trip in the back of an ambulance with suspension comparable to a troop carrier, then a cursory examination by a pathetically overworked resident, Hook makes his way out of St. Paul's Hospital with a cracked rib and a sprained wrist, keenly aware that it could have been much worse, and that whoever was driving the Studebaker would have preferred it that way.

What saved Hook from more serious injury or death were his attempts, all those years ago on the roads near Waldo, to imitate tricks performed by the daredevils at the Pacific Exhibition.

Education is a good thing. One never knows what will come in handy.

At present he doesn't feel particularly daredevilish. It hurts to breathe, and clearing his throat sends sharp spikes of pain down his chest. Laughing would be utter misery if he were in a humorous mood.

On the front steps, however, he experiences an unexpected brain wave that causes him to return to the nurse behind the registration desk. "I beg your pardon, nurse, but I wonder if I could make an inquiry?"

She gives him a look utterly devoid of curiosity, a woman in her sixties with plum-coloured circles beneath her eyes who has heard every imaginable request, many times over.

"I wish to ask about a patient. His name is John Lake. I expect you have him on record."

"Sir, you understand of course that a patient's privacy is—"

He produces his identification card: "Constable Hook of the Point Grey Police."

She examines it as though it might be counterfeit. "And you *are* on police business?"

"Most assuredly, madam."

She frowns slightly at the inconvenience, reaches for a ledger with alphabetical tabs stuck at intervals and leafs through pages under the letter *L*. Her finger stops partway down: "I have a John Lake—yes. In fact, I remember him signing out; it was some time ago. You may inform the family that his injuries were significant but not life threatening. The result of a beating, apparently." She shuts the book with a decisive slap. "That's all I can tell you, officer, without either a warrant or permission from a direct family member; a patient's privacy is, as you know..." She regards him with the official expression he has seen before when making unwelcome inquiries: *Why are you still here?*

"Only one more question, nurse. When he checked out, did Mr. Lake say where he was going?"

"As I recall, he didn't say anything. You see, his jaw was wired shut."

Constable Hook tips his hat and hobbles out of the hospital in good spirits; remembering a fistful of skinned knuckles, he mentally closes the file on Arthur Dawson and John Lake.

AT CUNNINGHAM DRUGS, a sympathetic clerk calls a flat-bed truck, which soon arrives for his motorcycle; then a taxi takes him to Fred Deeley Motorcycles on Broadway.

Another stroke of relatively good luck: he spilled on the left side of the BSA, the side that normally holds a sidecar, so that the twin tailpipes are undamaged—unlike his scorched, ripped trousers and jacket. In fact, as it turns out, the motorcycle is in acceptable running order, with only a series of unsightly scratches along the tank and fenders.

According to the repairman, someone tampered with the front wheel. The tyre tube had a three-inch split along the seam, directly beneath a weak spot in the tyre itself. Something or someone had scraped the tyre down to its paper-thin lining. At speed on a cobbled road, the tube pressure would push the thin rubber onto the cobbles and a few minutes of hard riding would cause it to blow.

This sabotage could easily have been accomplished in the minutes Hook spent inside the warehouse. But to do this they would have to have been prepared for his arrival.

Put another way, he was expected. Miss Hawthorn overheard Faulkner's telephone conversation because she was meant to.

35

It is more difficult to hide what one knows than to hide what one does not know.

"Hello, operator speaking, TRinity exchange. Is this SEymour 330?"

"Here is SEymour 330. The Hotel Vancouver, operator speaking."

"Here is TRinity 320. I will connect you now."

SWITCH

"SEymour 330, Hotel Vancouver, are you there?"

"Here is Inspector Caddell. I wish to speak to Attorney General Cunning, please."

"I will connect you, now."

SWITCH

"Hello, are you there?"

"Here is the operator speaking. Is this Suite 1420?"

"Suite 1420. Gordon Cunning speaking."

"Here is Inspector Caddell. Do you wish to make the connection?"

"I will speak to him."

"I will connect you now."

SWITCH

"Inspector, are you there?"

"Here is Caddell, sir. It's about our package."

"And which package is that?"

"The yellow one, sir—the package we discussed before it was... returned."

"Jesus Christ, inspector, you've got to tone this business down. The Orientals are in an uproar. Even the Chinese consulate has horned into it."

"Yes, I spoke to them yesterday. They refuse to accept our interpretation of events, and subsequent actions—holding, er, the package, incommunicado and so on."

"Damn it, do they not want to see a murderer caught and punished?"

"*Frankly, sir, they think we mean to hang the fellow no matter what.*"

"*Nonsense, inspector. This is the British justice system, not some kangaroo court.*"

"*Yes, sir. And with that in mind, one of the tongs hired Harry Stickler once again to defend, or should I say protect, the package. As you well know, sir, Stickler is well named. Nothing gets past him.*"

"*Excuse me a moment, would you?*"

"*Certainly, sir.*"

The Attorney General splashes another three fingers into his glass and drains it in one merciful swallow. The office chose Jollimore as Crown counsel, who hasn't lost a trial in two years—*except* to Harry Stickler. It's well known that Stickler has a way of unnerving Jollimore, of putting him off his game.

"*Inspector, are you still there?*"

"*I am here, sir. I wonder, do you think it possible to replace Crown counsel?*"

"*With the trial in a fortnight? That would be a wee bit transparent, don't you think?*"

"*Or maybe Mr. Jollimore could have some reason to withdraw—an unfortunate accident, maybe.*"

"*Inspector, I think we have gone far enough in that direction, given the results achieved.*"

"*If you say so, sir. It seems our, er, package has a relative who works for Stickler, a long-time employee so to speak. Seemingly, Stickler has developed a fondness for Chinamen.*"

"*So out of the goodness of his heart, Stickler is working pro bono? That would be a first.*"

"*No sir, the Chinese consulate has put up a good deal of money. I understand they're prepared for an international incident.*"

The Attorney General pours more whisky, this time until it slops over the rim of his old-fashioned glass. His head aches from the effort of imagining the bleakness of his future.

JANET STEWART CASTS A LONG SHADOW
Public Becoming Cynical about Government Itself
Ed McCurdy
Staff Writer
The Evening Star

The upcoming trial of Wong Sing Chi and the official missteps that preceded it have inspired a new level of cynicism in the mind of the man in the street.

To the stench of burners and fish plants has been added the unmistakable smell of mendacity. Like other bad smells of human origin, its source is not immediately apparent because nobody will own up. The trial of the Chinaman, sure to be sensational entertainment, is equally certain to fall far short of answering the myriad questions that have followed in Janet Stewart's wake—casting doubts about the province's leadership and, indeed, its entire political and legal apparatus.

Meanwhile, in the absence of trustworthy information, a renewed flood of imaginative reports pour in from near and far, which nobody can refute with certainty.

Inevitably, the wild party tales have come to life again, along with the rumour that guests were sniffing cocaine, injecting morphine and playing Russian roulette; not to mention the mysterious involvement of Scotland Yard, and even a Masonic connection—that the Attorney General, a high-degree Freemason, arranged for Wong Chi to be charged in order to protect a fellow Mason in Shaughnessy Heights.

The phantom party is said to have included a who's who of British Columbia, including the reputedly drug-addicted daughter of none other than General Hector Armstrong. (According to a highly placed official, the general plans to stand for election in the fall.)

Almost certainly, there is not a shred of truth to any of these rumours. At the same time, is it more believable that a houseboy murdered the nanny one morning after breakfast, while she was ironing baby clothes?

Certain Vancouver newspapers have tied themselves in knots attempting to supply a motive for the murder: that the houseboy murdered the nanny because she got wind of a drug deal of some sort, or because she was pregnant with his child. An intriguing report from Mr. Trotter, in a competing newspaper, claims that the Oriental was neither abducted nor beaten but arranged his own disappearance with the help of Chinese accomplices disguised as members of the Ku Klux Klan, their purpose being to defame members of the

Asiatic Exclusion League. What this has to do with the actual murder seems to be something he is keeping to himself.

The sober side to this farcical business is not only that an innocent girl is dead, but that a man could well hang for it purely to put an end to a tale that reflects poorly on all concerned.

A new level of cynicism has cast a pall over the city. To the man in the street, the police can no longer be trusted, the press no longer delivers facts, the legal system is biased in favour of power and money, and the governing of the province is nothing but a charade.

36

A dog will not find justice in a chicken's court.

THE VARNISHED HARDWOOD floor of the Crystal Ballroom reflects the light pouring from floor-to-ceiling windows, splattering off walls of encrusted gilt, chandeliers of gold and crystal, and a stage like an open mouth, draped with red velvet. There is even a separate balcony to accommodate musicians, so that guests may dance without looking at the players, or the players looking at them.

How is it possible to dance in a room like this and not feel superior?

After gaining entry to the Hotel Vancouver through the employee door (Miss Wickstram inadvertently left a small piece of kindling in the door jamb, free of charge for once), McCurdy made his way up the back stairs without being questioned. Now in the ballroom, he opens one of the double doors to the rooftop patio, steps outside, leans over the marble balustrade overlooking the courthouse, and scans the grounds and surrounding streets.

The perfect spot from which to describe the scene. It was Miss Wickstram's idea, he has to admit.

COURTHOUSE MOBBED
Shocking Start to the Wong Chi Murder Trial
Ed McCurdy
Staff Writer
The Evening Star

Viewed from the rooftop patio across the street, the court-house grounds appear as a sort of isthmus of grass, gravel and stone sculpture, faced with a tidal wave of seething humanity, a tide barely held back by a living dyke of VPD, Point Grey and Provincial Police officers. By nine o'clock on this September morning, countless concerned citizens have converged by auto and trolley to watch a grand procession of court officials, witnesses, jury members, representatives of the Chinese consul and of course the chief attraction— the Accused, whose guilt seems to them so certain that he might as well be wearing a noose and not a necktie. (As Wong Chi passes, spectators grow quiet, as if out of respect for the dead.)

At precisely a half-hour before the scheduled proceedings, the blue serge perimeter splits, the sluice gates open and, like a run of salmon, prospective spectators vie for the fifty empty seats in the courtroom.

As in a battle charge, teamwork wins the day. In this case, men and women from the Scottish Societies, having arrived *en masse* before dawn and having taken the vow of one for all, plow their way forward in a phalanx of raincoats, ever closer to their objective. Thanks to such tactics, almost every spectator seat will contain the buttocks of someone from the Scottish Societies.

With no possibility of watching the trial itself, Vancouver will rely on reports churned out by second-rate newspapers, whose editors already compete for readers with the most sensational prose their writers can muster. Having exhausted all possible versions of the crime itself, journalists have begun to portray the upcoming trial as a kind of boxing match between two lawyers of considerable renown.

Owen Jollimore's prosecutions are known to produce guilty verdicts at such a rate that defendants often collapse in tears when he enters the courtroom. Harry Stickler, in defending a client, makes full use of an encyclopedic knowledge of procedural rules, delivered in a voice seething with outrage, and a sincerity that has exculpated some of the shadiest characters in the province's history.

The event promises to be a duel to the death—the death being that of a third party, Wong Sing Chi.

THE SHERIFF HAS arranged for reporters to be granted standing room—a welcome gesture, in that McCurdy will not be required to sit next to Max Trotter.

Overwhelmingly dominated by the Scottish Societies, the

courtroom has fixed its attention on the Accused and his allies, with the fascination usually accorded to sideshow specimens and exotic reptiles.

Behind a low fence sit Wong Chi's relatives, Wong Gow and Wong Ling Sai Ken and their large families, near a representative of the Chinese consulate and a reporter from the *Chinese Times*. (Harry Stickler has not yet made his entrance.) In a corner stands the translator, Foon Sien, with his bowler hat tucked under his arm and a fresh coat of brilliantine slathered on his head.

There is an empty chair just behind the fence, dead centre, for the guest of honour.

Across from the Accused's seat and behind a similar fence sits the Crown prosecutor, in wig and robes, backed by representatives of the mayor and the chief of police. (The officials themselves have wisely maintained an appearance of neutrality.)

With a brisk rap of the gavel, Magistrate Wilcox calls the court in session, and in that same second Stickler strides into view, articulating his objection to the translator of the proceedings—who faithfully translated the demands of his client's abductors while they brutally assaulted their prisoner.

"Furthermore, I shall produce a source who will swear to having overheard this same Foon Sien bragging of his influence on both sides of the law, while offering his services to a certain importer of controversial Chinese medicines, including rhino horns and tiger's testicles."

Gasps from the women of the Scottish Societies, as Magistrate Wilcox raps his gavel: "I will not have that kind of language in my court. Mr. Stickler, I may agree with you, but I am overruling your objection as a point of principle."

Magistrate Wilcox pounds his desk again to indicate that the proceedings should continue, but another gasp erupts near the entrance, followed by a mumble, followed by silence.

Wong Sing Chi is escorted into the courtroom, wearing the same suit as at the previous two inquests, with a crisp white shirt and a paisley necktie. Two bailiffs guide the Accused to his seat, holding his arms firmly by the crook of the elbow. Some discolouration in the face is all that might remind the public of his earlier ordeal—not that he would garner much sympathy in any case.

He bows in the direction of a relative, then casts a glance toward the massed bulk of Scots spectators; feeling an urge to participate in the drama of the moment, a few hiss out loud.

For the next hour, McCurdy's notation skills are put to the test as Stickler and Jollimore continue to spar over the acceptability of Foon Sien and whether his alleged presence at the alleged kidnapping is relevant. Eager to move forward, an exasperated Magistrate Wilcox rules that Foon Sien should be replaced but can serve until a replacement is found.

The raps of the magistrate's gavel have already taken on a testy quality as Mr. Higgins, the court clerk, calls for Dr. Morris Blackwell, who takes the stand in a cream-coloured suit, purple bow tie and a gold Rolex watch.

From the first question and response it becomes evident that the doctor has acquired an understanding of the Crown's strategy: to catch someone in a contradiction or lie; an awareness that each witness is a potential suspect, a "person of interest." Each question could contain a hidden trap with which to catch one in a self-contradiction or otherwise cast a shadow of suspicion. For any witness it is a situation requiring utmost caution.

In this spirit, Dr. Blackwell delivers an impeccable, fully rehearsed account. He cannot speculate on the time of death, which is up to the forensic surgeon, Dr. Hunter. As for the electric iron on the floor near the body—that would be in Mr. Gorman's department. Nor is he prepared to state his thoughts about the condition of the corpse, which would be up to the coroner. He can, however, swear that a stream of Miss Stewart's blood flowed toward the door.

He can't recall where Mr. Faulkner and Constable Gorman went when they left the laundry room, if indeed they left the room at all; nor does he recall how the dead woman was taken from the premises. He does, however, remember that Constable Gorman conducted a thorough search of the basement floor and took extensive notes.

"I have no questions," Stickler says when Jollimore has retired. "There is no need for cross-examination, since nothing has been stated in the first place."

"Constable Joseph Gorman," announces the court clerk—to which Mr. Stickler also objects. "The witness is no longer with the police. He has left the force and can no longer give testimony in his official capacity."

(This is true. The former policeman recently purchased a half-interest in a small downtown hotel—a remarkable financial achievement for a man who earned twelve hundred dollars per year at most.)

On the stand, Constable Gorman takes offence at anything he construes as doubting his previous testimony. When asked by Mr. Jollimore to identify the murder weapon, the witness steps off the dais, picks up Frank Faulkner's service revolver from the evidence table and dramatically aims it at the audience; several spectators duck behind the chairs in front of them, while the sergeant-at-arms and the court clerk implore the former constable to point the gun someplace else. Gorman's point in doing this is never made clear.

Responding to Dr. Blackwell's testimony, Gorman denies having searched the laundry room at all. "It was not my responsibility to make a search of the premises."

As he is a light-skinned, nordic man, Jollimore's cheeks tend to flush when he becomes unnerved, a giveaway that has plagued him since childhood.

"Constable Gorman, as an officer of the law, why *wasn't* it your responsibility?"

"Because I did not expect to continue on the matter. I was to be replaced at any moment by Constable Hook."

"Why?"

"Constable Hook was the day man. The case was his responsibility."

"So you did nothing at all?"

"I stood by. Waiting for Constable Hook to arrive."

"Did Constable Hook do any looking around?"

"I don't think so. I considered his investigation inadequate, but it was not my place to say so."

"Did you take notes?"

"I was not told to take notes."

"I asked you, Mr. Gorman, *did you take notes?*"

"Not as such."

"Did you search the floor at any time?"

"No, I did not."

"Dr. Blackwell said that you searched the floor."

"I can't help what he says."

By this point Jollimore's cheeks are in full glow. The proceedings have turned in a bizarre direction and there is nothing he can do to right the course.

"While you were waiting for Mr. Hook, did you notice *anything*? Anything at all?"

"I did. I noted that Miss Stewart's blood flowed away from the door."

"Dear God, Mr. Gorman, are you aware that, just moments ago, Dr. Blackwell testified that her blood ran *toward* the door? Did you hear him say that?"

"Yes. Possibly some blood ran that way too."

Again, Stickler declines to cross-examine, since nothing relevant has been said.

The Crown's next witness, Nigel Edwards, reiterates his previous testimony but with less detail, to minimize the possibility of self-contradiction.

Following Mr. Edwards comes Dr. Hunter, the forensic surgeon who performed the autopsy on Miss Stewart. He too repeats the inconclusive testimony he presented during the two inquests. The women and men of the Scottish Societies begin to mutter darkly among themselves.

For no other reason than to regain the court's attention, Mr. Jollimore directs Dr. Hunter to perform a recitation of troubling particulars.

"Dr. Hunter, did you examine the genitals?"

"I did. This is standard procedure when there is a suspicion of ravishment."

"What did you find in there?"

"The vagina was plugged with absorbent cotton. There was a partial hymen present, and some blood."

"A *partial* hymen? Then you did suspect ravishment?"

"I thought such an injury was more likely caused by the embalming process itself."

"But *could* such findings be consistent with ravishment?"

"Any damage to the vagina may or may not have been due to forced sexual intercourse."

"Your worship," objects Mr. Stickler, "I ask that the latter testimony be struck as pointless and indecent. To idly speculate on whether there was or was not ravishment does not advance the issue."

"Sustained."

And so it continues. McCurdy has stopped taking notes; no reporter could explain the proceedings without hopelessly confusing his readers. The Janet Stewart story has become a maze with no way out, a diabolical road map where every route leads either to a head-on collision or a dead end.

THE SECOND DAY begins on a positive note, in the sense that a witness proves willing and able to present evidence consistent with her past statements—the only problem being that Cissie Braidwood's opinions, though strongly held, have no evidence to support them.

Miss Braidwood remains steadfast in her insistence that Janet Stewart was petrified of the houseboy and that she spoke of being afraid for her life. Her performance draws a round of applause from the Scottish Societies, not because it provides a shred of fact but because it is the story they came to hear.

In cross-examining Miss Braidwood, Mr. Stickler produces Miss Stewart's diary covering the past eight months, noting that they contain not a single word about her being afraid of Wong Sing Chi. In fact, when she refers to him at all it is with the patronizing affection one would expect between a white girl and an acquaintance of another race.

"Miss Braidwood, she mentions that the houseboy bought her film for her camera. Did she see this as a threatening act?"

"I picked up some photos for her at the drug store. I was so angry with him I tore them up."

This brings a round of applause from the spectators. "I felt I could have torn *him* up if I had him there."

A cheer erupts, stifled by the magistrate's gavel and a threat to clear the courtroom if such outbursts continue.

"If she was so afraid of the Chinaman, then why did she not write something about it in her diary?"

"Janet was a cheerful girl. She wouldn'a write but happy thoughts."

When she steps down from the witness stand, Miss Braidwood does not enhance her credibility by sitting beside Reverend McDougall, and by taking his hand.

Next to give evidence, Frank Faulkner makes an immediate impression on the entire room, in a lightweight Savile Row suit, a custom shirt from Jermyn Street and a regimental tie from the Royal Flying Corps. Miniatures of his service medals jingle beneath his chest pocket. The shape of his moustache is the work of a veteran barber, formerly attached to the upper ranks.

Unfortunately, the care he has given to his appearance has a paradoxical effect on the court. To the Scottish Societies, such impeccable grooming and tailoring speaks of a sly customer, and his smooth manner is that of a grifter.

Having failed to charm his audience, Faulkner initiates a sort of gas attack on the proceedings; to literally put the court to sleep, he expands his previous testimony in needless depth and detail. Even the prosecution is not immune to its soporific effect.

"I remember I was in and out that morning, very busy, opening an office is not an easy thing, believe you me, the office rental market is inflated beyond... let me give you an example...

"Ah yes, I remember one stop that morning: I went to see about some varnish for the floor. Spencer's store it was, and very good work they did, I must say, and I was reminded that..."

Massaging his eyes with finger and thumb, Prosecutor Jollimore tries to understand how it happened that with Frank Faulkner he has fallen victim to the most basic rule of examination: *Never let the witness take control.*

"You never told us about the varnish before, Mr. Faulkner. Why mention it now?"

"Because I thought of it since then. I remember because I passed through the parking lot and ran into Pat Fraser, who complimented me on a doubles match with Johnny Jukes—Pat will back me up on that—"

"But in your last testimony you said that you went to the Gregor Tire Company about an imported rubber purchase."

"Oh I don't recall that. But I may have done that too. We do business with Gregor Tire, a fine company and a quality product..."

"When you first saw Janet Stewart's body in the laundry room, was there any stiffening of the corpse?"

"No. I would say that she appeared fairly relaxed."

"You said at the inquest that it seemed to be, and I quote, 'stiffening.'"

"Upon reflection, I would say that she was both relaxed and stiffening."

Here Jollimore makes the decision to bring out the big guns.

"As well as the export of antiques, is your firm involved in the dope trade?"

A frisson of excitement erupts from the spectators; drug-smuggling rumours have been circulating for weeks.

"We handle general chemicals for medical purposes, if that's what you mean."

"Heroin, cocaine, morphine?"

"Among other medicines, yes. In the pharmaceutical business, we hardly refer to it as *dope*."

Stickler leaps to his feet, jaw set like a war monument. "Objection, My Lord. This line of questioning hasn't anything whatsoever to do with the Chinaman on trial."

"Objection sustained."

"I would request that the witness's entire testimony be put aside as irrelevant. The witness is not on trial for pushing illegal drugs."

Hisses from the spectators, who think otherwise. McCurdy would also like to see the Crown's probe continue along these lines.

Magistrate Wilcox raps his gavel briskly.

"I completely agree, Mr. Stickler. I rule an adjournment until tomorrow."

NEXT MORNING IT is announced that Mrs. Faulkner cannot give testimony due to illness—which is fine with the Scottish Societies, for the climax of the proceedings is about to occur: the interrogation and, many hope, the confession of the Chinaman who has become a living symbol of the Chinaman they fear. The fact that he is not a rat-faced creature with slanted eyes but a good-looking fellow only augments their horror that one day it might be possible for a Chinaman to pass himself off as white.

The room has become stifling. McCurdy loosens his tie and mops his face with his handkerchief. Beside him, a woman is fanning her face with a bible. Others appear to be either asleep or in a faint—bolt upright, there being no room to fall onto the floor.

Aware that his prosecution has so far failed to establish any case, let alone a lack of reasonable doubt, Crown counsel Jollimore resolves to wring the truth out of the Chinaman, right to the last drop. To set things off, he calls for a repeat performance of the Chicken Oath, which requires the sacrifice of another hen and which the public has already judged a waste of taxpayer money.

Following the oath, and after a roster of overruled objections from Mr. Stickler, the room turns its attention to the Accused.

Standing on the witness stand before a packed, unruly courtroom and with his life at stake, Wong Sing Chi displays an almost otherworldly calm, though his eyes narrow slightly at the sight of Foon Sien, his translator and tormentor. His speech, though distorted by missing teeth, comes with no undertone of apology or subservience. There are moments when, even to the Scottish Societies, Wong Sing Chi hardly seems to be Chinese at all.

Doggedly and with iron determination, Mr. Jollimore combs through the details of that Saturday morning, moment by moment, second by second, determined to pry loose the smallest inconsistency in the Chinaman's narrative.

"What were you doing when you heard the shot?"

"I was peeling potatoes."

"And where was Janet Stewart at the time?"

"I think she was upstairs."

"How long was she upstairs?"

"I don't remember."

"Did she come down again?"

"I saw her take clothes downstairs. Maybe ten o'clock."

"Yet you don't know how long she was upstairs"

"Some time I don't see her. Then I don't know."

"Until ten o'clock, when you heard the shot."

"I am not sure now."

"At what time *did* you hear the shot?"

"I not look at the clock."

"In other words, everything you say about Miss Stewart's actions that morning is pure guesswork."

"No."

His cheeks burning as though he were running a fever, Jollimore slumps behind the Prosecution table and massages his eyes with thumb and finger. "No more questions, Your Lordship."

Now it is Stickler's turn to mount a defence of Wong Chi—and, to the shock of spectators who like to see Stickler destroy witnesses as a form of blood sport, the defence opts not to call a single one.

Instead, he delivers a summation that turns the Crown's entire body of evidence into an argument for the defence. For his part, Mr. Jollimore gently holds his head in his hands, elbows on the table, eyes staring forward at the burnt husk that remains of his case.

"In conclusion, I submit to Your Lordship that the argument my friend has constructed, in his examination of witnesses and in his summation, point by point by point, leads us to the inescapable conclusion there is no evidence of murder here and that, even if there were, Wong Sing Chi had nothing to do with it."

MCCURDY RETURNS TO the courthouse the next morning, after a sleepless night listening to motorcars chattering back and forth in the street like ravenous insects. All night he was trying to envisage a thought process that might result in the conviction of Wong Chi for murder, other than the simple desire to hang a Chinaman—which cannot be dismissed out of hand.

The venue is surprisingly roomy for the day of a verdict and the room echoes with expressions of dashed hope as the spectators discuss the collapse of the Crown's case. And when the jury settles into their seats, the expression on their faces reflects either the seriousness of their task or that they have no other option, and the foreman, with regret, announces that they find no evidence to support charges against the Accused—indeed, they see no evidence that a homicide occurred at all.

Immediately, the Scottish Societies respond as one might expect—yet, this time around their indignation has a weariness to it, a suspicion that there must surely be something else to be outraged about. By investing so much energy, time and emotion in the Janet Stewart case, how many equally deserving injustices have been allowed to go fallow?

McCurdy walks out of the courthouse in a cloud of wonder at the sheer complexity of it all. He is no closer to knowing who killed Janet Stewart, or with what, or under what circumstances. He is no wiser than the moment he walked into the Faulkners' laundry room dressed as an undertaker's assistant. *Let someone smarter than me sort it out. Give it to Max Trotter. Let him gnaw at it until his teeth fall out.*

Back in his room with the window open to the street, he picks the Underwood off the floor, sets it on the table and rolls a sheet of paper into the carriage. He cleans his glasses with a fresh handkerchief, and begins to write.

NOT A SCANDAL BUT A SICKNESS
Max Trotter
Staff Writer
The Vancouver Sun

If there is anything to be learned from the Janet Stewart case, it is the corrosive effect of envy on the body politic.

Fired by sensational accounts by irresponsible journalists, with jealousy acting as kindling and rumour as gasoline, what began as the tragic demise of an innocent girl became an instrument for sub-normals with political agendas, waging class warfare against their betters in Shaughnessy Heights.

Meanwhile, like a man in a feverish dream, sick to death of his sleeping thoughts but compelled to dream on, the Vancouver public has become unutterably weary of the Janet Stewart case and all that has fallen along with it.

The citizens of Vancouver are thoroughly fed up with Wong Sing Chi. They are fed up with the hundreds of theories that have been force-fed to gullible readers. They are fed up with amateur sleuths who solve the entire case at the dinner table, and make the wine flat with their idle conjecture.

Surely, over the coming weeks, the fever will lift and the public temperature will return to normal, and Vancouver will be restored to health.

It will take much longer for this black mark to fade, this ugly blot on the city's reputation.

THE HALL TELEPHONE on McCurdy's floor rings approximately twenty times at around six in the morning.

"Hello, operator speaking, SEymour exchange. Is this SEymour 152? Mr. McCurdy, please."

"Operator, are you trying to have me evicted?"

"I am told this is an urgent call, sir. Mr. Sparrow calling for a Mr. McCurdy."

"Here is Ed McCurdy, damn him, and you. I will take the fucking call."

"I did not hear that, sir."

SWITCH

"Jesus, Howard, I hope you haven't had one of your premonitions."

"Quite the opposite, Ed. I have a retrieval to make—you m-might find it interesting."

"Where are we off to this time? Not Shaughnessy Heights again, please."

"No, b-but you're close. To Essondale Hospital. Jock West seems to have shot himself."

37

A drowning man is not bothered by rain.

SEATED IN—OR ON—the passenger seat, McCurdy squeezes into the white coat he wore when collecting Janet Stewart. The garment has some sort of brownish stain on the front.

Conversation is impossible in the hearse, due to the rattle of the coachwork, which threatens to disintegrate with every rut or pothole. Rain pours through nonexistent doors, and already McCurdy fears a back seizure.

Sparrow is driving with his chin resting on the steering wheel, staring through a sheet of rain, trying to see beyond the vibrating bonnet and down the road known as Kingsway, which extends straight ahead as though drawn with a ruler.

Once a wagon trail, Kingsway is now a strip of pock-marked desolation thanks to the ever-efficient Royal Engineers, who can transform any landscape to suit a convoy of tanks. The road leads all the way to Coquitlam, a town of twelve hundred with a modern lumber mill, a railway yard and Essondale Hospital for the Mind.

McCurdy wipes condensation from his glasses with his shirt-tail and closes his eyes, for the watery blur outside is giving him nausea. He will never understand why Sparrow feels it necessary to drive the hearse at such a clip. This is not an ambulance; time is not of the essence.

The vehicle veers violently sideways at unpredictable intervals, lurching McCurdy's back and sending electric jolts of pain down his right leg all the way to his foot. If only as a distraction, he puts his mind to potential links between the death of Captain Jock West and the death of Janet Stewart. Could she have been pregnant by Jock West? That might explain the botched autopsy, the inquests, the trial, the parade of stupidity—and all of it with a connection to General Hector Armstrong.

VIRTUALLY THE ONLY undamaged property in Coquitlam, Essondale is easy to locate.

The town has over the past few years suffered a fire, a flood and a giant logjam that destroyed wharves and knocked out two bridges. An unlucky place—no less so for the citizens of Essondale. As the hearse lurches up the driveway, McCurdy wonders what horrors go on behind the prison-like facade of the main building, an institution founded on the conviction that insanity is caused by syphilis, alcoholism or masturbation.

Since the war, doctors have been forced to re-evaluate their approach to "mental illness," as the cream of the Canadian crop returned home. Former teetotallers became alcoholics; former members of the Boys' Brigade ("Sure and Steadfast") exhibited a suicidal recklessness; former King's Scouts were regularly arrested for assaults and other crimes that they committed "for the fun of it." An epidemic of madness necessitated a second building for treating "seriously ill males."

McCurdy wonders, was there a change of staff to go with the change of clientele? Or is it still, in practice, a place of punishment?

As they pull up in front of Admitting, already the clatter of frantic little feet echo off the columned portico and down the stone steps, while a little man in a doctor's smock waves his arms frantically in a way that means, *Not here! Not here!*

With the hearse still in motion, McCurdy prepares to alight but is stopped by the man, who jumps onto the running board and pushes him back inside, hollering over the rattle of the motor: "Take this thing behind the building! You're upsetting the patients!"

By now the hearse has come to a full stop.

The man, who introduces himself as Superintendent Sharpe, jumps off the running board, runs around the bonnet and leaps onto the opposite running board, grips the stem of the rear-view mirror and with one hand directs Sparrow to a lane behind an adjacent brick building at the rear of Centre Lawn.

Sparrow pulls the brake lever and hops off the running board, while McCurdy and the superintendent hurry across the gravel driveway to an inconspicuous staff entrance. The three of them step onto the porch at about the same time, then pass through outer and inner doors and into a darkened hallway.

It takes a minute for McCurdy's eyes to adjust, and to discern the gauntlet of seated men in identical blue pajamas curled up on chairs, squatting or sprawled on the floor with their backs against the wall, a few wrapped in straitjackets as though holding together a stomach wound. They stare up at the visitors with the noncommittal gaze you get from a line of cattle behind a fence, waiting for milking, or for slaughter.

It seems clear to McCurdy that the new treatment facility for seriously ill men is not to inflict punishment but to provide storage, and that treatment occurs primarily to amuse the doctors in charge.

Patients shuffle erratic paths up and down the hall. At the far end a patient swabs the green linoleum floor with a rag mop and bucket. From both walls, waist height, eyes follow the undertakers as they make their way. Some patients mutter incomprehensible messages; others bark curses and imprecations to their unwelcome guests.

The morgue reveals itself to be a square windowless room at the far end of the hall, with a long wooden table in the middle, a sink in a corner and a bank of sixteen doors set into one wall— refrigerated cadaver drawers, though one might mistake them for safety deposit boxes, or a bank of files.

The electric lights have been switched off, and for some reason the superintendent makes no move to switch them on, leaving the occupants to squint through the trickle of sunlight seeping through a ceiling window of wired glass.

On the table lies an oblong package the size and shape of a human being. It contains the remains of Jock West, wrapped in a mattress cover for transportation, criss-crossed with baling twine so that it has the look of an Egyptian mummy.

"Here he is," the superintendent says. Then, in an unfortunate attempt to lighten the atmosphere, "All wrapped up and ready to go."

"Right-o," replies Sparrow. "B-But of course I have to inspect the face."

"You have to what?" The superintendent shuffles backwards on his little feet.

"An inspection, obviously for identification purposes. Company procedure."

"Of course." The superintendent's stubby fingers struggle with the knot; baling twine is the devil to untie.

Sparrow unfolds the fabric to expose the head and neck, down to the clavicle. The loose baling twine encircling the chest has coiled into a sort of wreath.

For his part, McCurdy heads straight for the corner sink (large enough to take a bath in) and quietly throws up his morning coffee.

Behind him, Sparrow lights a cigarette to mask the smell, leans over the corpse and examines the head, the top of which resembles a volcano. It's definitely Jock West. "Don't you see, Ed—the moustache. A real fighter pilot's moustache, you have to admire it."

From another drawer in the wall, the superintendent produces a waxed cotton bag with the unmistakable shape and heft of a service revolver. "The forensic surgeon might wish to examine this as well."

"It's a Webley," Sparrow remarks. "Nothing like a Webley to put a hole in a man."

McCurdy peers into the bag. The weapon is indistinguishable from the pistol he saw in the Faulkners' laundry room.

"Who gave him this weapon, Mr. Sharpe?"

"We have no idea. Access to Mr. West was tightly controlled at the family's insistence. It will be for the police to decide, I suppose. Or there may be some other explanation."

"Such as?" Sparrow asks, innocently. "Or are you keeping it to yourself?"

For the first time, the superintendent notices Sparrow's other eye.

"Gentlemen, I have nothing more to say on the matter."

HEADING SOUTH ON Kingsway, Sparrow has opted to drive at less than emergency speed so that the ride feels relatively smooth and is sufficiently quiet to allow for conversation.

"So? What did you notice?" McCurdy asks.

"About the b-body? Nothing special. Very common. I considered it myself, once."

"Surely you can do better than that. Or are you just pretending to be jaded?"

"I meant that it's a classic self-inflicted gunshot wound for someone in the military. A trained soldier puts the barrel in his mouth and fires upward. Civilians take a different approach—they worry about what they'll look like, for God's sake. But a shot to the temple can go straight through and miss the b-brain entirely. Aim between the eyes, and you'd better be steady or you can end up blind, deaf, dumb, stupid or all four at once. A shot to the roof of the mouth goes straight to the centre of the brain, does the job, and you don't have to aim, really. Of course it leaves a mess, b-but he was in a hospital; the orderlies can just hose it away."

"Howard, I've already thrown up once."

"You asked for specifics."

"If you'll remember, my original question was, what did you *notice*?"

"Someone smuggled him his service revolver, knowing full well that he would make a job of it—either someone from the Faulkner house, or someone from his home."

"Unless there's a third Webley."

"There isn't a third Webley."

"All this supports the theory that Jock was Miss Stewart's upper-class lover. He impregnated the nanny, took drastic action and is overcome with guilt."

"No, that's not quite what happened. It's m-more complicated as I see it."

"With which eye?"

"Both."

AFTER DELIVERING JOCK West's remains to Edwards Funeral Home, they head for the Lumberman's Club for what looks to be their last drink together.

"When are you thinking about making your move, Howard?"

"Tomorrow or the next day. It depends on the trains. Probably within three days."

"You're not coming back?"

"Can't see it. False exits are for slurgs and timmies." Sparrow takes a long drag of his thin cigarette.

"What do you plan to do for a living?"

"I might drive a hearse, or an ambulance. Always b-be dead people around, dead and wounded. The revolution is coming."

"Maybe it's called a revolution because you end up where you started."

"And besides, there's someone I need to see."

"Someone in France?"

"About the p-patch." Sparrow points to his left eye, unnecessarily.

"A painted piece of tin, Howard. What is there to know?"

"If I knew that I wouldn't b-be going to France."

He takes a long quaff of beer, produces a pocketknife and sharpens a stub of pencil. "So we keep in touch."

"Somehow I doubt that we will."

"You never know." He grins: "I m-might want to borrow m-money."

38

The whole of a serpent, the serpent knows.

THE *EMPRESS OF Russia* slows to three knots as she reaches Point Atkinson and heads toward Vancouver, a measure that lends the ship's entrance a stately quality. For anyone watching with binoculars from shore, she makes an impressive sight, nearly six hundred feet in length and seventeen thousand tons in weight, her prow slicing the water like a vertical axe, her three funnels aspirating a continuous stream of smoke from her coal-fed boilers.

Were the vessel arriving during daylight hours, hundreds would be lining the shoreline and packing the docks, even in heavy rain, waving to specks they take for passengers. As it is, the enthusiasts are fast asleep at home.

Aboard the *Empress of Russia* it is the same situation.

Were they in daylight, hundreds of passengers would be leaning over the railing and waving to shore. (The urge to wave to and from boats appears to be universal.) But at this early hour they are only just waking up, if that; just a few people stand on board, watching the lights of Vancouver grow nearer and clearer as the ship's engines slow to a low grumble, like an animal caged below.

On the bridge stand the captain and third officer, smoking in silence, waiting to mutter a routine order to the pilot, or ring the engine telegraph.

In the galley below stands a cook named Sin Lung, also awake. He peers anxiously through a porthole, then rechecks the white sacks by his feet to ensure that they are watertight and that they are securely tied to long ropes, with a floatation cork attached to each.

The ship passes among other vessels at anchor in the outer harbour, everything silent and still—except for the small gasoline launch chugging its way offshore some distance away, parallel to the ship. A man stands on deck, carrying a lantern, which swings with the motion of the water. The third officer waves to the man, who waves back. Unofficial escorts of fish boats and passenger boats are a common occurrence when a ship like the *Empress* hoves into port, even this early in the day.

The third officer returns his attention to the progress of the ship and thinks no more about the little boat.

For his part, Sin Lung has transferred his sacks across the galley to the garbage chute; gently he lowers them by their ropes until they reach the sea, being careful not to make an audible splash.

The gasoline launch holds its position. The man with the lantern, Wong Ling Sai Ken, waves goodbye as the vessel heads for Ballantyne Pier, while Wong Gow, at the stern, prepares to harvest fifty thousand dollars worth of opium, bobbing about in the *Empress*'s wake.

CONSTABLE HOOK ARRIVES at 3381 Osler at 10:00 AM, when Miss Hawthorn is out taking the baby for a walk. When a Redhat means to clobber a man with evidence, the fewer distractions the better, and you certainly don't want children looking on.

He kills the engine, sets the stand and dismounts, turns briskly (in case someone is watching) and strides up the walk to the verandah, pausing at the bottom of the steps to give his uniform a brush with one glove. When you are about to accuse a man of a crime it is best to stock up on official symbols.

Hook lifts and drops the brass door-knocker, set in the jaws of a lion. The sheer weight of it reverberates as though it signalled the angel of death.

JOCK WEST'S DEATH closed one line of inquiry for good; it may be difficult to interrogate a madman, but a dead man is impossible. Only one avenue remained: a visit to the Balmoral Hotel, to speak to the staff.

For any establishment in this part of the city, a police presence is bad for business. The longer a policeman remains on the property the greater the loss, not to mention the cost to one's reputation; so when a uniformed officer walks through the door with questions, the answers tend to come quickly.

In this case the uniform proved unnecessary. The desk man wore an army haircut and a tattoo of his regiment on his left forearm

(Lestock the Coyote). More obviously, his right arm bore another badge of service, having been amputated just above the elbow.

The desk man greets Hook with a cigarette in the corner of his mouth and the sarcasm a veteran reserves for all officers, including cops.

"Yes indeed, officer, lovely to see you, and how can I be of service today?" Only a veteran can form a phrase that seems inoffensive on paper and is therefore impossible to report but which, thrown in the right way, makes its point.

Hook is used to this. In reply he uses the Redhat voice that says *I could have you shot.* "To begin with, soldier, you can wipe that supercilious smile off your face."

In a classic case of conditioned reflex, the smile shuts down, overridden by a conditioned reflex to obey the superior officer. "Yes. Sir. Understood."

"Your tattoo, soldier. You were with the Princess Pats, I take it."

"Yes sir, I was, the Forty-Ninth from Edmonton." The desk clerk stands a bit taller now. He takes the cigarette out of his mouth.

"Trained at Midlands then, did you?"

"Yes, sir."

"And after that? Vimy? Yes?"

"Hill 70 actually, sir."

"Took some gas then, I dare say."

"That as well, sir, yes," with a self-deprecating grin.

"Trained at Midlands, you say. I was at Midlands myself..."

HOOK LIFTS THE brass knocker four more times, dropping it with increasing volume and is warming up for another set when he hears approaching footsteps—male and unsteady, neither Mrs. Faulkner nor Wong Chi.

The door swings open and above him stands Mr. Faulkner himself, exuding alcohol from every pore, sodden drunk, what-the-hell drunk—but in no danger of passing out, for he appears to have taken some sort of stimulant besides, probably cocaine. (His pupils are the colour and size of jaw breakers.)

Faulkner has not shaved his cheeks and jowls, nor has he changed his clothes for some time, to go by the smell. But even if wrinkled, the suit fits him perfectly, a tribute to his tailor. Likewise his moustache, though surrounded by stubble, forms a perfect inverted wing.

"Yes? What the devil do you want?"

"Good morning Mr. Faulkner, sir. I am Constable Hook, with the Point Grey Police."

Faulkner draws on a cigarette. "Oh, I know who you are." His mouth forms something like a smile, but there is no mirth in it. "You seem to have recovered from your accident, officer. You are most unfortunate."

"I appreciate your concern, sir. Is Wong Chi available?"

"No, he is not."

"Then I wonder if I might have a word with you about..."

"I *know* what you want to know about."

"Actually sir, I wonder if you do. May I come in for a moment?"

"No you may not. You've been a damned nuisance since this beastly business started." To emphasize the point, his body fills the doorframe so that, in effect, Faulkner becomes part of the door.

"Sir, I am not here to enquire about Janet Stewart. It's about a Miss Florence McNeil."

"Florence what?"

"McNeil, sir. She fell from a window at the Balmoral Hotel. I understand she recently worked as a maid at Canacraig."

"And what the hell has that to do with me?" Faulkner is becoming defensive. By his tone, Hook can tell that he knows precisely what it has to do with him.

"Sir, I spent some time with the desk man at the Balmoral Hotel. He recalled a gentleman who came to call on Miss McNeil around the day we think she died. The desk man admired the visitor's fine suit of clothes—an affluent man by the looks of him, so he said. It seems the gentleman stood about your height, sir, and had your manner of speaking. And it might have been pure coincidence, but a waitress named Eustace at the Good Eats Cafe claims she saw a McLaughlin parked in front of the hotel. It's an interesting combination of factors, Mr. Faulkner, wouldn't you say?"

"No, I wouldn't say that at all. It's a, a, a cluster of circumstances. Completely meaningless." Faulkner gives the policeman a look that says *I'm not as drunk as you think.*

"The other thing the desk clerk noticed, and admired may I say, was the gentleman's moustache—'a real airman's moustache,' was how he put it. A pilot's moustache. I wonder how many men in Vancouver possess such a moustache? I suppose, to answer that question, we would have to canvass the veterans list of airmen—specifically officers, which would narrow it down, then we would canvass the barbers, of course, a tedious business..."

"Officer," Faulkner interrupts. "I have one question for you."

"And what is that, sir?"

A pause follows. Hook realizes that, indeed, Mr. Faulkner is not as loaded as he appears. "Is the Balmoral Hotel in your jurisdiction?"

Extraordinary, how one's detailed plan can leave out of account a fundamental fact, a fact one should know well.

"Always wise to stay within one's own borders," Faulkner continues. "Especially on a motorcycle—traffic downtown can be very dangerous."

Faulkner smiles sideways, or possibly smirks, from his elevated position in the doorway; this tactical victory seems to have brightened his spirits somewhat. But only momentarily, for his face immediately reassumes its grim cast, while the pouches beneath his eyes seem to have taken on more weight.

"In any case, sir, I wonder if I might have a word with Mrs. Faulkner."

"No, I'm afraid you can't do that either."

"Sir, the Janet Stewart case is still an open murder inquiry. Though Mrs. Faulkner wasn't able to testify at the trial, she may be able to help us..."

At the mention of his wife, Faulkner's demeanour takes an abrupt turn for the worse; suddenly he is shouting, spitting brandy breath in Hook's face and over the front of his tunic.

"My wife isn't here! You idiot, do you fucking understand English? She isn't in the house! Nobody's home! She is gone! She won't be back for, for, for, for..." Mr. Faulkner's face seems to collapse in on itself, as though someone sucked the air out through a straw, reducing his resonant baritone to a hoarse whisper. "Mrs. Faulkner isn't here."

"When do you expect her back, sir?"

"I don't. Officer, whatever your half-baked suspicions, there is no information to be had here. The person in control of the situation has left, and she's not coming back. Doreen was always the one with the management skills, her father saw to that, and she has managed this situation expertly from beginning to end.

"Doreen emptied the contents of every account she had a key to—which was all of them, really. She ran the business, not me, and now she has taken it away. *The lady giveth, and the lady taketh away.* Here's to her!" He takes a solid swig from his bottle, using his sleeve as a napkin. "What I suggest to you is that, rather than beating your thick skull against a wall, your investigative energy might better be spent chasing after my wife. But of course, with the evidence well on its way... *To the evidence!*"

Faulkner raises his bottle, takes a deep swallow, admires the smoothness of the liquor, then looks down at Hook, an oily sheen to his gaze, and waxes philosophical, albeit in a supercilious way.

"Oh. Of course. Quite. The maternal instinct. How touching of you. She knows I can't be saddled with a brat. Advances will be made, through a third party, of course. Negotiations to follow, positions noted, incremental bargaining, a matter of give and take..." He smiles at the bottle, which is two-thirds empty.

Hook blurts a final question, which comes as a surprise even to himself: "When your wife left, Mr. Faulkner, was she alone? Or was she with someone... unexpected?"

"I have no idea what she sees in him. Chinamen all look alike to me."

Hook isn't listening anymore. An earlier combination of words has finally sunk in: *with the evidence well on its way...*

Ballantyne Pier.

Without another word, he fast-walks to the sidewalk, straddles his machine, jumps on the starter and performs a U-turn in the direction of The Crescent, leaving Faulkner standing in the doorway, drinking his brandy.

"Why the rush, officer?" Faulkner calls after him. "You know you're too late!"

BALLANTYNE PIER CONSISTS of a number of utilitarian sheds extending into the harbour, supported by thick pilings and fronted by a Beaux-Arts facade combining Art Deco and Romanesque elements—a grand entrance for what is essentially a warehouse.

The afternoon sky is the colour of wet wool, with patches of pale reflected light from an unknown source below. Clouds will cling to the nearby mountains as though sticky, like spider's webbing, which the city experiences as a damp mist, redolent of salt, creosote and the entrails of slaughtered salmon, and muffling the jagged clatter of shunting railway cars.

This morning near dawn, the *Empress of Russia* eased into

berth beside Pier B at barely perceptible speed. Onboard, over a thousand passengers were packing their suitcases, taking one last stroll around the deck or repairing to the Cossack Lounge for one last free drink. Meanwhile, crews onboard and ashore secured hawsers to the bollards, while cranes, hoists and winches swung into position and hatches opened for the unloading of freight and dunnage.

Now it is late afternoon. The passengers have disembarked, the holds have been unloaded and lading has begun, while squads of maids and janitors on each deck restore the staterooms, lounges, dining rooms and the decks themselves to pristine readiness.

Constable Hook trudges up the arched bridge that straddles the railway thirty feet below. At midpoint, he pauses to light a cigarette. He leans over the railing and looks down, careful to avoid the sore ribs on his left side. Below, on the track closest to the pier, a line of empty cars await high-priority shipments, either perishable or dangerous.

Today, the silk train has absolute priority.

The *Empress* contains approximately four thousand tons of cargo, including fifteen hundred bales of raw silk. For transporting this delicate, extremely valuable cargo, converted baggage cars have been sealed against moisture, refitted with hardwood lining and insulated with absorbent paper throughout.

Between each railway car on the silk train stands a man in a dark suit, holding a shotgun or a carbine across his stomach.

Leaving Vancouver, the silk train will steam non-stop across the continent to the markets of New York, having perpetual right-of-way over all other trains, including passenger trains, even the Limited. During a royal visit, the Prince of Wales was forced onto a siding to make way for the silk train.

To avoid becoming conspicuous, Hook parked his motorcycle on Clark Drive, a neighbourhood of recent Italian and Eastern European immigrants normally identified as Spicks, Bohunks and Polacks.

Since he is on personal and not police business—and, as he knows all too well, in VPD jurisdiction—he stowed his cap and insignia in his saddle bag. (In an hour he will change into his suit before calling on Miss Hawthorn. *The Humming Bird,* starring Gloria Swanson, has come to the Pantages.)

His suspicions don't matter. It's too late. Nothing a policeman can say now will delay the transfer of goods across continents and oceans, the backbone of the British Columbia economy. What harbourmaster would risk the spoilage of several million dollars' worth of silk, on the say-so of a member of the Point Grey Police?

Below, loaders are already packing the silk train with military dispatch, still closely supervised by heavily armed men.

Meanwhile, the cranes on Ballantyne Pier drop stuffed cargo nets into the maw of the *Empress of Russia*. One of the nets contains a load of cubical crates with *Faulkner and Partners* stencilled on the side; they too swing through the air and disappear into the hold. Nothing short of a full-scale search of it would produce any evidence now—and again, how would he convince the VPD, to say nothing of a judge, to seek and issue a warrant?

Hook crushes his cigarette beneath the heel of his shoe, turns and walks away.

Snookered again.

39

Never hire a handsome servant.

BY EIGHT O'CLOCK the next morning, the *Empress of Russia* is ready to receive passengers. The salt having been scrubbed off her hull's surface, her hold fully loaded with cargo, her passenger decks scrubbed inside and out (even steerage is hygienic) so that no trace remains of her former occupants, the *Empress of Russia* sits proudly by the pier, gleaming brown and white, God's spectator shoe.

Crowded outside the rococo entrance to Ballantyne Pier, well-wishers outnumber passengers by a good margin. (If you can't afford a ship, at least you can see one off.) An undifferentiated field of felt hats and raincoats surges toward the entrance, either to get aboard, wave at someone aboard or imagine going aboard themselves.

The McLaughlin crosses the bridge and gently but firmly eases its way to the curb, nudging the crowd this way and that. Mrs. Faulkner drives like a chauffeur—in fact she even looks the part, in a severe dress and with an empty seat beside her.

He watches her eyes, framed by the rear-view mirror, as she stops the automobile and sets the handbrake, leaving the engine running, despite the convenience of an electric starter.

Wong Sing Chi sits uneasily in the back seat, his view alternating between Mrs. Faulkner's eyes in the rear-view mirror and the back of her impeccably bobbed hair in front of his face—how effortlessly it falls into place at the nape of her neck.

At his side, like a scuffed brown wall, is a cardboard suitcase containing everything he owns.

Chung Young Lee reaches over the suitcase to proffer an open cigarette case, green enamel with gold trim.

"*Nǐ yào bùyào lái yī gēn yān?* Dunhill, very good English brand."

"*Bu yong le xie xie.* I do not smoke, Mr. Chung."

Chung Young Lee takes a cigarette for himself and the case snaps shut, in a way that signifies a closed subject. Mr. Chung lights up, without opening the window, a signal that the conversation will be short and private. Pocketing his lighter, he reaches into an inner chest pocket and produces a brown envelope, neatly folded and tied with baling twine; from another pocket he produces a folder containing a second-class, one-way ticket to Shanghai.

He places the envelope and ticket on top of Wong Chi's suitcase, the better to avoid touching hands.

"Here your ticket," he says. "And full payment. Inspect please. *Nǐ míngbái ma?*"

"Yes, I understand. I understand very well." Wong Chi's eyes have returned to the rear-view mirror and the violet eyes looking back at him.

"No, you do not seem to understand. I said to inspect now the money, please."

Forcing himself to look at the envelope, Wong Chi unties the string and counts the money, or appears to, for his employer's benefit. (What would either of them do if the amount were incorrect?)

"*Wǒ tóngyì.* All is fine, Mr. Chung. All is as it should be."

Mrs. Faulkner turns in her seat. "I hope so, Wong Chi. The past months have been difficult for all of us."

"Very hard, Mrs. Faulkner, yes."

Chung Young Lee peers over the suitcase as though looking for a sign of a double meaning but sees nothing to worry about. "Well then, now I think is good time to say goodbye, Wong Sing Chi," he says.

In the front seat, Mrs. Faulkner lights a Dunhill. "Very much so."

"Then I will say goodbye." Wong Chi turns, joins his palms over his chest and nods to Mr. Chung. "*Zàijiàn yǒngyuǎn.*"

"*Zàijiàn yǒngyuǎn,*" Chung Young Lee replies. "That is a good way to put it."

"Goodbye, Wong Chi," Mrs. Faulkner adds, taking a long last look in the rear-view mirror at the face of the houseboy. "I thank you for your discretion."

"Always discreet," Wong Chi replies, and opens the car door.

THE REAR DOOR of the McLaughlin swings open. Wong Chi

emerges with his suitcase, turns and, as gently as possible, slams the door shut. Immediately, the automobile revs its powerful engine and surges forward, forcing one pedestrian to hop out of the way; Mrs. Faulkner brakes sharply, then continues at a more stately speed.

Wong Chi pauses a moment to watch it go, then turns toward the pier entrance and eases his way through a break in the crowd making for the door—but something stops his progress. Something behind him that he should see. Instinctively he turns, looks back and is not surprised to see the McLaughlin stop on the pedestrian bridge, at the top of the arch, as though waiting for something. Do they want to make sure they are rid of him?

Then something happens that does surprise him. A woman, who must have been waiting next to the railing on the opposite side, steps off the sidewalk, crosses the bridge, opens the car door and climbs into the front passenger seat. The door slams shut. The auto accelerates forward and turns onto Alexander Street, heading west toward Japantown.

He doesn't know this woman, but he has seen her many times in the house. Family—*always the most important thing in life.*

He turns back to the pier and heads toward the entrance—but not quite. He stops at the black-and-gold post box beneath its small archway, covered with royal symbols, like a place of worship; he reaches into a side pocket and produces a white stamped envelope, then lifts the heavy brass flap and drops the envelope through the slot.

Wong Sing Chi returns to the main door and sidles inside to be met by his relatives, among them Wong Gow, Wong Ling Sai Ken and Harry Stickler, who have all come to wish him *bon voyage.*

40

Watch for the ending after the ending.

BESIDES A SEMI-RELIABLE pay packet, a staff writer with *The Evening Star* receives a mail slot and a cubby of his own. The cubby McCurdy can do without—he has no wish to bump into Shipley on a daily basis.

Amid the usual array of "shocked and outraged" and "you deserve to die" missives is an astonishing letter that is either genuine or an impeccable fake—seated at a table at the White Lunch, he has read it three times without touching his coffee:

Dear Mr. McCurdy Sir,

I write first to salute your observance and skill. You are a man who works with words. You write without looking at the page, and your words are fine enough to be printed for all to see. I salute your writing and I am hoping you will tell my story with your pen.

As I told you, I learned my poor English in my home village of Chin from an American lady missionary, Sai Zhenzhu, but her English name was Miss Buck. "When you go to America they will want you to speak English," Sai Zhenzhu said to me.

This was not so. When I landed in Vancouver cousin Wong Gow explained that white people do not prefer their servants speaking English except for commands a dog could obey. Trusted servants are best when not understanding what they overhear. Wong Gow knew this from work as a trusted servant at Canacraig.

So, in my new country my first lesson was that one must deceive for success. And from Wong Ling Sai Ken I learned that in this new country a good conscience pays badly.

290

Mr. Faulkner did not suspect that I understood his language, always he spoke to me in coolie talk. Mrs. Faulkner suspected but did not care. Missy knew but told no one. All three understandings had outcomes. With all three I became trusted but for different reasons.

A saying in my country goes *A cat loves fish, but hates to get his feet wet.* For Mr. Faulkner I was what you would call a middle man. I carried messages between Mr. Faulkner and Wong Gow and sometimes money too. Cousin Wong Gow was in the Chee Kung Tong of Chung Young Lee, and I joined as well. Mr. Chung said I could be trusted with money, an honour.

With Mrs. Faulkner trust was needed on other matters and I remain discreet. A secret between three is no secret.

It was another position with Missy Janet. Like you Mr. McCurdy, she knew I understood more words than I said. Alone in the house we talked about many things, I about China and Missy about gentlemen friends. Secrets there too, that died with the dead.

Her men friends amused Missy. They were so serious and needful like dogs, she said. I laughed and said they sound like apes to me and look like apes too, hair all over their bodies, and we laughed again.

One time Missy touched my hand and Miss Cissie walked in and saw this. Missy pulled her hand away and made disgusted talk to me. I did not blame her. I knew that it was discreet and honourable for her to do this. Nothing is more disgraceful than for a woman to touch a Chinaman.

If we are telling the truth, such nearness of a white person is not pleasant for a Chinese either.

You smell like sour cheese and rancid butter. Your breath smells like rotting flesh. Your eyes are flabby and pale and milky inside like the eyes of blind people. You have giant pink pointed noses and rough patches on your skin, like tree bark. One can see the veins beneath your skin like a sea-creature. Your skin turns green when you are afraid and red when you are angry and grey when you are sick. It is disgusting to watch you eat your plates of cow meat in such obscene quantities. Your teeth are yellow and crooked like wild dog's teeth. You grow coarse hair on your back like a boar. When you laugh you bray like donkeys. Your voices are loud, even when you whisper. You may be educated but you are easily fooled. You have poor concept of personal dignity.

To many Chinese you look like identical fat horses, even the women.

I do not know how Missy met Mr. Faulkner's friend Mr. West but he made her happy. Often she talked about her quality friend, her war hero. I heard he had a soldier's heart. I do not know if the name means bravery or a wound, or both.

For Mr. West I was the middle man too. I once gave Missy film for her camera but other presents came from Mr. West. Mr. West gave presents to Wong Gow. Wong Gow passed them to me. All was arranged by Mr. Faulkner, who thought Missy was good for his friend's health. I do not think he cared if his friend was good for Missy.

On the night of the party at Canacraig Missy worked as a servant and so did other nannies in Shaughnessy. Chinese servants were not desirable for the company.

Mr. Faulkner knew the party meant heavy traffic in Shaughnessy. It made a good time for an important meeting at Faulkner house with Chung Young Lee on import-export business. I am present with Wong Gow and other members of Chee Kung Tong.

It was to be a discreet meeting. Outside, Chee Kung Tong men watched for intruders and smoked cigarettes. Two in silk shirts stood guard on either side of the door to the front hall, also smoking. At a rosewood table near the big stone fireplace, Chung Young Lee sat in a black silk coat. Across the table, Mr. Faulkner wore a tuxedo for the party at Canacraig. The talk was in Mandarin and English. The interpreter was Foon Sien, whom I do not like.

Mr. McCurdy, you knew the shot in the morning was a lie. There was no shot in the morning. Everything was a lie, but not exactly, more arranging of true facts that does not tell the truth. To deceive is sometimes the necessary, good way. For family at home, it was the only way.

The disturbing sound was a man from Canacraig, shouting in Chinese and some English about urgent business. It was more disturbing because it was the middle of the night and neighbours might hear.

Chung Young Lee heard this and gave orders to his men, and all left for their cars. In seconds the living room was empty and Mr. Faulkner's business meeting with the Chee Kung Tong was over.

From outside I hear electric starters, tyres on the driveway, then silence. I see smoke drifting between the ceiling beams and a silver bowl containing the last of the white powder in question. Foon Sien has taken the razor and the rolled-up note.

Wong Gow ran to Canacraig, it was his responsibility. Mr. Faulkner told me to sit down and wait, and hurried to Canacraig as well.

Wong Gow later told me about terrible things that happened there.

Mr. West was very drunk. He saw Missy serving drinks. He said something to her. They later went upstairs to the lounge near the general's office. Nobody up there but Chinese housekeeping whose English was poor, and Miss McNeil serving in lounge, in case the general needed private meeting with a guest and there must be a white servant ready.

Miss McNeil was the only one who heard what Mr. West and Missy say and do in the lounge. Then second woman entered the room. Wong Gow said she was Mr. West's wife. Missy ran out of the lounge to the stairs. She turned back just as Mrs. West ran out of the lounge and pushed her backwards very hard. Missy flew backwards on hard marble stairs and hit her head. There was much blood.

Mrs. Faulkner go upstairs and said something to Mrs. West and something to Mr. West and they go into lounge and Miss McNeil served drinks. By now Wong Gow with other Chinese carried Missy away. Wong Gow's wife and other servants cleaned the stairs.

That I heard from Wong Gow. The rest I saw, and I can see now.

I am in the sitting room. It is still dark outside. I hear footsteps crunch on gravel and urgent voices at the back of the house. I hear commands, urgent orders from Mr. Faulkner, and Mrs. Faulkner too.

Then I hear a shot.

I did not lie when I said that I heard a gunshot. I did

not break the Chicken Oath. Nobody asked me if I heard a second shot. After hearing two shots I hurried down to the laundry room.

I am on the laundry room stairs and I see Mrs. Faulkner standing over Missy and holding a pistol. Her hands are shaking and so am I. Missy is dead. Mrs. Faulkner speaks angrily with Mr. Faulkner but I do not hear what she says. My mind makes a hiss like steam and my heart crashes. Mr. Faulkner tells me to bring Scotch whisky and I go upstairs. I am sick in the water closet and then I get Mr. Faulkner's Scotch whisky.

I come down with whisky. I am blinded by Missy's naked body, shining white and I have to look away but I see that Mrs. Faulkner is holding a hot iron against her skin.

Mrs. Faulkner tells me I must do this to Missy with the iron. Mr. Faulkner tells me I must choose between money and maybe hanging for murder, the Chinese suspect. Mrs. Faulkner tells me I cannot help Missy, no matter that people think she died later. All of this was true.

I hold the iron against her body for a long time to keep it warm. I cannot look at her, it is not decent.

I burn her once with the iron. I ask her forgiveness. I still wait for an answer.

When you read this I am in international waters.

I go home now. Goodbye.

HIS COFFEE IS as cold as the trail leading to Janet Stewart's murderer. He has no way of knowing whether the letter was written by Wong Chi or if it is a clever forgery by a murderer to bury his tracks once and for all. There is no handwriting sample for comparison, because Wong has never been known to write in English. Even if it's genuine, McCurdy has no way of knowing whether Wong Chi is telling the truth, for the man has for years maintained a semi-fictional existence; he could have fabricated this version so that his relatives in Vancouver would be spared further trouble, or because he simply wanted to shut down further inquiry once and for all. None of it can be confirmed or denied—and certainly the Faulkners will be of no help.

As material for the investigation, the letter means nothing.

He remembers as a child receiving an elementary puzzle book as a Christmas present: one of the puzzles involved dots on the page, with numbers on the dots which, when connected, created a picture of a man. How many pictures could he have created if there were no numbers on the dots?

He folds the letter and slips it inside an inside pocket, pays for his cold coffee and heads out the door onto Hastings Street.

And it is raining, again.

END

ACKNOWLEDGEMENTS

TO HOWARD WHITE—whose *Raincoast Chronicles* I've been looting for years.

To John Hughes—and his cache of *holy shit*! factoids.

To my editor Pam Robertson—nothing like having a smart, articulate reader on your side.

To my mate Beverlee—who accepts that I'm working when I'm lying on the couch.